Central High School
5199 Highway N
St. Charles, MO 63304

THE BEAN TREES

Barbara Kingsolver

WITH RELATED READINGS

THE EMC MASTERPIECE SERIES

Access Editions

EMC/Paradigm Publishing
St. Paul, Minnesota

Staff Credits

Laurie Skiba
Managing Editor

Brenda Owens
Editor

Chris Lee
Associate Editor

Nichola Torbett
Associate Editor

Jennifer J. Anderson
Associate Editor

Paul Spencer
Art and Photo Researcher

Valerie Murphy
Editorial Assistant

Gia Marie Garbinsky
Contributing Writer

Shelley Clubb
Production Manager

Lisa Beller
Design and Production Specialist

Leslie Anderson
Cover Designer

Parkwood Composition
Compositor

Sharon O'Donnell
Copy Editor

Jane Hilken
Proofreader

Cover image: *Cactus,* 1998, by Freshman Brown (b. 1940, American).
© Freshman Brown/SuperStock

Published by agreement with HarperCollins Publishers, Inc., 10 East 53rd Street, New York, New York. All rights reserved.

Library of Congress Cataloging-in-Publication Data

Kingsolver, Barbara.

The bean trees, with related readings / Barbara Kingsolver.

p. cm. – (EMC masterpiece series access editions)

ISBN 0-8219-2958-5

1. Kingsolver, Barbara. Bean trees. 2. Automobile travel—Fiction. 3. Indian children—Fiction. 4. Young women—Fiction. 5. West (U.S.)—Fiction. 6. Friendship—Fiction. 7. Orphans—Fiction. I. Title. II. Series.

PS3561.I496B44 2004

813'.54—dc22

2004053291

ISBN 0-8219-2958-5

Published by EMC/Paradigm Publishing
875 Montreal Way
St. Paul, Minnesota 55102
800-328-1452
www.emcp.com
E-mail: educate@emcp.com

Printed in the United States of America.
2 3 4 5 6 7 8 9 10 xxx 10 09 08 07 06 05

Table of Contents

THE LIFE AND WORKS OF

Barbara Kingsolver

© Steven L. Hopp

Barbara Kingsolver

Barbara Kingsolver, born April 8, 1955 in Annapolis, Maryland, spent much of her childhood in Carlisle, Kentucky. Like Taylor Greer in *The Bean Trees,* Kingsolver knew she wouldn't stay in rural Kentucky. "The options were limited," she has said: "Grow up to be a farmer or a farmer's wife."

But Kingsolver's love of storytelling and language is rooted deep in Kentucky soil. As she explained in a 1995 interview with *Salon* magazine, "Kentucky has, in common with the rest of the South, that captivation with language, that use of story in everyday life. You don't just say someone's 'ugly,' you say 'she's ugly as a mud-stick fence.' I grew up hearing that poetry that I didn't even recognize as poetry. . . . When I moved to Arizona, I found myself trying to write stories set in Arizona, but they always ended up back in Kentucky. . . . *The Bean Trees* finally began to work when I imported characters from Kentucky and put them in Tucson."

When Kingsolver was seven, her father took the family—including Barbara, nine-year-old Robert, and two-year-old Ann—to Africa. During the next year, her father practiced medicine in what was then called the Congo and is today known as the country of Zaire. "I came home with an acutely heightened sense of race, of ethnicity," she has said of the experience. "I got to live in a place where people thought I was noticeable and probably hideous because of the color of my skin."

Kingsolver also started writing while in Africa. "I have no idea why I started, only that I did, at age 8, daily, after somebody gave me for Christmas a small red diary with a tiny pencil & tiny gold lock (easily picked with a bobby pin, turns out)," she notes on her website. "I've continued to write frequently, if not daily, to this day. By the time I reached adolescence I was not just recording my life but also inventing poems and stories. Writing gave me a sense of accomplishment and satisfaction as a way to make sense of things and feel useful, at least to myself."

Kingsolver graduated from Nicholas County High School in Carlisle, Kentucky, and attended DePauw University in Greencastle, Indiana, where she earned degrees in biology and English in 1977. She also spent time abroad, living and studying in Athens, Greece, and Paris, France, and working as an archaeologist, a copy editor, an X-ray technician, a housecleaner, a biological researcher, and a translator of medical documents. At the age of twenty-two, Kingsolver moved from Europe to Tucson, Arizona. She earned a Masters of Science degree in ecology and evolutionary biology from the University of Arizona in 1981.

Working first as a science writer and then as a freelance journalist, she wrote articles that appeared in dozens of newspapers and magazines. She married in 1985 and, while pregnant with her first child in 1986, began writing about a young woman from the fictional Pittman, Kentucky, who heads west. *The Bean Trees,* Kingsolver's first novel, was published in 1988, and immediately gathered critical praise and enthusiastic readers. It also made the *New York Times* notable books list and won an American Library Association award. The book has never gone out of print and has been read by millions throughout the world.

Kingsolver's second book, *Holding the Line: Women in the Great Arizona Mine Strike of 1983,* focuses on the women of southern Arizona and the role they played in holding their families and the community together. This nonfiction account of an eighteen-month-long strike by copper miners was published in 1989, along with *Homeland and Other Stories*, a collection of short stories.

Two more novels followed: *Animal Dreams* in 1990, and *Pigs in Heaven* in 1993. *Animal Dreams* is set in Arizona, in the fictional mining town of Grace, Arizona. Kingsolver no longer had to import characters from Kentucky, however, because the time she spent among striking copper miners had developed her ear for their language and enabled her to capture the nuances of their Spanish-influenced English. In *Pigs in Heaven,* a sequel to *The Bean Trees,* Kingsolver returns to Tucson and the Cherokee Nation to continue Taylor and Turtle's story.

In 1995, Kingsolver published *High Tide in Tucson: Essays from Now and Never.* One of the related readings included in this edition, "In Case You Ever Want to Go Home Again," appears in that collection. In 1998, *The Poisonwood Bible,* the story of Nathan Price, a Baptist preacher who moves his family to the African Congo in 1959 to convert the natives to Christianity, earned Kingsolver the National Book Prize of South Africa and a nomination for the Pulitzer Prize for Literature.

In 2000, Kingsolver was awarded the National Humanities Medal, the United States' highest honor for service through the arts. Her fifth novel, *Prodigal Summer,* was also published that year. The novel is set in a rural farming community of southern Appalachia, a terrain similar to that where Barbara, her second husband Steven Hopp, and daughters Camille and Lily have resided since leaving Tucson in 2004.

Kingsolver considers herself a storyteller. "A novel has to entertain," she told *Publishers Weekly.* "That's the contract with the reader: You give me ten hours, and I'll give you a reason to turn every page." At the same time, she believes her contract with the reader involves more than a good story. "Literary fiction is a place you visit for the pleasure of being there," she explains on her website. "You go to hear the language and think new thoughts, and if you love it, you'll go back. The subtext is as important as the text. Without it you may have a story, but not the heart of the matter."

Kingsolver begins with a theme, and creates a world and characters who act out her theme, often examining cultural differences and social and political issues. She often puts her science background to good use, artfully weaving scientific explanations of the natural world into her stories.

Small Wonder, a collection of essays published in 2002, includes the author's thoughts on subjects ranging from nature to family to the origins of poverty to the tragedy of September 11, 2001. She believes that the stories we share can make the world a better place. "When you pick up a novel from the bedside table, you put down your own life at the same time and you become another person for the duration," she told Bill Moyers in a 2002 interview. "And so you live that person's life, and you understand in a way that you don't learn from reading a newspaper what it's like to live a life that's completely different from yours. And when you put that book down, you're changed. You have... something more expansive in your heart than you began with."

Time Line of Kingsolver's Life and Works

1955 Barbara Kingsolver is born in Annapolis, Maryland. Shortly thereafter, the family returns to her parents' native Kentucky and moves to the small, rural town of Carlisle.

1963 Kingsolver's family—older brother Robert, Barbara, younger sister Ann and parents—live in Africa, where her father practices medicine.

1972 Kingsolver graduates from Nicholas County High School in Carlisle, Kentucky.

1972–1977 Kingsolver attends DePauw University in Greencastle, Indiana. Kingsolver also spends time living and studying in Athens, Greece and Paris, France. In 1977, Kingsolver graduates from DePauw magna cum laude with a B.S. degree in biology.

1981 Kingsolver receives her M.S. in ecology and evolutionary biology from the University of Arizona in Tucson.

1981–1985 Kingsolver works as a scientific writer for the Office of Arid Lands Studies at the University of Arizona. During this time, she covers the 1983 strike of copper miners in southern Arizona.

1985–1987 Working as a freelance journalist, Kingsolver writes articles for numerous magazines and newspapers. In 1985, she marries Joseph Hoffmann. In 1986, pregnant with her first child, Kingsolver begins writing *The Bean Trees* at night. She receives an award for outstanding feature writing. Her daughter Camille is born in 1987.

1988 *The Bean Trees* is published.

1989 *Holding the Line: Women in the Great Arizona Mine Strike of 1983,* an oral history and social commentary of the copper miners' strike that Kingsolver covered as a journalist, and *Homeland and Other Stories,* a collection of short stories, are published.

1990 *Animal Dreams* is published.

1991-1992 Kingsolver and her family move to the Canary Islands, where she begins researching *The Poisonwood Bible.*

1992 *Another America/Otra America,* a collection of poems in English and Spanish, is published.

1993 *Pigs in Heaven,* the sequel to *The Bean Trees,* is published.

1995 *High Tide in Tucson: Essays from Now or Never* is published. Kingsolver is awarded an honorary Doctorate of Letters from DePauw University.

1996 Kingsolver's second daughter, Lily, is born.

1998 *The Poisonwood Bible* is published.

2000 Kingsolver is awarded the National Humanities Medal for her service to the country through the arts. Her fifth novel, *Prodigal Summer,* is published.

2002 Kingsolver publishes two nonfiction works: *Last Stand: America's Virgin Lands,* a collaboration with National Geographic photographer Annie Griffiths Belt, and *Small Wonder,* a collection of essays.

2004 Kingsolver and her family move from Tucson, Arizona, to their farm in southern Appalachia.

THE GEOGRAPHICAL AND HISTORICAL CONTEXT OF

The Bean Trees

Taylor Greer doesn't know who her daddy is, but she has a mama who loves her. She's not the smartest girl in high school, but she knows what she doesn't want: She doesn't want to end up like Newt Hardbine, whose daddy got thrown over the top of a Standard Oil sign, "like some old overalls slung over a fence," when a tractor tire blew up. And she doesn't want to get "hogtied to a future as a tobacco farmer's wife." What Taylor Greer wants is to get away.

The Bean Trees begins with Taylor Greer's odyssey west, which carries her from Pittman, Kentucky, to the Cherokee Nation in Oklahoma to Tucson, Arizona. This is a story of escapes and mutual rescues: most of the characters are running from something, and all find unlikely rescuers close at hand. Along the way, they breathe life into each other, and fill, as best they can and sometimes at great risk, the voids in each other's lives. *The Bean Trees* celebrates the power of human connectedness and reminds us that life perseveres under the harshest of conditions and in the most improbable places.

Geographical Context

You Won't Find Pittman, Kentucky on a Map

Taylor begins her westward trek from Pittman County, Kentucky, a fictional, rural farming community. On her website, Barbara Kingsolver describes Pittman as "a very real place of the kind that can't be found on a map. Its character and people are consistent with what you'd find in any number of small towns in the east-central part of Kentucky, including the one where I grew up."

In east-central Kentucky, the rolling hills of the central Bluegrass Region meet the foothills of the Appalachian Mountains that run through the eastern portion of the state. Kentucky, called "the Bluegrass State," takes its motto from the expanses of bluegrass that cover hills and pastures in the region. Actually, bluegrass is green, but small blue flowers in spring make it look blue from a distance. The Bluegrass Region is a rolling plateau bordered to the north and west by the Ohio River, and to the south and east by hills known as the Knobs. It is also home to Louisville and Lexington, Kentucky's two largest cities.

The Bluegrass Region is best known for tobacco farming and horses. Taylor's adamant refusal to being hogtied to a tobacco farmer and her musings over a swarm of ants milling around a discarded cigarette are references to her native state's primary crop. Burger Derby employee Sandi enthuses over Taylor's connection to Kentucky—home of the Kentucky Derby, the world-famous horse race. In fact, the Bluegrass Region, also known as the Thoroughbred Region, isn't far from the poorest part of the state. As Taylor tells Sandi, in the Kentucky she comes from, people don't own thoroughbreds; they just wish they could live as well as one. That's another echo from Kingsolver's own life: Her website biography notes that she grew up "'in the middle of an alfalfa field in the part of eastern Kentucky that lies between the opulent horse farms and the impoverished coalfields."

Eastern Kentucky, also known as the Eastern Coalfields/ Mountain Region or the Cumberland Plateau, is the westernmost edge of the Appalachian Mountain range that runs from Quebec to Georgia. Coal mining is the main industry, yet the region has the highest poverty and unemployment levels in the state. Taylor refers to the Appalachian Mountains when she observes, "In Kentucky you could never see too far, since there were always mountains blocking the other side of your view, and it left you the chance to think something good might be just over the next hill." Granny Logan's remark to Lou Ann, "I expect you'll be persuadin' the baby that his people's just ignorant hill folks," indicates she lives in or near this part of Kentucky.

Go West, Young Woman

The landscape of *The Bean Trees* changes dramatically as Taylor leaves Kentucky and heads across the Great Plains. As the lake-flat landscape of Oklahoma gives way to Arizona, she finds herself in the unfamiliar world of the arid Southwest.

Tucson, the setting for much of the novel, is Arizona's second largest city with a population of nearly 800,000. Situated in a high desert valley surrounded by mountains, Tucson is located in the Sonoran Desert, which covers 100,000 square miles, including much of the state of Sonora, Mexico, both sides of the Gulf of California, most of the southern half of Arizona, and the southeastern corner of California. According to *A Natural History of the Sonoran Desert,* published by the Arizona-Sonora Desert Museum, "two life forms . . . distinguish the Sonoran Desert from the other North

American deserts: legume [bean] trees and large columnar cacti."

The Cherokee Nation Isn't a Place

The Cherokee Nation refers to modern-day descendants of the original Cherokee Indians who once inhabited the southeastern United States. As a Cherokee teenager tells Taylor in *The Bean Trees*, "[T]he Cherokee Nation isn't any one place exactly. It's people. We have our own government and all."

In the novel, the Cherokee Nation also refers to physical boundaries in northeastern Oklahoma. The Cherokee Nation of Oklahoma is not a reservation, but a self-governed nation apart from the United States that has its own chief, constitution, and capital city of Talequah, Oklahoma. It is one of only three bands that are recognized by the U.S. government as self-governing nations. The Cherokee were forcibly relocated to Oklahoma by the U.S. government in 1838.

HISTORICAL CONTEXT

Native People of the Americas

The story of *The Bean Trees* presents three characters who are direct descendants of native cultures of the land that we now call the Americas: Estevan and Esperanza are Mayan, and Turtle is Cherokee.

The Cherokee

The Cherokee were one of the American Indian tribes of the Southeast United States. They called themselves *Ani-Yun' wiya,* which means "Principal People" or "Real Human Beings." For approximately 1,000 years before their first contact with white people, the Cherokee lived and prospered in what today are the southeastern states of Georgia, Tennessee, North and South Carolina, and parts of Kentucky and Alabama.

In 1540, the tribes of the Southeast first interacted with white people when Spanish conquistador Hernando de Soto and his men followed a Cherokee road into a Cherokee village. The contact between the Cherokee and de Soto is unremarkable. They gave him and his men food. He didn't find gold, and he left.

As de Soto moved west, through what is today Alabama, Mississippi, Louisiana, and Arkansas, he treated the native people brutally, killing, burning, and stealing anything he wanted. In 1542, as he was making his way out of America, he died of disease carried over from Spain. For Native Americans, with no immunity to the diseases of Europe, the next century was a plague of disease and devastation. The future would only bring worse.

The Trail of Tears

At the time of their first interaction with settlers in the mid-1600s, the Cherokee were the largest nation of the Southeast tribes with a territory of approximately 40,000 square miles around the Blue Ridge Mountains—part of the Appalachian Mountain range—of western North Carolina and eastern Tennessee. But treaty by treaty, the Cherokee were forced to surrender their land. The Cherokee signed the first treaty surrendering a portion of their territory to the governor of South Carolina in 1721. They did this to secure trade and to create a boundary between their territory and the settler's territory.

Each time they signed a treaty they were told that they would not be asked to give up any more of their land. But each time, white settlers ignored the new boundaries, moved into Cherokee territory, and refused to leave. In 1828, former Indian fighter Andrew Jackson became president and persuaded Congress to pass the 1830 Indian Removal Act, which set aside land west of the Mississippi River for the relocation of Indian tribes.

When the state of Georgia tried to force the Cherokee off their lands, the Cherokee filed a lawsuit against the state. Supreme Court Justice John Marshall upheld the Cherokee's right to remain on their land. But neither the settlers of Georgia nor President Jackson gave the ruling any authority. Jackson responded with words that have been handed down through history: "John Marshall has made his decision: now let him enforce it."

In the coming months, settlers in the state of Georgia, hungry to grab Cherokee land on which gold had just been discovered, held a public lottery. Cherokee territory was divided into "land lots" and "gold lots" and awarded to the citizens of Georgia. Winners of the lottery came in and took over the houses, land, and livestock of the Cherokee. One of the related readings in this edition, William Jay Smith's poem, "II. The Cherokee Lottery," depicts this event.

Between the summer of 1838 and the winter of 1838–1839, the U.S. government removed close to twenty thousand Cherokee from their lands. Many were held in detention camps before being relocated. In the winter of

1838–1839, eighteen thousand to twenty thousand Cherokee joined the Choctaws, Chickasaws, Creeks, and Seminoles in walking 1,200 miles under military escort to their new "home" in present-day Oklahoma. This forced journey, during which an estimated four thousand to eight thousand Cherokee died from disease or exhaustion, is known as the Trail of Tears. Taylor refers to the removal and forced march of the Cherokee when she remembers Mama's stories about her Cherokee grandfather, "one of the few that got left behind in Tennessee."

Guatemala, Home of the Mayans

Guatemala, the northernmost and most populous country in Central America, covers approximately forty-two thousand square miles, an area just larger than the state of Ohio. Guatemala is a beautiful country, with dramatic and diverse terrain that includes active volcanoes, rain forests, and coastal plains. But Guatemala is better known for its troubled and violent social and political history.

The Mayan civilization, one of the most advanced of the ancient world, thrived in the area between 250 and 900 AD. The Maya built hundreds of city-states in the areas today known as Mexico, Guatemala, Belize, and parts of El Salvador and Honduras. The ruins of these cities reveal a sophisticated architecture of pyramids, palaces, temples, libraries, and observatories. Particularly skilled in the subjects of math and astronomy, the Maya created a calendar as precise as the one we use today. They also invented the idea of "zero," traced the paths of the planets, calculated the lunar cycle, and accurately predicted eclipses of the sun and moon.

Around 900, Mayan civilization began to decline. The Maya deserted their city-states and resettled in the mountains of Guatemala and the Yucatán Peninsula region of Mexico. Fighting between Maya tribes and conquest by the Spanish marked the period from 1100 on.

First Spain and then descendants of the original Spanish settlers ruled Guatemala. When the country gained independence from Spain in 1821, the economy prospered but the Maya remained at the bottom of the social and economic structure. They were required to carry passbooks to prove they worked 150 days each year for wealthy landowners.

Hope for the Indians and the poor *ladinos* (people of both Spanish and Mayan ancestry) of the country came when Juan José Arévalo, a university professor, was elected president in 1944. Arévalo disposed of laws mandating the forced labor of the Indians. He raised the minimum wage, and he allowed workers to form labor unions.

In 1950, Colonel Jacobo Arbenz Guzmán, a former military officer, was elected president. Under Arbenz, the government purchased unused land from plantations of vast acreage and resold it at affordable prices to peasant cooperatives. Wealthy landowners didn't like this, and one American-owned company liked it even less.

The United Fruit Company, an influential American business in Guatemala and other parts of Central America, was one of the largest holders of unused land in Guatemala. When the government sought to purchase thousands of acres of the company's unused land, United Fruit complained to powerful friends in the U.S. government.

The United States, in the grips of the Cold War, became convinced that this redistribution of land was a communist plot directed by the Soviet Union. On June 18, 1954, the United States sent about 150 troops and six planes into Guatemala and threatened to bomb Guatemala City if the military didn't surrender their support for President Arbenz.

Colonel Carlos Castillo Armas, the successor to Arbenz preferred by the United States, quickly reversed the reforms that Arbenz had set in motion. The United Fruit Company got its land back. Castillo Armas tortured and jailed any who opposed him, and during his short time in power, thousands of Guatemalans were killed. Castillo Armas himself was killed in 1957.

This began in Guatemala, nearly four decades of civil war, characterized by brutal military dictatorships, death squads, atrocities, and suffering.

The Guatemalan Civil War

During the ten years that the country had been ruled by Arévalo and Arbenz, a quiet change had started to take place. Church leaders had begun to help landless Indians organize to form cooperative farming villages. Poor workers in urban areas had begun to form labor unions. University teachers and students had begun to talk of civil rights.

The civil war started in 1960, when Guatemalan opposition to the country's military dictatorship and power structure began to solidify. Since the time of Spanish colonization, a small group of wealthy European landowners had owned most of the land while the rest of the population was impoverished, virtually landless, and denied even the most basic civil rights.

This opposition to the government became an organized resistance spearheaded by guerrillas. The government's response to the resistance was a brutal campaign of killing and intimidation.

The government used "death squads" to terrorize the Guatemalan people. The names of poor *ladinos,* Indians, students, labor leaders, journalists, lawyers, and teachers—people thought likely to be sympathetic or give voice to the opposition—were placed on lists. The death squads, often off-duty policemen and soldiers, then invaded towns and villages, hunting down the people on the lists or anyone who might know them. Most of the victims targeted by the death squads had no connection to the guerrillas.

The violence reached new heights during the reign of General José Efraín Ríos Montt. In 1982, Ríos Montt took control of the country and put into action a "scorched earth policy": any region thought to harbor guerrilla activity was burned to the ground, its inhabitants tortured and killed. Between 1982 and 1983, more than four hundred villages were destroyed and more than one thousand people, mostly Guatemalan males, were killed each month. Ríos Montt launched "Beans and Guns," a strategy that promised food and protection to Guatemalan Indians who agreed to give up their land, homes, and villages to join the army—and fight against their neighbors who might be guerrillas.

In 1986, pressure from foreign countries over human rights violations being committed prompted the election of President Marcos Vinicio Cerezo Arévalo. In an effort to bring peace to the country, Cerezo met with representatives of the guerrilla groups. But the guerrillas wanted reforms that would give the Mayan Indians and poor *ladinos* civil rights, a voice in their own government, and access to land. Cerezo's hands were tied: if he tried to bring about the changes the guerrillas wanted, the military would overthrow him.

The Guatemalan Civil War finally ended in 1996, when government officials and rebel leaders signed a peace accord. Guerrilla groups agreed to lay down their weapons in return for promises by the government to end discrimination against Indians and *ladinos,* provide access to schools and health care, and institute land reform.

The Guatemalan Civil War claimed the lives of more than 200,000 Guatemalans, wiped out 440 Mayan villages, and left at least 45,000 listed as missing—these "disappeared" were most likely tortured and killed by government troops. Thousands more fled for their lives to Mexico, Canada, and the United States. These exiles are the real-life models for Estevan, Esperanza, and other Central American characters in *The Bean Trees* who find temporary refuge at Jesus Is Lord Used Tires in Tucson.

During and after the war, tribunal proceedings that summoned the testimony of Guatemalan citizens, human rights observers, and others were conducted. In 1999, the United Nations Commission for Historical Clarification issued findings charging the Guatemalan Army with genocide against the Mayan people.

The Sanctuary Movement

The Sanctuary Movement was an organized network of safe havens that sheltered refugees from Guatemala and other Central American countries, such as El Salvador, that were undergoing violent political upheaval. Though many of these people were running for their lives, the U.S. government refused to consider them political refugees and offer them asylum. Religious and social activists felt it was their moral and religious responsibility to break the law and aid the refugees.

In 1982, activists declared the Southside Presbyterian Church in Tucson the first public sanctuary for Central Americans fleeing death squads and oppression. Soon more than three hundred churches in cities across the United States declared themselves sanctuary churches, their members risking fines and jail terms to help refugees and pressure the United States to change its immigration policies. The Sanctuary Movement is credited with being a key influence in the government's decision to stop wholesale deportations of Salvadorans and Guatemalans in 1990.

Because the Sanctuary Movement has been compared to the Underground Railroad, through which abolitionists once led slaves to freedom before the U.S. Civil War, it is sometimes called the Overground Railroad. The Sanctuary Movement is the sanctuary to which Mattie refers in the novel.

The Bean Trees

Bean trees are a recurring image of renewal throughout the novel. The bean trees in the park that grow up the trellis and later develop the bean pods that Turtle notices are wisteria, a flowering vine of the bean family. Mattie's mysterious purple beans are most likely wisteria as well, since most wisteria have Asian origins.

The bean trees are also a symbol of Turtle's Cherokee heritage. Although Kingsolver specifies that corn, beans, and squash were the three staple food crops of traditional Cherokee society, she weaves many connections between Turtle and bean plants. In Chapter Seven, Turtle plants bean seeds that later emerge as a "ferocious thicket" that comes "plowing up through the squashes." In Chapter Eight, Turtle sings a recipe for succotash—a dish of beans and corn. The flourishing bean trees symbolize both Turtle's healing and Taylor's growing up.

Characters in *The Bean Trees*

Major Characters

Taylor Greer. The protagonist of *The Bean Trees*. Born in rural Kentucky, Taylor decides early in her life that she doesn't want to stay in Pittman and become a farmer's wife. Five years after graduating from high school, she sheds her given name (Marietta, though she's always been called Missy) and the Kentucky hill country as she heads west in a 1955 Volkswagen. Her life changes when her car breaks down inside the Cherokee Nation in Oklahoma, and she accepts responsibility for an abandoned Cherokee child whom she names Turtle.

Turtle. Turtle is the young Cherokee girl handed to Taylor during her brief stop in the Cherokee Nation of Oklahoma. Turtle becomes the center of Taylor's universe. Physically abused and emotionally traumatized, Turtle's gradual healing demonstrates the essential resilience of human beings and forms the redemptive heart of the novel.

Lou Ann Ruiz. Like Taylor, Lou Ann is a native Kentuckian who moved to Tucson. Lou Ann, who has been left by her husband, Angel, has a young son named Dwayne Ray. After Lou Ann takes Taylor and Turtle in as housemates, Lou Ann and Taylor become friends. Throughout the novel, Lou Ann struggles to come to terms with her failed marriage.

Mattie. A native of Tucson, Mattie is a widow who owns and runs Jesus Is Lord Used Tires. She befriends Taylor and Turtle early in the novel and gives Taylor a job at her tire shop. Mattie introduces Taylor to Estevan and Esperanza and to the natural world of the Arizona desert. Mattie is also part of the Sanctuary Movement; she shelters refugees from Central America in her home.

Estevan. A native of Guatemala and a Mayan Indian, Estevan was an English teacher in his home country. He and his wife, Esperanza, were forced to flee Guatemala during the civil war. They are taken in and sheltered by Mattie. Estevan develops a close friendship with Taylor.

Esperanza. A native of Guatemala and a Mayan Indian, Esperanza was forced to flee Guatemala during the civil war. She is Estevan's wife, and she is taken in and sheltered by Mattie.

Minor Characters

Mama. Taylor's mother. A single mother who worked hard all her life, Mama is a consistent source of encouragement and self-esteem for Taylor.

Lee Sing. The woman who runs the Chinese market in Lou Ann's neighborhood. Lee Sing's mother, who is never seen, is said to be more than one hundred years old. Lee Sing, who intimidates Lou Ann, predicts that Lou Ann will give birth to a baby girl. Lee Sing gave Mattie the bean plants that grow in her garden.

Mrs. Hoge. The woman who runs the Broken Arrow Motel. Mrs. Hoge lets Taylor stay in the hotel in exchange for help with the cleaning.

Irene. Mrs. Hoge's daughter-in-law.

Sandi. Taylor's first friend in Arizona. Sandi works at the Burger Derby, where Taylor gets a job for a short while. Sandi has an unsupportive family and young son named Seattle after the racehorse Seattle Slew.

Angel. Lou Ann's husband. Angel lost his leg in a truck accident. He leaves Lou Ann to follow the rodeo circuit and later tries to reconcile with her. The reader is never directly introduced to Angel, but hears plenty about him from Lou Ann.

Dwayne Ray. Lou Ann and Angel's son.

Granny Logan. Lou Ann's maternal grandmother. Granny Logan, a rural Kentuckian, is ornery, critical, and prejudiced.

Ivy. Lou Ann's mother. Ivy, also a rural Kentuckian, is domestic and likes to stick close to home. She visits Lou Ann to help her after the birth of her son and returns to Kentucky after a short stay in Tucson.

Fei. One of the women with whom Taylor has an interview while she is looking for a place to live.

Timothy. A housemate of Fei and La-Isha.

La-Isha. A housemate of Fei and Timothy.

Virgie Mae Parsons. A next-door neighbor of Lou Ann and Taylor. Virgie Mae lives with Edna Poppy. Virgie Mae is critical and prejudiced, but her nastiness is tempered by Edna's kind and gracious nature.

Edna Poppy. A next-door neighbor of Lou Ann and Taylor. Edna Poppy, who is blind, lives with Virgie Mae. Edna Poppy has dressed in all red since the age of sixteen. Edna and Virgie Mae frequently baby-sit Turtle and Dwayne Ray.

Ismene. The daughter of Estevan and Esperanza who is kidnapped by the Guatemalan government.

Cynthia. The social worker who shows up at Taylor and Lou Ann's to investigate the incident that happens to Turtle in the park. Cynthia informs Taylor that she has no legal claim to Turtle and probably doesn't have a good chance of being allowed to adopt her. Cynthia gives Taylor Mr. Armistead's name.

Mr. Armistead. The notary who authenticates the document that grants Taylor custody of Turtle. Mr. Armistead's office is near the Cherokee Nation of Oklahoma, yet he seems to have little knowledge or understanding of the Cherokee.

Echoes:

Quotations on Themes from The Bean Trees

"Empathy is really the opposite of spiritual meanness. It's the capacity to understand that every war is both won and lost. And that someone else's pain is as meaningful as your own."

—Barbara Kingsolver

"What is a family, after all, except memories?—haphazard and precious as the contents of a catch-all drawer in the kitchen."

—Joyce Carol Oates

"Family isn't about whose blood you have. It's about who you care about."

—Trey Parker and Matt Stone,
South Park, 1998

"If a child is to keep alive his inborn sense of wonder, he needs the companionship of at least one adult who can share it, rediscovering with him the joy, excitement and mystery of the world we live in."

—Rachel Carson

"A life isn't significant except for its impact on other lives."

—Jackie Robinson

"Never doubt that a small group of thoughtful, committed citizens can change the world. Indeed, it is the only thing that ever has."

—Margaret Mead

"The care of human life and happiness, and not their destruction, is the first and only legitimate object of good government."

—Thomas Jefferson

"They made us many promises, more than I can remember, but they never kept but one; they promised to take our land, and they took it."

—Red Cloud, Oglala Sioux

Images of The Bean Trees

Kevin R. Morris/CORBIS

A road winds through farmland near Carlisle, Kentucky, Barbara Kingsolver's childhood hometown.

Cherokee men, women and children, forcibly removed from their lands in Georgia in 1838, were marched 1,200 miles west to Oklahoma. During the journey that became known as the Trail of Tears, an estimated one-third of the Cherokees died from exhaustion or disease.

Painting by Robert Lindneux. Woolaroc Museum, Bartlesville, Okla.

Annie Griffiths Belt/CORBIS

The menu outside a fast-food restaurant in Tulsa, Oklahoma, is written in both English and Cherokee.

Douglas Kirkland/CORBIS

A homeless woman struggles to survive in gritty, urban Arizona.

Craig Aurness/CORBIS

Lightning over Monument Valley, Arizona, a high desert region of mesas, buttes, and colorful rock formations.

George H.H. Huey/CORBIS

The Organ Pipe Cactus National Monument in Arizona's Sonoran Desert blooms after a summer rain.

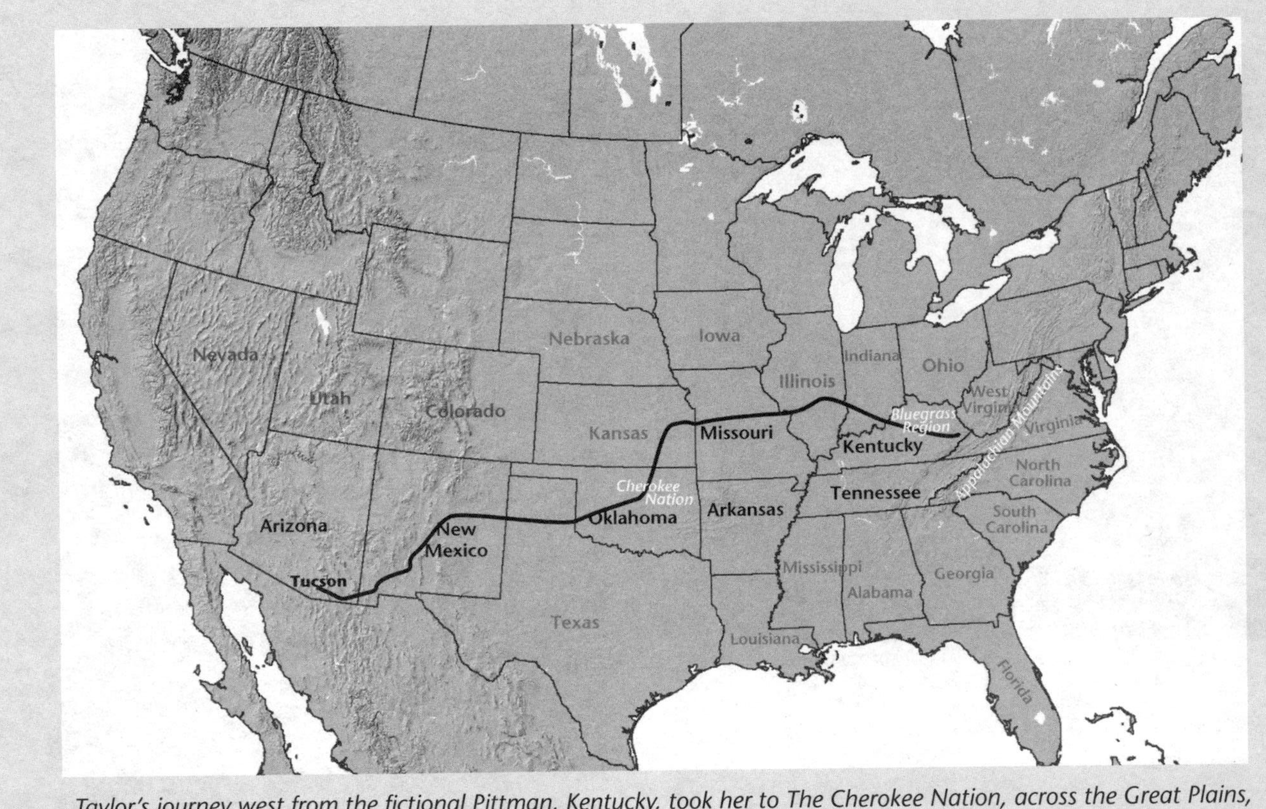

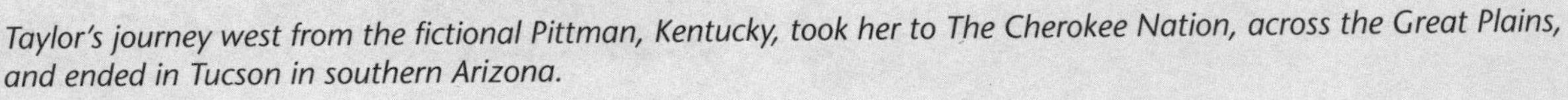
Taylor's journey west from the fictional Pittman, Kentucky, took her to The Cherokee Nation, across the Great Plains, and ended in Tucson in southern Arizona.

For Annie and Joe

One
The One to Get Away

I have been afraid of putting air in a tire ever since I saw a tractor tire blow up and throw Newt Hardbine's father over the top of the Standard Oil sign. I'm not lying. He got stuck up there. About nineteen people congregated during the time it took for Norman Strick to walk up to the Courthouse and blow the whistle for the volunteer fire department. They eventually did come with the ladder and haul him down, and he wasn't dead but lost his hearing and in many other ways was never the same afterward. They said he overfilled the tire.

◀ *What is Taylor afraid of? Why?*

Newt Hardbine was not my friend, he was just one of the big boys who had failed every grade at least once and so was practically going on twenty in the sixth grade, sitting in the back and flicking little wads of chewed paper into my hair. But the day I saw his daddy up there like some old overalls slung over a fence, I had this feeling about what Newt's whole life was going to amount to, and I felt sorry for him. Before that exact moment I don't believe I had given much thought to the future.

◀ *Who was Newt Hardbine? How did the narrator feel about him?*

My mama said the Hardbines had kids just about as fast as they could fall down the well and drown. This must not have been entirely true, since they were abundant in Pittman County and many survived to adulthood. But that was the general idea.

Which is not to say that we, me and Mama, were any better than Hardbines or had a dime to our name. If you were to look at the two of us, myself and Newt side by side in the sixth grade, you could have pegged us for brother and sister. And for all I ever knew of my own daddy I can't say we weren't, except for Mama swearing up and down that he was nobody I knew and was long gone besides. But we were cut out of basically the same mud,[1] I suppose, just two more dirty-kneed kids scrapping to beat hell and trying to land on our feet. You couldn't have said, anyway, which one would stay right where he was, and which would be the one to get away.

◀ *What does the narrator say about her father? What does she say about herself and Newt?*

1. **cut out of basically the same mud.** Come from the same background

words for everyday use

con • gre • gate (käŋ′ grə gāt) *v.*, gather, assemble, come together in a group. *I have noticed that people at parties often congregate by the food.*

a • bun • dant (ə bun′ dənt) *adj.*, plentiful, abounding. *Our small garden produced an abundant supply of vegetables that fed us all summer and fall.*

▶ By what name is the narrator called? Why?

Missy was what everyone called me, not that it was my name, but because when I was three supposedly I stamped my foot and told my own mother not to call me Marietta but *Miss* Marietta, as I had to call all the people including children in the houses where she worked Miss this or Mister that, and so she did from that day forward. Miss Marietta and later on just Missy.

The thing you have to understand is, it was just like Mama to do that. When I was just the littlest kid I would go pond fishing of a Sunday and bring home the boniest mess of bluegills and maybe a bass the size of your thumb, and the way Mama would carry on you would think I'd caught the famous big lunker[2] in Shep's Lake that old men were always chewing their tobacco and thinking about. "That's my big girl bringing home the bacon," she would say, and cook those things and serve them up like Thanksgiving for the two of us.

▶ While fishing, what did Missy sometimes see under the water?

I loved fishing those old mud-bottomed ponds. Partly because she would be proud of whatever I dragged out, but also I just loved sitting still. You could smell leaves rotting into the cool mud and watch the Jesus bugs[3] walk on the water, their four little feet making dents in the surface but never falling through. And sometimes you'd see the big ones, the ones nobody was ever going to hook, slipping away under the water like dark-brown dreams.

By the time I was in high school and got my first job and all the rest, including the whole awful story about Newt Hardbine which I am about to tell you, he was of course not in school anymore. He was setting tobacco alongside his half-crippled daddy and by that time had gotten a girl in trouble,[4] too, so he was married. It was Jolene Shanks and everybody was a little surprised at her, or anyway pretended to be, but not at him. Nobody expected any better of a Hardbine.

But I stayed in school. I was not the smartest or even particularly outstanding but I was there and staying out of trouble and I intended to finish. This is not to say that I was unfamiliar with the back seat of a Chevrolet. I knew the scenery of Greenup Road, which we called Steam-It-Up Road, and I knew what a pecker looked like, and none of

---

2. **lunker.** Largest fish
3. **Jesus bugs.** Refers to long-legged bugs called water striders that "walk on water"
4. **gotten a girl in trouble.** Made a girl who wasn't his wife pregnant

these sights had so far inspired me to get hogtied[5] to a future as a tobacco farmer's wife. Mama always said barefoot and pregnant was not my style. She knew.

It was in this frame of mind that I made it to my last year of high school without event. Believe me in those days the girls were dropping by the wayside like seeds off a poppy-seed bun and you learned to look at every day as a prize. You'd made it that far. By senior year there were maybe two boys to every one of us, and we believed it was our special reward when we got this particular science teacher by the name of Mr. Hughes Walter.

Now *him.* He came high-railing in there like some blond Paul McCartney,[6] sitting on the desk in his tight jeans and his clean shirt sleeves rolled up just so, with the cuffs turned in. He made our country boys look like the hand-me-down socks Mama brought home, all full of their darns and mends.[7] Hughes Walter was no Kentucky boy. He was from out of state, from some city college up north, which was why, everyone presumed, his name was backwards.

Not that I was moony over him, at least no more than the standard of the day, which was plain to see from the walls of the girls' bathroom. You could have painted a barn with all the lipstick that went into "H. W. enraptured forever" and things of that kind. This is not what I mean. But he changed my life, there is no doubt.

He did this by getting me a job. I had never done anything more interesting for a living than to help Mama with the for-pay ironing on Sundays and look after the brats of the people she cleaned for. Or pick bugs off somebody's bean vines for a penny apiece. But this was a real job at the Pittman County Hospital, which was one of the most important and cleanest places for about a hundred miles. Mr. Walter had a wife, Lynda, whose existence was ignored by at least the female portion of the high school but who was nevertheless alive and well, and was in fact one of the head nurses. She asked Hughes Walter if there was some kid in his classes that could do odd jobs down there after

◀ *What jobs did Missy have in the past?*

5. **hogtied.** To have one's feet tied together; to be made helpless
6. **Paul McCartney.** Singer, songwriter, and bass player for the musical group The Beatles
7. **darns and mends.** Spots on a sock where holes and worn areas have been sewn

words for everyday use

en • rap • ture (en rap′ chər) *v.*, to fill with joy or delight. *Petting the puppy seemed to enrapture the young child, and he began to smile and giggle uncontrollably.*

school and on Saturdays, and after graduation maybe it could work out to be a full-time thing, and he put the question to us just like that.

Surely you'd think he would have picked one of the Candy Stripers,[8] town girls with money for the pink-and-white uniforms and prissing around the bedpans on Saturdays like it was the holiest substance on God's green earth they'd been trusted to carry. Surely you would think he'd pick Earl Wickentot, who could dissect an earthworm without fear. That is what I told Mama on the back porch. Mama in her armhole apron in the caned porch chair and me on the stepstool, the two of us shelling out peas into a newspaper.

"Earl Wickentot my hind foot" is what Mama said. "Girl, I've seen you eat a worm whole when you were five. He's no better than you are, and none of them Candy Stripers either." Still, I believed that's who he would choose, and I told her so.

She went to the edge of the porch and shook a handful of pea hulls out of her apron onto the flowerbed. It was marigolds and Hot Tamale cosmos.[9] Both Mama and I went in for bright colors. It was a family trait. At school it was a piece of cake to pick me out of a lineup of town girls in their beige or pink Bobbie Brooks matching sweater-and-skirt outfits. Medgar Biddle, who was once my boyfriend for three weeks including the homecoming dance, used to say that I dressed like an eye test. I suppose he meant the type they give you when you go into the army, to see if you're color blind, not the type that starts with the big E. He said it when we were breaking up, but I was actually kind of flattered. I had decided early on that if I couldn't dress elegant, I'd dress memorable.

Mama settled back into the cane chair and scooped up another apronful of peas. Mama was not one of these that wore tight jeans to their kids' softball games. She was older than that. She had already been through a lot of wild times before she had me, including one entire husband by the name of Foster Greer. He was named after Stephen Foster, the sweet-faced man in the seventh-grade history book who wrote "My Old Kentucky Home," but twenty-two years after naming him that, Foster Greer's mother supposedly died of a broken heart. He was famous for drinking Old Grand Dad with a gasoline funnel, and always told Mama

8. **Candy Stripers.** Teenage volunteer workers at a hospital

9. **marigolds and Hot Tamale cosmos.** Two types of brightly colored flowers

never to pull anything cute like getting pregnant. Mama says trading Foster for me was the best deal this side of the Jackson Purchase.[10]

She snapped about three peas to every one of mine. Her right hand twisted over and back as she snapped a little curl of string off the end of each pod and rolled out the peas with her thumb.

"The way I see it," she said, "a person isn't nothing more than a scarecrow. You, me, Earl Wickentot, the President of the United States, and even God Almighty, as far as I can see. The only difference between one that stands up good and one that blows over is what kind of a stick they're stuck up there on."

◀ What is Mama's philosophy about the difference between one person and another?

I didn't say anything for a while, and then I told her I would ask Mr. Walter for the job.

There wasn't any sound but Henry Biddle using a hay mower on his front yard, down the road, and our peas popping open to deliver their goods out into the world.

She said, "Then what? What if he don't know you're good enough for it?"

I said, "I'll tell him. If he hasn't already given it to a Candy Striper."

Mama smiled and said, "Even if."

But he hadn't. After two days passed with nothing more said about it, I stayed after class and told him that if he didn't have his mind made up yet he'd just as well let me do it, because I would do a right smart job. I had stayed out of trouble this long, I said, and didn't intend to let my effort go to waste just because I was soon going to graduate. And he said all right, he would tell Lynda, and that I should go up there Monday afternoon and she would tell me what to do.

I had expected more of a fight, and when the conversation went straight down the road this way it took me a minute to think what to say next. He had to have about the cleanest fingernails in Pittman County.

I asked him how come he was giving the job to me. He said because I was the first one to ask. Just like that. When I think of all the time and effort girls in that school put into daydreaming about staying after school to make an offer to Hughes Walter, and I was the only one to do it. Though of course it was more a question of making the right kind of offer.

◀ Why does Mr. Walter give Missy the job?

10. **Jackson Purchase.** 1818 treaty between the U.S. government and the Chickasaw Indian Nation in which the Chickasaw were forced to sell some of their land; the land purchased by the government was added to the western portion of what today is the state of Kentucky and is now called the Jackson Purchase Region.

It turned out that I was to work mainly for Eddie Rickett, who was in charge of the lab—this was blood and pee and a few worse things though I was not about to complain—and the x-rays. Eddie was an old freckled thing, not really old but far enough along that everybody noticed he hadn't gotten married. And Eddie being the type that nobody made it their business to ask him why not.

He didn't treat me like teacher's pet or any kind of prize-pony thing, which was okay with me. With Eddie it was no horseradish, I was there to do business and I did it. Lab and x-ray were in two connected rooms with people always coming in and out through the swinging doors with their hands full and their shoes squeaking on the black linoleum. Before long I was just another one of them, filing papers in the right place and carrying human waste products without making a face.

I learned things. I learned to look in a microscope at red blood cells, platelets they are called though they aren't like plates but little catchers' mitts, and to count them in the little squares. It was the kind of thing I'm positive could make you go blind if you kept it up, but luckily there were not that many people in Pittman County who needed their platelets counted on any given day.

I hadn't been there even one whole week when hell busted loose. It was Saturday. These orderlies came in from the emergency room yelling for Eddie to get ready for a mess in x-ray. A couple of Hardbines, they said, just the way people always said that. Eddie asked how much of a hurry it was, and if he'd need help to hold them still, and they said half and half, one of them is hot and the other cold.[11]

I didn't have time to think about what that meant before Jolene Shanks, or Hardbine rather, was rolled in on a wheelchair and then came a stretcher right behind her, which they parked out in the hallway. Jolene looked like the part of the movie you don't want to watch. There was a wet tongue of blood from her right shoulder all the way down her bosom, and all the color was pulled out of her lips and face, her big face like a piece of something cut out of white dough. She was fighting and cursing, though, and clearly a far cry from dead. When I took one of her wrists to help her out of the wheelchair it twisted away under my fingers like a sleeve full of cables. She was still yelling at Newt: "Don't do it," and things like that. "Go ahead and kill your daddy for all I care, he's the one you want, not yourself and not

▶ *What has happened to Newt? What has happened to Jolene?*

11. **is hot and the other cold.** One patient is alive and the other is dead

me." Then she would go still for a minute, and then she'd start up again. I wondered what Newt's daddy had to do with it.

They said Doc Finchler was called and on his way, but that Nurse MacCullers had checked her over and it wasn't as bad as it looked. The bleeding was stopped, but they would need x-rays to see where the bullet was and if it had cracked anything on its way in. I looked at Eddie wanting to know would I have to get her out of her top and brassière into one of the gowns, and couldn't help thinking about bloodstains all over the creation, having been raised you might say in the cleaning-up business. But Eddie said no, that we didn't want to move her around that much. Doc would just have to see around the hooks and the snaps.

"Lucky for you he was a bad shot," Eddie was telling Jolene as he straightened her arm out on the table, which I thought to be rude under the circumstances but then that was Eddie. I held her by the elbows trying not to hurt her any more than she was already hurt, but poor thing she was hysterical and fighting me and wouldn't shut up. In my mind's eye I could see myself in my lead apron standing over Jolene, and this is exactly what I looked like: a butcher holding down a calf on its way to becoming a cut of meat.

Then Eddie said we were done, for me to keep her in the room next door until they could see if the pictures came out; they might have to do them over if she'd moved. Then he yelled for the other one, and two guys rolled in the long stretcher with the sheet over it and started hoisting it up on the table like something served up on a big dinner plate. I stood there like a damn fool until Eddie yelled at me to hold this one down because he wasn't going anyplace. Just another pretty picture for the coroner's office, Eddie said, but I couldn't stop staring. Maybe I'm slow. I didn't understand until just then that under that sheet, that was Newt.

◀ *What does it take a while for Missy to realize?*

In the room next door there was a stretcher intended for Jolene, but she would have none of it. She took one of the hard wooden seats that swung down from the wall, and sat there blubbering, saying, "Thank God the baby was at Mom's." Saying, "What am I going to do now?" She had on this pink top that was loose so it could have gone either way, if you were pregnant or if you weren't. As far as I

words for everyday use

hys • ter • i • cal (his ter′ i kəl) *adj.*, overwhelmed by fear, anger, sorrow, or other emotion; frantic; uncontrollable. *When the woman could not find her son at the playground, she became hysterical, and began yelling and pulling at her hair.*

know she wasn't just then. It had these little openings on the shoulders and bows on the sleeves, though of course it was shot to hell now.

Jolene was a pie-faced, heavy girl and I always thought she looked the type to have gone and found trouble just to show you didn't have to be a cheerleader to be fast. The trouble with that is it doesn't get you anywhere, no more than some kid on a bicycle going no hands and no feet up and down past his mother and hollering his head off for her to look. She's not going to look till he runs into something and busts his head wide open.

▶ *What does Jolene tell Missy about Newt's father?*

Jolene and I had never been buddies or anything, she was a year or two ahead of me in school when she dropped out, but I guess when you've just been shot and your husband's dead you look for a friend in whoever is there to hand you a Tylenol with codeine.[12] She started telling me how it was all Newt's daddy's fault, he beat him up, beat her up, and even had hit the baby with a coal scuttle.[13] I was trying to think how a half-dead old man could beat up on Newt, who was built like a side of beef. But then they all lived together in one house and it was small. And of course the old man couldn't hear, so it would have been that kind of life. There wouldn't be much talk.

I don't remember what I said, just "Uh-huh" mostly and "You're going to be okay." She kept saying she didn't know what was going to happen now with her and the baby and old man Hardbine, oh Lord, what had she got herself into.

It wasn't the kindest thing, maybe, but at one point I actually asked her, "Jolene, why Newt?" She was slumped down and rocking a little bit in the chair, holding her hurt shoulder and looking at her feet. She had these eyes that never seemed to open all the way.

What she said was "Why not, my daddy'd been calling me a slut practically since I was thirteen, so why the hell not? Newt was just who it happened to be. You know the way it is."

I told her I didn't know, because I didn't have a daddy. That I was lucky that way. She said yeah.

By the time it was over it seemed to me it ought to be dark outside, as if such a thing couldn't have happened in the daylight. But it was high noon, a whole afternoon ahead and everybody acting like here we are working for our money. I went to the bathroom and threw up twice, then came back and looked in the microscope at the little

12. **codeine.** Prescription pain reliever
13. **coal scuttle.** Metal pail used for carrying coal

catchers' mitts, counting the same ones over and over all afternoon. Nobody gave me any trouble about it. The woman that gave up that blood, anyway, got her money's worth.

I wanted Mama to be home when I got there, so I could bawl my head off and tell her I was quitting. But she wasn't and by the time she came in with a bag of groceries and a bushel basket of ironing for the weekend I was over it for the most part. I told her the whole thing, even Jolene's pink bow-ribbon top and the blood and all, and of course, Newt, and then I told her I'd probably seen the worst I was going to see so there was no reason to quit now.

◀ Why does Missy decide not to quit her job?

She gave me the biggest hug and said, "Missy, I have never seen the likes of you." We didn't talk too much more about it but I felt better with her there, the two of us moving around each other in the kitchen making boiled greens and eggs for dinner while it finally went dark outside. Every once in a while she would look over at me and just shake her head.

There were two things about Mama. One is she always expected the best out of me. And the other is that then no matter what I did, whatever I came home with, she acted like it was the moon I had just hung up in the sky and plugged in all the stars. Like I was that good.

◀ What two things does Missy reveal about Mama?

I kept that job. I stayed there over five and a half years and counted more platelets than you can think about. A person might think I didn't do much else with all that time other than keeping Mama entertained and off and on dating Sparky Pike—who most people considered to be a high-class catch because he had a steady job as a gas-meter man—until I got fed up with hearing who laid out in their backyards by their meters wearing what (or nothing-but-what) in the summertime.

But I had a plan. In our high school days the general idea of fun had been to paint "Class of '75" on the water tower, or maybe tie some farmer's goat up there on Halloween, but now I had serious intentions. In my first few years at Pittman County Hospital I was able to help Mama out with the rent and the bills and still managed to save up a couple hundred dollars. With most of it I bought a car, a '55 Volkswagen bug with no windows to speak of, and no back seat and no starter. But it was easy to push start without help once you got the hang of it, the wrong foot on the clutch and the other leg out the door, especially if you parked on a hill, which in that part of Kentucky you could hardly do

▶ *Why does Missy buy a 1955 Volkswagen bug?*

▶ *What does Mama know when she sees Missy's car? What does she make Missy do to the car?*

anything but. In this car I intended to drive out of Pittman County one day and never look back, except maybe for Mama.

The day I brought it home, she knew I was going to get away. She took one look and said, "Well, if you're going to have you an old car you're going to know how to drive an old car." What she meant was how to handle anything that might come along, I suppose, because she stood in the road with her arms crossed and watched while I took off all four tires and put them back on. "That's good, Missy," she said. "You'll drive away from here yet. I expect the last I'll see of you will be your hind end." She said, "What do you do if I let the air out of the front tire?" Which she did. I said, "Easy, I put on the spare," which believe it or not that damned old car actually had.

Then she let out the back one too and said, "Now what?" Mama had evidently run into trouble along these lines, at some point in her life with Foster and an Oldsmobile, and she wanted to be sure I was prepared.

I thought, and then I said, "I have a bicycle pump. I can get enough air in it to drive down to Norman Strick's and get it pumped up the rest of the way." And she just stood there with her arms crossed and I could see that she nor God nor nobody else was going to do it for me, so I closed my eyes and went at that tire for everything I was worth.

Mama hadn't been there that day. She couldn't know that all I was seeing behind those shut eyes was Newt Hardbine's daddy flying up into the air, in slow motion, like a fish flinging sideways out of the water. And Newt laid out like a hooked bass.

▶ *What is the first promise the narrator makes to herself?*

When I drove over the Pittman line I made two promises to myself. One I kept, the other I did not.

The first was that I would get myself a new name. I wasn't crazy about anything I had been called up to that point in life, and this seemed like the time to make a clean break. I didn't have any special name in mind, but just wanted a change. The more I thought about it, the more it seemed to me that a name is not something a person really has the right to pick out, but is something you're provided with more or less by chance. I decided to let the gas tank decide. Wherever it ran out, I'd look for a sign.

I came pretty close to being named after Homer, Illinois, but kept pushing it. I kept my fingers crossed through Sidney, Sadorus, Cerro Gordo, Decatur, and Blue Mound, and coasted into Taylorville on the fumes.[14] And so I am Taylor Greer. I suppose you could say I had some part in choosing this name, but there was enough of destiny in it to satisfy me.

What new name does the narrator take?

The second promise, the one that I broke, had to do with where I would end up. I had looked at some maps, but since I had never in my own memory been outside of Kentucky (I was evidently born across the river in Cincinnati, but that is beside the point), I had no way of knowing why or how any particular place might be preferable to any other. That is, apart from the pictures on the gas station brochures: Tennessee claimed to be the Volunteer State, and Missouri the Show-Me State, whatever that might mean, and nearly everyplace appeared to have plenty of ladies in fifties hairdos standing near waterfalls. These brochures I naturally did not trust as far as I could throw them out the window. Even Pittman, after all, had once been chosen an All-Kentucky City, on the basis of what I do not know. Its abundance of potato bugs and gossip, perhaps. I knew how people could toot their own horn without any earthly cause.

And so what I promised myself is that I would drive west until my car stopped running, and there I would stay. But there were some things I hadn't considered. Mama taught me well about tires, and many other things besides, but I knew nothing of rocker arms. And I did not know about the Great Plain.[15]

What is the second promise the narrator makes to herself, but does not keep?

The sight of it filled me with despair. I turned south from Wichita, Kansas, thinking I might find a way around it, but I didn't. There was central Oklahoma. I had never imagined that any part of a round earth could be so flat. In Kentucky you could never see too far, since there were always mountains blocking the other side of your view, and it left you the chance to think something good might be just over the next hill. But out there on the plain it was all laid out right in front of you, and no matter how far you looked it didn't get any better. Oklahoma made me feel there was nothing left to hope for.

How does Oklahoma make Taylor feel?

My car gave out somewhere in the middle of a great emptiness that according to the road signs was owned by the Cherokee tribe. Suddenly the steering wheel bore no

Where does Taylor's car break down?

14. **on the fumes.** Expression meaning that the gas tank of a car is so close to empty that the car is running just on the smell of the gas

15. **Great Plain.** Vast expanse of flat, treeless country ranging from Alberta and Saskatchewan in western Canada through Texas in the United States; the Great Plains cover central and eastern Montana, all of North and South Dakota, eastern Wyoming and Colorado, all of Nebraska and Kansas, central and western Oklahoma, eastern New Mexico, and a sizeable chunk of central Texas.

▶ *What did Taylor's mother tell Taylor about the Cherokee Nation and her great grandfather?*

▶ *What does Taylor believe is the reason the Cherokees were brought to Oklahoma? What did the Cherokees believe about trees? How many trees has Taylor seen in Oklahoma?*

relation to where the car was going. By the grace of some miracle I surely did not yet deserve, I managed to wobble off the highway all in one piece and find a service station.

The man who straightened out my rocker arm was named Bob Two Two. I am not saying he didn't ask a fair price—I should have been able to fix it myself—but he went home that night with his pocket full of something near half the money I had. I sat in the parking lot looking out over that godless stretch of nothing and came the closest I have ever come to cashing in and plowing under.[16] But there was no sense in that. My car was fixed.

I had to laugh, really. All my life, Mama had talked about the Cherokee Nation[17] as our ace in the hole.[18] She'd had an old grandpa that was full-blooded Cherokee, one of the few that got left behind in Tennessee because he was too old or too ornery to get marched over to Oklahoma. Mama would say, "If we run out of luck we can always go live on the Cherokee Nation." She and I both had enough blood to qualify. According to Mama, if you're one-eighth or more they let you in. She called this our "head rights."[19]

Of course, if she had ever been there she would have known it was not a place you'd ever go to live without some kind of lethal weapon aimed at your hind end. It was clear to me that the whole intention of bringing the Cherokees here was to get them to lie down and die without a fight.[20] The Cherokees believed God was in trees. Mama told me this. When I was a kid I would climb as high as I could in a tree and not come down until dinner. "That's your Indian blood," she would say. "You're trying to see God."

From what I could see, there was not one tree in the entire state of Oklahoma.

The sun was headed fast for the flat horizon, and then there would be nothing but twelve hours of headlights in front of me. I was in a hurry to get out of there. My engine was still running from Bob Two Two's jumper cables, and I hated to let a good start go to waste, but I was tired and

---

16. **cashing in and plowing under.** Giving up and going home
17. **Cherokee Nation.** Refers here to the physical boundaries of The Cherokee Nation of Oklahoma, whose capital city is Talequah, Oklahoma, and which is not a reservation but a self-governing nation recognized by the U.S. government
18. **ace in the hole.** Something good one holds onto in case it's needed later
19. **head rights.** Right to live on the Cherokee Indian Reservation, which requires proof of Cherokee descent
20. **bringing the Cherokees...without a fight.** Removal by U.S. troops of the Cherokee from their territory in Georgia to "Indian Territory," which is now the state of Oklahoma; this forced removal in 1838 and the Cherokee march to Oklahoma, in which nearly one-quarter of the population died from disease or exhaustion, is known as "The Trail of Tears."

didn't want to begin a night of driving without a cup of coffee and something to eat. I drove across the big patch of dirt that lay between the garage and another small brick-shaped building that had a neon Budweiser light in the window.

When I drove around to the front, a swarm of little boys came down on my car like bees on a bear.

"Wash your windows, lady," they said. "Dollar for the whole car."

"I got no windows," I told them. I reached back and put my hand through the side window hole to show them. "See, just the windshield. Lucky me, because I got no dollar either."

The boys went around the car putting their hands through all the window holes again and again. I thought twice about leaving my stuff in the car while I went into the restaurant. I didn't have anything worth taking, but then it was all I had.

I asked them, "You boys live around here?"

They looked at each other. "Yeah," one of them said. "He does. He's my brother. Them two don't."

"You ever hear of a Polaroid memory?"

The big one nodded. The others just stared.

"Well, I got one," I said. "It's just like a camera. My memory just took a picture of what y'all look like, so don't take any stuff out of my car, okay? You take any stuff, you're in for it."

The kids backed off from the car rubbing their hands on their sides, like they were wiping off anything their hands might have already imagined grabbing onto.

After the cool night, the hot air inside the bar hit me like something you could swim through. Near the door there was a wire rack of postcards. Some had Indians in various hokey poses, but most were views-from-the-air of Oral Roberts University, which apparently was in the vicinity—although I'm pretty sure if it had been within two hundred miles I could have seen it from the parking lot.

I picked out one with two Indian women on it, an older and a younger, pretty one, standing side by side next to some corn-grinding thing. I had often wondered which one-eighth of me was Cherokee, and in this picture I could begin

words for everyday use

hok • ey (hō kē) *adj.*, corny; phony. *Our school mascot is a giant ear of corn who performs hokey dances with the cheerleaders.*

to see it. The long, straight hair and the slender wrist bones. The younger one was wearing my two favorite colors, turquoise and red. I would write on it to Mama, "Here's us."

I sat down at the counter and gave the man a dime for the postcard. I nodded when he pointed the pot of coffee at me, and he filled my cup. The jukebox was playing Kenny Rogers and the TV behind the counter was turned on, although the sound was off. It was some program about, or from, Oral Roberts University, which I recognized from the postcards. Frequently a man with clean fat hands and a crest of hair like a woodpecker would talk on and on without sound. I presumed this was Oral Roberts himself, though of course I can't say for certain that it was. From time to time a line of blue writing would run across the bottom of the screen. Sometimes it gave a telephone number, and sometimes it just said "Praise the Lord." I wrote my postcard to Mama. "Grandpa had the right idea," I told her. "No offense, but the Cherokee Nation is crap. Headed west. Love, M." It didn't seem right just yet to sign it Taylor.

The place was cleared out except for two men at the counter, a white guy and an Indian. They both wore cowboy hats. I thought to myself, I guess now Indians can be cowboys too, though probably not vice versa. The Indian man wore a brown hat and had a brown, fine-looking face that reminded me of an eagle, not that I had ever actually seen an eagle. He was somewhere between young and not so young. I tried to imagine having a great grandpa with a nose like that and such a smooth chin. The other one in the gray hat looked like he had a mean streak to him. You can tell the kind that's looking for trouble. They were drinking beers and watching Oral on the silent TV, and once in a great while they would say something to each other in a low voice. They might have been on their first couple of beers, or they might have been drinking since sunup—with some types you can't tell until it's too late. I tried to recall where I had been at sunup that day. It was in St. Louis, Missouri, where they have that giant McDonald's thing towering over the city, but that didn't seem possible. That seemed like about a blue moon[21] ago.

▶ *What does Taylor think about the man in the gray hat, based on how he looks?*

"You got anything to eat that costs less than a dollar?" I asked the old guy behind the counter. He crossed his arms and looked at me for a minute, as if nobody had ever asked him this before.

21. **blue moon.** Very long period of time; refers to the *blue moon,* the second full moon in one month, which occurs roughly forty times every one hundred years

"Ketchup," the gray-hat cowboy said. "Earl serves up a mean bottle of ketchup, don't you, Earl?" He slid the ketchup bottle down the counter so hard it rammed my cup and spilled out probably five cents' worth of coffee.

"You think being busted is a joke?" I asked him. I slid the bottle back and hit his beer mug dead center, although it did not spill. He looked at me and then looked back to the TV, like I wasn't the kind of thing to be bothered with. It made me want to spit nails.[22]

◀ How does the man in the gray hat look at Taylor?

"He don't mean nothing by it, miss," Earl told me. "He's got a bug up his butt. I can get you a burger for ninety-nine cents."

"Okay," I told Earl.

Maybe ten or fifteen minutes passed before the food came, and I kept myself awake trying to guess what the fat-hands man was saying on the TV screen. Earl's place could have done with a scrub. I could see through the open door into the kitchen, and the black grease on the back of the stove looked like it had been there since the Dawn of Man. The air in there was so hot and stale I felt like I had to breathe it twice to get any oxygen out of it. The coffee did nothing to wake me up. My food came just as I was about to step outside for some air.

I noticed another woman in the bar sitting at one of the tables near the back. She was a round woman, not too old, wrapped in a blanket. It was not an Indian blanket but a plain pink wool blanket with a satin band sewed on the edge, exactly like one Mama and I had at home. Her hair lay across her shoulders in a pair of skinny, lifeless plaits.[23] She was not eating or drinking, but fairly often she would glance up at the two men, or maybe just one of them, I couldn't really tell. The way she looked at them made me feel like if I had better sense I'd be scared.

◀ How does the woman in the back of the bar look at the men at the bar?

Earl's ninety-nine-cent burger brought me around a little, though I still felt like my head had been stuffed with that fluffy white business they use in life preservers. I imagined myself stepping outside and the wind just scattering me. I would float out over the flat, dark plain like the silvery fuzz from a milkweed pod.

Putting it off, I read all the signs on the walls, one by one, which said things like THEY CAN'T FIRE ME, SLAVES HAVE TO BE SOLD and IN CASE OF FIRE YELL FIRE. The television kept on saying PRAISE THE LORD. 1-800-THE LORD. I tried to concentrate on keeping myself all in one place, even if it wasn't a spot

---

22. **want to spit nails.** Very angry
23. **plaits.** Braids

I was crazy about. Then I went outside. The air was cool and I drank it too fast, getting a little dizzy. I sat with my hands on the steering wheel for a few minutes trying to think myself into the right mood for driving all night across Oklahoma.

I jumped when she pecked on the windshield. It was the round woman in the blanket.

"No thanks," I said. I thought she wanted to wash the windshield, but instead she went around to the other side and opened the door. "You need a lift someplace?" I asked her.

Her body, her face, and her eyes were all round. She was someone you could have drawn a picture of by tracing around dimes and quarters and jar tops. She opened up the blanket and took out something alive. It was a child. She wrapped her blanket around and around it until it became a round bundle with a head. Then she set this bundle down on the seat of my car.

"Take this baby," she said.

It wasn't a baby, exactly. It was probably old enough to walk, though not so big that it couldn't be easily carried. Somewhere between a baby and a person.

"Where do you want me to take it?"

She looked back at the bar, and then looked at me. "Just take it."

I waited a minute, thinking that soon my mind would clear and I would understand what she was saying. It didn't. The child had the exact same round eyes. All four of those eyes were hanging there in the darkness, hanging on me, waiting. The Budweiser sign blinked on and off, on and off, throwing a faint light that made the whites of their eyes look orange.

▶ *According to the woman from the bar, who is the child's mother?*

"Is this your kid?"

She shook her head. "My dead sister's."

"Are you saying you want to give me this child?"

"Yes."

"If I wanted a baby I would have stayed in Kentucky," I informed her. "I could have had babies coming out my ears by now."

A man came out of the bar, gray hat or brown hat I couldn't tell because my car was parked some distance from the door. He got into a pickup truck but didn't start the ignition or turn on the lights.

"Is that your man in there, in the bar?" I asked her.

"Don't go back in there. I'm not saying why. Just don't."

"Look," I said, "even if you wanted to, you can't just give somebody a kid. You got to have the papers and stuff. Even a car has papers, to prove you didn't steal it."

"This baby's got no papers. There isn't nobody knows it's alive, or cares. Nobody that matters, like the police or nothing like that. This baby was born in a Plymouth."

◀ *What does the woman tell Taylor about the child?*

"Well, it didn't happen this morning," I said. "Plymouth or no Plymouth, this child has been around long enough for somebody to notice." I had a foggy understanding that I wasn't arguing the right point. This was getting us nowhere.

She put her hands where the child's shoulders might be, under all that blanket, and pushed it gently back into the seat, trying to make it belong there. She looked at it for a long time. Then she closed the door and walked away.

As I watched her I was thinking that she wasn't really round. Without the child and the blanket she walked away from my car a very thin woman.

I held the steering wheel and dug my fingernails into my palms, believing the pain might force my brain to wake up and think what to do. While I was thinking, the woman got in the pickup truck and it drove away without lights. I wondered if that was for a reason, or if it just didn't have headlights. "Praise the Lord," I said out loud. "At least my car has headlights."

I thought: I can take this Indian child back into that bar and give it to Earl or whichever of those two guys is left. Just set it on the counter with the salt and pepper and get the hell out of here. Or I can go someplace and sleep, and think of something to do in the morning.

◀ *What two options is Taylor trying to decide between?*

While I was deciding, the lights in the bar flickered out. The Budweiser sign blinked off and stayed off. Another pickup truck swung around in the gravel parking lot and headed off toward the highway.

It took everything I had to push-start the car. Naturally I had not found a hill to park on in Oklahoma. "Shit!" I said. "Shit fire son of a bitch!" I pushed and pushed, jumped in and popped the clutch, jumped out and pushed some more. I could see the child's big eyes watching me in the dark.

"This isn't as dumb as you think," I said. "It's easier in Kentucky."

My car has no actual way of keeping track of miles, but I believe it must have been fifty or more before we came to a town. It was getting cold with no windows, and the poor little thing must have been freezing but didn't make a peep.

"Can you talk?" I said. I wondered if maybe it spoke something besides English. "What am I supposed to do with you tonight?" I said. "What do you eat?"

I believe that flat places are quieter than hilly ones. The sounds of the cars on the highway seemed to get sucked straight out over the empty fields where there was nothing, not even a silo,[24] to stop them from barreling on forever into the night. I began to think that if I opened my mouth nothing would come out. I hummed to myself to keep some sound in my ears. At the same time I would have paid my bottom dollar for a radio. I would even have listened to Oral Roberts. I talked to the poor, dumb-struck child to stay awake, although with every passing mile I felt less sleepy and more concerned that I was doing something extremely strange.

We passed a sign that said some-odd number of miles to the Pioneer Woman Museum. Great, I thought. Now we're getting somewhere.

"Are you a girl or a boy?" I asked the child. It had a cereal-bowl haircut, like pictures you see of Chinese kids. She or he said nothing. I supposed I would find out eventually.

▶ *About what does Taylor begin to worry as she is driving with the silent child?*

After a while I began to wonder if perhaps it was dead. Maybe the woman had a dead child, murdered or some such thing, and had put it in my car, and I was riding down the road beside it, talking to it. I had read a story in Senior English about a woman who slept with her dead husband for forty years. It was basically the same idea as the guy and his mother in *Psycho,* except that Norman Bates in *Psycho*[25] was a taxidermist and knew how to preserve his mother so she wouldn't totally rot out. Indians sometimes knew how to preserve the dead. I had read about Indian mummies out West. People found them in caves. I told myself to calm down. I remembered that the baby's eyes had been open when she put it down on the seat. But then again, so what if its eyes were open? Had it blinked? What was the penalty for carrying a dead Indian child across state lines?

▶ *What does Taylor smell? What does this tell her?*

After a while I smelled wet wool. "Merciful heavens," I said. "I guess you're still hanging in there."

My plan had been to sleep in the car, but naturally my plans had not taken into account a wet, cold kid. "We're really in trouble now, you know it?" I said. "The next phone booth we come to, I'm going to have to call 1-800-THE LORD."

24. **silo.** Tall cylinder used to make and store food for cattle

25. **Norman Bates in *Psycho*.** Main character in Alfred Hitchcock's 1960 horror movie

The next phone booth we did come to, as a matter of fact, was outside the Mustang Motel. I drove by slowly and checked the place out, but the guy in the office didn't look too promising.

There were four or five motels pretty much in a row, their little glass-fronted offices shining out over the highway like TV screens. Some of the offices were empty. In the Broken Arrow Motor Lodge there was a gray-haired woman. Bingo.

I parked under the neon sign of a pink arrow breaking and unbreaking, over and over, and went into the office.

"Hi," I said to the lady. "Nice evening. Kind of chilly, though."

She was older than she had looked from outside. Her hands shook when she lifted them off the counter and her head shook all the time, just slightly, like she was trying to signal "No" to somebody behind my back, on the sly.

But she wasn't, it was just age. She smiled. "Winter's on its way," she said.

"Yes, ma'am, it is."

"You been on the road long?"

"Way too long," I said. "This place is real nice. It's a sight for sore eyes. Do you own this place?"

"My son owns it," she said, her head shaking. "I'm over here nights."

"So it's kind of a family thing?"

"Kind of like. My daughter-in-law and me, we do most of the cleaning up and all, and my son does the business end of it. He works in the meat-packing plant over at Ponca City. This here's kind of a sideline thing."

"You reckon it's going to fill up tonight?"

She laughed. "Law, honey, I don't think this place been filled up since President Truman."[26] She slowly turned the pages of the big check-in book.

"President Truman stayed here?"

She looked up at me, her eyes swimming through her thick glasses like enormous tadpoles. "Why no, honey, I don't think so. I'd remember a thing like that."

"You seem like a very kind person," I said, "so I'm not going to beat around the bush. I've got a problem. I can't really afford to pay for a room, and I wouldn't even bother you except I've got a child out in that car that's wet and cold and looking to catch pneumonia if I don't get it to bed someplace warm."

---

26. **President Truman.** Harry Truman, the thirty-second president of the United States, who held office from 1945–1953

▶ *What does Taylor offer to do in exchange for a room at the motel?*

▶ *What does Taylor say is the most amazing thing about the child?*

She looked out toward the car and shook her head, but of course I couldn't tell what that meant. She said, "Well, honey, I don't know."

"I'll take anything you've got, and I'll clean up after myself, and tomorrow morning I'll change every bed in this place. Or anything else you want me to do. It's just for one night."

"Well," she said, "I don't know."

"Let me go get the baby," I said. "You won't mind if I just bring the poor kid in here to warm up while you decide."

The most amazing thing was the way that child held on. From the first moment I picked it up out of its nest of wet blanket, it attached itself to me by its little hands like roots sucking on dry dirt. I think it would have been easier to separate me from my hair.

It's probably a good thing. I was so tired, and of course I was not in the habit anyway of remembering every minute where I had put down a child, and I think if it had not been stuck to me I might have lost it while I was messing with the car and moving stuff into the little end room of the Broken Arrow. As it was, I just ended up carrying it back and forth a lot. It's like the specimens back at the hospital, I told myself. You just have to keep track. It looked like carrying blood and pee was to be my lot in life.

Once we were moved in I spread the blanket over a chair to dry and ran a few inches of warm water in the tub. "First order of business," I said, "is to get you a bath. We'll work out the rest tomorrow." I remembered the time I had found a puppy and wanted to keep it, but first Mama made me spend thirty-five cents a word to run an ad in the paper. "What if it was yours?" she had said. "Think how bad you'd want it back." The ad I wrote said: FOUND PUPPY, BROWN SPOTS, NEAR FLOYD'S MILL ROAD. I had resented how Floyd's Mill Road was three whole words, a dollar and five cents.

I thought to myself, I'd pay a hundred and five to get this one back to its rightful owner. But what kind of ad would you run to find out if anybody had lost an Indian child?

All of the baby's clothes were way too big, with sleeves rolled up and shirt tails wrapped around, and everything wet as mud boots and as hard to get off. There was a bruise twice the size of my thumb on its inner arm. I threw the soggy shirt in the sink to soak. The child's hands constantly caught my fingers and wouldn't let go. "You little booger," I said, shaking my finger and the little fist. "You're like a mud turtle. If a mud turtle bites you, it won't let go till it thunders." I hadn't any sooner gotten the hands pried loose from my fingers before they grabbed onto my shirt sleeves and my hair. When I pulled off the pants and the diapers there were more bruises.

Bruises and worse.

The Indian child was a girl. A girl, poor thing. That fact had already burdened her short life with a kind of misery I could not imagine. I thought I knew about every ugly thing that one person does to another, but I had never even thought about such things being done to a baby girl. She sat quietly in the bathtub watching me, and I just prayed she had enough backbone not to fall over and drown, because I had to let her go. I doubled up on the floor at the base of the toilet and tried not to throw up. The floor was linoleum in a pattern that looked like rubber bricks set in mortar. Nothing, not Newt Hardbine or anything else I had ever seen, had made me feel like this.

◀ *What does Taylor realize has happened to the child?*

◀ *How does this make Taylor feel?*

The kid was splashing like a toad frog. Her fingers were wiggling and slapping at the surface of the water, no doubt trying to grab hold of something. "Here," I said, and handed her a washcloth that had BROKEN ARROW written on the selvage[27] in indelible magic marker. She hugged that wash cloth and smiled. I swear to God.

After I washed and dried her I put her to bed in a T-shirt that one of Mama's people had brought me one summer from Kentucky Lake. It was tight on me, and said DAMN I'M GOOD. I am skinny and flat-chested like a model, and always looked great in that T-shirt if I say so myself. It was turquoise with red letters, and came down past the baby's knees. "These are good colors," I said, trying to pull it over her sleepy, bobbing head. "Indian colors." Finally her hands were empty and relaxed. She was asleep.

I took out the stamps I had brought from home wrapped in waxed paper, and licked one and stuck it on my souvenir postcard from the Cherokee Nation. I added a line at the bottom:

"I found my head rights, Mama. They're coming with me."

---

27. **selvage.** Edge or border of a piece of fabric that keeps it from unraveling

words for everyday use

in • del • i • ble (in de' lə bəl) *adj.*, lasting; unforgettable; that which cannot be removed, erased, or washed off. *As Jerome looked out from the top of the mountain he had just climbed, he knew he was creating an indelible memory.*

Two

New Year's Pig

▶ *How does Lou Ann Ruiz think of herself?*

Lou Ann Ruiz lived in Tucson,[1] but thought of herself as just an ordinary Kentuckian a long way from home. She had acquired her foreign last name from her husband, Angel. As it turned out, this was the only part of him that would remain with her. He left on Halloween.

Three years before on Christmas Day Angel had had a bad accident in his pickup truck. It left him with an artificial leg below the knee, and something else that was harder to pin down. Lou Ann often would get the feeling that he didn't really like her, or anyone else for that matter. He blamed people for things beyond their control. Lou Ann was now pregnant with her first, which was due in two months. She hoped more than anything that it wouldn't be born on Christmas Day.

▶ *What had Lou Ann been thinking about for a long time? What did she do about it?*

She had been thinking about herself and Angel splitting up for even longer than she had been pregnant, but she didn't particularly do anything about it. That was Lou Ann's method. She expected that a divorce would just develop, like a pregnancy—that eventually they would reach some kind of agreement without having to discuss it. This isn't how it worked out.

▶ *What quality did the arguments between Angel and Lou Ann take on? How did they make Lou Ann feel?*

When she began to turn away from him in bed at night, and to get up quietly in the mornings to cook his eggs, Angel seemed to accept this. Possibly he thought she was worried about the baby. Later, when the arguments resumed, they had a hopeless quality that Lou Ann had not experienced before. The arguments made her feel that her bones were made of something like the rubber in a Gumby[2] doll, that her body could be bent into any shape and would stay that way. She would sit at the kitchen table tracing her fingers over the artificial knots in the wood-look Formica table top while Angel paced back and forth and accused her of thinking he wasn't good enough. He listed names of people, mostly friends of his she could barely remember having met, and asked her if she had slept with them, or if she had wanted to. Angel limped so slightly it was barely noticeable, but there was just the faintest jingling sound with every other step. It was probably something he could have gotten adjusted if he hadn't been too proud to take it into

1. **Tucson.** City in southeastern Arizona
2. **Gumby.** Animated clay figure that was the main character of a television show for children in the 1950s

the prosthetic shop. No matter how loud his voice became, Lou Ann could still hear the jingle. She could never think of anything to say that would change the course of these arguments, and so they went on and on. Once, several years before, she had become so frustrated with Angel that she threw a package of baloney at him. They both laughed, and it ended the argument. Now she didn't have the strength to get up and open the refrigerator.

Finally he had said it was because of his leg, and no matter what she said he wouldn't hear it any other way. She more or less gave up talking, and when she lay on her back at night she felt it was the guilt weighing down on her aching spine, instead of the baby.

She could remember wheeling him down the white corridor at the hospital to bring him home, just two and a half weeks after the accident. She had felt filled-up and proud; everything she loved in the world was in that chair. Having nearly lost Angel made him all the more precious. One of the doctors said that his boot had probably saved his life, and she felt like kissing it, although in all the confusion no one knew exactly where it had ended up. The boot had caught on the door frame, causing him to be dragged several hundred yards along with the truck as it spun into an irrigation ditch along Highway 86 west of Tucson. The damage to the truck was surprisingly minor. There was a bottle of Jim Beam[3] in the cab that wasn't even broken. He lost his leg because of being twisted and dragged, but the doctor said if he had been thrown from the vehicle at such a high speed he would have died instantly. It crossed Lou Ann's mind that he might have just been saying this because Angel was so upset about losing a leg, but she decided it would be best to take the doctor's word for it.

◀ *How did Lou Ann feel when she picked Angel up at the hospital to bring him home?*

When he came home Lou Ann gave up her part-time job at the Three Bears Day School to be with him, insisting that they would get along fine on his disability pay until he was able to go back to work at the bottling plant. She spent weeks playing gin rummy with Angel on the bed and running out to Lee Sing's market to get whatever he wanted. She loved the way he asked for things specifically, like Mrs. Smith's pound cake or Beefaroni. She wouldn't have guessed Angel had even noticed that things came in different brand names, other than beer. It was their best time together.

Never at any time was Lou Ann repulsed by the amputation. After his stump had healed it did not bother her to

3. **Jim Beam.** Brand of bourbon, a type of alcoholic beverage

touch it, which Angel himself would never do. It had a smooth, defenseless look to it that reminded her of a penis, something she had always thought seemed out of place on a man's body. When he got the prosthesis she was fascinated at first by the way it was put together, and then thought nothing of it at all. It was something that lay on the floor by his side of the bed at night while the cat, Snowboots, lay curled up by hers. It took Angel some time to get used to the new leg, but in the long run there was very little he couldn't do with it, except that he was no longer able to wear cowboy boots. For some reason the ankle hinges were not flexible enough to fit into a boot. Other than this, Lou Ann could never see why the accident needed to change his life at all. He hadn't been a cowboy for years, anyway.

▶ *What couldn't Lou Ann understand about Angel's accident? Why?*

On the Friday Angel left, he had long since gone back to work. He probably didn't think about it being Halloween, only that it was payday. Lou Ann didn't think of any of this, of course, since she had no idea that it was the particular day her husband had decided to leave her.

▶ *Where is Lou Ann on the day that Angel leaves her?*

Lou Ann was in Dr. Pelinowsky's waiting room waiting for her seventh-month prenatal exam. She had a magazine on her lap, or what was left of her lap, but preferred to stare instead at an enormous wall calendar that showed all the months at once. She was anxious about her child's birthday. Christmas had been difficult for Angel and Lou Ann since the accident, naturally, and they had just about stopped celebrating it altogether. Having a baby on that day would just be a reminder. And besides she had read in *McCall's*[4] that children with Christmas birthdays often feel cheated out of having their own special day. Lou Ann thought being born the day after, when everybody is fed up with celebrating, would just be that much worse. She decided to ask the doctor if there was some way to make sure the baby would come before Christmas, although she was pretty sure there wasn't.

Dr. Pelinowsky's nurses seemed to like him, and called him "Dr. P." Lou Ann thought this was a hoot because he was OB-GYN, a maternity doctor, which all starts when you bring in a jar of pee. She had to keep from laughing out loud when-

4. ***McCall's.*** Magazine with articles about raising a family, cooking, and sewing

words for everyday use

pros • the • sis (präs thē′ səs) *n.*, an artificial device to replace a missing part of the body. *Iliana, who lost her leg in an automobile accident and wears a prosthesis, is one of the most physically active people I know.*

pre • na • tal (prē na′ təl) *adj.*, occurring, existing, or performed before birth. *A wholesome diet, exercise, and regular visits to the doctor are important prenatal responsibilities that contribute to a healthy pregnancy and baby.*

ever she heard the nurses call out over the intercom, "Doctor Pee, Doctor Pee."

A nurse with crispy-looking white hair and a lavender pants suit came out and called Lou Ann's name. She called her Mrs. Angel Ruiz. Angel would always correct Anglos when they pronounced his name wrong. "Ahn-*hel!*" he would say. "I'm not a damn baseball team!" But Lou Ann rarely corrected anybody on anything. Her mother, Mrs. Logan, still pronounced neither Angel's first name nor their last name correctly, saying it something like Ruins. She hadn't wanted Lou Ann to marry Angel in the first place, but for the wrong reasons. She disliked him because he was Mexican, which didn't make the slightest difference to Lou Ann. In Tucson, she tried to explain to her mother, there were so many Mexicans that people didn't think of them as a foreign race. They were doctors, bank clerks, TV personalities, and even owned hotels. "You can see them any day of the week eating in a Black Angus Steak House," she told her mother. Mrs. Logan, who lived in eastern Kentucky and had never seen a Mexican, thought Lou Ann was making this up.

◀ *Why does Lou Ann's mother dislike Angel? How does Lou Ann feel about this?*

When Dr. Pelinowsky examined her he warned again that she was gaining too much weight. Originally he had thought it might be twins, but now they knew for sure it was just Lou Ann and the baby. This time his warning about her weight was more severe. For Lou Ann, who had always been practically underweight according to the doctor's office charts, it was impossible to imagine she wouldn't be exactly the same after it was all over. But she had to admit the baby made her want to eat constantly. She told Dr. Pelinowsky that it's hard when you're in the kitchen cooking for someone all the time. He told her to put her husband on a diet too. He meant it as a joke.

On her way out the nurse gave her a pamphlet with a special diet written out in both English and Spanish. She thought about asking for a second copy to send to her mother. After four years Lou Ann still felt that she had to prove her point about Mexicans, and so she would send clippings from the newspaper when they were promoted to company vice presidents and such. Lou Ann realized, though, that this pamphlet didn't fall into that category. Her mother was no doubt already convinced that Mexicans had babies like anyone else. In fact, she had told Lou Ann that from what she heard they had too many, that they were trying to take over the world like the Catholics.

Lou Ann hadn't yet broken the news that, when the baby was born, the plan was to give it a Catholic baptism.[5] This would be for the sake of Angel's mother, who frequently claimed to be dying from any one of various causes. The only English words she knew were the names of diseases. Lou Ann made the baptism decision purely for practical reasons: if one of the grandmothers was going to have a conniption,[6] it might as well be the one who was eighteen hundred miles away rather than the one who lived right across town.

Lou Ann looked over the pamphlet while she waited for the bus. Like most of the other literature she had received, it had a picture on the front of a mother holding a baby. Sometimes the women in the pictures were white, sometimes Mexican, and sometimes black. They were shown holding their babies in various positions, but they were never shown as pregnant. Lou Ann wondered about this, since all the pamphlets were about prenatal care.

On the bus she decided it must have to do with the fact that the pamphlets were put together by men, who in her opinion liked the looks of a mother and baby better than a pregnant woman. She was fairly sure about this. On the bus, for instance, several men would stand up to offer her a seat, but they wouldn't quite look at her. The high school boys didn't make remarks under their breath or try to rub up against her when the bus made sudden stops and turns. To be able to relax this way on a crowded bus was a new experience for Lou Ann, and she thought that in some ways it would not be so bad to go through your life as a pregnant lady.

She watched the houses and telephone poles go sailing by. Some of the telephone poles had advertisements for Tania Maria, a woman leaning forward in a loose sweater and spike heels. She was a singer, and had enough hair for at least two people. Other telephone poles had black posters with letters that appeared to be cut out of a newspaper, like the ransom notes in mystery novels, but they were ads for bands with names like Audio Confusion and Useless Turmoil and the Meat Puppets. She thought of naming her baby Tania Maria. Angel would suggest naming it something like Meat Puppet. That would be his idea of a joke.

It was pure pleasure not to have men pushing into her and touching her on the bus. It allowed her mind to drift

---

5. **baptism.** Religious ceremony in which a person, usually a baby, is dipped into water to symbolize spiritual cleansing and initiation into the religious community

6. **conniption.** Fit of rage, hysteria, or alarm

far away from her strange, enormous body. When she was nine her Grandfather Ormsby had given her a jackknife, and had told her that for safety's sake she should always keep a magic circle around her when she used it. She would sit in the backyard and draw a circle in the dirt that no one could come into while she whittled for hours and hours on thick brown bars of soap. The jackknife was long gone now, but once again there was something like a magic circle around her.

She got off at the Roosevelt Park shop, which was a half block from the park itself. Sprawled over the large corner lot was a place called Jesus Is Lord Used Tires. You couldn't make a mistake about the name—it was painted in big, cramped blue letters over the door, with periods inserted between the words: JESUS.IS.LORD.USED.TIRES. On the side of the pleated tin building there was a large picture of Jesus with outstretched hands and yellow streamers of light emanating from His head. There was also a whitewall tire, perhaps added to the mural as an afterthought and probably meant to have no direct connection with the Lord, but it hung in the air below His left hand very much like a large yoyo. Jesus appeared to be on the verge of performing an Around the World[7] or some other fancy trick.

◀ *What is the name of the used tire store?*

Top-heavy, chin-high stacks of Firestones and Michelins[8] at the edge of the paved lot formed a wall between Jesus Is Lord and a combination nightclub and pornography shop next door called Fanny Heaven. There was no mistaking this place either. The front windows were whitewashed, and large signs painted over them declared GIRLS GIRLS GIRLS on one side of the door and TOTAL NUDITY on the other. On the front door of Fanny Heaven was a life-size likeness of a woman with long red hair and a leopard-skin bikini. Public art of various types was popular on this block.

Lou Ann walked past both of these establishments nearly every day. Something about the Jesus Is Lord place reminded her of Kentucky, and she always meant to ask (if she only had the nerve) if the people there came from her part of the country. Fanny Heaven she just tried to ignore. There was something innocent and primitive about the

7. **Around the World.** Yo-yo trick
8. **Firestones and Michelins.** Brands of tires

words for everyday use

em • a • nate (em′ ə nāt) *v.*, flow from; spring; come out from a source. *People are surprised to find that feelings of joy often emanate from doing selfless things for others.*

painting on the door, as though the leopard-bikini lady might have been painted by a schoolchild, except that she was positioned in such a way that the door handle, when a person pushed it, would sink into her crotch. This door always gave Lou Ann the shivers, though she tried not to give it a second thought.

▶ Why doesn't Lou Ann buy all the items recommended by the diet pamphlet?

She rounded the corner and stopped to do some grocery shopping at the Lee Sing Market, which faced the park directly across from where she and Angel lived. She bought most of the items recommended by the diet pamphlet, but some of them, like yogurt, were too expensive. She bought a package of macaroons[9] because they were Angel's favorite.

▶ What does Lee Sing tell Lou Ann?

The Chinese woman at the cash register was Lee Sing. Her mother, who was said to be more than one hundred years old, lived with her in the back of the store. Lee Sing told Lou Ann she was going to have a girl. "She's high, up here," Lee Sing said, tapping her bony fist above her stomach. She said this to Lou Ann every time she came in.

"Either way is okay with me," Lou Ann said, although she was somewhat curious to see if Lee Sing would be right.

Lee Sing shook her head as she rang the cash register, and muttered something that sounded to Lou Ann like "New Year pig."

"Beg your pardon?" Lou Ann was a little afraid of Lee Sing, who often said peculiar things like this.

▶ What does Lee Sing say about feeding a girl? How does Lou Ann feel about Lee Sing's comment?

▶ Where does Lou Ann's brother live? Whom did he marry?

"Feeding a girl is like feeding the neighbor's New Year pig. All that work. In the end, it goes to some other family."

Lou Ann felt offended, but didn't really know how to answer. She was a long way from her own family in Kentucky, but she didn't see this as being entirely her fault. And it wasn't as if her brother had stuck any closer to home, either. He had gone north to work on the Alaska Pipeline and had married a Canadian dog trainer. They had four daughters with Eskimo names that Lou Ann couldn't keep straight—things that sounded like Chinook and Winnebago.

Outside it was beginning to get dark. Lou Ann crossed the park in a hurry, skirting around an olden wooden <u>trellis</u> where several <u>transients</u> were congregating. As usual she

9. **macaroons.** Cookie made with egg whites and coconut

words for everyday use

trel • lis (tre′ ləs) *n.,* frame or structure of crossed wood or metal strips usually used as a support for climbing plants. *Each summer, Maria was surprised anew at how lovely her wild roses looked climbing up the <u>trellis</u>.*

tran • si • ent (tran′ zē ənt) *n.,* person traveling about usually in search of work. *After years in the same city, Kate is ready to become a <u>transient</u>, traveling from city to city, and working at any job she can find.*

tried to concentrate on not being afraid. Angel had told her that some people, like dogs, can smell fear.

When she got home she saw that Angel had already been home from work and had left again, for good. She was confused at first and thought they had been robbed, until she began to see a pattern to what was taken. She wandered around the house with her grocery bag looking at the half-empty house. After four years there was very little, other than clothes, that she thought of as belonging clearly to one or the other. In a strange way she was fascinated to see what he had claimed for his own. It revealed more to her about his personality, she thought, than she had learned during their whole marriage.

◀ *What does Lou Ann realize when she returns home?*

◀ *What is Lou Ann fascinated to see? Why?*

He left all of the sheets and blankets, the knickknacks, and all the kitchen things except for three matching beer mugs. He had taken some of the old magazines and paperback mysteries from the shelf. She didn't miss the books so much as she was hurt by the ugly empty spaces left behind, like missing teeth, the books on either side falling and crowding into the gaps.

Gone from the bedroom was a picture of Angel taken at a rodeo[10] in 1978. In the picture he was sitting on top of a bull named S.O.B., which was supposed to be the meanest bull in the history of rodeo. In the entire year of 1978 only one rider had stayed on S.O.B. for eight seconds. Angel wasn't the one. At the time of this particular photo the animal was doped up on PCP,[11] which the rodeys[12] used to drug the bulls and horses when they moved them around. PCP was common as dirt in that line of work. Angel's rodeo name had been Dusty, which was short for Angel Dust.

He also had taken one clean towel, the only tube of toothpaste, and the TV.

Lou Ann had forgotten it was Halloween, and was completely bewildered when a mob of children came to the door. She was frightened by their dark, darting pupils peering through the little holes in their bright plastic masks. She knew they were neighborhood children she had seen a thousand times, but in their costumes she couldn't tell who they were. To calm herself down she talked to them and tried to guess whether each one was a boy or a girl. She guessed correctly on the princess, the green-faced witch,

10. **rodeo.** Public performance featuring mustang and bull riding, calf roping, and steer wrestling
11. **PCP.** Illegal drug
12. **rodeys.** Workers employed by the rodeo

Frankenstein, and the Incredible Hulk (also green). The Extra Terrestrial[13] she got wrong.

Now she remembered why she had needed to go to the Lee Sing Market: she didn't have any candy to give out. She considered giving them pieces of fruit or macaroons, but this would be a waste of money. Their mothers would probably go through their bags and throw things like that away, fearing cyanide[14] and razor blades. On television they said everything should be sealed in the original wrapper. The children seemed to feel sorry for her, but were growing impatient. They expected adults to be prepared.

"You better give us something or we'll have to soap your windows, Mrs. Ruiz," the Extra Terrestrial said half-heartedly. Lou Ann decided to go and shake out the Mickey Mouse bank, in which she had been saving pennies to buy a washing machine for the baby's diapers. Angel had laughed at her, saying the baby would have kids of its own before she could save that many pennies.

The children seemed satisfied with the pennies and went away. She left Mickey by the door so she would be better organized for the next round.

▶ *Why will Lou Ann have to go to sleep with her shoes on?*

By eleven o'clock Lou Ann's feet were killing her. She could feel her heartbeat in her ankles. For three or four weeks Lou Ann's feet had been so swollen that she could only wear one particular pair of shoes, which had a strap across the ankle, and now she was going to have to go to bed with these shoes on. She couldn't bend over far enough to unbuckle the straps, and Angel was not there to do it for her. If she had thought of it she might have asked the last bunch of trick-or-treat kids to do it, but it was too late now.

As she was getting ready for bed she caught sight of herself in the mirror and thought she looked disgusting and pornographic in her nightgown and panty hose and shoes, like someone who would work at Fanny Heaven. Though of course they wouldn't have pregnant women there. Still, the thought upset her. She turned out the light but kept listening for sounds that might be more kids coming to the door, or might be Angel changing his mind, coming home. In her other ear, pressed against the pillow, she could hear the blood pumping all the way down to her feet. It sounded something like the ocean, which she had seen once with Angel in Mexico. The baby nudged and poked at her with what felt like fingers, but must be tiny elbows or feet. She

13. **Extra Terrestrial.** Creature from another planet
14. **cyanide.** Poisonous substance

thought about the baby playing in waves of her blood, on the smooth, dark beach of her insides. Her feet hurt and she couldn't find a comfortable place in the bed.

Finally, late in the night, she cried until her eye sockets felt empty. At the beach she had gotten seawater in her eyes and they felt like this. Angel had warned her to keep them shut, but she had wanted to see where she was going. You never knew what kind of thing could be down there under the water.

◀ *How did Lou Ann's eyes feel when she got seawater in them? What had Angel told her to do? Why hadn't she listened to him?*

Three

Jesus Is Lord Used Tires

▶ *How does Taylor describe the scenery as she crosses into Arizona?*

We crossed the Arizona state line at sunup. The clouds were pink and fat and hilarious-looking, like the hippo ballerinas in a Disney movie. The road took us through a place called Texas Canyon that looked nothing like Texas, heaven be praised for that, but looked like nothing else I had ever seen either. It was a kind of forest, except that in place of trees there were all these puffy-looking rocks shaped like roundish animals and roundish people. Rocks stacked on top of one another like piles of copulating[1] potato bugs. Wherever the sun hit them, they turned pink. The whole scene looked too goofy to be real. We whizzed by a roadside sign on which I could make out a dinosaur. I wondered if it told what kind of rocks they were, or if it was saying that they were actually petrified[2] dinosaur turds. I was laughing my head off. "This is too much," I said to the Indian child. "This is the best thing I've seen in years." Whether my car conked out or not, I made up my mind to live in Arizona.

▶ *About what does she make up her mind?*

It was the second day of the new year. I had stayed on at the Broken Arrow through most of the holidays, earning some money changing beds. The older woman with the shakes, whose name was Mrs. Hoge, was determined that I should stay awhile. She said they could use the extra help during the Christmas season, especially since her daughter-in-law's ankles were giving her trouble. Which is no wonder. A human ankle is not designed to hold up two hundred and fifty pounds. If we were meant to weigh that much we would have big round ankles like an elephant or a hippopotamus.

They did get quite a few folks at Christmastime passing through on their way to someplace on one side or the other of Oklahoma, which was where I longed to be. But on the other hand, I was glad for the chance to make some bucks before I headed on down the pike.[3] Mrs. Hoge's ulterior motive,[4] I believe, was the child, which she looked after a great deal of the time. She made it plain that her fondest wish was to have a grandbaby. Whenever fat Irene would pick up the baby, which was not too often, Mrs.

▶ *What does Taylor think is the real reason Mrs. Hoge asked her to stay at the Broken Arrow through the holidays?*

1. **copulating.** Engaging in sexual intercourse
2. **petrified.** Rock-like; turned to stone
3. **down the pike.** Down the road; into the future
4. **ulterior motive.** Reason (for doing something) that one does not reveal that is often inappropriate and selfish

Hoge would declare, "Irene, you don't know how becoming that looks." As if someone ought to have a kid because it looked good on them.

By this time I had developed a name for the child, at least for the time being. I called her Turtle, on account of her grip. She still wasn't talking but she knew her name about as far as a cat ever does, which means that when you said it she would look up if she was in the right mood. Mrs. Hoge hinted in every imaginable way that she was retarded, but I maintained that she had her own ways of doing things and wasn't inclined to be pushed. She had already been pushed way too far in her lifetime, though of course I didn't tell this to old Mrs. Hoge or her daughter-in-law.

◀ What name does Taylor give to the child she has taken on? Why?

◀ What does Mrs. Hoge hint about the child? What is Taylor's response to this?

I was in hog heaven[5] to be on the road again. In Arizona. My eyes had started to hurt in Oklahoma from all that flat land. I swear this is true. It felt like you were always having to look too far to see the horizon.

By the time we were in sight of Tucson it became clear what those goofy pink clouds had been full of: hail. Within five minutes the car was covered with ice inside and out, and there was no driving on that stuff. The traffic was moving about the speed of a government check. I left the interstate at an off ramp and pulled over next to what looked like the Flying Nun's hat made out of bumpy concrete, held up by orange poles. Possibly it had once been a gas station, although there were no pumps and the building at the back of the paved lot looked abandoned. All over the walls and boarded-up windows someone had painted what looked like sperms with little smiles in red spray paint, and sayings like "Fools Believe."

I rubbed my hands on my knees to keep them from freezing. There was thunder, though I did not see lightning. I thought of all the mud turtles in Arizona letting go. Did Arizona even have mud turtles? An old man my mama used to clean for would say if it thunders in January it will snow in July. Clearly he had never been to Arizona. Or perhaps he had.

We got out of the open car and stood under the concrete wings to stay dry. Turtle was looking interested in the

5. **hog heaven.** Extremely satisfying state or situation

words for everyday use

re • tard • ed (ri tär′ dəd) *adj.*, slow or limited in intellectual or emotional development. *Ian is mildly retarded, and though he may be slow at absorbing new information, he is a bright and funny person with great artistic talent.*

in • clined (in klīnd′) *adj.*, tending toward; of a mind; likely. *Bernardo always says what he thinks and is rarely inclined to be silent when people are debating an issue.*

▶ *What does Taylor say to Turtle about Arizona?*

scenery, which was a first. Up to then the only thing that appeared to interest her was my special way of starting the car.

"This is a foreign country," I told her. "Arizona. You know as much about it as I do. We're even steven."

The hail turned to rain and kept up for half an hour. A guy came out of the little boarded-up building and leaned against one of the orange poles near us. I wondered if he lived there, or what. (If he did live there, did he paint the sperms?) He had on camouflage army pants and a black baseball cap with cloth flaps hanging down in the back, such as Gregory Peck or whoever it was always wore in those old Foreign Legion movies.[6] His T-shirt said VISITOR FROM ANOTHER PLANET. That's me, I thought. I should be wearing that shirt.

"You from out of town?" he asked after a while, eying my car.

"No," I said. "I go to Kentucky every year to get my license plate." I didn't like his looks.

He lit a cigarette. "What'd you pay for that bucket of bolts?"

"A buck two-eighty."

"Sassy one, aren't you?"

"You got that one right, buster," I said. I wished to God I wasn't going to have to make such a spectacle of myself later on, starting the car.

The sun came out even before the hail stopped. There was a rainbow over the mountains behind the city, and over that another rainbow with the colors upside down. Between the two rainbows the sky was brighter than everywhere else, like a white sheet lit from the back. In a few minutes it was hot. I had on a big red pullover sweater and was starting to sweat. Arizona didn't do anything halfway. If Arizona was a movie you wouldn't believe it. You'd say it was too corny for words.

I knew I had better stay put for a few more minutes to give the engine a chance to dry out. The guy was still hanging around, smoking and making me nervous.

---

6. **Gregory Peck...Foreign Legion movies.** Taylor confuses American actor Gregory Peck (1916–2003) with American actor Gary Cooper (1901–1961), who starred in movies such as *Beau Geste* (1939) about the French Foreign Legion; the French Foreign Legion was founded in 1831 for service in Algeria.

words for everyday use

spec • ta • cle (spek′ ti kəl) *n.,* unusual, entertaining, or dramatic public display; an object of curiosity or contempt. *The waitress was embarrassed at the spectacle she created when she dropped a large tray of food.*

"Watch out," he said. There was this hairy spider about the size of a small farm animal making its way across the pavement. Its legs jerked up and down like the rubber spiders on a string that you get from a gumball machine.

"I've seen worse," I said, although to tell you the truth I hadn't. It looked like something that might have crawled out of the Midnight Creature Feature.

"That's a tarantula," he said. "You got to watch out for them suckers. They can jump four feet. If they get you, you go crazy. It's a special kind of poison."

This I didn't believe. I never could figure out why men thought they could impress a woman by making the world out to be such a big dangerous deal. I mean, we've got to live in the exact same world every damn day of the week, don't we?

"What's it coming around here for?" I said. "Is it your pet, or your girlfriend?"

"Nah," he said, squashing out his cigarette, and I decided he was dumber than he was mean.

◀ *What does Taylor decide about the guy she is talking to?*

There were a lot more bugs crawling up on the cement slab. A whole swarm of black ants came out of a crack and milled around the cigarette butt trying, for reasons I could not imagine, to take it apart. Some truck had carried that tobacco all the way from Kentucky maybe, from some Hardbine's or Richey's or Biddle's farm, and now a bunch of ants were going to break it into little pieces to take back to their queen. You just never knew where something was going to end up.

"We had a lot of rain lately," the guy said. "When the ground gets full of water, the critters drown out of their holes. They got to come up and dry off." He reached out with his foot and squashed a large, shiny black bug with horns. Its wings split apart and white stuff oozed out between. It was the type that you wouldn't have guessed had wings, although I knew from experience that just about every bug has wings of one kind or another. Not including spiders.

He lit another cigarette and threw the match at the tarantula, missing it by a couple of inches. The spider raised its two front legs toward the flame like a scared lady in an old movie.

"I got things to do," I said. "So long." I put Turtle in the car, then went around to the other side and put it in neutral and started to push.

He laughed. "What is that, a car or a skateboard?"

"Look, Buster, you can help give me a push, or you can stand and watch, but either way I'm out of here. This car got me here from Kentucky, and I reckon she's got a few thousand left in her."

"Not on them tires, she don't," he said. I looked back to see the rear tire flapping empty on the wheel. "Shit," I said, just as the engine caught and the car zoomed forward. In the rear-view mirror I could see broken glass glistening on the off ramp, dropping away behind me like a twinkly green lake.

I had no intention of asking the dumb guy for help. The tire looked like it was done-for anyway so I drove on it for a few blocks. There were a bank, some houses, and a park with palm trees and some sick-looking grass. Some men with rolled-up blankets tied around their waists were kicking at the dirt, probably looking for bugs to step on. Just beyond the park I could see a stack of tires. "Will you look at that," I said. "I'm one lucky duck. We should have gone to Las Vegas."

▶ *What is the woman using to chase the bugs away?*

The stacked-up tires made a kind of wall on both sides of a big paved corner lot. Inside the walls a woman was using an air hose to chase bugs off the pavement, herding them along with little blasts of air. She was wearing blue jeans and cowboy boots and a red bandana on her head. A long gray braid hung down the middle of her back.

"How do," I said. I noticed that the name of the place was Jesus Is Lord Used Tires. I remembered wanting to call 1-800-THE LORD, just to see who you'd get. Maybe this was it.

▶ *Why doesn't the woman kill the bugs?*

"Hi, darlin," she said. "These bugs aggravate the dickens[7] out of me after it rains, but I can't see my way clear to squashing them. A bug's just got one life to live, after all. Like us."

"I know what you mean," I said.

"Oh, bless your heart. Looks like you've got a couple of flats."

I did. I hadn't seen the rear on the right side.

"Drive it up onto the big jack," she ordered. "We'll get them off and have a look. We'll fix your little wagon right up."

I asked if Turtle could ride up on the jack, but she said it wasn't safe, so I took her out of the car and looked for a place to put her down. All those tires around made me nervous. Just out of instinct, more or less, I looked up to

7. **dickens.** Devil

see if there was anything tall overhead to get thrown up onto. There was nothing but clear blue sky.

Off to one side there were some old wheel rims and flat tires. An empty tire couldn't possibly explode, I reasoned, so I sat Turtle down in one of those.

"What's your little girl's name?" the woman wanted to know, and when I told her she didn't bat an eye. Usually people would either get embarrassed or give me a lecture. She told me her name was Mattie.

"She's a cute little thing," Mattie said.

"How do you know she's a girl?" I wasn't lipping off, for once. Just curious. It's not as if I had her dressed in pink.

"Something about the face."

We rolled the tires over to a tub of water. Mattie rubbed Ivory soap on the treads and then dunked them in like big doughnuts. Little threads of bubbles streamed up like strings of glass beads. Lots of them. It looked like a whole jewelry store in there.

"I'm sorry to tell you, hon, these are bad. I can tell you right now these aren't going to hold a patch. They're shot through." She looked concerned. "See these places here along the rim? They're sliced." She ran her hand along the side of the tire under the water. She had a gold wedding band settled into the flesh of her finger, the way older women's rings do when they never take them off.

"I'm sorry," she said again, and I could tell she really was. "There's a Goodyear place down the road about six blocks. If you want to roll them down there for a second opinion."

"That's okay," I said. "I'll take your word for it." Turtle was slapping at the side of her flat whitewall with one hand. The other had caught hold of the doohickey[8] where the air goes in. I tried to think what in the world we were going to do now. "How much for new ones?" I asked.

Mattie considered for a minute. "I could give you a pair of good retreads,[9] five thousand miles guaranteed, put on and balanced for sixty-five."

"I'll have to think on that one," I said. She was so nice I didn't want to tell her flat out that I couldn't afford new tires.

"It's too early in the morning for bad news," Mattie said. "I was just brewing up a pot of coffee. You want a cup of coffee? Come sit."

---

8. **doohickey.** Word that people use to refer to something when they don't know or can't remember the actual name of the thing

9. **retreads.** Used tires that have had new treads—the surface of the tire that meets the road—put on them

"Okay," I said. I collected Turtle out of the tire and carried her to the back of the shop. It was a big old two-story place, and there at the back of the garage was an area with a sink and some shelves, some folding chairs painted blue, a metal table, and a Mr. Coffee. I scooted another flat over next to the chairs and set Turtle down in it. I was glad to be away from that wall of tires, all of them bulging to burst. Hanging around here would be like living in a house made of bombs. The sound of the air hose alone gave me the willies.[10]

"These come in pretty handy," I said, trying to be cheerful. "I know what I can use those two flat tires for."

"I've got some peanut-butter crackers," Mattie said, leaning over Turtle. "Will she eat peanut butter?"

"She eats anything. Just don't let her get hold of anything you don't want to part with. Like your hair," I said. Mattie's braid was swinging into the danger zone.

She poured coffee into a mug that said "BILL with a capital B," and handed it to me. She poured a cup for herself in a white mug with cartoon rabbits all over it. They were piled all over each other like the rocks in Texas Canyon. After a minute I realized that the rabbits were having sex in about a trillion different positions. I couldn't figure this woman out. This was definitely not 1-800-THE LORD.

"You must have come a ways," she said. "I saw your plates were Kentucky. Or plate, rather. You don't have to have them both front and back in Kentucky?"

"No. Just the back."

"Here you've got to have one on the front too. I guess so the cops can get you coming and going." She handed Turtle a peanut-butter cracker, which she grabbed with both hands. It broke to smithereens, and she got such big sad eyes I thought she was going to cry.

"It's all right, honey," Mattie said. "You put that one in your mouth and I'll give you another one." Turtle did. I was amazed. She had never been this kind to Mrs. Hoge. Mattie was clearly accustomed to dealing with kids.

"Are you on the road?" she asked me.

"Have been up to now. From Kentucky, with a stopover in Oklahoma. We're out to see what we can see. Now I guess we'll see how we like Tucson."

"Oh, you will. I ought to know, I've lived my whole life here. And that's a rare breed, let me tell you. I don't think there's hardly a soul in Tucson anymore that was born here.

10. **willies.** Jitters; a fit of nervousness

Most of them come, you know, from out of state. My husband, Samuel, was from Tennessee. He came out as a young man for his asthma and he never could get used to the dry. I love it, though. I guess it's all in what you're used to."

"I guess," I said. I was dying to know about the name of the place, but couldn't think of a polite way to bring it up. "Is this tire place part of a national chain, or something like that?" I finally asked. That sounded polite, but dumb.

She laughed. "No, me and my husband started it up. His dad was a mechanic, so Sam was a grease monkey[11] born and raised. He was the one that named the place. He was kind of fanatical, you might say. Bless his soul." She handed Turtle another cracker. The kid was eating like a house on fire. "He got some Mexican kids to do the painting out front. I never did change it, it's something different. Lots of people stop in for curiosity. Does that baby want some juice? She needs something to wash that peanut butter down with."

"Don't put yourself out. I can get her some water out of the tap."

"I'll run get some apple juice. I won't be a minute." I had thought she meant she was actually going to a store, but she went through a door at the back of the shop. Apparently there was more to this building, including a refrigerator with apple juice in it. I wondered if Mattie lived on the premises, maybe upstairs.

While she was gone two men stopped by, almost at exactly the same time, although they were not together. One of them asked for Matilda. He wanted an alignment[12] and to pick up a tire for his ORV.[13] He said it as though everybody ought to know what an ORV was, and maybe have one or two at home. The other man had on a black shirt with a white priest's collar, and blue jeans, of all things. I wondered if maybe he was some kind of junior-varsity priest. I really had no idea. They didn't have Catholics in Pittman.

---

11. **grease monkey.** Slang term for an automobile mechanic
12. **alignment.** Process of adjusting the tires on a car so that they are properly positioned in relation to each other
13. **ORV.** Off Road Vehicle

words for everyday use

asth • ma (az′ mə) *n.*, allergic condition marked by difficult breathing, tightening in the chest, and attacks of wheezing, coughing, and gasping. *Most people with asthma carry a small device called an* inhaler, *through which they inhale medicine into their lungs so they can breathe normally.*

fa • nat • i • cal (fa na′ ti kəl) *adj.*, marked by excessive enthusiasm and intense, uncritical devotion. *The fanatical fans of the rock band surrounded the stage, singing and dancing to all the songs.*

► *How does the priest seem to Taylor? Who does she see in the back of his station wagon?*

► *How does Taylor feel when she sees Mattie working on Roger's car? Why?*

► *What small prayer does Taylor say for Mattie and for herself?*

► *Why is Taylor embarrassed?*

► *What does Taylor admit to Mattie? How does Mattie respond?*

"She'll be back in about two seconds," I told them. "She just went to get something."

The ORV fellow waited, but the priest said he would come back later. He seemed a little jumpy. As he drove away I noticed there was a whole family packed into the back of his station wagon. They looked like Indians.

"Well, how in the world are you, Roger?" Mattie said when she came back. "Just make yourself at home, hon, this won't take a minute," she told me, and handed me an orange cup with a little drinking spout, which must have been designed especially for small children. I wondered if it was hard to fill it through that little spout. Once Turtle got her hands on this cup she wasn't going to want to give it up.

Roger drove his car onto a platform that was attached to a red machine with knobs and dials on it. Mattie started up the machine, which made the front tires of Roger's Toyota spin around, and after a minute she lay down on one shoulder and adjusted something under the front. She didn't get that dirty, either. I had never seen a woman with this kind of know-how. It made me feel proud, somehow. In Pittman if a woman had tried to have her own tire store she would have been run out of business. That, or the talk would have made your ears curl up like those dried apricot things. "If Jesus is indeed Lord," I said to myself, "He surely will not let this good, smart woman get blown sky-high by an overfilled tire. Or me either, while He's at it."

The two of them went out to the wall of tires and pulled down a couple of smallish fat ones. They hit the ground with a smack, causing both Turtle and me to jump. Roger picked one of them up and dribbled it like a basketball. He and Mattie were talking, and Roger was making various vibrating sounds with his lips. I supposed he was trying to describe something that was wrong with his ORV. Mattie listened in an interested way. She was really nice to Roger, even though he was bald and red-faced and kind of bossy. She didn't give him any lip.

When she came back Turtle had drunk all her juice and was banging the cup against the tire, demanding more in her speechless way. I was starting to get embarrassed.

"You want more juice, don't you?" Mattie said to Turtle in a grownup-to-baby voice. "It's a good thing I brought the whole bottle down in the first place."

"Please don't go out of your way," I said. "We've put you out enough already. I have to tell you the truth, I can't even afford to buy one tire right now, much less two. Not for a while, anyway, until I find work and a place for us to live." I picked up Turtle but she went on banging the cup against my shoulder.

"Why, honey, don't feel bad. I wasn't trying to make a sale. I just thought you two needed some cheering up." She pried the cup out of Turtle's hand and refilled it. The top snapped right off. I hadn't thought of that.

"You must have grandbabies around," I said.

"Mmm-hmmm. Something like that." She handed the cup back to Turtle and she sucked on it hard, making a noise like a pond frog. I wondered what, exactly, would be "something like" grandbabies.

◀ How does Mattie answer when Taylor asks her if she has grandchildren? What does Taylor wonder about Mattie's response?

"It's so dry out here kids will dehydrate real fast," Mattie told me. "They'll just dry right up on you. You have to watch out for that."

"Oh, right," I said. I wondered how many other things were lurking around waiting to take a child's life when you weren't paying attention. I was useless. I was crazy to think I was doing this child a favor by whisking her away from the Cherokee Nation. Now she would probably end up mummified[14] in Arizona.

◀ How does Mattie's caution that children can dehydrate make Taylor feel?

"What kind of work you looking for?" Mattie rinsed the coffee cups and set them upside down on a shelf. A calendar above the shelf showed a bare-chested man in a feather headdress and heavy gold arm bracelets carrying a woman who looked dead or passed out.

"Anything, really. I have experience in housecleaning, x-rays, urine tests, and red blood counts. And picking bugs off bean vines."

Mattie laughed. "That's a peculiar résumé."

"I guess I've had a peculiar life," I said. It was hot, Turtle was spilling or spitting juice down my shoulder blade, and I was getting more depressed by the minute. "I guess you don't have bean vines around here," I said. "That kind of limits my career options."

"Well, heck yes, girl, we've got bean vines!" Mattie said. "Even purple ones. Did you ever see purple beans?"

14. **mummified.** Dried up and shriveled like a mummy

words for everyday use

de • hy • drate (dē hī′ drāt) *v.,* lose water or body fluids and become dry and thirsty. *You don't want to dehydrate, so be sure to drink plenty of water while exercising.*

ré • su • mé (re′ zə mā) *n.,* summary of a person's educational and/or employment history. *Because the job advertisement mentions experience working with children, I will write a résumé that emphasizes the summers I worked as a camp counselor.*

"Not that were alive," I said.

"Come on back here and let me show you something."

We went through the door at the back, which led through a little room jam-packed with stuff. There was a desk covered with papers, and all around against the walls there were waist-high stacks of old *National Geographics* and *Popular Mechanics* and something called *The Beacon,* which showed Jesus in long, swirling robes floating above a lighthouse. Behind the desk there was a staircase and another door that led out the back. I could hear someone thumping around overhead in stocking feet.

▶ *What does Taylor hear above her?*

▶ *What is Mattie's garden like?*

Outside was a bright, wild wonderland of flowers and vegetables and auto parts. Heads of cabbage and lettuce sprouted out of old tires. An entire rusted-out Thunderbird, minus the wheels, had nasturtiums blooming out the windows like Mama's hen-and-chicks pot on the front porch at home. A kind of teepee frame made of CB[15] antennas was all overgrown with cherry-tomato vines.

"Can you believe tomatoes on the second of January?" Mattie asked. I told her no, that I couldn't. Frankly that was only the beginning of what I couldn't believe. Mattie's backyard looked like the place where old cars die and go to heaven.

"Usually we'll get a killing frost by Thanksgiving, but this year it's stayed warm. The beans and tomatoes just won't quit. Here, doll, bite down, don't swallow it whole." She handed me a little tomato.

"Okay," I said, before I realized she had popped one into Turtle's mouth, and was talking to her. "It hailed this morning," I reminded Mattie. "We just about froze to death for a few minutes there."

"Oh, did it? Whereabouts?"

"On the freeway. About five blocks from here."

"It didn't get here; we just had rain. Hail might have got the tomatoes. Sometimes it will. Here's the beans I was telling you about."

Sure enough, they were one hundred percent purple: stems, leaves, flowers and pods.

"Gosh," I said.

▶ *What does Taylor notice about the purple beans?*

"The Chinese lady next door gave them to me." She waved toward a corrugated tin fence that I hadn't even noticed before. It was covered with vines, and the crazy-quilt garden kept right on going on the other side, except without the car parts. The purple beans appeared to go

15. **CB.** Citizen's Band, a range of radio-wave frequencies that in the United States are set aside for private radio communication between citizens

trooping on down the block, climbing over anything in their path.

"They're originally from seeds she brought over with her in nineteen-ought-seven," Mattie told me. "Can you picture that? Keeping the same beans going all these years?"

I said I could. I could picture these beans marching right over the Pacific Ocean, starting from somebody's garden in China and ending up right here.

What can Taylor picture?

Mattie's place seemed homey enough, but living in the hustle-bustle of downtown Tucson was like moving to a foreign country I'd never heard of. Or a foreign decade. When I'd crossed into Rocky Mountain Time,[16] I had set my watch back two hours and got thrown into the future.

For Taylor, how is Tucson different from Pittman County?

It's hard to explain how this felt. I went to high school in the seventies, but you have to understand that in Pittman County it may as well have been the fifties. Pittman was twenty years behind the nation in practically every way you can think of, except the rate of teenage pregnancies. For instance, we were the last place in the country to get the dial system. Up until 1973 you just picked up the receiver and said, Marge, get me my Uncle Roscoe, or whoever. The telephone office was on the third floor of the Courthouse, and the operator could see everything around Main Street square including the bank, the drugstore, and Dr. Finchler's office. She would tell you if his car was there or not.

In Tucson, it was clear that there was nobody overlooking us all. We would just have to find our own way.

Turtle and I took up residence in the Hotel Republic, which rented by the week and was within walking distance of Jesus Is Lord's. Mattie said it would be all right to leave my car there for the time being. This was kind of her, although I had visions of turnips growing out of it if I didn't get it in running order soon.

Life in the Republic was nothing like life at the Broken Arrow, where the only thing to remind you you weren't dead was the constant bickering between old Mrs. Hoge and Irene. Downtown Tucson was lively, with secretaries clicking down the sidewalks in high-heeled sandals, and banker and lawyer types puffy-necked in their ties, and in the evenings, prostitutes in get-ups you wouldn't believe. There was one who hung out near the Republic who wore a miniskirt that looked like Reynolds Wrap and almost every day a new type

16. **Rocky Mountain Time.** Time zone used in the Rocky Mountain states of the United States; also called Mountain Standard Time

of stockings: fishnets in all different colors, and one pair with actual little bows running down the backs. Her name was Cheryl.

There was also a type of person who lived downtown full time, not in the Republic but in the bus station or on the sidewalk around the Red Cross plasma[17] center. These people slept in their clothes. I know that living in the Republic only put me a few flights of stairs above such people, but at least I did sleep in pajamas.

And then there was this other group. These people did not seem to be broke, but they wore the kinds of clothes Mama's big-house ladies used to give away but you would rather go naked than wear to school. Poodle skirts[18] and things of that kind. Standing in line at the lunch counters and coffeeshops they would rub the backs of each other's necks and say, "You're holding a lot of tension here." They mainly didn't live downtown but had studios and galleries in empty storefronts that had once been J.C. Penney's and so forth. Some of these still had old signs on the faces of the brick buildings.

Which is to say that at first I had no idea what was going on in those storefronts. One of them that I passed by nearly every day had these two amazing things in the front window. It looked like cherry bombs[19] blowing up in boxes of wet sand, and the whole thing just frozen mid-kaboom. Curiosity finally got the better of me and I walked right in. I knew this was no Woolworth's.[20]

Inside there were more of these things, one of them taller than me and kind of bush-shaped, all made of frozen sand. A woman was writing something on a card under one of the sand things that was hanging on the back wall, kind of exploding out of a metal frame. The woman had on a pink sweater, white ankle socks, pink high heels, and these tight pants made out of the skin of a pink silk leopard. She came over with her clipboard and kind of eyed Turtle's hands, which were sticky I'll admit, but a good two feet clear of the sand bush.

"This is terrific," I said. "What's it supposed to be?"

"It's non-representational,"[21] she said, looking at me like I was some kind of bug she'd just found in her bathroom.

---

17. **plasma.** Fluid part of blood
18. **Poodle skirts.** Long, full skirts with fabric patches of poodles that have become a symbol of the 1950s
19. **cherry bombs.** Powerful red firecrackers
20. **Woolworth's.** American chain of "five-and-dime" stores that opened in 1879 in New York and closed in the late 1980s; most of the items they sold could be purchased for five or ten cents.
21. **non-representational.** Refers to nonrepresentational art, which depicts abstract and not recognizable objects

"Excuse me for living," I said. She was about my age, no more than twenty-five anyway, and had no reason I could see for being so snooty. I remembered this rhyme Mama taught me to say to kids who acted like they were better than me: "You must come from Hog-Norton, where pigs go to church and play the organ."

◀ *How did Taylor's mother teach her to react to people who act as though they are better than she is?*

The thing was sitting on a square base covered with brown burlap, and a little white card attached said BISBEE DOG #6. I didn't see the connection, but I acted like I was totally satisfied with that. "Bisbee Dog #6," I said. "That's all I wanted to know."

Turtle and I went all around checking out the ones on the walls. Most of them were called something relief: ASCENDANT RELIEF, ENDOGENOUS RELIEF, MOTIVE RELIEF, GALVANIC RELIEF.[22] After a while I realized that the little white cards had numbers on them too. Numbers like $400. "Comic Relief," I said to Turtle. "This one is Instant Relief," I said. "See, it's an Alka-Seltzer, frozen between the plop and the fizz."

On some days, like that one, I was starting to go a little bit crazy. This is how it is when all the money you have can fit in one pocket, and you have no job, and no prospects. The main thing people did for money around there was to give plasma, but I drew the line. "Blood is the body's largest organ," I could just hear Eddie Ricketts saying, and I wasn't inclined to start selling my organs while I was still alive. I did inquire there about work, but the head man in a white coat and puckery white loafers looked me over and said, "Are you a licensed phlebotomist[23] in the state of Arizona?" in this tone of voice like who was I to think I could be on the end of the needle that doesn't hurt, and that was the end of that.

Down the block from the plasma center was a place called Burger Derby. The kids who worked there wore red caps, red-and-white-striped shirts, and what looked like red plastic shorts. One of them, whose name tag said, "Hi I'm Sandi," also wore tiny horse earrings, but that couldn't have been

22. **ASCENDANT RELIEF, ENDOGENOUS RELIEF, MOTIVE RELIEF, GALVANIC RELIEF.** *Relief* refers to works of sculpture, and *ascendant, endogenous, motive,* and *galvanic* are titles the artists have given their works.
23. **phlebotomist.** Person professionally trained to take blood

words for everyday use

pros • pect (prä′ spekt) *n.,* outlook for the future; good chance; well-grounded hope. *With all my schoolwork, the prospect of a relaxing weekend at the beach does not seem possible.*

part of the uniform. They couldn't make you pierce your ears; that would have to be against some law.

Sandi usually worked the morning shift alone, and we got to know each other. My room in the Republic had a hot plate for warming cans of soup, but sometimes I ate out just for the company. The Burger Derby was safe. No one there was likely to ask you where you were holding your tension.

Sandi turned out to be horse-crazy. When she found out I was from Kentucky she treated me like I had personally won the Derby.[24] "You are so lucky," she said. "My absolute *dream* is to have a horse of my own, and braid flowers in its mane and prance around in a ring and win ribbons and stuff." She had this idea that everyone in Kentucky owned at least one Thoroughbred, and it took me some time to convince her that I had never even been close enough to a horse to get kicked.

▶ *What idea does Sandi have about the people who live in Kentucky?*

▶ *What does Taylor tell Sandi about the part of Kentucky that she is from?*

"In the part of Kentucky I come from people don't own Thoroughbreds," I told her. "They just wish they could live like one." The Thoroughbreds had their own swimming pools. My whole county didn't even have a swimming pool. I told her what a hoot we all thought it was when these rich guys paid six million for Secretariat after his running days were over, since he was supposedly the most valuable stud on the face of the earth, and then he turned out to be a reticent breeder, which is a fancy way of saying homosexual. He wouldn't go near a filly[25] for all the sugar in Hawaii.

Sandi acted kind of shocked to hear this news about Secretariat's sex life.

"Didn't you know that? I'm sure that made the national news."

"No!" she said, scouring the steam table like a fiend. She kept looking around to see if anyone else was in the restaurant, but no one was, I'm sure. I always went there around ten-thirty, which is a weird time of day to eat a hot dog, but I was trying to get Turtle and me onto two meals a day.

▶ *Why does Taylor go to the Burger Derby at ten-thirty?*

"What's it like to work here?" I asked her. There had been a HELP WANTED sign in the window for going on two weeks.

---

24. **the Derby.** Refers to the Kentucky Derby, a famous horse race, which began in 1875 in Louisville, Kentucky, and takes place annually on the first Saturday in May

25. **filly.** Young female horse

words for everyday use

ret • i • cent (re′ tə sənt) *adj.*, reluctant; unresponsive. *At first, Kara was a reticent participant in the karaoke contest, but by the end of the night we could not get the microphone away from her.*

"Oh, it's fan*tas*tic," she said.

I'll bet, I thought. Serving up Triple Crown Chili Dogs and You Bet Your Burgers and chasing off drunks and broke people who went around the tables eating nondairy creamer straight out of the packets would be fan*tas*tic. She looked about fourteen.

"You should apply for it, really. They couldn't turn you down, being from Kentucky."

"Sure," I said. What did she think, I was genetically programmed to fry chicken? "What's it pay?"

"Three twenty-five an hour. *Plus* your meals."

"What am I even talking about? I've got this kid," I said. "I'd have to pay somebody more than that to take care of her."

"Oh no! You could just do what I do, take her to Kid Central Station."

"You've got a kid?"

"Yeah, a little boy. Twenty-one months."

I had thought Pittman was the only place on earth where people started having babies before they learned their multiplication tables. I asked her what Kid Central Station was.

"It's free. See, it's this place in the mall where they'll look after your kids while you shop, but how do they know? See what I mean? The only thing is you have to go and check in every two hours, to prove you're still shopping, so I just dash over there on my breaks. The number five bus just goes right straight there. Or I'll get some friend to go. The people that work there don't know the difference. I mean, they've got these jillion kids crawling all over the place, how are they going to know if somebody's really one of 'em's mother?"

◀ *What is Kid Central Station? What does Sandi tell Taylor about it?*

Sandi was sliding the little white buckets of cauliflower and shredded carrots and garbanzo beans into the holes in the salad bar, getting ready for the lunch crowd. For some odd reason they had artificial grapes strewed out over the ice all around the buckets.

"I'll go check it out," I said, although I already had a good notion of what it would be like.

"If you're going right now, could you check in for my little boy? His name's Seattle. I'm sure he's the only one there named Seattle. Just make sure he's okay, will you?"

"Like Seattle, Washington?"

"No, like Seattle Slew, the racehorse. He's a little towhead, you can't miss him, he looks just like me only his hair's blonder. Oh, they have a requirement that they have to be able to walk. Can your daughter walk?"

"Sure she walks. When there's someplace she wants to go."

A celery stick fell out of the bucket onto the floor, and Sandi swiped it up and took a bite. "Well, I couldn't very well let a customer eat it," she said.

"Don't look at me," I said. "It's no skin off my teeth if you want to eat the whole bucket of celery, and the artificial grapes besides. For three twenty-five an hour I think you're entitled."

She munched kind of thoughtfully for a minute. Her eyelashes were stuck together with blue mascara and sprung out all around her eyes like flower petals. "You, know, your little girl doesn't look a thing like you," she said. "I mean, no offense, she's cute as a button."

What does Taylor tell Sandi about Turtle? How does Sandi respond?

"She's not really mine," I said. "She's just somebody I got stuck with."

Sandi looked at both of us, her elbow cocked on her hip and the salad tongs frozen in midair. "Yeah, I know exactly what you mean."

words for everyday use

en • ti • tle (en tī′ təl) *v.*, authorize; give a right or claim to. *Being a guest at someone's house does not entitle you to make long distance phone calls without their permission.*

Respond to the Selection

What do you think of the choices Taylor has made in the story so far?

Investigate, Inquire, and Imagine

Recall: GATHERING FACTS

1a. What was Taylor's attitude toward finishing high school? Why did Taylor get the job at the hospital? Why doesn't she quit after the Hardbine incident?

Interpret: FINDING MEANING

→ 1b. Based on these details, what can you tell about the type of person Taylor is?

2a. How did Mama act when Taylor came home with tiny fish? What does Mama say about Taylor asking Mr. Walter for the job? What does Mama do and say when she sees Taylor's car?

→ 2b. What do these details tell you about the type of mother Mama is?

3a. How does the woman in the bar look at the men at the bar? In the parking lot, what does she tell Taylor about going back into the bar? Who is the child's mother? What does the woman tell Taylor about the child's papers? Later, in the motel, what does Taylor discover about the child?

→ 3b. Why does the woman in the bar give the child to Taylor?

Analyze: TAKING THINGS APART

4a. Look back to Chapter 2 and collect details about Lou Ann Ruiz. How does she think of herself? What is Lou Ann's "method"? How did Angel treat Lou Ann? Provide examples from the text. How did Lou Ann respond to the opinions expressed by her mother and Angel's mother?

Synthesize: BRINGING THINGS TOGETHER

→ 4b. Based on the details you collected, what can you tell about the type of person Lou Ann is? In what ways is Lou Ann different from Taylor? In what ways are Lou Ann and Taylor similar? Do the differences and similarities between Lou Ann and Taylor hint at a future event in the plot? Explain.

Evaluate: MAKING JUDGMENTS

5a. Taylor makes a decision when she takes Turtle from the woman in the bar parking lot in Oklahoma. How might Taylor's decision be considered risky or irresponsible? How might her decision be considered responsible? Do you think Taylor's decision can be judged as right or wrong? Explain.

Extend: CONNECTING IDEAS

5b. The first chapter of the book is titled "The One to Get Away." Based on your reading of the first chapter, who is "the one to get away"? Support your answer using details from the story. Do other characters in the first three chapters "get away"? Explain.

Understanding Literature

NARRATOR. **A narrator** is the teller of a story. A narrator can be a character in the story or someone outside the story who sees or hears about the events being related.

POINT OF VIEW. **Point of view** is the vantage point from which a story is told.

In a story written from the **first-person point of view,** the narrator is a participant or witness of the action, uses the pronouns *I* and *we* to tell what happened, and offers the reader a *limited point of view* in which all the events reported to the reader are seen only through the eyes of the narrator.

In a story written from the **third-person point of view,** the narrator is not a character in the story, but someone outside the story. The third-person narrator uses pronouns such as *he, she, it,* and *they* to tell the story, and may offer the reader a *limited point of view,* showing the reader the private internal thoughts of one or two characters, or an *omniscient point of view,* showing the reader the private internal thoughts of any character.

You may want to recreate the chart below in your notebook so you can refer to it at any time. You can also record your answers to the following questions in your chart.

Chapter	Points of View		Pronouns Used		Narrator is	
	First Person	Third Person	*I, we, me, us, my, our*	*he, she, it, they, him, her, them*	A character in the story	Not a character in the story
Chapter 1						
Chapter 2						
Chapter 3						

Review the first three chapters. From which point of view is the story narrated in each chapter? Which pronouns are used in each chapter? Who is the narrator of each chapter?

IMAGE AND MOTIF. An **image** is the vivid mental picture of an object or experience that language creates in a reader's mind. The author frequently uses descriptive language to create images of the natural world and often refers to elements in nature.

A **motif** is any element that recurs in one or more works of literature, art, or music. Barbara Kingsolver uses nature in all its varying forms—land and sky, plants, insects, and animals—as a motif throughout *The Bean Trees.*

Find three examples of descriptions of natural elements in the first three chapters. Which of these descriptions create particularly strong pictures in your mind? As you read, think about what the author wants to accomplish by using nature as a constant, vivid presence.

Four

Tug Fork Water

▶ *What has Granny Logan done for the last two weeks? Why?*

Lou Ann's Grandmother Logan and Lou Ann's new baby were both asleep in the front room with the curtains drawn against the afternoon heat. For the last two weeks Granny Logan had stomped around the house snapping the curtains shut just as fast as Lou Ann could open them, until finally Lou Ann gave up the effort and they all moved around in the gloom of a dimly lit house. "You'd think somebody had died, instead of just being born," Lou Ann complained, but the old woman declared that the heat was unnatural for January and would cause the baby to grow up measly and unwholesome.

When she woke up, Granny Logan would deny she had been sleeping. She had said she only needed to rest her eyes for the trip back to Kentucky, three days on the Greyhound.

In the kitchen Ivy Logan and Lou Ann were packing a paper bag with baloney sandwiches and yellow apples and a Mason jar of cold tea. Ivy's heavy arms and apron-covered front moved around like she was the boss, even in her daughter's unfamiliar kitchen. Under her breath she hummed one line of a hymn, "All our sins and griefs to bear," over and over until Lou Ann thought she would scream. It was an old habit.

▶ *Why does Lou Ann wish her mother would stay a few more days?*

Lou Ann pushed her damp blond hair back from her face and told her mother she wished she would stay a few days more. Whenever Ivy looked at her Lou Ann could feel the tired half-moons under her own eyes.

"You haven't hardly had time to say boo to Angel. He'll have Tuesday off and we could take the truck and all go someplace. We could all fit in some way. Or otherwise I could stay here with Dwayne Ray, and you all go. It's a shame for you to come all this way from home and not see what you can see."

▶ *What did Angel agree to do?*

Surprisingly, Angel had agreed to move back in until after her mother and grandmother's visit. He might be hard to talk to and unreasonable in every other way but at least, Lou Ann realized, he knew the power of mothers and grandmothers.

words for everyday use

mea • sly (mēz′ lē) *adj.*, of small size or little value; contemptibly small. *The fancy restaurant has big prices, but measly portions.*

If Granny Logan had known they were getting a divorce she would have had an apoplectic.[1] At the very least, she and Ivy would insist that Lou Ann come back home.

"Oh, honey, we seen plenty from the bus," Ivy said. "Them old big cactus and every kind of thing. Lordy, and them big buildings downtown, all glass it looked to me like. I expect we'll see a good sight more on the way home."

"I guess, but it seems like we haven't done a thing since you got here but set around and look at the baby."

"Well, that's what we come for, honey. Now we've done helped you have him, and get settled with him, and we're anxious to get on home. The heat puts Mother Logan in a mood."

"I know it." Lou Ann breathed in slowly through her nose. She was beginning to believe that the hot, dry air in her chest might be the poison her grandmother claimed it to be. "I wish I could have put you up better than we did," she said.

"You put us up just fine. You know her, it wouldn't make no difference if it was the Queen a Sheba[2] a-putting us up, she'd be crosspatch.[3] She just don't sleep good out of her own bed." Ivy untied the borrowed apron and smoothed down the front of her navy-blue dress. Lou Ann remembered the dress from about a hundred church potluck suppers. Just the sight of it made her feel stuffed with potato-chip casseroles and Coca-Cola cake.

"Mama," she said, and then started over because her voice was too low to hear. "Mama, when Daddy was alive . . ." She was not sure what she meant to ask. Did you talk to each other? Was he the person you saved things up to say to, or was it like now? A houseful of women for everything, for company. Ivy was not looking at her daughter but her hands were still, for once. "Did Granny Logan always live with you, from the beginning?"

Ivy peered into the brown bag and then rolled the top down tightly. "Not her with us. We lived with her."

"Is that how you wanted it?" Lou Ann felt embarrassed.

"I guess I always thought it would have been something to go off on our own, like you done. But there was so much work in them days, no time for fun, and besides I'd of been scared to death out someplace all by myself."

◀ *What would Granny and Ivy insist if they knew Lou Ann were getting a divorce?*

◀ *What does Lou Ann's mother say she came to do?*

◀ *What did Ivy always think would have been something? Why didn't she do it?*

1. **apoplectic.** Of, relating to, or causing a stroke
2. **Queen a Sheba.** Queen of Sheba, queen of an ancient kingdom in southwestern Arabia
3. **crosspatch.** Grouch; someone who is cranky and unable to be pleased

"It wouldn't be all by yourself. You would have been with Daddy."

"I s'pose," Ivy said. "But we didn't think about it that way." She turned back to the sink to wash her hands, then pulled the dish towel down from the wooden ring over the sink, refolded it, and hung it back up. "I want you to run on in there now and tell Mother Logan we've got to get ready to go."

Ivy and her mother-in-law were not speaking, on account of one thing or another. Lou Ann could never keep track. She wondered what the trip would be like for them, all those days and nights on the Greyhound. But they were sure to find some way of having a conversation. In the past, in times of necessity, she had seen her mother and grandmother address one another through perfect strangers.

"Granny Logan." Lou Ann put her hand gently on the old woman's shoulder, feeling the shoulder bones through the dark, slick cloth of her dress. At the same time she opened her eyes the baby started to cry. "You have a nice catnap,[4] Granny?" she asked, hurrying to pick up the baby and bounce him on her hip. She always thought he sounded like he was choking.

"It was just my eyes, needed a rest. I weren't sleeping." She held tightly to the arms of the chair until she knew where she was. "I told you, the heat's done put that baby into a colic.[5] He needs a mustart plaster[6] to draw out the heat."

"Mama says tell you it's time to get your grip packed. She says you all are fixing to leave tonight."

"My grip's[7] done packed."

"All right then. You want a bite of supper before you go?"

"Why don't you come on home with us, honey? You and the baby."

▶ *How does Lou Ann feel about lying to Granny and Ivy? Why does she do it?*

"Me and *Angel* and the baby, Granny. I've been married now for practically five years, remember?" She felt like such a sneak, letting on as though her marriage was just fine. It was like presenting her mother and grandmother with a pretty Christmas package to take back with them, with nothing but tissue paper inside. She had never lied to them before, that she could remember, but something in her would not let them be right about Angel.

---

4. **catnap.** Very short nap

5. **colic.** Condition of unknown cause that gives babies stomach pain and causes them to cry uncontrollably

6. **mustart plaster.** Mustard plaster, a plaster containing powdered mustard that is mixed with water and rubbed on the skin

7. **grip.** Suitcase

"Angel's got good work at the bottling plant," she told Granny Logan. This, at least, was true. "We like it here."

"I don't see how a body could like no place where it don't rain. Law,[8] I'm parched. Get me a glass of water."

"I'll get it for you in a minute," she said, switching the baby to her other hip, knowing that in a minute Granny Logan would have forgotten her request. "You get used to it. When we first moved out I had sore throats all the time. I was scared to death I'd caught throat cancer like that what's her name on TV. You know, that had to stop singing?" Lou Ann realized Granny Logan wouldn't know NBC from pinto beans. "But I turned out to be fine, of course. And it don't bother him one bit, does it?" She crooked a finger under the baby's chin and looked into the foggy blue eyes. "Dwayne Ray's a Tucson boy, aren't you?"

Lou Ann's baby had not been born on Christmas, or even the day after. He had come early on the morning of January 1, just missing First Baby of the Year at St. Joseph's Hospital by about forty-five minutes. Lou Ann later thought that if she had just pushed a little harder she might have gotten the year of free diapers from Bottom Dollar Diaper Service. That was the prize. It would have come in handy now that her washing-machine fund, which was meager enough to begin with, had been parceled out to all the neighborhood kids.

"I don't see how a body can grow no tobaccy if it don't rain," Granny Logan said.

"They don't grow tobacco here. No crops hardly at all, just factories and stuff, and tourists that come down here for the winter. It's real pretty out in the mountains. We could have showed you, if you hadn't had to go back so soon." The baby coughed again and she jiggled him up and down. "And it's not usually this hot in January, either. You heard it yourself, Granny, the man on the radio saying it was the hottest January temperatures on record."

"You talk different. I knowed you was going to put on airs."[9]

◀ *What does Granny say she knew Lou Ann was going to do?*

"Granny, I do not."

8. **Law.** Lord
9. **to put on airs.** To act superior; to pretend to be better than you are

words for everyday use

par • cel (pär′ səl) *v.,* divide into parts and distribute. *We waited eagerly for Mama to parcel out the peach pie.*

▶ *What does Granny fear Lou Ann will persuade the baby to think?*

▶ *What is in the bottle that Granny has brought? What is it for?*

"Don't talk back to me, child, you do. I can hear it. I expect you'll be persuadin' the baby that his people's just ignorant hill folks."[10]

Ivy brought in the bags of food and her suitcase, which was held together with a leather belt. Lou Ann recognized the belt as one she had been whipped with years ago, when her father was alive.

"Honey," Ivy said, "tell Mother Logan not to start in on you again. We've got to git."

"Tell Ivy to mind her business and I'll mind mine. Here, I brung you something for the baby." Granny Logan retrieved her black velvet purse, purpled with age and wear around the clasp, and rummaged through it with slow, swollen knuckles. Lou Ann tried not to watch.

After a minute the old woman produced a Coke bottle filled with cloudy water. The bent metal cap had been pushed back on and covered with cellophane, tied around and around with string.

Lou Ann shifted the baby onto her hip, pushed her hair behind her ear, and took the bottle with her free hand. "What is it?"

"That's Tug Fork water. For baptizing the baby."

The water inside the bottle looked milky and cool. A fine brown sediment stuck to the glass bottom when she tipped it sideways.

"I remember when you was baptized in Tug Fork, you was just a little old bit of a thing. And scared to death. When the reverend went to dunk you over, you hollered right out. Law, I remember that so good."

"That's good, Granny. You remember something I don't." Lou Ann wondered how Granny Logan was picturing a baptism in one bottle of water. Of course, the original plan had been to have Dwayne Ray sprinkled as a Catholic, but Granny would die if she knew that. And everything was up in the air now, anyway, with Angel gone.

"Doll baby, I reckon we're all set," Ivy said. "Oh, I hate to go. Let me hold my grandbaby again. You see he gets enough to eat now, Lou Ann. I always had plenty of milk for you and

10. **hill folks.** People who live in the mountains; in Granny Logan's case, people who live in the Appalachian Region of eastern Kentucky where most people are poor and have little education

words for everyday use

rum • mage (rum' ij) *v.*, to search thoroughly or to search carelessly. *It took Katrina an hour to rummage through the piles of clothing in her messy room so that she could find her favorite skirt.*

your brother, but you're not as stout as I was. You never was a stout girl. It's not my fault you wouldn't eat what I put down in front of you." She gave the baby a bounce on her pleated bosom. "Lordy mercy, he'll be all growed up before we see him again, I expect."

"I'm as fat as a hog since I had him, Mama, and you know it."

"Remember you have to use both sides. If you just nurse him on one side you'll go dry."

"Don't expect I'll see him again a-tall," Granny Logan grunted. "Not his old great-grandmaw."

"Mama, I wish you'd wait till Angel gets home and we could drive you down to the station. You're going to get all confused if you try to take the bus. You've got to change downtown." The way they had both managed to avoid Angel he might as well not have moved back in.

"It's a sin to be working on Sunday. He ought to be home with his family on the Lord's day," Granny Logan said, and sighed. "I guess I oughtn't expect better from a heathern Mexican."[11]

◀ *What does Granny say about working on Sunday? What does Granny say about Angel for working on Sunday?*

"It's shift work," Lou Ann explained again. "He's just got to go in when they tell him to, and that's that. And he's not a heathen. He was born right here in America, same as the rest of us." Just because he wasn't baptized in some old dirty crick, Lou Ann added in a voice way too low for Granny Logan to hear.

◀ *How does Lou Ann respond to Granny's remarks about Angel?*

"Who tells him to?" the old woman demanded. Lou Ann looked at her mother.

"We'll manage, with the bus and all," Ivy said.

"That don't make it right, do it? Just because some other heathern tells him to work on the Lord's day?"

Lou Ann found a scrap of paper and wrote down the name of the stop and the number of the bus they would have to take downtown. Ivy handed back the baby and took the paper. She looked at it carefully before she folded it twice, tucked it in her purse, and began helping Granny Logan on with her coat.

"Granny, you're not going to need that coat," Lou Ann said. "I swear it's eighty degrees out there."

"You'll swear yourself to tarnation[12] if you don't watch out. Don't tell me I'm not going to need no coat, child. It's January." Her old hand pawed the air for a few seconds

11. **heathern.** Heathen, a disapproving term used to refer to someone who does not believe in the Christian God
12. **tarnation.** Mild swear word meaning "damnation"

before Ivy silently caught it and corralled it in the heavy black sleeve.

"Lou Ann, honey, don't let him play with that ink pen," Ivy said over her shoulder. "He'll put his eyes out before he even gets a good start in life."

The baby was waving his fist vaguely in the direction of the blue pen in Lou Ann's breast pocket, although he couldn't have grabbed it or picked it up if his little life depended on it.

"All right, Mama," Lou Ann said quietly. She wrapped the baby in a thin blanket in spite of the heat because she knew one or the other of the two women would fuss if she didn't. "Let me help you with the stairs, Granny," she said, but Granny Logan brushed her hand away.

Heat waves rising from the pavement made the brown grass and the palm tree trunks appear to wiggle above the sidewalk, making Lou Ann think of cartoons she had seen of strange lands where palm trees did the hula.[13] They reached the little bus stop with its concrete bench.

"Don't sit on it," she warned. "It'll be hot as a poker in this sun." Granny Logan and Ivy stepped back from the bench like startled children, and Lou Ann felt pleased that she was able to tell them something they didn't already know. The three women stood beside the bench, all looking in the direction from which the bus would come.

"Pew, don't they make a stink," Mother Logan said when the bus arrived. Ivy put her arms around both Lou Ann and the baby, then picked up the two bags and boarded the bus, lifting her feet high for the two big steps. At the top she turned and reached down for her mother-in-law, her sturdy, creased hand closing around the old knuckles. The bus driver leaned on his elbows over the steering wheel and stared ahead.

"I just wish you wasn't so far away," Ivy said as the doors hissed together.

"I know," she mouthed. "Wave bye to your great-grandmaw," Lou Ann told the baby, but they were on the wrong side to see.

---

13. **hula.** Polynesian dance marked by swaying hips and arms

words for everyday use

cor • ral (kə ral′) *v.*, collect; gather. *I ran around the yard frantically trying to corral the pages of newspaper that were blowing away.*

She imagined herself running after the bus and banging on the door, the bus driver letting her climb up and settle herself and the baby onto the wide seat between her mother and grandmother. "Tell your mother to hand me that jar of tea," Granny Logan would say to her. "I'll be dry as a old stick fence before we get back to Kentucky."

◀ What scene does Lou Ann imagine as the bus pulls away?

One block down and across the street, old Bobby Bingo sold vegetables out of his dilapidated truck. Lou Ann had been tempted by his tomatoes, which looked better than the hard pink ones at the grocery; those didn't seem like tomatoes at all, but some sickly city fruit maybe grown inside a warehouse. She had finally collected the nerve to ask how much they cost and was surprised that they were less than grocery tomatoes. On her way home she made up her mind to buy some more.

"Hi, tomato lady," Bingo said. "I remember you."

She flushed. "Are they still forty-five a pound?"

"No, fifty-five. End of the season."

"That's okay," she said. "It's still a good price." She looked at every one in the box and picked out six, handing them to the old man one at a time with her free hand. With her other hand she adjusted the baby on her hip taking extra care, as she had been instructed, to support his wobbly head. "Your tomatoes are the first good ones I've had since back home." She felt her heart do something strange when she said "back home."

Bobby Bingo had skin like a baked potato. A complete vegetable man, Lou Ann thought, though she couldn't help liking him.

He squinted at her. "You're not from here? I didn't think so." He shook out a wad of odd-sized plastic bags, chose one with red letters on it, and bagged the tomatoes. "Seventy-five," he said, weighing them up and down in his hand before he put them on the scales. "And an apple for Johnny," he said, picking out a red apple and shaking it at the baby.

"His name's Dwayne Ray, and he thanks you very much I'm sure but he don't have any teeth yet." Lou Ann laughed. She was embarrassed, but it felt so good to laugh that she was afraid next she would cry.

words for everyday use

di • lap • i • dat • ed (də la′ pə dāt ed) *adj.*, decayed; fallen into ruin due to neglect; broken-down. *The dilapidated barn had no roof and leaned heavily to one side.*

"That's good," Bingo said. "Soon as they get teeth, they start to bite. You know my boy?"

Lou Ann shook her head.

"Sure you do. He's on TV every night, he sells cars. He's a real big guy in cars."

▶ *What does Lou Ann admit to Bobby Bingo? Why is she surprised that she does this?*

"Sorry," she said. "I don't have a TV. My husband took it to his new apartment." She couldn't believe, after deceiving her own mother and grandmother for two entire weeks, that she was admitting to a complete stranger on the street that her marriage had failed.

He shook his head. "Don't worry about it. Makes me sick every time he comes on. Don't even call himself by his own name—'Bill Bing' he says. 'Come on down to Bill Bing Cadillac,' he says. 'Bill Bing has just the thing.' I always wanted him to be a real big guy, you know. Well, look at him now. He don't even eat vegetables. If he was here right now he would tell you he don't know who I am. 'Get rid of that old truck,' he says to me. 'What you need to sell this garbage for? I could buy you a house in Beverly Hills right now,' he says to me. 'What?' I tell him. 'You crazy? Beverly Hills? Probably they don't even eat vegetables in Beverly Hills, just Alaska King Crab and bread sticks!' I tell him. 'You want to make me happy, you give me a new Cadillac and I can sell my vegetables out of the trunk.'" Bingo shook his head. "You want grapes? Good grapes this week."

▶ *What does Bobby say his son could do that would make him happy?*

"No, just the tomatoes." She handed him three quarters.

"Here, take the grapes. Johnny can eat the grapes. Seedless." He put them in the bag with the tomatoes. "Let me tell you something, tomato lady. Whatever you want the most, it's going to be the worst thing for you."

Back at the house she laid down the baby for his nap, then carefully washed the produce and put it in the refrigerator, all the while feeling her mother's eyes on her hands. "The worst thing for you," she kept repeating under her breath until she annoyed herself. She moved around the edges of the rooms as though her big mother and demanding grandmother were still there taking up most of the space; the house felt both empty and cramped at the same time, and Lou Ann felt a craving for something she couldn't put a finger on, maybe some kind of food she had eaten a long time ago. She opened the curtains in the front room to let in the light. The sky was hard and bright, not a blue sky full of water. Strangely enough, it still surprised her sometimes to open that window and not see Kentucky.

▶ *What can Lou Ann feel on her hands?*

She noticed the Coke bottle sitting on the low wooden bureau along with two of Granny Logan's hairpins. The old-fashioned hairpins gave her a sad, spooky feeling. Once she had found a pair of her father's work gloves in the tobacco barn, still molded to the curved shape of his hands, long after he was dead.

◀ What memory does finding Granny's hairpins remind Lou Ann of?

The bottle had leaked a wet ring on the wood, which Lou Ann tried to wipe up with the hem of her jumper. She was concerned about it staining, since the furniture wasn't actually hers. The house had come furnished. She thought for a long time about what to do with the bottle and finally set it on the glass shelf of the medicine cabinet in the bathroom.

Later, while she was nursing the baby in the front room, she closed her eyes and tried to remember being baptized in Tug Fork. She could see the child in a white dress, her sunburned arms stiff at the elbows, and could hear her cry out as she went over backwards, but she could not feel that child's terror as the knees buckled and the green water closed over the face. The strong light from the window took on a watery look behind her closed eyelids and she could see it all perfectly. But couldn't feel it. She thought of her mother and automatically switched the baby to her other breast.

She was still nursing when Angel came home. She opened her eyes. The late-afternoon light on the mountains made them look pink and flat like a picture postcard.

She heard Angel in the kitchen. He moved around in there for quite a while before he said anything to Lou Ann, and it struck her that his presence was different from the feeling of women filling up the house. He could be there, or not, and it hardly made any difference. Like a bug or a mouse scratching in the cupboards at night—you could get up and chase after it, or just go back to sleep and let it be. This was good, she decided.

◀ What hardly makes a difference to Lou Ann?

When he came into the front room she could hear the jingle of his leg.

"They gone?" he asked behind her.

"Yes."

"I'm packing my shaving stuff," he said. Angel had a moustache but shaved the rest of his face often, sometimes twice a day. "Did you see my belt buckle? The silver one with the sheepshank on it?" he asked her.

"The what on it?"

"Sheepshank. It's a rope tied in a knot."

"Oh. I wondered what that was on there."

"So did you see it?"
"No. Not lately, I mean."
"What about my Toros cap?"
"Is that the blue one?"
"Yeah."
"You left that in Manny Quiroz's car. Remember?"
"Damn it, Manny moved to San Diego."
"Well, I can't help it. That's what you did with it."
"Damn."

He was standing close enough behind her so she could smell the faint, sweet smell of beer on his breath. It was a familiar smell, but today it made Lou Ann wonder about bars and the bottling plant and the other places Angel went every day that she had never seen. She turned her head in time to watch him leave the room, his work shirt rolled up at the elbows and dirty from doing something all day, she did not know exactly what. For a brief instant, no longer than a heartbeat, it felt strange to be living in the same house with this person who was not even related to her.

▶ *For an instant, how does it feel to Lou Ann to be living with Angel?*

But of course he's related. He's my husband. Was my husband.

"What the hell is this?" he called from the bathroom.

She leaned back in the rocking chair where she sat facing east out the big window. "It's water from Tug Fork, the crick at home that I was baptized in. Me and I guess practically everybody else in my family. Granny Logan brought it for baptizing Dwayne Ray. Wouldn't you know she'd bring something weird like that?"

She heard the chugging sound of the water as he poured it down the drain. The baby's sucking at her felt good, as if he might suck the ache right out of her breast.

▶ *What does Angel do with the bottle of water that Granny brought?*

Five

Harmonious Space

The Republic Hotel was near the exact spot where the railroad track, which at one time functioned as a kind of artery, punctured Tucson's old, creaky chest cavity and prepared to enter the complicated auricles[1] and ventricles[2] of the railroad station. In the old days I suppose it would have been bringing the city a fresh load of life, like a blood vessel carrying platelets to circulate through the lungs. Nowadays, if you could even call the railroad an artery of Tucson, you would have to say it was a hardened one.

◀ At one time, Tucson's railroad track could have been compared to what? Today, to what could you compare the railroad track?

At the point where it entered the old part of downtown, the train would slow down and let out a long, tired scream. Whether the whistle was for warning the cars at the crossings up ahead, or just letting the freeloaders[3] know it was time to roll out of the boxcars, I can't say. But it always happened very near six-fifteen, and I came to think of it as my alarm clock.

Sometimes the sound of it would get tangled up into a dream. I would hear it whistling through my sleep for what seemed like days while I tried to lift a heavy teakettle off a stove or, once, chased a runaway horse that was carrying off Turtle while she hollered bloody murder (something I had yet to hear her do in real life). Finally the sound would push out through my eyes and there was the daylight. There were the maroon paisley[4] curtains made from an Indian bedspread, there was the orange-brown stain on the porcelain sink where the faucet dripped, there was the army cot where Turtle was asleep, safe and sound in the Republic Hotel. Some mornings it was like that.

On other days I would wake up before the whistle ever sounded and just lie there waiting, feeling that my day couldn't begin without it. Lately it had been mostly this second way.

---

1. **auricles.** Two chambers of the heart that connect the veins to the ventricles
2. **ventricles.** Two chambers of the heart that connect the auricles and the arteries
3. **freeloaders.** People who take advantage of free offerings and the generosity of others
4. **paisley.** Pattern that features teardrop-shaped forms

words for everyday use

ar • ter • y (är′ tə rē) *n.*, any of the tubular, branching muscular and elastic-walled vessels that carry blood from the heart through the body; a channel of transportation, such as a river or highway. *An artery carries blood through the body just as a main highway carries traffic through a city.*

▶ *How long did Taylor work at the Burger Derby? What happened?*

▶ *What did Sandi's son's father tell everyone about Sandi?*

▶ *What did Sandi's mother make her do when she found out she was pregnant?*

We were in trouble. I lasted six days at the Burger Derby before I got in a fight with the manager and threw my red so-called jockey cap in the trash compactor[5] and walked out. I would have thrown the whole uniform in there, but I didn't feel like giving him a free show.

I won't say that working there didn't have its moments. When Sandi and I worked the morning shift together we'd have a ball. I would tell her all kinds of stories I'd heard about horse farms, such as the fact that the really high-strung horses had TVs in their stalls. It was supposed to lower their blood pressure.

"Their favorite show is old reruns of Mr. Ed,"[6] I would tell her with a poker[7] face.

"No! You're kidding. Are you kidding me?"

"And they *hate* the commercials for Knox gelatin."[8]

She was easy to tease, but I had to give her credit, considering that life had delivered Sandi a truckload of manure[9] with no return address. The father of her baby had told everyone that Sandi was an admitted schizophrenic[10] and had picked his name out of the high school yearbook when she found out she was pregnant. Soon afterward the boy's father got transferred from Tucson and the whole family moved to Oakland, California. Sandi's mother had made her move out, and she lived with her older sister Aimee, who was born again[11] and made her pay rent. In Aimee's opinion it would have been condoning sin to let Sandi and her illegitimate[12] son stay there for free.

---

5. **trash compactor.** Appliance that compacts pieces of trash into one small, tightly packed square
6. **Mr. Ed.** 1960s television show that featured a talking horse named Mr. Ed
7. **poker face.** Refers to a face that shows no expression so as not to give away whether one has good or bad cards during the game of poker
8. **commercials for Knox gelatin.** Made from the bones, skins, and tissue of animals, including horses
9. **manure.** Material that fertilizes land, especially livestock excrement
10. **schizophrenic.** One who suffers from schizophrenia, a psychotic disorder characterized by loss of contact with one's immediate environment, noticeable deterioration in one's ability to function in everyday life, and the disintegration of one's personality
11. **born again.** Christian who has made a renewed commitment of faith, especially after an intense religious experience
12. **illegitimate.** Born of parents not married to each other

words for everyday use

jock • ey (jä kē) *n.,* person who rides a horse, typically a person whose profession is to ride horses during races. *A jockey has to be very careful about his or her weight because races have different limits for how much weight a horse can carry.*

con • done (kən dōn′) *v.,* overlook; excuse; pardon. *My teacher assigned me detention because she could not condone how rude I had been to a classmate.*

But nothing really seemed to throw Sandi. She knew all about things like how to rub an ice cube on kids' gums when they were teething, and where to get secondhand baby clothes for practically nothing. We would take turns checking on Turtle and Seattle, and at the end of our shift we'd go over to the mall together to pick them up. "I don't know," she'd say real loud, hamming it up[13] while we waited in line at Kid Central Station. "I can't decide if I want that Lazyboy[14] recliner in the genuine leather or the green plaid with the stainproof finish." "Take your time deciding," I'd say. "Sleep on it and come back tomorrow."

Turtle would be sitting wherever I set her down that morning, with each hand locked onto some ratty, punked-out stuffed dog or a torn book or another kid's jacket and her eyes fixed on some empty point in the air, just the way a cat will do. It's as though they live in a separate universe that takes up the same space as ours, but is full of fascinating things like mice or sparrows or special TV programs that we can't see.

◀ *How does Taylor describe what Turtle would be doing when she picked her up at Kid Central Station?*

Kid Central Station was not doing Turtle any good. I knew that.

◀ *What does Taylor know about Kid Central Station?*

After six days the Burger Derby manager Jerry Speller, this little twerp who believed that the responsibility of running a burger joint put you a heartbeat away from Emperor of the Universe, said I didn't have the right attitude, and I told him he was exactly right. I said I had to confess I didn't have the proper reverence for the Burger Derby institution, and to prove it I threw my hat into the Mighty Miser and turned it on. Sandi was so impressed she burned the french fries twice in a row.

The fight had been about the Burger Derby uniform. The shorts weren't actually plastic, it turned out, but cotton-polyester with some kind of shiny finish that had to be dry-cleaned. Three twenty-five an hour plus celery and you're supposed to pay for dry-cleaning your own shorts.

◀ *About what did Taylor and Jerry, the Burger Derby manager, fight?*

My one regret was that I didn't see much of Sandi anymore. Naturally I had to find a new place to eat breakfast. There were half a dozen coffeeshops in the area, and

◀ *What is Taylor's one regret about leaving the Burger Derby?*

---

13. **hamming it up.** Acting in an exaggerated or theatrical way, usually to gain attention and create humor

14. **Lazyboy.** Brand of furniture

words for everyday use

rev • er • ence (rev′ rənts) *n.*, honor or respect that is felt or shown; devotion. *Different religions have different customs for showing reverence to their God.*

although I didn't really feel at home in any of them I discovered a new resource: newspapers. On the tables, along with their gritty coffee cups and orange rinds and croissant[15] crumbs, people often left behind the same day's paper.

There was a lady named Jessie with wild white hair and floppy rainboots who would dash into the restaurants and scrounge the leftover fruit and melon rinds. "It's not to eat," she would explain to any- and everybody as she clumped along the sidewalk pushing an interesting-smelling shopping cart that had at some point in history belonged to Safeway. "It's for still-lifes."[16] She told me she painted nothing but madonnas:[17] Orange-peel madonna. Madonna and child with strawberries. Together we made a sort of mop-up team. I nabbed the newspapers, and she took the rest.

Looking through the want ads every day gave new meaning to my life. The For Rents, on the other hand, were a joke as far as I was concerned, but often there would be ads looking for roommates, a possibility I hadn't considered. I would circle anything that looked promising, although people seemed unbelievably picky about who they intended to live with:

"Mature, responsible artist or grad student wanted for cooperative household; responsibilities shared, sensitivity a must."

"Female vegetarian nonsmoker to share harmonious space with insightful Virgo and cat."

I began to suspect that sharing harmonious space with an insightful Virgo might require even greater credentials than being a licensed phlebotomist in the state of Arizona.

The main consideration, though, was whether or not I could locate the address on my Sun-Tran maps of all the various bus routes. At the end of the week I made up my mind to check out a couple of possibilities. One ad said, among other things, "Must be open to new ideas." The other said, "New mom needs company. Own room, low rent, promise I won't bother you. Kids ok." The first sounded like an adventure, and the second sounded like I wouldn't have to pass a

▶ *What is Taylor's assessment of the two ads she decides to follow up on?*

15. **croissant.** Flaky, rich, crescent-shaped roll
16. **still-lifes.** Painting, drawing, or photo of inanimate objects; fruit is often the subject of still-life art
17. **madonnas.** Refers to the Virgin Mary

words for everyday use

scrounge (skrounj') *v.*, steal; swipe; scavenge. *Johnny was able to scrounge one dollar and fifteen cents out of the cushions of his friend's couch.*

test. I put on a pair of stiff, clean jeans and braided my hair and gave Turtle a bath in the sink. She had acquired clothes of her own by now, but just for old time's sake I put her in my DAMN I'M GOOD T-shirt from Kentucky Lake. Just for luck.

Both places were near downtown. The first was a big old ramshackle house with about twelve kinds of wind chimes hanging on the front porch. One was made from the silver keys of some kind of musical instrument like a flute or clarinet, and even Turtle seemed interested in it. A woman came to the door before I even knocked.

She let me inside and called out, "The prospective's[18] here." Three silver earrings—a half moon, a star, and a grinning sun—dangled from holes in her left ear so that she clinked when she walked like some human form of wind chime. She was barefoot and had on a skirt that reminded me of the curtains in my room at the Republic. There was no actual furniture in the room, only a colorful rug and piles of pillows here and there, so I waited to see what she would do. She nested herself into one of the piles, flouncing her skirt out over her knees. I noticed that she had thin silver rings on four of her toes.

◀ How does Taylor describe the woman who answers the door?

Another woman came out of the kitchen door, through which I was relieved to see a table and chairs. A tall, thin guy with a hairless chest hunkered in another doorway for a minute, rubbing a head of orange hair that looked like a wet cat. He had on only those beachcomber-type pants held up by a fake rope. I really couldn't tell how old these people were. I kept expecting a parent to show in another doorway and tell Beach Blanket Bingo to put on his shirt, but then they could have been older than me. We all settled down on the pillows.

"I'm Fay," the toe-ring woman said, "spelled F-E-I, and this is La-Isha and that's Timothy. You'll have to excuse Timothy; he used caffeine yesterday and now his homeostasis[19] is out of balance." I presumed they were talking about his car, although I was not aware of any automotive uses for caffeine.

◀ Why is Timothy's homeostasis out of balance?

"That's too bad," I said. "I wouldn't do anything with caffeine but drink it."

18. **prospective.** Refers to Taylor as the prospective, or likely, new tenant
19. **homeostasis.** Relatively stable state of equilibrium or balance

words for everyday use

ram • shack • le (ram′ sha kəl) *adj.*, appearing as if ready to collapse. *The windows of the ramshackle house were boarded up, and all the kids in the neighborhood said it was haunted.*

They all stared at me for a while.

"Oh. I'm Taylor. This is Turtle."

"Turtle. Is that a spirit name?" La-Isha asked.

"Sure," I said.

La-Isha was thick-bodied, with broad bare feet and round calves. Her dress was a sort of sarong,[20] printed all over with black and orange elephants and giraffes, and she had a jungly-looking scarf wrapped around her head. And to think they used to stare at me for wearing red and turquoise together. Drop these three in Pittman County and people would run for cover.

F-E-I took charge of the investigation. "Would the child be living here too?"

"Right. We're a set."

▶ *How do Fei, La-Isha, and Timothy respond to the idea of Turtle living with them?*

"That's cool. I have no problem with small people," she said. "La-Isha, Timothy?"

"It's not really what I was thinking in terms of, but I can see it happening. I'm flex on children," La-Isha said, after giving it some thought. Timothy said he thought the baby was cute, asked if it was a boy or a girl.

"A girl," I said, but I was drowned out by Fei saying, "Timothy, I *really* don't see that that's an issue here." She said to me, "Gender is not an issue in this house."

"Oh," I said. "Whatever."

"What does she eat?" La-Isha wanted to know.

"Mainly whatever she can get her hands on. She had half a hot dog with mustard for breakfast."

There was another one of those blank spells in the conversation. Turtle was grumpily yanking at a jingle bell on the corner of a pillow, and I was beginning to feel edgy myself. All those knees and chins at the same level. It reminded me of an extremely long movie I had once seen about an Arabian sheik. Maybe La-Isha is Arabian, I thought, though she looked very white, with blond hair on her arms and pink rims around her eyes. Possibly an albino[21] Arabian. I realized she was giving a lecture of some kind.

"At least four different kinds of toxins," she was saying, more to the room in general than to me. Her pink-rimmed

20. **sarong.** Loose garment made of a long strip of cloth that is wrapped around the body and worn as a skirt or dress

21. **albino.** Organism that displays a lack of coloration; albino mammals have translucent skin, white hair, and eyes with a pink or blue iris.

words for everyday use

tox • in (täk' sən) *n.*, poisonous substance. *Swimming in the lake is banned because recent tests showed a high level of toxins in the water.*

eyes were starting to look inflamed. "In a hot dog." Now she was definitely talking to me. "Were you aware of that?"

"I would have guessed seven or eight," I said.

"Nitrites,"[22] said Timothy. He was gripping his head between his palms, one on the chin and one on top, and bending it from side to side until you could hear a little pop. I began to understand about the unbalanced homeostasis.

"We eat mainly soybean products here," Fei said. "We're just starting a soy-milk collective.[23] A house requirement is that each person spend at least seven hours a week straining curd."[24]

"Straining curd," I said. I wanted to say, Flaming nurd. Raining turds. It isn't raining turds, you know, it's raining violets.

"Yes," Fei went on in this abnormally calm voice that made me want to throw a pillow at her. "I guess the child . . ."

"Turtle," I said.

"I guess Turtle would be exempt. But we would have to make adjustments for that in the kitchen quota. . . ."

I had trouble concentrating. La-Isha kept narrowing her eyes and trying to get Fei's attention. I remembered Mrs. Hoge with her shakes, always looking like she was secretly saying, "Don't do it" to somebody behind you.

"So tell us about you," Fei said eventually. I snapped out of my daydreams, feeling like a kid in school that's just been called on. "What kind of a space are you envisioning for yourself?" she wanted to know. Those were her actual words.

"Oh, Turtle and I are flex," I said. "Right now we're staying downtown at the Republic. I jockeyed fried food at the Burger Derby for a while, but I got fired."

La-Isha went kind of stiff on that one. I imagined all the little elephants on her shift getting stung through the heart with a tiny stun gun. Timothy was trying to get Turtle's attention by making faces, so far with no luck.

"Usually little kids are into faces," he informed me. "She seems kind of spaced out."

◀ What observations does Timothy make about Turtle? How does Taylor respond to them?

22. **Nitrites.** Substances found in many foods considered unhealthy
23. **soy milk collective.** Cooperative unit or organization whose members share the responsibilities of making "milk" from soybeans to drink themselves and/or to sell to others
24. **curd.** Soft vegetable "cheese"

words for everyday use

quo • ta (kwō tə) *n.,* share or proportion assigned to each member of a group. *If you want to participate in the walk-a-thon, you have to meet the quota of $50 in sponsored donations.*

"She makes up her own mind about what she's into."

"She sure has a lot of hair," he said. "How old is she?"

"Eighteen months," I said. It was a wild guess.

"She looks very Indian."

"Native American," Fei corrected him. "She does. Is her father Native American?"

"Her great-great-grandpa was full-blooded Cherokee," I said. "On my side. Cherokee skips a generation, like red hair. Didn't you know that?"

The second house on my agenda turned out to be right across the park from Jesus Is Lord's. It belonged to Lou Ann Ruiz.

▶ *Within ten minutes of meeting, what do Taylor and Lou Ann find themselves doing?*

Within ten minutes Lou Ann and I were in the kitchen drinking diet Pepsi and splitting our gussets[25] laughing about homeostasis and bean turds. We had already established that our hometowns in Kentucky were separated by only two counties, and that we had both been to the exact same Bob Seger concert at the Kentucky State Fair my senior year.

"So then what happened?" Lou Ann had tears in her eyes. I hadn't really meant to put them down, they seemed like basically good kids, but it just got funnier as it went along.

"Nothing happened. In their own way, they were so polite it was pathetic. I mean, it was plain as day they thought Turtle was a dimwit and I was from some part of Mars where they don't have indoor bathrooms, but they just kept on asking things like would I like some alfalfa[26] tea?" I had finally told them no thanks, that we'd just run along and envision ourselves in some other space.

Lou Ann showed me the rest of the house except for her room, where the baby was asleep. Turtle and I would have our own room, plus the screened-in back porch if we wanted it. She said it was great to sleep out there in the summer. We had to whisper around the house so we wouldn't wake the baby.

"He was just born in January," Lou Ann said when we were back in the kitchen. "How old's yours?"

"To tell you the truth, I don't even know. She's adopted."

"Well, didn't they tell you all that stuff when you adopted her? Didn't she come with a birth certificate or something?"

---

25. **splitting our gussets.** Splitting our sides from laughing so hard
26. **alfalfa.** Deep-rooted plant that is a member of the legume, or bean, family

"It wasn't an official adoption. Somebody just kind of gave her to me."

"You mean like she was left on your doorstep in a basket?"

"Exactly. Except it was in my car, and there wasn't any basket. Now that I think about it, there should have at least been a basket. Indians make good baskets. She's Indian."

"Wasn't there even a note? How do you know her name's Turtle?"

"I don't. I named her that. It's just temporary until I can figure out what her real name is. I figure I'll hit on it sooner or later."

Turtle was in a high chair of Lou Ann's that must have been way too big for a kid born in January. On the tray there were decals of Kermit the Frog and Miss Piggy, which Turtle was slapping with her hands. There was nothing there for her to grab. I picked her up out of the chair and hefted her onto my shoulder, where she could reach my braid. She didn't pull it, she just held on to it like a lifeline. This was one of our normal positions.

"I can't get over it," Lou Ann said, "that somebody would just dump her like an extra puppy."

"Yeah, I know. I think it was somebody that cared for her, though, if you can believe it. Turtle was having a real rough time. I don't know if she would have made it where she was." A fat gray cat with white feet was sleeping on the windowsill over the sink. Or so I thought, until all of a sudden it jumped down and streaked out of the kitchen. Lou Ann had her back to the door, but I could see the cat in the next room. It was walking around in circles on the living-room rug, kicking its feet behind it again and again, throwing invisible sand over invisible cat poop.

◀ *What does Taylor think about the woman who gave Turtle to her? Why?*

"You wouldn't believe what your cat is doing," I said.

"Oh yes, I would," Lou Ann said. "He's acting like he just went potty, right?"

"Right. But he didn't, as far as I can see."

"Oh, no, he never does. I think he has a split personality. The good cat wakes up and thinks the bad cat has just pooped on the rug. See, we got him as a kitty and I named him Snowboots but Angel thought that was a stupid name so he always called him Pachuco instead. Then a while back, before Dwayne Ray was born, he started acting that way. Angel's my ex-husband, by the way."

It took some effort here to keep straight who was cats and who was husbands.

Lou Ann went on. "So just the other day I read in a magazine that a major cause of split personality is if two parents treat a kid in real different ways, like one all the time tells the kid it's good and the other one said it's bad. It gives them this idea they have to be both ways at once."

"That's amazing," I said. "Your cat ought to be in *Ripley's Believe It or Not*. Or one of those magazine columns where people write in and tell what cute things their pets do, like parakeets that whistle Dixie[27] or cats that will only sleep on a certain towel with pictures of goldfish on it."

"Oh, I wouldn't want anyone to know about Snowboots, it's too embarrassing. It's just about proof-positive that he's from a broken home, don't you think?"

"What does Pachuco mean?"

"It means like a bad Mexican boy. One that would go around spray-painting walls and join a gang."

Pachuco alias Snowboots was still going at it in the living room. "Seriously," I said, "you should send it in. They'd probably pay good money—it's unbelievable what kinds of things you can get paid for. Or at the very least they'd send you a free case of cat chow."

"I almost won a year of free diapers for Dwayne Ray. Dwayne Ray's my son."

"Oh. What does he do?"

Lou Ann laughed. "Oh, he's normal. The only one in the house, I guess. Do you want some more Pepsi?" She got up to refill our glasses. "So did you drive out here, or fly, or what?"

I told her that driving across the Indian reservation was how I'd ended up with Turtle. "Our paths would never have crossed if it weren't for a bent rocker arm."

"Well, if something had to go wrong, at least you can thank your stars you were in a car and not an airplane," she said, whacking an ice-cube tray on the counter. I felt Turtle flinch on my shoulder.

"I never thought of it that way," I said.

"I could never fly in an airplane. O Lord, never! Remember that one winter when a plane went right smack dab into that frozen river in Washington, D.C.? On TV I saw them pulling the bodies out frozen stiff with their knees and arms bent like those little plastic cowboys that are supposed to be riding horses, but then when you lose the horse they're useless. Oh, God, that was so pathetic. I

---

27. **Dixie.** 1859 song about the Southern states in which the Southern states were referred to as "Dixie"

can just hear the stewardess saying, 'Fasten your seat belts, folks,' calm as you please, like 'Don't worry, we just have to say this,' and then next thing you know you're a hunk of ice. Oh, shoot, there's Dwayne Ray just woke up from his nap. Let me go get him."

I did remember that airplane crash. On TV they showed the rescue helicopter dropping down a rope to save the only surviving stewardess from an icy river full of dead people. I remember just how she looked hanging on to that rope. Like Turtle.

In a minute Lou Ann came back with the baby. "Dwayne Ray, here's some nice people I want you to meet. Say hi."

He was teeny, with skin you could practically see through. It reminded me of the Visible Man[28] we'd had in Hughes Walter's biology class. "He's adorable," I said.

"Do you think so, really? I mean, I love him to death of course, but I keep thinking his head's flat."

"They all are. They start out that way, and then after a while their foreheads kind of pop out."

"Really? I never knew that. They never told me that."

"Sure. I used to work in a hospital. I saw a lot of newborns coming and going, and every one of them's head was flat as a shovel."

She made a serious face and fussed with the baby for a while without saying anything.

"So what do you think?" I finally said. "Is it okay if we move in?"

"Sure!" Her wide eyes and the way she held her baby reminded me for a minute of Sandi. The lady downtown could paint either one of them: "Bewildered Madonna with Sunflower Eyes." "Of course you can move in," she said. "I'd love it. I wasn't sure if you'd want to."

"Why wouldn't I want to?"

"Well, my gosh, I mean, here you are, so skinny and smart and cute and everything, and me and Dwayne Ray, well, we're just lumping along here trying to get by. When I put that ad in the paper, I thought, Well, this is sure four dollars down the toilet; who in the world would want to move in here with us?"

◀ *Why doesn't Lou Ann think that Taylor would want to move in with her?*

28. **Visible Man.** Classroom model of the human skeleton and its organs

words for everyday use

bi • ol • o • gy (bī ′ä lə jē) *n.*, branch of science that deals with living organisms. *In biology, we used a microscope to view the tiny creatures that live in a drop of water.*

"Stop it, would you? Quit making everybody out to be better than you are. I'm just a plain hillbilly from East Jesus Nowhere with this adopted child that everybody keeps on telling me is dumb as a box of rocks. I've got nothing on you, girl. I mean it."

Lou Ann hid her mouth with her hand.

"What?" I said.

"Nothing." I could see perfectly well that she was smiling.

"Come on, what is it?"

"It's been so long," she said. "You talk just like me."

What about the way Taylor talks makes Lou Ann smile?

Six

Valentine's Day

The first killing frost[1] of the winter came on Valentine's Day. Mattie's purple bean vines hung from the fence like long strips of beef jerky drying in the sun. It broke my heart to see that colorful jungle turned to black slime, especially on this of all days when people everywhere were sending each other flowers, but it didn't faze Mattie. "That's the cycle of life, Taylor," she said. "The old has to pass on before the new can come around." She said frost improved the flavor of the cabbage and Brussels sprouts. But I think she was gloating. The night before, she'd listened to the forecast and picked a mop bucket full of hard little marbles off the tomato vines, and this morning she had green-tomato pies baking upstairs. I know this sounds like something you'd no more want to eat than a mud-and-Junebug[2] pie some kid would whip up, but it honestly smelled delicious.

◀ What do Mattie's beans vines look like after the killing frost?

◀ What does Mattie tell Taylor about the cycle of life? What does the frost do to the cabbage and Brussels sprouts?

I had taken a job at Jesus Is Lord Used Tires.

◀ Where has Taylor taken a job? Why did she try to avoid doing this?

If there had been any earthly way around this, I would have found it. I loved Mattie, but you know about me and tires. Every time I went to see her and check on the car I felt like John Wayne[3] in that war movie where he buckles down his helmet, takes a swig of bourbon, and charges across the minefield yelling something like "Live Free or Bust!"

But Mattie was the only friend I had that didn't cost a mint in long distance to talk to, until Lou Ann of course. So when she started telling me how she needed an extra hand around the place I just tried to change the subject politely. She had a lot of part-time help, she said, but when people came and went they didn't have time to get the knack of things like patching and alignments. I told her I had no aptitude whatsoever for those things, and was that

1. **killing frost.** Frost that kills all but the most hardy, cold-tolerant plants
2. **Junebug.** Large, leaf-eating beetle
3. **John Wayne.** Legendary American film star, 1907–1979

words for everyday use

faze (fāz') *v.*, to disturb the composure of; disconcert, daunt. *The lightning storm scared Katy, but it didn't faze Sarah.*

gloat (glōt') *v.*, take great pleasure in; brag; triumph; revel in. *I listened to Martin gloat over beating me in tennis by bragging about his game-winning serve.*

knack (nak') *n.*, talent; aptitude; gift; a special talent that is difficult to analyze or teach. *Tyrell has a knack for communicating with young children, so he became a kindergarten teacher.*

ap • ti • tude (ap' tə tüd) *n.*, natural ability; talent. *Velma has an incredible aptitude for math, and though only a junior in high school, she is taking college-level math classes.*

a real scorpion[4] on that guy's belt buckle that was just in here? Did she think we'd get another frost? How did they stitch all those fancy loops and stars on a cowboy boot, was there a special kind of heavy-duty sewing machine?

But there was no steering Mattie off her course. She was positive I'd be a natural at tires. She chatted with me and Turtle between customers, and then sent us on our way with a grocery bag full of cabbage and peas, saying, "Just think about it, hon. Put it in your swing-it-till-Monday basket."[5]

When Mattie said she'd throw in two new tires and would show me how to fix my ignition, I knew I'd be a fool to say no. She paid twice as much as the Burger Derby, and of course there was no ridiculous outfit to be dry-cleaned. If I was going to get blown up, at least it would be in normal clothes.

In many ways it was a perfect arrangement. You couldn't ask for better than Mattie. She was patient and kind and let me bring Turtle in with me when I needed to. Lou Ann kept her some days, but if she had to go out shopping or to the doctor, one baby was two hands full. I felt a little badly about foisting her off on Lou Ann at all, but she insisted that Turtle was so little trouble she often forgot she was there. "She doesn't even hardly wet her diapers," Lou Ann said. It was true. Turtle's main goal in life, other than hanging on to things, seemed to be to pass unnoticed.

▶ *What does the main goal in Turtle's life seem to be?*

Mattie's place was always hopping. She was right about people always passing through, and not just customers, either. There was another whole set of people who spoke Spanish and lived with her upstairs for various lengths of time. I asked her about them once, and she asked me something like had I ever heard of a sanctuary.

▶ *Who lives upstairs with Mattie? When Taylor asks her about them, how does Mattie respond?*

I remembered my gas-station travel brochures. "Sure," I said. "It's a place they set aside for birds, where nobody's allowed to shoot them."

"That's right. They've got them for people too." This was all she was inclined to say on the subject.

4. **scorpion.** Nocturnal arachnid that has a long body and a segmented tail with a poisonous stinger at the tip

5. **swing-it-till-Monday basket.** Creative way of saying "think about it over the weekend and decide on Monday"

words for everyday use

foist (fòist′) *v.*, to force another to accept; thrust upon; impose upon. *I overheard my sister making plans to go to the beach, and I knew she would try to foist her weekend chores on me.*

sanc • tu • ary (saŋ k′ chə wer ē) *n.*, place of refuge and protection; holy place; shrine; haven; shelter. *For some, the woods are a sanctuary from the stress and noise of everyday life.*

Usually the people were brought and taken away by the blue-jeans priest in the station wagon I'd seen that first day. He also wore an interesting belt buckle, not with a scorpion but with an engraving of a small stick figure lost in a kind of puzzle. Mattie said it was an Indian symbol of life: the man in the maze. The priest was short, with a muscular build and white-blond, unruly hair, not really my type but handsome in a just-rolled-out-of-bed kind of way, though I suppose that saying such things about a priest must be some special category of sin. His name was Father William.

◀ *How do the people get to and leave Mattie's?*

◀ *What is the figure on the priest's belt buckle?*

When Mattie introduced us I said, "Pleased to meet you," making an effort not to look at his belt buckle. What had popped into my head was "You are old, Father William." Now where did *that* come from? He was hardly old, and even if he were, this isn't something you'd say.

He and Mattie went to the back of the shop to discuss something over coffee and pie while I held down the fort. It came to me a little later while I was testing a stack of old whitewalls, dunking them in the water and marking a yellow chalk circle around each leak. I remembered three drawings of a little round man: first standing on his head, then balancing an eel straight up on his nose, then kicking a boy downstairs. "You Are Old, Father William"[6] was a poem in a book I'd had as a child. It had crayon scribbles on some pages, so it must have been a donation from one of Mama's people whose children had grown up. Only a rich child would be allowed to scribble in a hardback book.

I decided that after work I would go down to one of Sandi's New To You toy stores and find a book for Turtle. New To You was just like Mama's people, only you had more choice about what you got.

After I had marked all the tires I rolled them across the lot and stacked them into leaky and good piles. I congratulated myself on my steady hand, but later in the day Mattie saw me jump when some hot-dog Chevy backfired out in the street. She was with a customer, but later she came over and said she'd been meaning to ask what I was always so jumpy about. I thought of that column in *Reader's Digest* where you write in and tell your most embarrassing moment. Those were all cute: "The Day My Retriever Puppy Retrieved the Neighbor's Lingerie Off the Clothes Line." In real life, your most embarrassing moment is the last thing in the world you would want printed in *Reader's Digest.*

6. **"You Are Old, Father William."** Children's poem by Lewis Carroll, the author of *Alice in Wonderland*

▶ *To what does Taylor compare Mattie? Why?*

▶ *What does Mattie have enough of on her hands?*

"Nothing," I said.

We stood for a minute with our hands folded into our armpits. Mattie's gray bangs were more salt than they were pepper, cut high and straight across, and her skin always looked a little sunburned. The wrinkles around her eyes reminded me of her Tony Lama boots.[7]

Mattie was like a rock in the road. You could stare at her till the cows come home, but it wouldn't budge the fact of her one inch.

"Just don't tell me you're running from the law," she said finally. "I've got enough of that on my hands."

"No." I wondered what exactly she meant by that. Out on the street a boy coasted by on a bicycle, his elbow clamped over a large framed picture of a sportscar. "I have a fear of exploding tires," I said.

"Well, of all things," she said.

"I know. I didn't ever tell you because it sounds chickenshit." I stopped to consider if you ought to say "chickenshit" in a place called Jesus Is Lord's, but then the damage was done. "Really it's not like it sounds. I don't think there's a thing you could name that I'm afraid of, other than that."

"Of all things," she said again. I imagined that she was looking at me the way you do when you first notice someone is deformed. In sixth grade we had a new teacher for three weeks before we realized his left hand was missing. He always kept his hanky over it. We'd just thought it was allergies.

"Come over here a minute," Mattie said. "I'll show you something." I followed her across the lot. She took a five-gallon jerry can,[8] the type that Jeeps have strapped on their backs, and filled it a little better than halfway up with water.

"Whoa!" I said. While I wasn't paying attention she'd thrown the heavy can at me. I caught it, though it came near to bowling me over.

"Knocked the wind out of you, but it didn't kill you, right?"

"Right," I said.

"That's twenty-eight pounds of water. Twenty-eight pounds of air is about what you put in a tire. When it hits you, that's what it feels like."

"If you say so," I said. "But I saw a guy get blown up in the air once by a tire. All the way over the Standard Oil sign. It was a tractor tire."

7. **Tony Lama boots.** Brand of cowboy boots
8. **jerry can.** Container for holding gasoline

"Well that's another whole can of beans," Mattie said. "If we get a tractor tire in here, I'll handle it."

I had never thought of tire explosions in relative terms, though it stood to reason that some would be worse than others. By no means did this put my fears to rest, but still I felt better somehow. What the hell. Live free or bust.

"Okay," I said. "We'll handle it together, how's that?"

"That's a deal, hon."

"Can I put this down now?"

"Sure, put it down." She said it in a serious way, as if the can of water were some important damaged auto part we'd been discussing. I blessed Mattie's soul for never laughing at any point in this conversation. "Better yet," she said, "pour it out on those sweet peas."

There was a whole set of things I didn't understand about plants, such as why hadn't the sweet peas been killed by the frost? The same boy sped by again on his bike, or possibly a different boy. This time he had a bunch of roses in a white paper funnel tucked under his arm. While the water glugged out over the sweet peas I noticed Mattie looking at me with her arms crossed. Just watching. I missed Mama so much my chest hurt.

◀ *What doesn't Taylor understand about the sweet peas?*

◀ *When Taylor notices Mattie watching her, what effect does it have on Taylor?*

Turtle had managed to get through her whole life without a book, I suppose, and then had two of them bought for her in one day. I got her one called *Old MacDonald*[9] *Had an Apartment House,* which showed pictures of Old MacDonald growing celery in windowboxes and broccoli in the bathtub and carrots under the living-room rug. Old MacDonald's downstairs neighbors could see the carrots popping down through the ceiling. I bought it because it reminded me of Mattie, and because it had stiff pages that I hoped might stand up to Turtle's blood-out-of-turnips grip.[10]

◀ *What kind of pictures does the Old MacDonald book have? Why did Taylor choose the book?*

While I was downtown I also looked for a late Valentine's card to send Mama. I still felt kind of awful about leaving her, and changing my name just seemed like the final act of betrayal, but Mama didn't see it that way. She said I was smarter than anything to think of Taylor, that it fit me like a pair of washed jeans. She told me she'd always had second thoughts about Marietta.

◀ *How does Taylor think that changing her name must seem to Mama? What does Mama say about Taylor changing her name?*

I found just the right card to send her. On the cover there were hearts, and it said, "Here's hoping you'll soon

9. **Old MacDonald.** Name of a farmer who is the subject of the children's song "Old MacDonald Had a Farm"

10. **blood-out-of-turnips grip.** Very tight grip; refers to squeezing hard enough to get juice out of a turnip

have something big and strong around the house to open those tight jar lids." Inside was a picture of a pipe wrench.

Lou Ann, meanwhile, had bought one of those name-your-baby books in the grocery checkout line. When I came home she had it propped open on the stove and was calling out names from the girl section while she made dinner. Both Turtle and Dwayne Ray were propped up at the table in chairs too big for them. Dwayne Ray's head was all flopped over, he was too little to hold it up by himself, and he was wiggling toward the floor like Snake Man escaping from his basket. Turtle just sat and stared at nothing. Or rather, at something on the table that was as real to her as Snowboots's invisible poop was to him.

Lou Ann was banging pot lids to wake the dead and boiling bottles. She had stopped nursing and put Dwayne Ray on formula, saying she was petrified she wouldn't have enough milk for him.

"Leandra, Leonie, Leonore, Leslie, Letitia," she called out, watching Turtle over her shoulder as though she expected her to spew out quarters like a slot machine when she hit the right combination of letters.

"Lord have mercy," I said. "Have you been doing this all the way from the Agathas and Amys?"

"Oh, hi, I didn't hear you come in." She acted a little guilty, like a kid caught using swear words. "I thought I'd do half today and the rest tomorrow. You know what? Lou Ann is on the exact middle page. I wonder if my mother had a book like this."

"The book our mothers had was the Bible, not some fifty-cent dealie they sell from the same rack as the *National Enquirer.*" I knew very well that none of my various names had come out of a Bible, nor Lou Ann's either, but I didn't care. I was just plain in a bad mood. I put Turtle over my shoulder. "What do you really expect her to do if you say the right name, Lou Ann? Jump up and scream and kiss you like the people on those game shows?"

▶ *Why does Turtle worry Lou Ann? How does Taylor respond to this?*

"Don't be mad at me, Taylor, I'm just trying to help. She worries me. I'm not saying she's dumb, but it seems like she doesn't have too much personality."

"Sure she does," I said. "She grabs onto things. That's her personality."

▶ *What does Lou Ann say babies do automatically? What does she say about personality?*

"Well, no offense, but that's not personality. Babies do that automatically. I haven't worked in a hospital or anything, but at least I know that much. Personality has to be something you learn."

"And reading off a list of every name known to humankind is going to teach her to have personality?"

"Taylor, I'm not trying to tell you what to do, but all the magazines say that you have to play with children to develop their personality."

"So? I play with her. I bought her a book today."

"Okay, you play with her. I'm sorry." Lou Ann ladled soup out of the big pot on the stove and brought bowls over to the table. Her bowl held about two teaspoons of the red-colored broth. She was starving herself to lose the weight she'd gained with Dwayne Ray, which was mostly between her ears as far as I could see.

"This is Russian cabbage-and-beet soup," she announced. "It's called borscht. It's the beets that turn it pink. You're supposed to put sour cream on top but that just seemed like calories up the kazoo. I got it out of *Ladies' Home Journal.*"

I could imagine her licking her index finger and paging through some magazine article called "Toasty Winter Family Pleasers," trying to find something to do with all that cabbage I kept bringing home from Mattie's. I fished out a pink potato and mushed it up in Turtle's bowl.

"It's good, Lou Ann. Nothing personal, I'm just in a crappy mood."

"Watch out, there's peas in there. A child's windpipe can be blocked by anything smaller than a golf ball."

For Lou Ann, life itself was a life-threatening enterprise. Nothing on earth was truly harmless. Along with her clip file of Hispanic[11] bank presidents (which she had started to let slide, now that Angel was talking divorce), she saved newspaper stories of every imaginable type of freak disaster. Unsuspecting diners in a restaurant decapitated[12] by a falling ceiling fan. Babies fallen head-first into the beer cooler and drowned in melted ice while the family played Frisbee. A housewife and mother of seven stepping out of a Wick 'N' Candle store, only to be shot through the heart by a misfired high-pressure nail gun at a construction site across the street. To Lou Ann's way of thinking, this proved not only that ice chests and construction sites were dangerous, but also Wick 'N' Candle stores and Frisbees.

◀ *According to Taylor, what is life for Lou Ann?*

I promised her that I wouldn't give Turtle anything smaller than a golf ball. I amused myself by thinking about the cabbage: would you have to take into account the size of one leaf compressed into golf-ball shape? Or could you

11. **Hispanic.** Person of Latin American—especially Cuban, Mexican, or Puerto Rican—descent, living in the United States
12. **decapitated.** Beheaded; had their heads cut off

just consider the size of the entire cabbage and call the whole thing safe?

Lou Ann was fanning a mouthful that was still too hot to swallow. "I can just hear what my Granny Logan would say if I tried to feed her Russian cabbage soup. She'd say we were all going to turn communist."

▶ *Later that night, what does Taylor realize?*

Later that night when the kids were in bed I realized exactly what was bugging me: the idea of Lou Ann reading magazines for child-raising tips and recipes and me coming home grouchy after a hard day's work. We were like some family on a TV commercial, with names like Myrtle and Fred. I could just hear us striking up a conversation about air fresheners.

Lou Ann came in wearing her bathrobe and a blue towel wrapped around her hair. She curled up on the sofa and started flipping through the book of names again.

"Oh, jeez, take this away from me before I start looking at the boy section. There's probably fifty thousand names better than Dwayne Ray, and I don't even want to know about them. It's too late now."

"Lou Ann, have a beer with me. I want to talk about something, and I don't want you to get offended." She took the beer and sat up like I'd given her an order, and I knew this wasn't going to work.

"Okay, shoot." The way she said it, you would think I was toting an M-16.[13]

▶ *What does Taylor tell Lou Ann about Lou Ann cooking dinner and taking care of Turtle? How does Lou Ann respond?*

"Lou Ann, I moved in here because I knew we'd get along. It's nice of you to make dinner for us all, and to take care of Turtle sometimes, and I know you mean well. But we're acting like Blondie and Dagwood[14] here. All we need is some ignorant little dog named Spot to fetch me my slippers. It's not like we're a *family,* for Christ's sake. You've got your own life to live, and I've got mine. You don't have to do all this stuff for me."

"But I want to."

"But I don't *want* you to."

---

13. **M-16.** Type of rifle
14. **Blondie and Dagwood.** Husband and wife comic strip characters

words for everyday use

com • mu • nist (käm′ yə nist) *n.,* one who adheres to the theory or system of communism, under which private property is eliminated, and all goods are owned in common and available to all as needed. *According to the theory of communism, a communist society eliminates the rich and the poor and creates a classless society.*

tote (tōt′) *v.,* carry by hand. *Jennifer would have liked to walk to the grocery store, but she did not want to have to tote her grocery bags back home.*

It was like that.

By the time we had worked through our third beers, a bag of deep-fried tortilla chips, a pack of individually-wrapped pimiento-cheese slices and a can of sardines in mustard, Lou Ann was crying. I remember saying something like "I never even *had* an old man, why would I want to end up acting like one?"

It's the junk food, I kept thinking. On a diet like this the Bean Curd kids would be speaking in tongues.[15]

All of a sudden Lou Ann went still, with both hands over her mouth. I thought she must be choking (after all her talk about golf balls), and right away thought of the Heimlich Maneuver[16] poster on the wall at Mattie's store. That's how often she fed people there. I was trying to remember if you were or were not supposed to slap the person on the back. But then Lou Ann moved her hands from her mouth to her eyes, like two of the three No-Evil monkey brothers.[17]

"Oh, God," she said. "I'm drunk."

"Lou Ann, you've had three beers."

"That's all it takes. I *never* drink. I'm scared to death of what might happen."

I was interested. This house was full of surprises. But this turned out to be nothing like the cat. Lou Ann said what she was afraid of was just that she might lose control and do something awful.

"Like what?"

"I don't know. How do I know? Just something. I feel like the only reason I have any friends at all is because I'm always careful not to say something totally dumb, and if I blow it just one time, then that's it."

◀ *What is the only reason that Lou Ann thinks she has any friends?*

"Lou Ann, honey, that's a weird theory of friendship."

"No, I mean it. For the longest time after Angel left I kept thinking back to this time last August when his friend Manny and his wife Ramona came over and we all went out to the desert to look at the shooting stars?[18] There was

---

15. **speaking in tongues.** Speaking in tongues is a religious practice of charismatic Christians whereby they are inspired to such states of religious fervor that they begin speaking in unknown languages; here, Taylor uses the expression to mean "lose their minds" or "go crazy."

16. **Heimlich Maneuver.** Procedure of applying sudden upward pressure on the upper abdomen of a choking victim to force a foreign object from the windpipe

17. **No-Evil monkey brothers.** Three monkeys—one with hands over his eyes, one with hands over his ears, and one with hands over his mouth—who illustrate the Buddhist proverb "See no evil, hear no evil, speak no evil"

18. **shooting stars.** Meteors that appear as temporary streaks of light in the night sky; a meteor is any of the small particles of matter in the solar system that can only be seen because of the white-hot glow it gives off when it enters the earth's atmosphere.

supposed to be a whole bunch of them, a shower, they were saying on the news. But we kept waiting and waiting, and in the meantime we drank a bottle of José Cuervo[19] plumb down to the worm.[20] The next morning Angel kept saying, 'Man, can you believe the meteor shower? What, you don't even remember it?' I honestly couldn't remember a thing besides looking for the star sapphire[21] from Ramona's ring that had plunked out somewhere. It turned out she'd lost it way before. She found it at home in their dog's dish, can you believe it?"

I was trying to fit Angel into some pigeonhole[22] or other in the part of my brain that contained what I knew about men. I liked this new version of an Angel who would go out looking for shooting stars, but hated what I saw of him the next morning, taunting Lou Ann about something that had probably never even happened.

▶ *What version of Angel does Taylor like? What version of Angel does she hate?*

▶ *What does Taylor suggest to Lou Ann about the meteor shower?*

"Maybe he was pulling your leg,"[23] I said. "Maybe there never was any meteor shower. Did you ask Ramona?"

"No. I never thought of that. I just assumed."

"Well, why don't you call her up and ask?"

"She and Manny moved to San Diego," she wailed. You'd think they had moved for the sole purpose of keeping this information from Lou Ann.

"Well, I'm sorry."

She persisted. "But that's not even really the point. It wasn't just that I'd missed something important. I kept on thinking that if I could miss a whole meteor shower, well, I'd probably done something else ridiculous. For all I know I could've run naked through the desert singing 'Skip to My Lou.'"

I shuddered. All those spiny pears and prickly whatsits.[24]

She stared mournfully into the empty bag of chips. "And now it's Valentine's Day," she said. "And everybody

---

19. **José Cuervo.** Brand of tequila, a Mexican liquor
20. **down to the worm.** Refers to the bottom of the bottle, where the agave worm rests in bottles of Mezcal, a traditional Mexican liquor made from the agave cactus
21. **star sapphire.** Blue gem that, when cut and polished, reveals pale white streaks that give the look of a star
22. **pigeonhole.** Narrow category
23. **pulling your leg.** Teasing you; trying to fool you by telling you something that isn't true
24. **spiny pears and prickly whatsits.** Cactuses

words for everyday use

mourn • ful • ly (mōrn′ fəl le) *adv.,* full of sorrow; sad; gloomy. *Knowing we wouldn't see each other again for a year, my fiancé and I mournfully drove to the airport.*

else in the whole wide world is home with their husband smooching on the couch and watching TV, but not Lou Ann, no sir. I ran off both my husband *and* the TV."

I couldn't even think where to begin on this one. I thought of another one of Mama's hog sayings: "Hogs go deaf at harvest time." It meant that people would only hear what they wanted to hear. Mama was raised on a hog farm.

Lou Ann looked abnormally flattened against the back of the sofa. I thought of her father, who she'd told me was killed when his tractor overturned. They'd found him pressed into a mud bank, and when they pulled him out he left a perfect print. "A Daddy print" she'd called it, and she'd wanted to fill the hole with plaster of Paris to keep him, the way she'd done with her hand print in school for Mother's Day.

"I always wondered if that night we got drunk had something to do with why I lost him," she said. I was confused for a second, still thinking of her father.

"I thought you were glad when Angel left."

"I guess I was. But still, you know, something went wrong. You're supposed to love the same person your whole life long till death do you part and all that. And if you don't, well, you've got to have screwed up somewhere."

"Lou Ann, you read too many magazines." I went into the kitchen and checked the refrigerator for about the fifteenth time that night. It was still the same: cabbages and peanut butter. I opened a cabinet and peered behind the cans of refried beans and tomato sauce. There was a bottle of black-strap molasses, a box of Quick Hominy Grits, and a can of pink salmon. I considered all of these things in various combinations, then settled for another bag of tortilla chips. This is what happens to people without TVs, I thought. They die of junk food.

When I came back to the living room she was still depressed about Angel. "I'll tell you my theory about staying with one man your whole life long," I said. "Do you know what a flapper ball is?"

She perked up. "A whatter ball?"

"Flapper ball. It's that do-jobbie in a toilet tank that goes up and down when you flush. It shuts the water off."

"Oh."

"So one time when I was working in this motel one of the toilets leaked and I had to replace the flapper ball. Here's what it said on the package; I kept it till I knew it by heart: 'Please Note. Parts are included for all installations, but no installation requires all of the parts.' That's kind of my philosophy about men. I don't think there's an installation out there that could use all of my parts."

Lou Ann covered her mouth to hide a laugh. I wondered who had ever told her laughing was a federal offense.

"I'm serious, now. I'm talking mental capacity and everything, not just parts like what they cut a chicken into." By this time she was laughing out loud.

"I tell you my most personal darkest secret and you laugh," I said, playing vexed.

"They can always use a breast or a thigh or a leg, but nobody wants the scroungy old neckbones!"

"Don't forget the wings," I said. "They always want to gobble up your wings right off the bat." I dumped the rest of the bag of chips out into the bowl on the ottoman[25] between us. I was actually thinking about going for the jar of peanut butter.

"Here, let me show you this Valentine's card I got for Mama," I said, digging through my purse until I found it. But Lou Ann was already having such a fit of giggles I could just as well have shown her the electric bill and she would have thought it was the funniest thing in recorded history.

"Oh, me," she said, letting the card fall in her lap. Her voice trailed down from all those high-pitched laughs like a prom queen floating down the gymnasium stairs. "I could use me a good wrench around here. Or better yet, one of them . . . what do you call 'ems? That one that's shaped like a weenie?"

I had no idea what she meant. "A caulking gun? An angle drill? A battery-head cleaner?" Come to think of it, just about every tool was shaped like either a weenie or a pistol, depending on your point of view. "The Washington Monument?" I said. This set Lou Ann off again. If there really had been a law against laughing, both of us would have been on our way to Sing Sing by now.

"Oh, Lordy, they ought to put that on a Valentine's card," she said. "I can just see me sending something like that to *my* Mama. She'd have a cow right there on the

25. **ottoman.** Overstuffed footstool

words for everyday use

in • stal • la • tion (in stə lā′ shən) *n.,* act of setting up for use or service. *As soon as the serviceperson completes the installation of the stove, I am going to cook something delicious for dinner.*

vex (veks′) *v.,* distress; agitate; trouble; harass. *The fact that my sister will not stop singing loudly while I try to study is really beginning to vex me!*

kitchen floor. And Granny Logan jumping and twisting her hands saying, 'What is it? I don't get it.' She'd go running after the mailman and tell him, 'Young man, come back in here this minute. Ask Ivy what's supposed to be so funny.'

"Oh, Lordy, Lordy," Lou Ann said again, drying her eyes. She put a chip in her mouth with a flourish, licking each of her fingers afterward. She was draped out on the sofa in her green terry bathrobe and blue turban like Cleopatra[26] cruising down the Nile, with Snowboots curled at her feet like some insane royal pet. In ancient Egypt, I'd read somewhere, schizophrenics were worshiped as gods.

"I'll tell you one thing," Lou Ann said. "When something was bugging Angel, he'd never of stayed up half the night with me talking and eating everything that wasn't nailed down. You're not still mad, are you?"

What does Lou Ann say Angel never would have done?

I held up two fingers. "Peace, sister," I said, knowing full well that only a complete hillbilly would say this in the 1980s. Love beads came to Pittman the same year as the dial tone.

"Peace and love, get high and fly with the dove," she said.

26. **Cleopatra.** Queen of Egypt from 69 to 30 BC

words for everyday use

flour • ish (flər′ ish) *n.*, wave; dramatic or showy motion. *The smug student solved the difficult math equation at the blackboard, then with a flourish of his chalk hand, he took a small bow and headed for his seat.*

Seven

How They Eat In Heaven

"A red Indian thought he might eat tobacco in church!" Lou Ann had closed her eyes and put herself in a trance to dig this item out of her fourth-grade memory, the way witnesses at a holdup will get themselves hypnotized to recollect the color of the getaway car. "That's it! Arithmetic!" she cried, bouncing up and down. Then she said, "No offense to anyone present, about the Indian." No one seemed offended.

"Oh, sure, I remember those," Mattie said. "There was one for every subject. Geography was: George eats old gray rutabagas[1] and picks his—something. What would it be?"

"Oh, gross," Lou Ann said. "Gag a maggot."

I couldn't think of a solitary thing George might pick that started with Y. "Maybe you haven't got it quite right," I told Mattie. "Maybe it's something else, like 'pulls his yarn.'"

"Plants his yard?" offered Lou Ann.

"Pets his yak," said the dark, handsome man, who was half of a young couple Mattie had brought along on the picnic. Their names I had not yet gotten straight: Es-something and Es-something. The man had been an English teacher in Guatemala City.[2] This whole conversation had started with a rhyme he used to help students remember how to pronounce English vowels. Then we'd gotten onto spelling.

▶ *What was the profession, when he lived in Guatemala City, of the man Mattie invites to the picnic?*

"What's a yak?" Lou Ann wanted to know.

"It's a type of very hairy cow," he explained. He seemed a little embarrassed. Lou Ann and I had already told him three or four times that he spoke better English than the two of us combined.

▶ *What embarrasses the man?*

1. **rutabagas.** Root vegetable
2. **Guatemala City.** Capital city of the Central American country of Guatemala

words for everyday use

trance (trants') *n.*, hypnotic state; state of deep mental absorption or distraction; daze. *When Hendrick watches action movies, he falls into a trance, and he doesn't see or hear anything that is going on around him.*

hyp • no • tize (hip' nə tīz) *v.*, to cause to go into a state that resembles sleep, but during which, a person becomes readily accepting of suggestions made by the person who induced, or put the person into, the state. *On television, people dangle a pocket watch and say, "You are getting very sleepy" when they want to hypnotize someone; then they make them cluck like a chicken.*

rec • ol • lect (rek' ə lekt) *v.*, remember. *When I asked Angela to return my sweater, she said she didn't recollect borrowing it.*

We were flattened and sprawled across the rocks like a troop of lizards stoned on the sun, feeling too good to move. Lou Ann's feet dangled into the water. She insisted that she looked like a Sherman tank[3] in shorts but had ended up wearing them anyway, and a pink elastic tube top which, she'd informed us, Angel called her boob tube. I'd worn jeans and regretted it. February had turned mild again right after the frost, and March was staying mainly on the sweaty end of pleasant. Lou Ann and Mattie kept saying it had to be the warmest winter on record. The old-timers, somewhere down the line, would look back on this as the year we didn't have a winter, except for that freeze God sent on Valentine's Day so we'd have green-tomato pie. When the summer wildflowers started blooming before Easter, Mattie said the Lord was clearly telling us to head for the hills and have us a picnic. You never could tell about Mattie's version of the Lord. Mainly, He was just one damn thing after another.

We'd come to a place you would never expect to find in the desert: a little hideaway by a stream that had run all the way down the mountains into a canyon, where it jumped off a boulder and broke into deep, clear pools. White rocks sloped up out of the water like giant, friendly hippo butts. A ring of cottonwood trees cooled their heels in the wet ground, and overhead leaned together, then apart, making whispery swishing noises. It made me think of Gossip, the game we played as kids where you whisper a message around a circle. You'd start out with "Randy walks to the hardware store" and end up with "Granny has rocks in her underwear drawer."

It had been Lou Ann's idea to come here. It was a place she and Angel used to go when she first came to Tucson with him. I didn't know if her choice was a good or bad sign, but she didn't seem unhappy to be here without him. She seemed more concerned that the rest of us would like it.

"So is this place okay? You're sure?" she asked us, until we begged her to take our word for it, that it was the most wonderful picnic spot on the face of the earth, and she relaxed.

"Me and Angel actually talked about getting married up here," she said, dipping her toes in and out. There were Jesus bugs here, but not the long-legged, graceful kind we had back home. These were shaped like my car and more

3. **Sherman tank.** Battle tank designed, built, and widely used by the United States during World War II.

or less <u>careened</u> around on top of the water. The whole gang of them together looked like graduation night in Volkswagen land.

"That would have been a heck of a wedding," Mattie said. "A hefty hike for the guests."

"Oh no. We were going to do the whole thing on horseback. Can't you just see it?"

I could see it in *People Magazine,* maybe. What with my disgust for anything horsy, I always forgot that Angel had won Lou Ann's heart and stolen her away from Kentucky during his days as a rodeo man.

▶ *How did Angel's mother respond to Lou Ann's idea for a horseback wedding?*

"Anyway," she went on, "we could never have gone through with it on account of Angel's mother. She said something like, 'Okay, children, go ahead. When I get thrown off a horse and bash my brains out on the rocks, just step over me and go on with the ceremony.'"

The English teacher spoke softly in Spanish to his wife, and she smiled. Most of our conversation seemed to be getting lost in the translation, like some international form of the Gossip game. But this story had come from Mrs. Ruiz's Spanish (Lou Ann claimed that the only English words her mother-in-law knew were names of diseases) into English, and went back again without any trouble. A certain kind of mother is the same in any language.

▶ *Why are Angel's mother's comments easily understood by the guests Mattie has brought?*

Esperanza and Estevan were their names. It led you to expect twins, not a young married couple, and really there was something twinnish about them. They were both small and dark, with the same high-set, watching eyes and strongboned faces I'd admired in the bars and gas stations and postcards of the Cherokee Nation. Mattie had told me that more than half the people in Guatemala were Indians. I had no idea.

▶ *How does Taylor describe the faces of Estevan and Esperanza? What had Mattie told Taylor about Guatemala?*

But where Estevan's smallness made him seem compact and springy, as though he might have steel bars inside where most people have flab and sawdust, Esperanza just seemed to have shrunk. Exactly like a wool sweater washed in hot. It seemed impossible that her hands could be so small, that all the red and blue diamonds and green birds that ran across the bosom of her small blouse had been embroidered with regular-sized needles. I had this <u>notion</u>

▶ *What does Taylor think seems impossible about Esperanza?*

words for everyday use

ca • reen (kə rēn′) *v.*, lurch; swerve. *Malcolm hit a large pebble, which caused him to <u>careen</u> off the bike path, and ride right into the lake.*

no • tion (nō′ shən) *n.*, person's impression of something; idea; opinion. *Around midnight, Nadia expressed the <u>notion</u> that a swim in the pool followed by ice cream would be the best way to guarantee the success of the slumber party.*

that at one time in life she'd been larger, but that someone had split her in two like one of those hollow wooden dolls, finding this smaller version inside. She took up almost no space. While the rest of us talked and splashed and laughed she sat still, a colorful outgrowth of rock. She reminded me of Turtle.

◀ Of whom does Esperanza remind Taylor?

There had been something of a scene between her and Turtle earlier that day. We'd driven up in two cars, Lou Ann and me and the kids leading the way on my brand-new retreads and the other three following in Mattie's pickup. When we got to the trail head we parked in the skimpy shade you find under mesquite trees[4]—like gray lace petticoats—and pulled out the coolers and bedspreads and canteens. The last two things out of the car were Dwayne Ray and Turtle.

Esperanza was just stepping out of the cab, and when she saw the kids she fell back against the seat, just as if she'd been hit with twenty-eight pounds of air. For the next ten minutes she looked blanched, like a boiled vegetable. She couldn't take her eyes off Turtle.

◀ How did Esperanza respond to seeing Turtle for the first time?

As we hiked up the trail I fell in behind Estevan and made small talk. Lou Ann was in the lead, carrying Dwayne Ray in a pouch on her back and holding his molded-plastic car seat over her head like some space-age sunbonnet. Behind her, ahead of us, went Esperanza. From behind you could have mistaken her for a schoolgirl, with her two long braids swinging across her back and her prim walk, one small sandal in front of the other. The orange plastic canteen on her shoulder looked like some burden thrust upon her from another world.

Eventually I asked Estevan if his wife was okay. He said certainly, she was okay, but he knew what I was talking about. A little later he said that my daughter looked like a child they'd known in Guatemala.

◀ What does Estevan tell Taylor about Turtle?

"She could be, for all I know." I laughed. I explained to him that she wasn't really my daughter.

Later, while we sat on the rocks and ate baloney sandwiches, Esperanza kept watching Turtle.

4. **mesquite trees.** Tree that is part of the legume, or bean, family

words for everyday use

can • teen (kan tēn') *n.,* portable container for carrying liquid. *The thirsty hikers passed around the canteen filled with water until it was empty.*

blanch (blanch') *v.,* to take the color out of; to boil or steam for a brief period so that the skin can be easily removed. *If you blanch a tomato in boiling water for thirty seconds, the skin will peel right off.*

prim (prim') *adj.,* stiff; formal; neat. *We were used to seeing Celia in prim white shirts and neatly cuffed pants, so were surprised when she wore a flowing red dress to the dance.*

Estevan and I eventually decided to brave the cold water. "Don't look," I announced, and stripped off my jeans.

"Taylor, no! You mustn't," Lou Ann said.

"For heaven's sake, Lou Ann, I've got on decent underwear."

"No, what I mean is, you're not supposed to go in for an hour after you eat. You'll drown, both of you. It's something about the food in your stomach makes you sink."

"I know I can depend on you, Lou Ann," I said. "If we sink, you'll pull us out." I held my nose and jumped in.

The water was so cold I couldn't imagine why it hadn't just stayed frozen up there on the snow-topped mountain. The two of us caught our breath and whooped and splashed the others until Lou Ann was threatening our lives. Mattie, more inclined to the direct approach, was throwing rocks the size of potatoes.

"If you think I'd go in there to drag either one of you out, you're off your rocker," Mattie said. Lou Ann said, "If you all want to go and catch pee-namonia, be my guest."

Estevan went from whooping to singing in Spanish, hamming it up in this amazing yodely[5] voice. He dog-paddled over to Esperanza and rested his chin on the rock by her feet, still singing, his head moving up and down with the words. What kind of words, it was easy to guess: "My sweet nightingale, my rose, your eyes like the stars." He was unbelievably handsome, with this smile that could just crack your heart right down the middle.

▶ *How does Taylor describe Estevan's appearance?*

▶ *What does Taylor notice about Esperanza as Estevan sings to her?*

But she was off on her own somewhere. From time to time she would gaze over to where the kids were asleep on the blue bedspread. And who could blame her, really? It was a sweet sight. With the cottonwood shade rippling over them they looked like a drawing from one of those old-fashioned children's books that show babies in underwater scenes, blowing glassy bubbles and holding on to fishes' tails. Dwayne Ray had on a huge white sailor hat and had nodded forward in his car seat, but Turtle's mouth was open to the sky. Her hair was damp and plastered down in dark cords on her temples, showing more of her forehead than usual. Even from a distance I could see her eyes dancing around under eyelids as thin as white grape skins. Turtle always had desperate, active dreams. In sleep, it seemed, she was free to do all the things that during her waking life she could only watch.

▶ *What kinds of dreams does Turtle have? What does Taylor believe about Turtle's sleep?*

5. **yodely.** Characterized by the repeated changing of the voice from low to high

We went back at that time of evening when it's dusky but the headlights don't really help yet. Mattie said she was stoneblind this time of night, so Estevan drove. "Be careful now," she warned him as the three of them climbed into the cab. "The last thing we need is to get stopped." Lou Ann and the kids and I followed in my car.

Fortunately the parking lot had a good slant to it so getting started was a piece of cake. I hardly had time to curse, and we caught right up. Mattie needn't have worried; Estevan was a careful driver. As we puttered along Lou Ann had to keep reaching into the back seat, which wasn't really a seat but a kind of pit where one used to be, to get the kids settled down. They had both slept through the entire hike back, but now were wide awake.

"Oh, shoot, I've sunburned the top half of my boobs," she said, frowning down her chest. "Stretch marks and all."

Mattie's pickup stopped so fast I nearly rear-ended it. I slammed on the brakes and we all pitched forward. There was a thud in the back seat, and then a sound, halfway between a cough and a squeak.

"Jesus, that was Turtle," I said. "Lou Ann, that was her, wasn't it? She made that sound. Is her neck broken?"

◀ *How does Taylor react to the thud in the back seat?*

"She's fine, Taylor. Everybody's fine. Look." She picked up Turtle and showed me that she was okay. "She did a somersault. I think that sound was a laugh."

It must have been true. She was hanging on to Lou Ann's boob tube for dear life, and smiling. We both stared at her. Then we stared at the tailgate of the truck in front of us, stopped dead in the road.

"What in the tarnation?" Lou Ann asked.

I said I didn't know. Then I said, "Look." In the road up ahead there was a quail,[6] the type that has one big feather spronging out the front of its head like a forties-model ladies' hat. We could just make out that she was dithering back and forth in the road, and then we gradually could see that there were a couple dozen babies running around her every which way. They looked like fuzzy ball bearings[7] rolling around in a box.

◀ *What is in the road that caused Mattie to hit her brakes?*

6. **quail.** Type of bird
7. **ball bearings.** Steel balls that roll easily

words for everyday use

dus • ky (dəs' kē) *adj.*, somewhat dark in color; shadowy. *Characters in horror movies always try to find out what lurks in the dusky corners of basements.*

Our mouths opened and shut and we froze where we sat. I suppose we could have honked and waved and it wouldn't have raised any more pandemonium than this poor mother already had to deal with, but instead we held perfectly still. Even Turtle. After a long minute or two the quail got her family herded off the road into some scraggly bushes. The truck's brakelights flickered, like a wink, and Estevan drove on. Something about the whole scene was trying to make tears come up in my eyes. I decided I must be about to get my period.

▶ How does the scene affect Taylor?

"You know," Lou Ann said a while later, "if that had been Angel, he would've given himself two points for every one he could hit."

▶ What brings Taylor great relief? Why?

Knowing that Turtle's first uttered sound was a laugh brought me no end of relief. If I had dragged her halfway across the nation only to neglect and entirely botch[8] her upbringing, would she have laughed? I thought surely not. Surely she would have bided her time while she saved up whole words, even sentences. Things like "What do you think you're doing?"

I suppose some of Lou Ann had rubbed off on me, for me to take this laugh as a sign. Lou Ann was the one who read her horoscope[9] every day, and mine, and Dwayne Ray's, and fretted that we would never know Turtle's true sign[10] (which seemed to me the least of her worries), and was sworn to a strange kind of logic that said a man could leave his wife for missing a meteor shower or buying the wrong brand of cookies. If the mail came late it meant someone, most likely Grandmother Logan, had died.

▶ What is Turtle's first word?

But neither of us could interpret the significance of Turtle's first word. It was "bean."

We were in Mattie's backyard helping her put in the summer garden, which she said was way overdue considering the weather. Mattie's motto seemed to be "Don't let the

8. **botch.** Mess up
9. **horoscope.** General forecast of the future events of one's life based on one's birth date, the positions of the planets, and signs of the zodiac
10. **sign.** Zodiac sign; the zodiac is an imaginary band in the heavens that is divided into twelve constellations or signs: Aries, Taurus, Gemini, Cancer, Leo, Virgo, Libra, Scorpio, Sagittarius, Capricorn, Aquarius, and Pisces.

words for everyday use

pan • de • mo • ni • um (pan də mō′ nē əm) *n.,* wild uproar; chaos; commotion; turmoil. *Pandemonium broke out in the stadium as fans stormed the field after their team won the championship.*

grass grow under your feet, but make sure there's something growing everywhere else."

"Looky here, Turtle," I said. "We're planting a garden just like Old MacDonald in your book." Mattie rolled her eyes. I think her main motive, in insisting that Turtle watch us do this, was to straighten the child out. She was concerned that Turtle would grow up thinking carrots grew under the rug.

"Here's squash seeds," I said. "Here's pepper seeds, and here's eggplants." Turtle looked thoughtfully at the little flat disks.

"That's just going to discombobble her," Mattie said. "Those seeds don't look anything like what you're saying they'll grow into. When kids are that little, they don't take much on faith."

"Oh," I said. It seemed to me that Turtle had to take practically everything on faith.

"Show her something that looks like what you eat."

I scooped a handful of big white beans out of one of Mattie's jars. "These are beans. Remember white bean soup with ketchup? Mmm, you like that."

"Bean," Turtle said. "Humbean."

I looked at Mattie.

"Well, don't just sit there, the child's talking to you," Mattie said.

I picked up Turtle and gave her a hug. "That's right, that's a bean. And you're just about the smartest kid alive," I told her. Mattie just smiled.

As I planted the beans, Turtle followed me down the row digging each one up after I planted it and putting it back in the jar. "Good girl," I said. I could see a whole new era arriving in Turtle's and my life.

Mattie suggested that I give her some of her own beans to play with, and I did, though Lou Ann's warning about windpipes and golf balls was following me wherever I went these days. "These are for you to keep," I explained to Turtle. "Don't eat them, these are playing-with beans. There's eating beans at home. And the rest of these in here are putting-in-the-ground beans." Honest to God, I believe she understood that. For the next half hour she sat quietly between two squash hills, playing with her own beans. Finally she buried them there on the spot, where they were forgotten by all until quite a while later when a ferocious thicket of beans came plowing up through the squashes.[11]

◀ *What does Mattie's motto seem to be?*

◀ *What does Taylor believe is Mattie's main motive for having Turtle watch them plant her garden?*

◀ *What order does Mattie give Taylor after Turtle says her first word?*

◀ *How does Taylor respond to Turtle's first word?*

◀ *What happens to the beans Taylor gives Turtle to play with?*

---

11. **beans came plowing...the squashes.** Beans, corn, and squash were the three most important food crops of the traditional agricultural society of the Cherokee.

On the way home Turtle pointed out to me every patch of bare dirt beside the sidewalk. "Humbean," she told me.

Lou Ann was going through a phase of cutting her own hair every other day. In a matter of weeks it had gone from shoulder length to what she referred to as "shingled," passing through several stages with figure-skaters' names in between.

"I don't know about shingled," I said, "but you've got to draw the line somewhere or you're going to end up like this guy that comes into Mattie's all the time with a Mohawk. He has 'Born to Die' tattooed onto the bald part of his scalp."

"I might as well just shave it off," said Lou Ann. I don't think she was really listening.

She was possessed of the type of blond, bone-straight hair that was, for a brief period in history, the envy of every teenaged female alive. I remember when the older girls spoke so endlessly of bleaching and ironing techniques you'd think their hair was something to be thrown in a white load of wash. Lou Ann would have been in high school by then, she was a few years older than me, but she probably missed this whole craze. She would have been too concerned with having the wrong kind of this or that. She'd told me that in high school she prayed every night for glamour-girl legs, which meant that you could put dimes between the knees, calves, and ankles and they would stay put; she claimed her calves would have taken a softball. I'm certain Lou Ann never even noticed that for one whole year her hair was utterly perfect.

▶ *What is Taylor sure that Lou Ann never noticed?*

"It looks like it plumb *died,*" she said, tugging on a straight lock over one eyebrow.

I was tempted to remind her that anything subjected so frequently to a pair of scissors wouldn't likely survive, but of course I didn't. I always tried to be positive with her, although I'd learned that even compliments were a kind of insult to Lou Ann, causing her to wrinkle her face and advise me to make an appointment with an eye doctor. She despised her looks, and had more ways of saying so than anyone I'd ever known.

"I ought to be shot for looking like this," she'd tell the mirror in the front hall before going out the door. "I look like I've been drug through hell backwards," she would say on just any ordinary day. "Like death warmed over. Like something the cat puked up."

I wanted the mirror to talk back, to say, "Shush, you do not," but naturally it just mouthed the same words back at her, leaving her so forlorn that I was often tempted to stick little notes on it. I thought of my T-shirt, Turtle's now, from Kentucky Lake. Lou Ann needed a DAMN I'M GOOD mirror.

◀ *What kind of mirror does Taylor think Lou Ann needs?*

On this particular night we had invited Esperanza and Estevan over for dinner. Mattie was going to be on TV, on the six-o'clock news, and Lou Ann had suggested inviting them over to watch it on a television set we didn't have. She was constantly forgetting about the things Angel had taken, generously offering to loan them out and so forth. We'd settled it, however, by also inviting some neighbors Lou Ann knew who had a portable TV. She said she'd been meaning to have them over anyway, that they were very nice. Their names were Edna Poppy and Virgie Mae Valentine Parsons, or so their mailbox said. I hadn't met them, but before I'd moved in she said they had kept Dwayne Ray many a time, including once when Lou Ann had to rush Snowboots to the vet for eating a mothball.

Eventually Lou Ann gave up on berating her hair and set up the ironing board in the kitchen. I was cooking. We had worked things out: I cooked on weekends, and also on any week night that Lou Ann had kept Turtle. It would be a kind of payment. And she would do the vacuuming, because she liked to, and I would wash dishes because I didn't mind them. "And on the seventh day we wash bean turds," I pronounced. Before, it had seemed picayune[12] to get all bent out of shape organizing the household chores. Now I was beginning to see the point.

◀ *How have Taylor and Lou Ann worked out the household chores?*

The rent and utilities we split fifty-fifty. Lou Ann had savings left from Angel's disability insurance settlement—for some reason he hadn't touched this money—and also he sent checks, but only once in a blue moon. I worried about what she would do when the well ran dry, but I'd decided I might just as well let her run her own life.

For the party I was making sweet-and-sour chicken, more or less on a dare, out of one of Lou Ann's magazines. The folks at Burger Derby should see me now, I thought. I had originally planned to make navy-bean soup, in celebration of Turtle's first word, but by the end of the week she had

12. **picayune.** Petty, of little value

words for everyday use

for • lorn (fər lȯrn′) *adj.*, sad or lonely because of isolation or desertion; pathetic; abandoned. *The two dogs had lived together for ten years, and the death of one left the other forlorn.*

be • rate (bi rāt′) *v.*, scold; criticize; curse. *After dinner, I knew my mother would berate my brother for making rude comments in front of our guests.*

said so many new words I couldn't have fit them all in Hungarian goulash.[13] She seemed to have a one-track vocabulary, like Lou Ann's hypochondriac[14] mother-in-law, though fortunately Turtle's ran to vegetables instead of diseases. I could just imagine a conversation between these two: "Sciatica, hives, roseola, meningomalacia,"[15] Mrs. Ruiz would say in her accented English. "Corns, 'tato,[16] bean," Turtle would reply.

"What's so funny?" Lou Ann wanted to know. "I hope I can even fit into this dress. I should have tried it on first, I haven't worn it since before Dwayne Ray." I had noticed that Lou Ann measured many things in life, besides her figure, in terms of Before and After Dwayne Ray.

"You'll fit into it," I said. "Have you weighed yourself lately?"

"No, I don't want to know what I weigh. If the scale even goes up that high."

"I refuse to believe you're overweight, that's all I'm saying. If you say one more word about being fat, I'm going to stick my fingers in my ears and sing 'Blue Bayou' until you're done."

She was quiet for a minute. The hiss of the steam iron and the smell of warm, damp cotton reminded me of Sunday afternoons with Mama.

"What's Mattie going to be on TV about? Do you know?" she asked.

▶ *Why is Mattie going to be on television?*

"I'm not sure. It has something to do with the people that live with her."

"Oh, I'd be petrified to be on TV, I know I would," Lou Ann said. "I'm afraid I would just blurt out, 'Underpants!' or something. When I was a little girl I would get afraid in church, during the invocation[17] or some other time when it got real quiet, and I'd all of a sudden be terrified that I was going to stand up and holler, 'God's pee-pee!'"

I laughed.

"Oh, I know it sounds ridiculous. I mean, I didn't even know if God had one. In the pictures He's always got on all those robes and things. But the fact that I even wondered about it seemed like just the ultimate sin. If I was bad enough to think it, how did I know I wasn't going to stand up and say it?"

---

13. **Hungarian goulash.** Stew of meat, assorted vegetables, and paprika
14. **hypochondriac.** One who suffers from hypochondria, extreme depression of mind or spirits often centered on imaginary physical ailments
15. **Sciatica, hives, roseola, meningomalacia.** Various medical ailments
16. **'tato.** Potato
17. **invocation.** Prayer in which one asks for help

"I know what you mean," I said. "There's this Catholic priest that comes to Mattie's all the time, Father William. He's real handsome, I think he's your type, maybe not. But sometimes I get to thinking, What if I were to strut over and say something like, 'Hey good looking, whatcha got cooking?'"

"Exactly! It's like, did you ever have this feeling when you're standing next to a cliff, say, or by an upstairs window, and you can just picture yourself jumping out? The worst time it happened to me was in high school. On our senior trip we went to the state capitol, which is at Frankfort. Of course, you know that, what am I saying? So, what happened was, you can go way up in the dome and there's only this railing and you look down and the people are like little miniature ants. And I saw myself just hoisting my leg and going over. I just froze up. I thought: if I can think it, I might do it. My boyfriend, which at that time was Eddie Tubbs, it was way before I met Angel, thought it was fear of heights and told everybody on the bus on the way home that I had ackero-phobia, but it was way more complicated than that. I mean, ackero-phobia[18] doesn't have anything to do with being afraid you'll holler out something god-awful in church, does it?"

"No," I said. "I think what you mean is a totally different phobia. Fear that the things you imagine will turn real."

Lou Ann was staring at me, transfixed. "You know, I think you're the first person I've ever told this to that understood what I was talking about."

I shrugged. "I saw a *Star Trek* episode one time that was along those lines. All the women on this whole planet end up naked. I can't remember exactly, but I think Captain Kirk gets turned into a pipe wrench."

The six o'clock news was half over by the time we got the TV plugged in. There had been a mix-up with the women next door, who were waiting for us to come over and get the television. They didn't realize they had been invited for dinner.

Meanwhile, Estevan and Esperanza arrived. Estevan played the gentleman flirt, saying how nice I looked, and didn't he perhaps know my tomboy sister who worked with a used-tire firm? "Exquisite" was what he actually said, and "tom boy" as if it were two words. I batted my eyelashes and

18. **ackero-phobia.** Acrophobia; fear of heights

said yes indeed, that she was the sister who got all the brains of the family.

I suppose I did look comparatively elegant. Lou Ann had parted my hair on the side ("What you need is one of those big blowzy white flowers behind one ear," she said, and "God, would I kill for black hair like yours." "Kill what?" I asked. "A skunk?") and forced me into a dress she had purchased "before Dwayne Ray" in an uptown thrift shop. It was one of those tight black satin Chinese numbers you have to try on with a girlfriend—you hold your breath while she zips you in. I only agreed to wear it because I thought sharing our clothes might shut her up about being a Sherman tank. And because it fit.

But Esperanza was the one who truly looked exquisite. She wore a long, straight dress made of some amazing woven material that brought to mind the double rainbow Turtle and I saw on our first day in Tucson: twice as many colors as you ever knew existed.

"Is this from Guatemala?" I asked.

She nodded. She looked almost happy.

"Sometimes I get homesick for Pittman and it's as ugly as a mud stick fence," I said. "A person would have to just ache for a place where they make things as beautiful as this."

▶ *What does Taylor say Esperanza must feel for Guatemala? Why?*

Poor Lou Ann was on the phone with Mrs. Parsons for the fourth time in ten minutes, and apparently still hadn't gotten it straight because Mrs. Parsons and Edna walked in the front door with the TV just as Lou Ann ran out the back to get it.

One of the women led the way and the other, who appeared to be the older of the two, carried the set by its handle, staggering a little with the weight like a woman with an overloaded purse. I rushed to take it from her and she seemed a little startled when the weight came up out of her hands. "Oh my, I thought it had sprouted wings," she said. She told me she was Edna Poppy.

I liked her looks. She had bobbed, snowy hair and sturdy, wiry arms and was dressed entirely in red, all the way down to her perky patent-leather shoes.

"Pleased to meet you," I said. "I love your outfit. Red's my color."

"Mine too," she said.

Mrs. Parsons had on a churchy-looking dress and a small, flat white hat with a dusty velveteen bow. She didn't seem too friendly, but of course we were all dashing around trying to get set up. I didn't even know what channel we were looking for until Mattie's face loomed up strangely in black and white.

Signatory to the United Nations[19] something-something on human rights,[20] Mattie was saying, and that means we have a legal obligation to take in people whose lives are in danger.

A man with a microphone clipped to his tie asked her, What about legal means? And something about asylum. They were standing against a brick building with short palm trees in front. Mattie said that out of some-odd thousand Guatemalans and Salvadorans who had applied for this, only one-half of one percent of them had been granted it, and those were mainly relatives of dictators, not the people running for their lives.

Then the TV showed both Mattie and the interview man talking without sound, and another man's voice told us that the Immigration and Naturalization Service[21] had returned two illegal aliens,[22] a woman and her son, to their native El Salvador last week, and that Mattie "claimed" they had been taken into custody when they stepped off the plane in San Salvador and later were found dead in a ditch. I didn't like this man's tone. I had no idea how Mattie would know such things, but if she said it was so, it was.

◀ *What does Mattie say we have a legal obligation to do?*

◀ *What does Mattie say about the people who have applied for asylum and the people who have received it?*

◀ *What does "another man's" voice tell viewers about two illegal aliens? What does the man say that Mattie "claimed" about the illegal aliens? What is Taylor's reaction to what the man had to say?*

---

19. **Signatory to the United Nations.** A signatory is a government bound with other governments by a signed convention. The United Nations is an international organization that was created in 1945 to maintain world peace and security and to promote economic, social, and cultural cooperation among nations. Mattie's interrupted comment refers to the United States being a signatory to the United Nations Universal Declaration of Human Rights, which was adopted in 1948 and pledges to promote and protect the human rights of all people around the world.

20. **human rights.** Basic rights that should belong to every person, such as the right to be free from slavery, torture, and groundless imprisonment, the right to move freely within the borders of one's country; the right to seek asylum from persecution; the right to start a family and have it protected by government and society; the right to freedom of thought and religion

21. **Immigration and Naturalization Service.** Now known as the Bureau of Citizenship and Immigration Services, the government agency that manages everything related to the influx of people from other countries into the United States, such as issuing temporary work visas, granting U.S. citizenship, granting political asylum, and detecting people who have entered the United States illegally

22. **illegal aliens.** People who have entered the United States illegally, without permission from the Bureau of Citizenship and Immigration Services

words for everyday use

a • sy • lum (ə sī′ ləm) *n.*, protection from arrest and extradition—surrender to another state or country for trial or prosecution—given especially to political refugees by a nation or embassy. *The family fled their country to escape persecution by the government, and if they are not granted political asylum by the United States, they will be forced to return to the country from which they are running.*

dic • ta • tor (dik′ tā tər) *n.*, ruler who holds all the power and often oppresses his or her people. *People who live in countries that are ruled by a dictator lack many freedoms, including the right to free speech.*

But it was all garbled anyhow. Mrs. Parsons had been talking the whole time about not being able to sit in a certain type of chair or her back would go out, and then Lou Ann flew in the back door and called out, "Damn it, they're not home. Oh."

Mrs. Parsons made a little sniffing sound. "We're here, if you want to know."

"What program did you want to see?" Edna asked. "I hope we haven't spoiled it by coming late?"

"That was it, we just saw it," I said, though it seemed ridiculous. Thirty seconds and it was all over. "She's a friend of ours," I explained.

▶ *What is Mrs. Parsons's comment about what she heard on the television?*

"All I could make out was some kind of trouble with illegal aliens and dope peddlers,"[23] said Mrs. Parsons. "Dear, I need a pillow for the small of my back or I won't be able to get out of bed tomorrow. Your cat has just made dirt in the other room."

I went for a cushion and Lou Ann rushed to put the cat out. Estevan and Esperanza, I realized, had been sitting together on the ottoman the whole time, more or less on the fringe of all the commotion. I said, "I'd like you to meet my friends . . ."

▶ *By what names does Estevan introduce Esperanza and himself?*

"Steven," Estevan said, "and this is my wife, Hope." This was a new one on me.

"Pleased to make your acquaintance," Edna said.

▶ *What does Mrs. Parsons say about Turtle?*

Mrs. Parsons said, "And is this naked creature one of theirs? She looks like a little wild Indian." She was talking about Turtle, who was not naked, although she didn't exactly have a shirt on.

▶ *How does Esperanza look when Estevan says they have no children?*

"We have no children," Estevan said. Esperanza looked as though she had been slapped across the face.

"She's mine," I said. "And she *is* a little wild Indian, as a matter of fact. Why don't we start dinner?" I picked up Turtle and stalked off into the kitchen, leaving Lou Ann to fend for herself. Why she would call this old pruneface a nice lady was beyond my mental powers. I did the last-minute cooking, which the recipe said you were supposed to do "at the table in a sizzling wok[24] before the admiring guests." A sizzling wok, my hind foot. Who did they think read those magazines?

23. **dope peddlers.** Drug sellers
24. **wok.** Bowl-shaped Chinese cooking pot used for stir-frying

words for everyday use

gar • ble (gär′ bəl) *v.*, distort; jumble; run together; confuse. *Turning the volume up really high on my stereo will only garble the sound of the music.*

A minute later Esperanza came into the kitchen and quietly helped set the table. I touched her arm. "I'm sorry," I said.

It wasn't until everyone came in and sat down to dinner that I really had a chance to look these women over. The fact that they couldn't possibly have had time to dress up for dinner made their outfits seem to tell everything. (Though of course Mrs. Parsons would have had time to powder her nose and reach for the little white hat.) Edna even had red bobby pins in her hair, two over each ear. I couldn't imagine where you would buy such items, a drugstore I suppose. I liked thinking about Edna finding them there on the rack, along with the purple barrettes and Oreo-cookie hair clips, and saying, "Why, look, Virgie Mae, red bobby pins! That's my color." Virgie Mae would be the type to sail past the douche aisle with her nose in the air and lecture the boy at the register for selling condoms.

Estevan produced a package, which turned out to be chopsticks. There were twenty or so of them wrapped together in crackly cellophane with black Chinese letters down one side. "A gift for the dishwasher," he said, handing each of us a pair of sticks. "You use them once, then throw them away." I couldn't think how he knew we were going to have Chinese food, but then I remembered running into him a day or two ago in the Lee Sing Market, where we'd discussed a product called "wood ears."[25] The recipe called for them, but I had my principles.

"The dishwasher thanks you," I said. I noticed Lou Ann whisking a pair out of Dwayne Ray's reach, and could hear the words "put his eyes out" as plainly as if she'd said them aloud. Dwayne Ray started squalling, and Lou Ann excused herself to go put him to bed.

"What is it, eating sticks?" Edna ran her fingers along the thin shafts. "It sounds like a great adventure, but I'll just stick to what I know, if you don't mind. Thank you all the same." I noticed that Edna ate very slowly, with gradual, exact movements of her fork. Mrs. Parsons said she wasn't game for such foolishness either.

"I never said it was foolishness," Edna said.

The rest of us gave it a try, spearing pieces of chicken and looping green-pepper rings and chasing the rice around our plates. Even Esperanza tried. Estevan said we were being too aggressive.

---

25. **wood ears.** Type of mushroom

"They are held this way." He demonstrated, holding them like pencils in one hand and clicking the ends together. I loved his way of saying, "It is" and "They are."

Turtle was watching me, imitating. "Don't look at me, I'm not the expert." I pointed at Estevan.

Lou Ann came back to the table. "Where'd you learn how to do that?" she asked Estevan.

▶ *Where does Estevan work? What does he do?*

"Ah," he said, "this is why I like chopsticks: I work in a Chinese restaurant. I am the dishwasher."

"I didn't know that. How long have you worked there?" I asked, realizing that I had no business thinking I knew everything about Estevan. His whole life, really, was a mystery to me.

"One month," he said. "I work with a very kind family who speak only Chinese. Only the five-year-old daughter speaks English. The father has her explain to me what I must do. Fortunately, she is very patient."

Mrs. Parsons muttered that she thought this was a disgrace. "Before you know it the whole world will be here jibbering and jabbering till we won't know it's America."

"Virgie, mind your manners," Edna said.

▶ *What does Mrs. Parsons think about people from other countries coming to live in the United States?*

"Well, it's the truth. They ought to stay put in their own dirt, not come here taking up jobs."

"Virgie," Edna said.

▶ *What does Taylor want to scream at Mrs. Parsons?*

I felt like I'd sat on a bee. If Mama hadn't brought me up to do better, I think I would have told that old snake to put down her fork and get her backside out the door. I wanted to scream at her: This man you are looking at is an English teacher. He did not come here so he could wash egg foo yung[26] off plates and take orders from a five-year-old.

▶ *What does Taylor realize is the reason that Estevan doesn't seem bothered by Mrs. Parsons's comments?*

But Estevan didn't seem perturbed, and I realized he must hear this kind of thing every day of his life. I wondered how he could stay so calm. I would have murdered somebody by now, I thought, would have put a chopstick to one of the many deadly uses that only Lou Ann could imagine for it.

"Can I get anybody anything?" Lou Ann asked.

"We're fine," Edna said, obviously accustomed to being Virgie Mae's public-relations department.[27] "You children have made a delightful meal."

Esperanza pointed at Turtle. It was the first time I ever saw her smile, and I was struck with what a lovely woman

26. **egg foo yung.** Chinese dish of egg pancakes with a rich brown sauce
27. **public-relations department.** Department responsible for handling communications between a public figure, business, or institution and the general public

she was when you really connected. Then the smile left her again.

Turtle, wielding a chopstick in each hand, had managed to pick up a chunk of pineapple. Little by little she moved it upward toward her wide-open mouth, but the sticks were longer than her arms. The pineapple hung in the air over her head and then fell behind her onto the floor. We laughed and cheered her on, but Turtle was so startled she cried. I picked her up and held her on my lap.

"Tortolita,[28] let me tell you a story," Estevan said. "This is a South American, wild *Indian* story about heaven and hell." Mrs. Parsons made a prudish face, and Estevan went on. "If you go to visit hell, you will see a room like this kitchen. There is a pot of delicious stew on the table, with the most delicate aroma you can imagine. All around, people sit, like us. Only they are dying of starvation. They are jibbering and jabbering," he looked extra hard at Mrs. Parsons, "but they cannot get a bite of this wonderful stew God has made for them. Now, why is that?"

"Because they're choking? For all eternity?" Lou Ann asked. Hell, for Lou Ann, would naturally be a place filled with sharp objects and small round foods.

"No," he said. "Good guess, but no. They are starving because they only have spoons with very long handles. As long as that." He pointed to the mop, which I had forgotten to put away. "With these ridiculous, terrible spoons, the people in hell can reach into the pot but they cannot put the food in their mouths. Oh, how hungry they are! Oh, how they swear and curse each other!" he said, looking again at Virgie. He was enjoying this.

◀ *Why are the people in hell starving?*

"Now," he went on, "you can go and visit heaven. What? You see a room just like the first one, the same table, the same pot of stew, the same spoons as long as a sponge mop. But these people are all happy and fat."

"Real fat, or do you mean just well-fed?" Lou Ann asked.

"Just well-fed," he said. "Perfectly, magnificently well-fed, and very happy. Why do you think?"

He pinched up a chunk of pineapple in his chopsticks, neat as you please, and reached all the way across the table to offer it to Turtle. She took it like a newborn bird.

28. **Tortolita.** Spanish for "Turtle"

Respond to the Selection

Consider the relationships that Taylor has formed since leaving Pittman. In what ways, if any, do these relationships provide a sense of family for the people involved in them?

Investigate, Inquire, and Imagine

Recall: GATHERING FACTS

1a. What does Lou Ann ask her mother about her father? When Angel comes home after Lou Ann's mother and grandmother have left, what does he say and do? To what does Lou Ann compare his presence? In what way does Lou Ann find his presence in the house different from that of her mother and grandmother?

Interpret: FINDING MEANING

→ 1b. Why do you think Lou Ann is envious about her mother and father's marriage? How do you think Angel makes Lou Ann feel? What might Lou Ann want in her life that Angel doesn't seem to provide?

2a. What questions do Fei and her housemates ask Taylor? What are some of the topics that Lou Ann and Taylor discuss? What are some of the things that they have in common?

→ 2b. How does Taylor's experience meeting Fei and her housemates differ from her experience meeting Lou Ann?

3a. What is Lou Ann's theory about friendship? What is Lou Ann's theory about marriage? What is Taylor's flapper ball theory?

→ 3b. What do Lou Ann's theories about friendship and marriage reveal about her? What does Taylor's flapper ball theory reveal about her?

4a. Summarize the South American story that Estevan tells during dinner.

→ 4b. Why do the people in hell starve when the people in heaven are well fed and happy? Why do you think Estevan tells the story?

Analyze: TAKING THINGS APART

5a. In what ways has Taylor changed since she left Pittman?

Synthesize: BRINGING THINGS TOGETHER

→ 5b. How do you think Taylor will continue to change? Explain.

Evaluate: MAKING JUDGMENTS

6a. How does Taylor's attitude toward caring for Turtle change in chapters 4–7? How well do you think Taylor will take care of Turtle? Explain, using examples from the story to support your answers.

Extend: CONNECTING IDEAS

→ 6b. In Estevan's story about heaven and hell, people who help each other are well fed, while those who do not starve. How does the relationship between Taylor and Lou Ann show the same idea? What other relationships in the novel demonstrate the same idea?

Understanding Literature

CHARACTERIZATION. **Characterization** is the use of literary techniques to create characters. Writers use multiple techniques to bring their characters to life: direct description; portraying what characters do, say, or think; and showing what other characters say or think about them. Consider the characters of Taylor, Mama, Lou Ann, and Ivy. What characterization techniques does the author use to reveal the relationship between Taylor and Mama? What characterization techniques does the author use to reveal the relationship between Lou Ann and Ivy? Provide examples from the story.

DIALECT AND DIALOGUE. A **dialect** is a version of language spoken by the people of a particular place, time, or social group. **Dialogue** is conversation involving two or more people or characters. Kingsolver uses both dialect and dialogue to develop her major and minor characters. How does the author's use of dialect help develop the character of Taylor? How does it develop the character of Granny Logan? Examine the author's use of dialect and dialogue in the scene in Chapter 5, in which Taylor meets Fei and her housemates. How does dialect affect the conversation between Taylor and Fei, La-Isha, and Timothy? How does dialect affect the first meeting between Taylor and Lou Ann?

SYMBOL. A **symbol** is a thing that stands for or represents both itself and something else. For example, a red rose is a symbol of love, and a white dove is a symbol of peace. In Chapter 3, how do the bean vines appear to Taylor? What do the bean plants seem to symbolize? As Chapter 6 opens, what has happened to Mattie's bean plants? How does the author create a clear connection between the bean plants and Turtle in Chapter 7? Why do you think the author creates this connection? What might be the significance of the bean plants being killed by a frost and then replanted by Mattie and Taylor?

Eight

The Miracle Of Dog Doo Park

▶ *What is Mama doing? What does Taylor think about it?*

Of all the ridiculous things, Mama was getting married. To Harland Elleston no less, of El-Jay's Paint and Body fame. She called on a Saturday morning while I'd run over to Mattie's, so Lou Ann took the message. I was practically the last to know.

When I called back Mama didn't sound normal. She was out of breath and kept running on about Harland. "Did I get you in out of the yard?" I asked her. "Are you planting cosmos?"

"Cosmos, no, it's not even the end of April yet, is it? I've got sugar peas in that little bed around to the side, but not cosmos."

"I forgot," I told her. "Everything's backwards here. Half the stuff you plant in the fall."

"Missy, I'm in a tither,"[1] she said. She called me Taylor in letters, but we weren't accustomed to phone calls. "With Harland and all. He treats me real good, but it's happened so fast I don't know what end of the hog to feed.[2] I wish you were here to keep me straightened out."

"I do too," I said.

"You plant things in the fall? And they don't get bit?"

"No."

At least she did remember to ask about Turtle. "She's great," I said. "She's talking a blue streak."[3]

▶ *In what way does Mama say Turtle is the way Taylor used to be? What does Taylor think of Mama's comment?*

"That's how you were. You took your time getting started, but once you did there was no stopping you," Mama said.

I wondered what that had to do with anything. Everybody behaved as if Turtle was my own flesh and blood daughter. It was a conspiracy.

Lou Ann wanted to know every little detail about the wedding, which was a whole lot more than I knew myself, or cared to.

"Everybody deserves their own piece of the pie, Taylor," Lou Ann insisted. "Who else has she got?"

"She's got me."

---

1. **in a tither.** frazzled, confused, overly excited, anxious
2. **I don't know what end of the hog to feed.** Implies being frazzled or confused and not sure of what to do
3. **talking a blue streak.** Talking excessively
4. **Red Taiwan.** Inplies communist Taiwan, but Lou Ann's metaphor is scrambled. Taiwan, an island off the coast of China has long opposed the communist government of the mainland.

"She does not, you're here. Which might as well be Red Taiwan,[4] for all the good it does her."

"I always thought I'd get Mama out here to live. She didn't even consult me, just ups and decides to marry this paint-and-body yahoo."[5]

"I do believe you're jealous."

"That is so funny I forgot to laugh."

"When my brother got married I felt like he'd deserted us. He just sends this letter one day with a little tiny picture, all you could make out really was dogs, and tells us he's marrying somebody by the name of She-Wolf Who Hunts by the First Light." Lou Ann yawned and moved farther down the bench so her arms were more in the sun. She'd decided she was too pale and needed a tan.

"Granny Logan liked to died. She kept saying, did Eskimos count as human beings? She thought they were half animal or something. And really what are you supposed to think, with a name like that? But I got used to the idea. I like to think of him up there in Alaska with all these little daughters in big old furry coats. I've got in my mind that they live in an igloo, but that can't be right."

◀ *What did Granny Logan keep asking about Eskimos? What did Granny Logan think about Eskimos?*

We were sitting out with the kids in Roosevelt Park, which the neighbor kids called such names as Dead Grass Park and Dog Doo Park. To be honest, it was pretty awful. There were only a couple of shade trees, which had whole dead parts, and one good-for-nothing palm tree so skinny and tall that it threw its shade onto the roof of the cooler-pad factory down the block. The grass was scraggly, struggling to come up between shiny bald patches of dirt. Mostly it put me in mind of an animal with the mange.[6] Constellations of gum-wrapper foil twinkled around the trash barrels.

◀ *What is the name of the park Lou Ann and Taylor are visiting? What do the neighborhood kids call the park? Why? Of what does the park remind Taylor?*

"Look at it this way, at least she's still kicking,"[7] Lou Ann said. "I feel like my mama's whole life stopped counting when Daddy died. You want to know something? They even got this double gravestone. Daddy's on the right hand side, and the other side's already engraved for Mama. 'Ivy Louise Logan, December 2, 1934—to blank.' Every time I see it it gives me the willies. Like it's just waiting there for her to finish up her business and die so they can fill in the blank."

"It does seem like one foot in the grave,"[8] I said.

"If Mama ever got married again I'd dance a jig at her wedding. I'd be thrilled sideways. Maybe it would get her off

5. **yahoo.** Crude and stupid person; bumpkin, an unrefined person
6. **mange.** Contagious skin disease marked by inflammation and loss of hair
7. **still kicking.** Still alive
8. **one foot in the grave.** Near death

my back about moving back in with her and Granny." Dwayne Ray coughed in his sleep, and Lou Ann pushed his stroller back and forth two or three times. Turtle was pounding the dirt with a plastic shovel, a present from Mattie.

"Cabbage, cabbage, cabbage," she said.

Lou Ann said, "I know a guy that would just love her. Did you ever know that fellow downtown that sold vegetables out of his truck?" But Turtle and Bobby Bingo would never get to discuss their common interest. He had disappeared, probably to run off with somebody's mother.

"Your mother wouldn't be marrying Harland Elleston," I told Lou Ann, getting back to the subject at hand.

"Of course not! That big hunk is already spoken for."

"Lou Ann, you're just making a joke of this whole thing."

"Well, I can't help it, I wouldn't care if my mother married the garbage man."

"But Harland Elleston! He's not even . . ." I was going to say he's not even related to us, but of course that wasn't what I meant. "He's got warts on his elbows and those eyebrows that meet in the middle."

▶ *How does Lou Ann say Taylor talks about men?*

▶ *Who does Taylor like?*

I'll swan,[9] Taylor, you talk about men like they're a hangnail. To hear you tell it, you'd think man was only put on this earth to keep urinals from going to waste."

"That's not true, I like Estevan." My heart sort of bumped when I said this. I knew exactly how it would look on an EKG[10] machine: two little peaks and one big one.

"He's taken. Who else?"

"Just because I don't go chasing after every Tom's Harry Dick that comes down the pike."

"Who else? You never have one kind thing to say about any of your old boyfriends."

"Lou Ann, for goodness' sakes. In Pittman County there was nothing in pants that was worth the trouble, take my word for it. Except for this one science teacher, and the main thing he had going for him was clean fingernails." I'd never completely realized how limited the choices were in Pittman. Poor Mama. If only I could have gotten her to Tucson.

"Well, where in the heck do you think I grew up, Paris, France?"

"I notice you didn't stick with home-grown either. You had to ride off with a Wild West rodeo boy."

9. **I'll swan.** I swear

10. **EKG.** Electrocardiograph, an instrument used for diagnosing abnormalities of heart action

"Fat lot of good it did me, too."

"Well, you did get Dwayne Ray out of the deal." I remembered what Mama always said about me and the Jackson Purchase.

What good thing does Taylor say came out of Lou Ann's relationship with Angel? Why does Taylor say this?

"But oh, Taylor, if you could have seen him. How handsome he was." She had her eyes closed and her face turned up toward the sun. "The first time I laid eyes on him he was draped on this fence like the Marlboro man, with his arms out to the sides and one boot up on the bottom rung. Just chewing on a match and hanging out till it was time to turn out the next bull. And do you know what else?" She sat up and opened her eyes.

"What?" I said.

"Right at that exact moment there was this guy in the ring setting some kind of a new world's record for staying on a bull, and everybody was screaming and throwing stuff and of course me and my girlfriend Rachel had never seen a rodeo before so we thought this was the wildest thing since Elvis joined the army. But Angel didn't even look up. He just squinted off at the distance toward the hay field behind the snack bar. Rachel said, 'Look at that tough guy over by that fence, what an asshole, not even paying attention.' And you know what I thought to myself? I thought, I bet I could get him to pay attention to me."

A child in a Michael Jackson tank shirt rumbled down the gravel path on a low-slung trike with big plastic wheels, making twice as much noise as his size would seem to allow for. "This is a O-R-V," he told us. Now I knew.

"I know you." He pointed at Lou Ann. "You're the one gives out money at Halloween."

Lou Ann rolled her eyes. "I'm never going to live that down. This year they'll be coming in from Phoenix and Flagstaff to beat down our door."

"Watch out when the bums come," he told us. "Go straight home." He tore off again, pedaling like someone possessed.

The gravel path cut through the middle of the park from a penis-type monument, up at the street near Mattie's, down to the other end where we liked to sit in a place Lou Ann called the arbor. It was the nicest thing about the park. The benches sat in a half-circle underneath an old wooden trellis that threw a shade like a cross-stitched tablecloth. The trellis had thick, muscly vines twisting up its support poles and fanning out overhead. Where they first came out of the ground, they reminded me of the arms of this guy who'd delivered Mattie's new refrigerator

What had Taylor thought about the vines growing up the trellis in the winter? What had Lou Ann told her?

▶ *What is the miracle of Dog Doo Park?*

▶ *What does Lou Ann say Taylor's mama will do if she's anything like Taylor?*

▶ *What does Turtle sing?*

by himself. All winter Lou Ann had been telling me they were wisteria[11] vines. They looked dead to me, like everything else in the park, but she always said, "Just you wait."

And she was right. Toward the end of March they had sprouted a fine, shivery coat of pale leaves and now they were getting ready to bloom. Here and there a purplish lip of petal stuck out like a pout from a fat green bud. Every so often a bee would hang humming in the air for a few seconds, checking on how the flowers were coming along. You just couldn't imagine where all this life was coming from. It reminded me of that Bible story where somebody or other struck a rock and the water poured out.[12] Only this was better, flowers out of bare dirt. The Miracle of Dog Doo Park.

Lou Ann went on endlessly about Mama. "I can just see your mama. . . . What's her name, anyway?"

"Alice," I said. "Alice Jean Stamper Greer. The last thing she needs is an Elleston on top of all that."

". . . I can just see Alice and Harland running for the sugar shack. If she's anything like you, she goes after what she wants. I guess now she'll be getting all the paint and body jobs she needs."

"He's only half owner, with Ernest Jakes," I said. "It's not like the whole shop belongs to him."

"Alice and Harland sittin' in a tree," she sang, "K-I-S-S-I-N-G!"

I plugged my ears and sang, "I'm going back someday! Come what may! To Blue Bayou!" Turtle whacked the dirt and sang a recipe for succotash.[13]

I spotted Mrs. Parsons and Edna Poppy coming down the gravel path with their arms linked. From a great distance you could have taken them for some wacked-out geriatric[14] couple marching down the aisle in someone's sick idea of a garden wedding. We waved our arms at them, and Turtle looked up and waved at us.

"No, we're waving at them," I said, and pointed. She turned and folded and unfolded her hand in the right direction.

Now and again these days, not just in emergencies, we were leaving the kids with Edna and Virgie Mae on their

---

11. **wisteria.** Woody, flowering vine that is a member of the legume, or bean, family

12. **Bible story...water poured out.** Biblical reference to the Book of Exodus in the Old Testament, which tells of Moses leading the Jews out of slavery in Egypt. At one point during their journey through the desert, Moses strikes a rock, and it gives forth water for all to drink.

13. **succotash.** Beans and green corn cooked together

14. **geriatric.** Old, elderly

front porch to be looked after. Edna was so sweet we just hoped she would cancel out Virgie's sour, like the honey and vinegar in my famous Chinese recipe. It was awfully convenient, anyway, and Turtle seemed to like them okay. She called them Poppy and Parsnip. She knew the names of more vegetables than many a greengrocer, I'd bet. Her favorite book was a Burpee's catalogue from Mattie's, which was now required reading every night before she would go to bed. The plot got old, in my opinion, but she was crazy about all the characters.

◀ What does Taylor say about Edna? What effect does she hope Edna will have on Virgie Mae Parsons?

◀ What is Turtle's favorite "book"?

"Ma Poppy," Turtle said when they were a little closer. She called every woman Ma something. Lou Ann was Ma Wooahn, which Lou Ann said sounded like something you'd eat with chopsticks, and I was just Ma. We never told her these names, she just came to them on her own.

◀ What does Turtle call every woman? What does she call Taylor?

The two women were still moving toward us at an unbelievably slow pace. I thought of a game we used to play in school at the end of recess: See who can get there last. Edna had on a red knit top, red plaid Bermuda shorts, and red ladies' sneakers with rope soles. Virgie had on a tutti-frutti hat and a black dress printed all over with what looked like pills. I wondered if there was an actual place where you could buy dresses like that, or if after hanging in your closet for fifty years, regular ones would somehow just transform.

"Good afternoon, Lou Ann, Taylor, children," Mrs. Parsons said, nodding to each one of us. She was so formal it made you want to say something obscene.[15] I thought of Lou Ann's <u>compulsions</u> in church.

"Howdy do," Lou Ann said, and waved at a bench. "Have a sit." But Mrs. Parsons said no thank you, that they were just out for their constitutional.[16]

"I see you're wearing my favorite color today, Edna," I said. This was a joke. I'd never seen her in anything else. When she said red was her color, she meant it in a way most people don't.

"Oh, yes, always." She laughed. "Do you know, I started to dress in red when I was sixteen. I decided that if I was to be a Poppy, then a Poppy I would be."

◀ What did Edna start to do when she was sixteen? Why?

15. **obscene.** Offensive, indecent, vulgar
16. **constitutional.** Walk taken for one's health

words for everyday use

com • pul • sion (kəm pəl′ shən) *n.,* irresistible impulse to perform an irrational act; urge; drive. *As Gheta stood in front of the class to present her oral report, she was suddenly overtaken by the <u>compulsion</u> to sing and dance.*

▶ *Who does Mrs. Parsons say was looking for Lou Ann?*

Edna said the most surprising things. She didn't exactly look at you when she spoke, but instead stared above you as though there might be something wonderful hanging just over your head.

"Well, we've heard all about that before, haven't we?" said Mrs. Parsons, clamping Edna's elbow in a knucklebone vice-grip. "We'll be going along. If I stand still too long my knees are inclined to give out." They started to move away, but then Mrs. Parsons stopped, made a little nod, and turned around. "Lou Ann, someone was looking for you this morning. Your husband, or whatever he may be."

"You mean Angel?" She jumped so hard she bumped the stroller and woke up Dwayne Ray, who started howling.

"I wouldn't know," Virgie said, in such a way that she might as well have said, "How many husbands do you have?"

"When, this morning while I was at the laundromat?"

"I have no idea where *you* were, my dear, only that *he* was *here*."

"What did he say?"

"He said he would come back later."

Lou Ann bounced the baby until he stopped crying. "Shit," she said, quite a few minutes later when they'd moved out of earshot. "What do you think that means?"

"Maybe he wanted to deliver a check in person. Maybe he wants to go on a second honeymoon."

"Sure," she said, looking off at the far side of the park. She was still jiggling Dwayne Ray, possibly hadn't noticed he'd stopped crying.

"Why do you think she puts up with that coot?"[17] I asked.

"What coot, old Vicious Virgie you mean? Oh, she's harmless." Lou Ann settled the baby back into his stroller. "She reminds me of Granny Logan. She's that type. One time Granny introduced me to some cousins by marriage of hers, I was wearing this brand-new midi-skirt I'd just made? And she says, 'This is my granddaughter Lou Ann. She isn't bowlegged, it's just her skirt makes her look that way.'"

"Oh, Lou Ann, you poor thing."

She frowned and brushed at some freckles on her shoulder, as though they might suddenly have decided to come loose. "I read a thing in the paper this morning about the sun giving you skin cancer," she said. "What does it look like in the early stages, do you know?"

17. **coot.** Eccentric or crotchety person

"No. But I don't think you get it from sitting out one afternoon."

She pushed the stroller back and forth in an absent-minded way, digging a matched set of ruts into the dust. "Come to think of it, though, I guess that's a little different from the way Mrs. Parsons is. Somehow it's more excusable to be mean to your own relatives."

She rubbed her neck and turned her face to the sun again. Lou Ann's face was small and rounded in a pretty way, like an egg sunny side up.[18] But in my mind's eye I could plainly see her dashing out the door on any given day, stopping to say to the mirror: "Ugly as homemade sin in the heat of summer." No doubt she could see Granny Logan in there too, staring over her shoulder.

After a while I said, "Lou Ann, I have to know something for Turtle's and my sake, so tell me the honest truth. If Angel wanted to come back, I mean move back in and have everything the way it was before, would you say yes?"

◀ *What does Taylor need to know for her sake and for Turtle's sake? How does Lou Ann answer her?*

She looked at me, surprised. "Well, what else could I do? He's my husband, isn't he?"

There may have been a world of things I didn't understand, but I knew when rudeness passed between one human being and another. The things Mrs. Parsons had said about aliens were wrong and unkind, and I still felt bad even though weeks had passed. Eventually I apologized to Estevan. "She's got a mean streak in her," I told him. "If you're unlucky enough to get ahold of a dog like that, you give it away to somebody with a big farm. I don't know what you do about a neighbor."

◀ *What does Taylor know about the comments Mrs. Parsons made about the illegal aliens from El Salvador? What does Taylor tell Estevan about Mrs. Parsons?*

Estevan shrugged. "I understand," he said.

"Really, I don't think she knew what she was saying, about how the woman and kid who got shot must have been drug dealers or whatever."

"Oh, I believe she did. This is how Americans think." He was looking at me in a thoughtful way. "You believe that if something terrible happens to someone, they must have deserved it."

◀ *How does Estevan say Americans think?*

I wanted to tell him this wasn't so, but I couldn't. "I guess you're right," I said. "I guess it makes us feel safe."

◀ *Why does Taylor say Americans think that way?*

Estevan left Mattie's every day around four o'clock to go to work. Often he would come down a little early and we'd

18. **egg sunny side up.** Lightly fried egg in which the yolk is cooked on top, and remains bright yellow and unbroken

chat while he waited for his bus. "Attending my autobus" was the way he put it.

"Can I tell you something?" I said. "I think you talk so beautifully. Ever since I met you I've been reading the dictionary at night and trying to work words like constellation and scenario[19] into the conversation."

He laughed. Everything about him, even his teeth, were so perfect they could have come from a book about the human body. "I have always thought you had a wonderful way with words," he said. "You don't need to go fishing for big words in the dictionary. You are poetic, mi'ija."

"What's miha?"

"Mi hija," he pronounced it slowly.

"My something?"

▶ *What does mi'ija mean in English? What does it mean in Spanish?*

"My daughter. But it doesn't work the same in English. We say it to friends. You would call me mi'ijo."

"Well, thank you for the compliment," I said, "but that's the biggest bunch of hogwash,[20] what you said. When did I ever say anything poetic?"

▶ *What does Estevan say is poetic?*

"Washing hogs is poetic," he said. His eyes actually twinkled.

His bus pulled up and he stepped quickly off the curb, catching the doorway and swinging himself in as it pulled away. That is just how he would catch a bus in Guatemala City, I thought. To go teach his classes. But he carried no books, no graded exams, and the sleeves of his pressed white shirt were neatly rolled up for a night of dishwashing.

▶ *After whom is Roosevelt Park named?*

I felt depressed that evening. Mattie, who seemed to know no end of interesting things, told me about the history of Roosevelt Park. I had just assumed it was named after one of the Presidents, but it was for Eleanor. Once when she had been traveling across the country in her own train she had stopped here and given a speech right from a platform on top of her box car. I suppose it would have been a special type of box car, decorated, and not full of cattle and bums and such. Mattie said the people sat out in folding chairs in the park and listened to her speak about those less fortunate than ourselves.

Mattie didn't hear Eleanor Roosevelt's speech, naturally, but she had lived here a very long time. Thirty years ago, she said, the homes around this park belonged to some of the most fortunate people in town. But now the houses all seemed a little senile,[21] with arthritic hinges and window

19. **scenario.** Sequence of events, especially when imagined
20. **hogwash.** Nonsense
21. **senile.** Exhibiting old age

screens hanging at embarrassing angles. Most had been subdivided[22] or otherwise transformed in ways that favored function over beauty. Many were duplexes.[23] Lee Sing's was a home, grocery, and laundromat. Mattie's, of course, was a tire store and sanctuary.

◀ What is Taylor slowly coming to understand?

Slowly I was coming to understand exactly what this meant. For one thing, people came and went quietly. And stayed quietly. Around to the side of Mattie's place, above the mural Lou Ann and I called Jesus Around the World, there was an upstairs window that looked out over the park. I saw faces there, sometimes Esperanza's and sometimes others, staring across the empty space.

◀ How do people come, go, and stay at Mattie's?

Mattie would occasionally be gone for days at a time, leaving me in charge of the shop. "How can you just up and go? What if I get a tractor tire in here?" I would ask her, but she would just laugh and say, "No chance." She said that tire dealers were like veterinarians. There's country vets, that patch up horses and birth calves, and there's the city vets that clip the toenails off poodles. She said she was a city vet.

And off she would go. Mattie had numerous cars that ran, but for these trips she always took the four-wheel Blazer and her binoculars, and would come back with the fenders splattered with mud. "Going birdwatching" is what she always told me.

◀ What things does Mattie always take on her "birdwatching trips"? What does Taylor always notice about Mattie's truck when she returns?

After she returned, a red-haired man named Terry sometimes came by on his bicycle and would spend an hour or more upstairs at Mattie's. He didn't look any older than I was, but Mattie told me he was already a doctor. He carried his doctor bag in a special rig on the back of his bike.

"He's a good man," she said. "He looks after the ones that get here sick and hurt."

◀ What does Mattie tell Taylor about the red-haired man named Terry?

"What do you mean, that get here hurt?" I asked.

"Hurt," she said. "A lot of them get here with burns, for instance."

I was confused. "I don't get why they would have burns," I persisted.

She looked at me for so long that I felt edgy. "Cigarette burns," she said. "On their backs."

The sun was setting, and most of the west-facing windows on the block reflected a fierce orange light as if the houses were on fire inside, but I could see plainly into Mattie's upstairs. A woman stood at the window. Her hair was threaded with white and fell loose around her shoulders, and she was folding a pair of men's trousers. She

22. **subdivided.** Divided into building lots
23. **duplexes.** Two-family houses

moved the flats of her hands slowly down each crease, as if folding these trousers were the only task ahead of her in life, and everything depended on getting it right.

▶ *Why has Angel come back?*

True to his word, Angel came back. He didn't come to move in, but to tell Lou Ann he was going away for good. I had taken Turtle for a doctor's appointment so I didn't witness the scene; all I can say is that the man had a genuine knack for dropping bombshells at home while someone was sitting in Dr. Pelinowsky's waiting room. But of course, I had no real connection to Angel's life. It was just a coincidence.

▶ *Why does Taylor decide to take Turtle to the doctor?*

Turtle was healthy as corn, but as time went by I got to thinking she should have been taken to a doctor, in light of what had been done to her. (Lou Ann's main question was: Shouldn't you tell the police? Call 88-CRIME or something? But of course it was all in the past now.) I had thought of asking Terry, the red-haired doctor on the bicycle, but couldn't quite get up the gumption. Finally I called for an appointment with the famous Dr. P., on Lou Ann's recommendation, even though he wasn't exactly the right kind of doctor. His nurse agreed that he could see my child this once.

▶ *Why can't Taylor fill out Turtle's medical form?*

We found the doctor's office all right, but checking her in was another story. They gave me a form to fill out which contained every possible question about Turtle I couldn't answer. "Have you had measles?"[24] I asked her. "Scabies?[25] Date of most recent polio vaccination?"[26] The one medical thing I did know about her past was not on the form, unless they had a word for it I didn't know.

Turtle was in my lap but had turned loose of me completely, since she needed both arms to turn through the pages of her magazine in search of vegetables. She wasn't having much luck. Every other woman in that waiting room was pregnant, and every magazine was full of nursing-bra ads.

I knew how to trample my way through most any situation, but you can't simply invent a person's medical history. I went up and tapped on the glass to get the

24. **measles.** Contagious disease
25. **scabies.** Contagious skin disease caused by parasitic mites
26. **polio vaccination.** Vaccine given to help resist the polio virus

words for everyday use

tram • ple (tram′ pəl) *v.*, to tread heavily so as to bruise, crush, or injure; trudge; bully. *I have always been considerate of Ben's feelings, but, lately, I feel like he has done nothing but trample our friendship.*

nurse's attention. I saw that she was actually pregnant too, and I felt an old panic. In high school we used to make jokes about the water fountains outside of certain home rooms.

"Yes?" she said. Her name tag said Jill. She had white skin and broad pink stripes of rouge in front of her ears.

"I can't answer these questions," I said.

"Are you the parent or guardian?"

"I'm the one responsible for her."

"Then we need the medical history before we can fill out an encounter form."

"But I don't know that much about her past," I said.

"Then you are not the parent or guardian?"

This was getting to be a trip around the fish pond.[27] "Look," I said. "I'm not her real mother, but I'm taking care of her now. She's not with her original family anymore."

"Oh, you're a foster home."[28] Jill was calm again, shuffling through a new stack of papers. She blinked slowly in a knowing way that revealed pink and lavender rainbows of makeup on her eyelids. She handed me a new form with far fewer questions on it. "Did you bring in your DES medical and waiver forms?"[29]

◀ *What conclusion does the nurse make about Taylor's relationship to Turtle?*

"No," I said.

"Well, remember to bring them next time."

By the time we got in to see Dr. Pelinowsky I felt as though I'd won this man in one of those magazine contests where you answer fifty different questions about American cheese. He was fiftyish and a little tired-looking. His shoulders slumped, leaving empty space inside the starched shoulders of his white coat. He wore black wingtip shoes, I noticed, and nylon socks with tiny sea horses above the ankle bones.

Turtle became clingy again when I pulled off her T-shirt. She squeezed wads of my shirt tail in both fists while Dr. Pelinowsky thumped on her knees and shined his light into her eyes. "Anybody home?" he asked. The only time

27. **trip around the fish pond.** Circular discussion that never gets to the point
28. **foster home.** Household that takes in and cares for orphaned or neglected children
29. **DES medical and waiver forms.** Forms from the Arizona Department of Economic Security that show Turtle is a foster child and that the state will pay for her medical care

words for everyday use

guard • i • an (gär' dē ən) *n.,* one responsible for caring for the person or property of another. *My sister and her husband have asked my husband and me to be the legal guardian of their daughter should anything happen to them before she is eighteen.*

she perked up at all was when he looked in her ears and said, "Any potatoes in there?" Her mouth made a little O, but then she spaced out again.

"I didn't really think she'd turn out to be sick, or anything like that. She's basically in good shape," I said.

"I wouldn't expect to turn up anything clinically. She appears to be a healthy two-year-old." He looked at his clip board.

"The reason I brought her in is I'm concerned about some stuff that happened to her awhile ago. She wasn't taken care of very well." Dr. Pelinowsky looked at me, clicking his ballpoint pen.

"I'm a foster parent," I said, and then he raised his eyebrows and nodded. It was a miracle, this new word that satisfied everyone.

"You're saying that she was subjected to deprivation or abuse[30] in the biological parents' home," he said. His main technique seemed to be telling you what you'd just said.

▶ *What does Taylor tell the doctor she thinks happened to Turtle?*

"Yes. I think she was abused, and that she was," I didn't know how to put this. "That she was molested.[31] In a sexual way."

Dr. Pelinowsky took in this information without appearing to notice. He was scribbling something on the so-called encounter form. I waited until he finished, thinking that I was going to have to say it again, but he said, "I'll give her a complete exam, but again I wouldn't expect to turn up anything now. This child has been in your care for five months?"

"More or less," I said. "Yes."

While he examined her he explained about abrasions[32] and contusions[33] and the healing process. I thought of how I'd handled Jolene Shanks exactly this way, as calm as breakfast toast, while her dead husband lay ten feet away under a sheet. "After this amount of time we might see behavioral evidence," Dr. P. said, "but there is no residual physical damage." He finished scribbling on the form and decided it would be a good idea to do a skeletal survey,[34]

---

30. **abuse.** To mistreat, harm, damage, take advantage of
31. **molested.** Had inappropriate physical and sexual contact forced on her
32. **abrasions.** Scrapes
33. **contusions.** Bruises
34. **skeletal survey.** X-rays

words for everyday use

re • sid • u • al (ri zi' jə wəl) *adj.*, remaining; leftover. *Although we both apologized after our argument, there is still some residual awkwardness between us.*

and that sometime soon we ought to get her immunizations[35] up to date.

I was curious to see the x-ray room, which was down a hall in another part of the office. Everything was large and clean, and they had a machine that turned out the x-rays instantly like a Polaroid camera. I don't believe Dr. Pelinowsky really understood how lucky he was. I used to spend entire afternoons in a little darkroom developing those things, sopping the stiff plastic sheets through one and another basin of liquid, then hanging them up on a line with tiny green clothespins. I used to tell Mama it was nothing more than glorified laundry.

We had to wait awhile to see him again, while he saw another patient and then read Turtle's x-rays. I hung around asking the technician questions and showing Turtle where the x-rays came out, though machines weren't really her line. She had one of her old wrestling holds on my shoulder.

When we were called back to Dr. Pelinowsky's office again he looked just ever so slightly shaken up. "What is it?" I asked him. All I could think of was brain tumors, I suppose from hanging around Lou Ann, who had learned all she knew about medicine from *General Hospital.*

He laid some of the x-rays against the window. Dr. Pelinowsky's office window looked out onto a garden full of round stones and cactus. In the dark negatives I could see Turtle's thin white bones and her skull, and it gave me the same chill Lou Ann must have felt to see her living mother's name carved on a gravestone. I shivered inside my skin.

"These are healed fractures, some of them compound,"[36] he said, pointing with his silver pen. He moved carefully through the arm and leg bones and then to the hands, which he said were an excellent index of age. On the basis of height and weight he'd assumed she was around twenty-four months, he said, but the development of cartilage[37] in the carpals[38] and metacarpals[39] indicated that she was closer to three.

◀ *What does the doctor point out to Taylor as they are looking at Turtle's X-rays?*

"Three years?"

35. **immunizations.** Vaccinations
36. **fractures, some of them compound.** Broken bones that result in bone fragments protruding through the skin
37. **cartilage.** Translucent and elastic tissue that composes most of the skeletal system during the early years of growth and development and eventually converts to bone
38. **carpals.** Wrist bones
39. **metacarpals.** Bones of the hands or feet

▶ *What does the doctor say sometimes happens to children who are raised in environments of physical or emotional deprivation? What is the condition called?*

"Yes." He seemed almost undecided about telling me this. "Sometimes in an environment of physical or emotional deprivation a child will simply stop growing, although certain internal maturation does continue. It's a condition we call failure to thrive."

"But she's thriving now. I ought to know, I buy her clothes."

"Well, yes, of course. The condition is completely reversible."

"Of course," I said.

▶ *While the doctor continues to review the X-rays, to what does Taylor turn her attention? What does she see? What can't she imagine?*

He put up more of the x-rays in the window, saying things like "spiral fibular fracture[40] here" and "excellent healing" and "some contraindications[41] for psychomotor[42] development." I couldn't really listen. I looked through the bones to the garden on the other side. There was a cactus with bushy arms and a coat of yellow spines as thick as fur. A bird had built her nest in it. In and out she flew among the horrible spiny branches, never once hesitating. You just couldn't imagine how she'd made a home in there.

Mattie had given me the whole day off, so I had arranged to meet Lou Ann at the zoo after Turtle's appointment. We took the bus. Mattie and I hadn't gotten around to fixing the ignition on my car, so starting it up was a production I saved for special occasions.

On the way over I tried to erase the words "failure to thrive" from my mind. I prepared myself, instead, for the experience of being with Lou Ann and the kids in a brand-new set of hazards. There would be stories of elephants going berserk[43] and trampling their keepers; of children's little hands snapped off and swallowed whole by who knows what seemingly innocent animal. When I walked up to the gate and saw her standing there with tears streaming down her face, I automatically checked Dwayne Ray in his stroller to see if any of his parts were missing.

---

40. **spiral fibular fracture.** Break in one of the bones between the knee and the ankle
41. **contraindications.** Something that makes a particular treatment not advisable
42. **psychomotor.** Relating to muscular movement directly proceeding from mental activity
43. **berserk.** Insane, violent

words for everyday use

dep • ri • va • tion (dep rə vā′ shən) *n.*, withholding; removal; loss; need. *Research shows that people with many friends live longer and that social deprivation is not healthy.*

thrive (thrīv′) *v.*, grow vigorously; flourish. *After the much-needed rain, all the plants in the garden began to thrive.*

People were having to detour around her to get through the turnstile, so I led her to one side. She sobbed and talked at the same time.

"He says he's going to join up with any rodeo that will take a one-legged clown,[44] which I know isn't right because the clown's the hardest job, they jump around and distract them so they won't tromple on the cowboys' heads."

What has Angel told Lou Ann that has made her cry?

I was confused. Was there an elephant somewhere in this story? "Lou Ann, honey, you're not making sense. Do you want to go home?"

She shook her head.

"Then should we go on into the zoo?"

She nodded. I managed to get everybody through the turnstile[45] and settled on a bench in the shade between the duck pond and the giant tortoises. The sound of water trickling over a little waterfall into the duck pond made it seem cool. I tried to get the kids distracted long enough for Lou Ann to tell me what was up.

"Look, Turtle, look at those old big turtles," I said. The words "childhood identity crisis" from one of Lou Ann's magazines sprang to mind, but Turtle seemed far more interested in the nibbled fruit halves strewn around their pen. "Apple," she said. She seemed recovered from her doctor's visit.

"He said something about the Colorado-Montana circuit,[46] which I don't even know what that means, only that he's leaving town. And he said he might not be sending any checks for a while until he'd got on his feet. He actually said on his foot, can you believe that? The way Angel sees himself, it's like he's an artificial leg with a person attached."

Where does Angel say he is going? What does he tell her he won't be sending for a while? How does Lou Ann say Angel sees himself?

A woman on a nearby bench stopped reading and tilted her head back a little, the way people do when they want to overhear your conversation. She had on white sneakers, white shorts, and a visor. It looked as if she must have been on her way to a country club to play tennis before some wrongful bus change landed her here.

"It's her husband that's the problem," I told the woman. "He's a former rodeo man."

---

44. **clown.** The rodeo clown is responsible for distracting the bull away from the rider and helping the rider safely exit the rodeo ring in the event that the rider falls off the bull.

45. **turnstile.** Post with pivoting arms on the top through which people pass one by one as in the entryway to an amusement park or a stadium

46. **Colorado-Montana circuit.** One of the regional circuits in amateur or professional rodeo

"Taylor!" Lou Ann whispered, but the woman ignored us and took a drag from her cigarette, which she balanced beside her on the front edge of the bench. She shook out her newspaper and folded back the front page. It showed a large color picture of Liz Taylor with a black man in a silver vest and no shirt, and there was a huge block headline that said, WORLD'S YOUNGEST MOM-TO-BE: INFANT PREGNANT AT BIRTH. Apparently the headline wasn't related to the picture.

A kid with orange foam-rubber plugs in his ears whizzed by on a skateboard. Another one whizzed right behind him. They had a fancy way of tipping up their boards to go over the curbs.

"They shouldn't allow those in here. Somebody will get killed," Lou Ann said, blowing her nose. I noticed that one of the giant tortoises in the pen was pursuing another one around and around a clump of shrubby palm trees.

"So what about Angel?" I asked.

A woman in a flowery dress sat down on the bench with the country-club woman. She had very dark, tightly wrinkled skin and wore enormous green high-heeled pumps. The country-club woman's cigarette, on the bench between them, waved up a little boundary line of smoke.

"He said there would be papers to sign for the divorce," Lou Ann said.

"So what's the problem, exactly?" I didn't mean to be unkind. I really didn't know.

"Well, what am I going to do?"

"Well, to be honest, I don't think it much matters what you do. It probably doesn't make any difference what kind of a divorce you get, or even if you get one at all. The man is gone, honey. If he stops sending checks I don't imagine there's anything to be done, not if he's out riding the range in God's country. I guess you'll have to look for a job, sooner or later."

► *What does Taylor tell Lou Ann she's going to have to do? How does Lou Ann respond?*

Lou Ann started sobbing again. "Who would want to hire me? I can't do anything."

"You don't necessarily have to know how to do something to get a job," I reasoned. "I'd never made a french fry in my life before I got hired at the Burger Derby." She blew her nose again.

"So how'd she get born pregnant?" the green-shoes woman asked the woman with the newspaper.

"It was twins, a boy and a girl," the woman told her. "They had sexual intercourse in the womb. Doctors say the chances against it are a million to one."

"Yeah," the green-shoes woman said in a tired way. She bent over and shuffled through a large paper shopping bag, which was printed with a bright paisley pattern and had sturdy-looking green handles. All three of us waited for her to say something more, or to produce some wonderful answer out of her bag, but she didn't.

Lou Ann said to me, in a quieter voice, "You know, the worst thing about it is that he wouldn't ask me to come with him."

"Well, how in the world could you go with him? What about Dwayne Ray?"

"It's not that I'd *want* to, but he could have asked. He did say if I wanted to come along he wouldn't stop me, but he wouldn't actually say he wanted me to."

"I don't follow you, exactly."

"You know, that was always just the trouble with Angel. I never really felt like he would put up a fight for me. I would have left him a long time ago, but I was scared to death he'd just say, 'Bye! Don't let the door hit your butt on the way out.'"

◀ What does Lou Ann say was always the trouble with Angel? Why didn't she leave him a long time ago?

"Well, maybe it's not that he doesn't want you, Lou Ann. Maybe he's just got better sense than to ask you and a four-month-old baby to come along on the Montana-Colorado circuit, or whatever. I can just see it. Dwayne Ray growing up to be one of those tattooed midgets that do somersaults in the sideshow and sell the popcorn at intermission."

"It's not a circus, for God's sake, it's a rodeo." Lou Ann honked in her handkerchief and laughed in spite of herself.

At the edge of the pond there was a gumball machine full of peanuts, for feeding to the ducks, I presumed. But these ducks were so well fed that even where peanuts were scattered by the fistful at the water's edge they just paddled right on by with beady, bored eyes.

Turtle dug one out of the mud and brought it to me. "Bean," she said.

"This is a peanut," I told her.

"Beanut." She made trip after trip, collecting peanuts and mounding them into a pile. Dwayne Ray, in his stroller, was sleeping soundly through his first zoo adventure.

I couldn't stop thinking about the x-rays, and how Turtle's body was carrying around secret scars that would always be there. I wanted to talk to Lou Ann about it, but this wasn't the time.

◀ What can't Taylor stop thinking about?

"So why are you taking his side?" Lou Ann wanted to know.

"I'm not taking his side. Whose side?"

"You are too. Or at least you're not taking mine. Whenever I complain about Angel you won't agree with me that he's a scum bucket. You just listen and don't say anything."

I picked up a green bottle cap and threw it in the duck pond. The ducks didn't even turn their heads. "Lou Ann," I said, "in high school I used to lose friends that way like crazy. You think he's a scum bucket now, but sooner or later you might want him back. And then you'd be too embarrassed to look me in the eye and admit you're still in love with this jerk whose anatomical parts we've been laughing about for the last two months."

"It's over between me and Angel. I know it is."

"Just the same. I don't want you to have to choose him or me."

She dug through her purse looking for a clean handkerchief. "I just can't get over him leaving like that."

"When, now or last October?" I was starting to get annoyed. "He moved out over six months ago, Lou Ann. Did you think he'd just stepped out for some fresh air? It's April now, for God's sake."

▶ What does Lou Ann notice when Taylor says the word "April"?

"Did you see that?" Lou Ann pointed at Turtle. Her head had bobbed up like an apple on a string, and her eyes fixed on me as if she had seen the Lord incarnate.[47]

"What's up, Turtle?" I asked, but she just stared fearfully from her pile of peanuts.

"She did that one other time that I know of. When we were talking about the phone bill you thought we'd got gypped[48] on," Lou Ann said.

"So what are you saying, that she understands when we're mad? I already knew that."

"No, I'm saying that bill was for April. She looks up when you say April, especially if you sound mad."

Turtle did look up again.

"Don't you get it?" Lou Ann asked.

I didn't.

▶ What does Lou Ann say is Turtle's name?

"That's her name! April's her name!" Now Lou Ann was kind of hopping in her seat. "April, April. Looky here, April. That's your name, isn't it? April!"

If it was her name, Turtle had had enough of it. She had gone back to patting the sides of her peanut mound.

"You have to do it scientifically," I said. "Say a bunch of other words and just casually throw that one in, and see if she looks up."

47. **incarnate.** Invested with bodily form

48. **gypped.** Cheated

"Okay, you do it. I can't think of enough words."

"Rhubarb,"[49] I said. "Cucumber. Porky Pig. Budweiser. April." Turtle looked up right on cue.

"May June July August September!" Lou Ann shouted. "April!"

"Lord, Lou Ann, the child isn't deaf."

"It's April," she declared. "That's her legal name."

"Maybe it's something that just sounds like April. Maybe it's Mabel."

Lou Ann made a face.

"Okay, April, that's not bad. I think she's kind of used to Turtle though. I think we ought to keep calling her that now."

A fat duck with a shiny green head had finally decided Turtle's cache of peanuts was too much to ignore. He came up on shore and slowly advanced, stretching his neck forward.

"Ooooh, oooh!" Turtle shouted, shaking her hands so vigorously that he wheeled around and waddled back toward the water.

"Turtle's okay for a nickname," Lou Ann said, "but you have to think of the future. What about when she goes to school? Or like when she's eighty years old? Can you picture an eighty-year-old woman being called Turtle?"

◀ What does Lou Ann say about the name "Turtle"? What does Taylor say Lou Ann needs to remember?

"An eighty-year-old Indian woman, I could. You have to remember she's Indian."

"Still," Lou Ann said.

"April Turtle, then."

"No! That sounds like some weird kind of air freshener."

"So be it," I said, and it was.

We sat for a while listening to the zoo sounds. There were more trees here than most places in Tucson. I'd forgotten how trees full of bird sounds made you sense the world differently: that life didn't just stop at eye level. Between the croaks and whistles of the blackbirds there were distant cat roars, monkey noises, kid noises.

◀ What had Taylor forgotten?

"I'll swan, the sound of that running water's making me have to go," Lou Ann said.

"There's bathrooms over by where we came in."

Lou Ann took a mirror out of her purse. "Death warmed over," she said, and went off to find a bathroom.

The giant tortoise, I noticed, had caught up to its partner and was proceeding to climb on top of it from behind. Its neck and head strained forward as it climbed, and to tell

49. **rhubarb.** Plant whose leaves are poisonous but whose stems are used for making pies and jams

the truth, it looked exactly like a bald, toothless old man. The knobby shells scraping together made a hollow sound. By the time Lou Ann came back from the bathroom, the old fellow on top was letting out loud grunts that rang out all the way down to the military macaws.[50]

"What on earth? I could hear that noise up by the bathrooms," Lou Ann declared. "Well, I'll be. I always did wonder how they'd do it in those shells. That'd be worse than those panty girdles we used to wear in high school to hold our stockings up. Remember those?"

A teenage couple holding hands bounced up to investigate, giggled, and moved quickly away. A woman with an infant on her hip turned the baby's head away and walked on. Lou Ann and I laughed till we cried. The country-club woman gave us a look, folded her paper, stabbed out her cigarette, and crunched off down the gravel path.

---

50. **macaws.** Type of South or Central American parrot

Nine

Ismene

Esperanza tried to kill herself. Estevan came to the back door and told me in a quiet voice that she had taken a bottle of baby aspirin.

◀ *What did Esperanza do?*

I couldn't really understand why he had come. "Shouldn't you be with her?" I asked.

He said she was with Mattie. Mattie had found her almost immediately and rushed her to a clinic she knew of in South Tucson where you didn't have to show papers.[1] I hadn't even thought of this—all the extra complications that must have filled their lives even in times of urgency. Mattie once told me about a migrant lemon picker in Phoenix who lost a thumb in a machine and bled to death because the nearest hospital turned him away.

◀ *Where did Mattie take her? What did Mattie once tell Taylor about a migrant lemon picker in Phoenix?*

"Is she going to be all right?"

How could he know? But he said yes, that she was. "They might or might not have to vacuum her stomach," he explained. He seemed to know the whole story, including the ending, and I began to suspect it was something that had happened before.

◀ *What does Estevan seem to know? What does Taylor begin to suspect?*

It was after sunset and the moon was already up. A fig grew by the back door, an old, stubborn tree that was slow to leaf out. The moon threw shadows of fig branches that curled like empty hands across Estevan's face and his chest. Something inside this man was turning inside out.

◀ *What curls across Estevan's face and chest? What does Taylor see happening to Estevan?*

He followed me into the kitchen where I had been cutting up carrots and cubes of cheese for Turtle's lunch tomorrow.

To keep my hands from shaking I pushed the knife carefully through stiff orange carrot flesh against the cutting board. "I don't really know what to say when something like this happens," I told him. "Anything I can think of to talk about seems ridiculous next to a person's life or death."

He nodded.

"Can I get you something? Did you eat?" I opened the refrigerator door, but he waved it shut. "At least a beer, then," I said. I opened two beers and set one on the table in front of him. From my earliest memory, times of crisis seemed to end up with women in the kitchen preparing food for men. "I can see right now that I'm going to do one of two things here," I told Estevan. "Either shove food at

1. **show papers.** Show identification or insurance papers

▶ *When Taylor tells Estevan she will do one of two things, what does he tell her to do?*

▶ *What does Taylor ask Estevan if he knew? How does he answer?*

you, or run off at the mouth. When I get nervous I fall back on good solid female traditions."

"It's okay," he said. "I'm not hungry, so talk." I had never heard him say, "It's okay," before. Restaurant work was corrupting Estevan's perfect English.

I took his statement to mean that it was okay to talk about things that weren't especially important, so I did. "Lou Ann took the baby over to her mother-in-law's for some kind of a weekend-long reunion," I said, swallowing too much beer. "They still consider her part of the family, but of course she won't go over when Angel's there so they have to work it all out, but now of course it's easier since Angel's left town. It's totally nuts. See, they're Catholic, they don't recognize divorce." I felt my face go red. "I guess you're Catholic too."

But he wasn't offended. "More or less," he said. "Catholic by birth."

"Did you have any idea she was going to do this?"

"No. I don't know."

"There's not a thing you could have done, anyway. Really." I swept the carrot pieces into a plastic bag and put it in the refrigerator. "I knew this kid in high school, Scotty Richey? Everybody said Scotty was a genius, mainly because he was real quiet and wore these thick glasses and understood trigonometry.[2] He killed himself on his sixteenth birthday, just when everybody else was thinking, 'Well, now Scotty'll learn to drive and maybe get a car and go out on dates,' you know, and that his complexion was bound to clear up and so forth. Bang, they find him dead in a barn with all these electrical wires strung around his neck. In the paper they said it was an accident but nobody actually believed that. Scotty had done probably five hundred different projects with electricity for 4-H."

"Four-H?"

"It's a club for farm kids where you raise lambs or make an apron or wire a den lamp out of a bowling pin, things like that. I never was in it. You had to pay."

"I see."

"Do you want to sit in the living room?" I asked him. He followed me into the other room and I scooted Snowboots off the sofa. When Estevan sat down next to me my heart was bumping so hard I wondered if I was going to have a heart attack. Just what Estevan needed would be another woman falling apart on him.

2. **trigonometry.** Study of the mathematical properties of triangles

"So nobody could understand about Scotty," I said. "But the way I see it is, he just didn't have anybody. In our school there were different groups you would run with, depending on your station in life. There were the town kids, whose daddies owned the hardware store or what have you—they were your cheerleaders and your football players. Then there were hoodlums, the motorcycle types that cut down trees on Halloween. And then there were the rest of us, the poor kids and the farm kids. Greasers, we were called, or Nutters. The main rule was that there was absolutely no mixing. Do you understand what I mean?"

◀ *Why does Taylor think Scotty killed himself?*

◀ *What was the group that Taylor was part of in high school called? What was the main rule that the different groups followed?*

"Yes," he said. "In India they have something called the caste system.[3] Members of different castes cannot marry or even eat together. The lowest caste is called the Untouchables."

◀ *To what does Estevan compare the groups in Taylor's high school? What can't members of different castes do? What is the lowest caste called?*

"But the Untouchables can touch each other?"

"Yes."

"Then that's it, exactly. The Nutters were the bottom of the pile, but we had each other. We all got invited to the prom and everything, from inside our own group. But poor Scotty with his electricity and his trigonometry, he just didn't belong to any group. It was like we were all the animals on Noah's ark that came in pairs, except of his kind there was only the one."

◀ *According to Taylor, how do the Untouchables and the Nutters differ from Scotty?*

It struck me how foolishly I was chattering about something that was neither here nor there. Mama would call this "rattling your teeth." I drank about half my beer without saying another word.

Then I said, "I could kind of see it with Scotty, but Esperanza had somebody. Has somebody. How could she want to leave you? It's not fair." I realized I was furious with Esperanza. I wondered if he was too, but didn't dare ask. We sat there in the shadowy living room thinking our thoughts. You could hear us swallowing beer.

◀ *What does Taylor realize she feels toward Esperanza? What does she wonder but not dare to ask Estevan?*

Then out of the clear blue sky he said, "In Guatemala City the police use electricity for interrogation. They have something called the 'telephone,' which is an actual tele-

◀ *What does Estevan say the police in Guatemala use electricity for?*

3. **caste system.** System of rigid social division based on hereditary social classes that restrict the occupation of their members and their association with members of other castes

words for everyday use

in • ter • ro • ga • tion (in ter′ ə gā′ shən) *n.,* act of formal and systematic questioning; examination; investigation; inquisition. *Breaking our curfew by more than an hour without calling resulted in an hour-long interrogation by our parents.*

phone of the type they use in the field. It has its own generator,[4] operated by a handle." He held up one hand and turned the other one in a circle in front of the palm.

"A crank? Like the old-fashioned telephones?"

"Operated with a crank," he said. "The telephones are made in the United States."

"What do you mean, they use them for interrogation? Do you mean they question you over the telephone?"

▶ *When Taylor asks Estevan how the telephone is used for interrogation, how does Estevan answer her?*

Estevan seemed annoyed with me. "They disconnect the receiver wire and tape the two ends to your body. To sensitive parts." He just stared at me until it hit me like a truck. I felt it in my stomach muscles, just the way I did when I realized that for nearly an hour I had been in the presence of Newt Hardbine's corpse. There is this horrible thing staring you in the face and you're blabbering about bowling-pin lamps and 4-H.

"I'll get us another beer," I said. I went to the kitchen and brought back the rest of the six pack, carrying it by the plastic rings like a purse. I popped two of them open and plumped back down on the sofa, no longer caring what I looked like. The schoolgirl nerves that had possessed me half an hour ago seemed ridiculous now; this was like having a crush on some guy only to find out he's been dating your mother or your math teacher. This man was way beyond me.

▶ *What does Taylor keep finding out? What does Estevan say would be easier?*

▶ *What does Taylor say Estevan thinks, and why does she tell him that it is not true?*

"I don't know exactly how to say this," I said. "I thought I'd had a pretty hard life. But I keep finding out that life can be hard in ways I never knew about."

"I can see that it would be easier not to know," he said.

"That's not fair, you don't see at all. You think you're the foreigner here, and I'm the American, and I just look the other way while the President or somebody sends down this and that, shiploads of telephones to torture people with. But nobody asked my permission, okay? Sometimes I feel like I'm a foreigner too. I come from a place that's so different from here you would think you'd stepped right off the map into some other country where they use dirt for decoration and the national pastime is having babies. People don't look the same, talk the same, nothing. Half the time I have no idea what's going on around me here."

A little shadow moved in the doorway and we both jumped. It was Turtle.

"You're a rascal," I said. "You hop back to bed this minute."

She took one hop backwards, and both Estevan and I tried not to smile. "This minute," I said, in the meanest

4. **generator.** Machine that changes mechanical energy into electrical energy

voice I could muster. She hopped backwards through the door, clapping her hands one time with each hop. We could hear her hopping and clapping all the way back through the kitchen and into bed. Snowboots jumped onto the back of the sofa and sat behind my neck, waiting for something. He made me nervous.

"All I am saying is, don't be so sure until you have all the facts," Estevan said. "You cannot know what Esperanza has had to live through."

What does Estevan say Taylor cannot know?

I was confused. He was picking up the middle of a conversation I didn't even know we'd started.

"No," I said. "I don't. Or you either."

He looked away from me and touched the corners of his eyes, and I knew he was crying in the secret way men feel they have to do. He said something I couldn't hear very well, and a name, "Ismene."

I shoved Snowboots gently away from the back of my neck. "What?" I asked.

"Do you remember the day we walked in the desert? And you asked why Esperanza was staring at Turtle, and I told you she looked very much like a child we knew in Guatemala." I nodded. "The child was Ismene."

I was afraid to understand this. I asked him if he meant that Ismene was their daughter, and Estevan said yes, that she was. She was taken in a raid[5] on their neighborhood in which Esperanza's brother and two friends were killed. They were members of Estevan's teachers' union.[6] He told me in what condition they had found the bodies. He wasn't crying as he told me this, and I wasn't either. It's hard to explain, but a certain kind of horror is beyond tears. Tears would be like worrying about watermarks on the furniture when the house is burning down.

Who is Ismene? What happened to her? What happened to Esperanza's brother and Esperanza and Estevan's two friends during the raid?

Ismene wasn't killed; she was taken.

Try as I would, I couldn't understand this. I was no longer so stupid as to ask why they didn't call the police, but still I couldn't see why they hadn't at least tried to get her back if they knew the police had taken her, and where. "Don't be upset with me," I said. "I know I'm ignorant, I'm sorry. Just explain it to me."

But he wasn't upset. He seemed to get steadier and more patient when he explained things, as if he were teaching a class. "Esperanza and I knew the names of twenty other

5. **raid.** Surprise attack by a small force, a hostile or predatory entrance into a territory, an invasion

6. **teachers' union.** During this time in Guatemala, members of teachers' unions risked their lives to help those being persecuted by the government.

union members," he said. "The teachers' union did not have open meetings. We worked in cells,[7] and communicated by message. Most people knew only four other members by name. This is what I am saying: In Guatemala, you are careful. If you want to change something you can find yourself dead. This was not the—what do you call? The P.T.A."[8]

"I understand."

"Three members had just been killed, including Esperanza's brother, but seventeen were still alive. She and I knew everyone of those seventeen, by name. Can you understand that this made us more useful alive than dead? For us to go after Ismene is what they wanted."

▶ Why does Estevan say he and Esperanza were more useful alive than dead?

"So they didn't kill her, they just held her? Like . . . I don't know what. A worm on a goddamn hook?"

"A god damn hook." He was looking away from me again. "Sometimes, after a while, usually . . . these children are adopted. By military or government couples who cannot have children."

▶ What did Estevan and Esperanza assume would happen to Ismene? Why did Estevan and Esperanza choose not to try to get Ismene back?

I felt numb, as if I had taken some drug. "And you picked the lives of those seventeen people over getting your daughter back?" I said. "Or at least a chance at getting her back?"

"What would you do, Taylor?"

"I don't know. I hate to say it, but I really don't know. I can't even begin to think about a world where people have to make choices like that."

"You live in that world," he said quietly, and I knew this, but I didn't want to. I started to cry then, just tears streaming out all over and no stopping them. Estevan put his arm around me and I sobbed against his shoulder. The dam had really broken.

▶ What does Taylor say she can't even begin to think about? How does Estevan respond?

I was embarrassed. "I'm going to get snot on your clean shirt," I said.

"I don't know what it is, snot."

"Good," I said.

There was no way on earth I could explain what I felt, that my whole life had been running along on dumb luck and I hadn't even noticed.

▶ How does Taylor suddenly feel about her whole life?

"For me, even bad luck brings good things," I told him finally. "I threw out a rocker arm on my car and I got Turtle. I drove over broken glass on an off ramp and found Mattie." I crossed my arms tightly over my stomach, trying to stop myself from gulping air. "Do you know, I spent the first half of my life avoiding motherhood and tires, and now I'm counting them as blessings?"

7. **cells.** Smallest organizational units of a centralized group or movement
8. **P.T.A.** Parent-Teacher Association

Turtle showed up in the doorway again. I don't know how long she had been there, but she was looking at me with eyes I hadn't seen on her since that night on the Oklahoma plain.

"Come here, pumpkin," I said. "I'm okay, just sprung a leak, don't you worry. Do you want a drink of water?" She shook her head. "Just want to cuddle a few minutes?" She nodded, and I took her on my lap. Snowboots jumped onto the sofa again. I could feel the weight of him moving slowly across the back and down the other arm, and from there he curled into Estevan's lap. In less than a minute Turtle was asleep in my arms.

When I was a child I had a set of paper dolls. They were called the Family of Dolls, and each one had a name written on the cardboard base under the feet. Their names were Mom, Dad, Sis, and Junior. I played with those dolls in a desperate, loving way until their paper arms and heads disintegrated. I loved them in spite of the fact that their tight-knit little circle was as far beyond my reach as the football players' and cheerleaders' circle would be in later years.

But that night I looked at the four of us there on the sofa and my heart hurt and I thought: in a different world we could have been the Family of Dolls.

Turtle wiggled. "No," she said, before she was even awake.

"Yes," I said. "Time for bed." I carried her in and tucked her under the sheet, prying her hand off my T-shirt and attaching it to her yellow stuffed bear, which had a pink velvet heart sewed onto its chest.

"Sleep tight, don't let the potato bugs bite."

"Tato bite," she said.

When I came back Snowboots had moved from Estevan's lap and curled into the little depression where I had been. I sat in the space between them with my feet tucked under me. I no longer felt self-conscious, though I could feel almost a pull, like a flow of warm water, at the point where our knees touched.

"It seems like, if you get to know them well enough, everybody has had something awful happen to them. All

words for everyday use

dis • in • te • grate (di sin′ tə grāt) *v.*, break down or decompose; fall apart; decay. *Packing peanuts are now made out of starch so they simply disintegrate when you put water on them.*

this time I've been moping around because of having the responsibility of Turtle forced on me, and now I feel guilty."

"That responsibility is terrible if you don't want it."

"Oh, big deal. The exact same thing happened to about sixty percent of the girls in my high school, if not the whole world."

"If you look at it that way," he said. He was falling asleep.

"I guess that's just the way the world has got to go around. If people really gave it full consideration, I mean, like if you could return a baby after thirty days' examination like one of those Time-Life books, then I figure the entire human species would go extinct in a month's time."

"Some people wouldn't send them back," he said. "I would have kept Ismene." His eyes were closed.

"Did you get up in the middle of the night to do the feeding and diapering?"

"No," he said, smiling a little.

"I can't believe I'm even asking you that. Does it hurt you a lot to talk about Ismene?"

▶ *What helps Estevan most in thinking about Ismene? What does Taylor realize is the other side to knowing that Ismene is growing up?*

"At first, but not so much now. What helps me the most is to know her life is going on somewhere, with someone. To know she is growing up."

"Sure," I said, but I knew there was another side to this, too. Where she was growing up, what they would raise her to be. I thought of Turtle being raised by Virgie Mae Parsons, learning to look down her nose and wear little hats, and then I got it mixed up with police uniforms. A little later I realized I had been asleep. We both rolled in and out of sleep in a friendly way. You can't be nervous if you're sleeping on the same sofa with somebody, I thought. Letting your mouth fall open any old way.

Snowboots jumped off the sofa. I heard his claws scratch the carpet as he covered up his sins.

"Why did they call you Nutters?" I remembered Estevan asking at some point. I thought and thought about it, trying to fight my way out of some dream where Turtle and I were trying to get to the other side of a long, flat field. We had to follow the telephone wires to get to civilization.

"Nutters," I said finally. "Oh, because of walnuts. In the fall, the kids that lived in the country would pick walnuts to earn money for school clothes."

"Did you have to climb the trees?" Estevan amazed me. That he would be interested in details like that.

"No. Basically you waited till they fell, and then picked them up off the ground. The worst part was that to get the hulls off you'd have to put them in the road for cars to run over, and then you'd pick the nuts out of the mess. It stained your hands black, and then you were marked. That was the worst part, to go to school with black hands and black fingernails. That was proof positive you were a Nutter."

"But otherwise you would have no new clothes."

"Right. So you were damned if you didn't and damned if you did. I guess the ideal thing," I conjectured, half dreaming, "would have been to get clothes with good, deep pockets." I meant so that you could hide your hands, but I had a picture in my mind of skirts and trousers with pockets full of pounds and pounds of walnuts. Ten cents a pound is what we got for them. A hundred and fifty pounds equaled one pair of Levi's.

Later I woke up again, feeling the pressure of Snowboots's feet walking down my leg, then hearing them thump on the floor. Estevan and I were curled like spoons on the sofa, his knees against the backs of my knees and his left hand on my ribs, just under my breast. When I put my hand on top of his I could feel my heart beating under his fingers.

I thought of Esperanza, her braids on her shoulders. Esperanza staring at the ceiling. She would be lying on a cot somewhere, sweating the poison out of her system. Probably they had given her syrup of ipecac,[9] which makes you keep throwing up until you can feel the sides of your stomach banging together. All of Esperanza's hurts flamed up in my mind, a huge pile of burning things that the world just kept throwing more onto. Somewhere in that pile was a child that looked just like Turtle. I lifted Estevan's hand from my ribcage and kissed his palm. It felt warm. Then I slid off the sofa and went to my own bed.

◀ *How does Taylor picture Esperanza's hurts? Who is in the middle of them?*

Moonlight was pouring in through the bedroom window like a watery version of my mother's potato soup. Moon soup, I thought, hugging myself under the covers. Somewhere in the neighborhood a cat yowled like a baby, and somewhere else, closer by, a rooster crowed, even though it was nowhere near daybreak.

9. **syrup of ipecac.** Drug made from the dried roots of two tropical American plants and used for treatment of accidental poisoning

words for everyday use

con • jec • ture (kən jek' chər) *v.*, guess; imagine; suspect. *I can't even begin to conjecture about the theme they'll come up with for the party.*

Ten

The Bean Trees

Even a spotted pig looks black at night. This is another thing Mama used to tell me quite often. It means that things always look different, and usually better, in the morning.

▶ What does Mattie call first thing in the morning to say?

And they did. Mattie called first thing to say that Esperanza was going to be all right. They hadn't pumped her stomach after all because she hadn't taken enough to do much harm. I made Estevan a big breakfast, eggs scrambled with tomatoes and peppers and green chile sauce, and sent him home before I could start falling in love with him again over the breakfast dishes. Turtle woke up in one of those sweet, eye-rubbing moods that kids must know by instinct as a means of saving the human species from extinction. Lou Ann came home from the Ruiz family reunion singing "La Bamba."

▶ What observation does Taylor make about the bird world?

▶ Why doesn't Taylor argue with Lou Ann about the noise the pigeony bird makes?

It's surprising, considering Roosevelt Park, but we always heard birds in the morning. There must be transients in the bird world too, rumple-feathered outcasts that naturally seek out each other's company in inferior and dying trees. In any case, there were lots of them. There was a type of woodpecker that said, "Ha, ha, ha, to hell with you!" I swear it did. And another one, a little pigeony-looking bird, said, "Hip hip hurroo." Lou Ann insisted that it was saying "Who Cooks for Who?" She said she had read it in a magazine. I had a hard time imagining what kind of magazine would go into something like that, but I wasn't about to argue. It was the first time I could remember her hanging on to her own opinion about something—Lou Ann not normally being inclined in that direction. One time in a restaurant, she'd once told me, a waiter mistakenly brought her somebody else's dinner and she just ate it, rather than make trouble. It was beef shingles on toast.

Gradually Lou Ann and I were changing the house around, filling in the empty spaces left behind by Angel with ABC books and high chairs and diaper totes and all manner of toys, all larger than a golf ball. I had bought Turtle a real bed, junior size, from New To You. We turned the screen porch in the back into a playroom for the kids, not that Dwayne Ray did any serious playing yet, but he liked to sit out there strapped in his car seat watching Turtle plant her cars in flowerpots. The fire engine she called "domato," whereas the orange car was "carrot." Or sometimes she called it "Two-Two," which is what I had named my Volkswagen, after the man who profited from my rocker arm disaster.

I had considered putting Turtle's bed out there on the porch too, but Lou Ann said it wouldn't be safe, that someone might come along and slash the screen and kidnap her before you could say Jack Robinson. I never would have thought of that.

But it didn't matter. The house was old and roomy; there was plenty of space for Turtle's bed in my room. It was the type of house they called a "rambling bungalow"[1] (the term reminded me somehow of Elvis Presley movies), with wainscoting[2] and steam radiators and about fifty coats of paint on the door frames, so that you could use your thumbnail to scrape out a history of all the house's tenants as far back as the sixties, when people were fond of painting their woodwork apple green and royal blue. The ceilings were so high you just learned to live with the cobwebs.

It wasn't unreasonably hot yet, and the kids were bouncing around the house like superballs (this was mainly Turtle, with Dwayne Ray's participation being mainly vocal), so we took them out to sit under the arbor for a while. The wisteria vines were a week or two past full bloom, but the bees and the perfume still hung thick in the air overhead, giving it a sweet purplish hue. If you ignored the rest of the park, you could imagine this was a special little heaven for people who had lived their whole lives without fear of bees.

Lou Ann was full of gossip from her weekend with the Ruiz cousins. Apparently most of them spoke English, all the men were good-looking and loved to dance, and all the women had children Dwayne Ray's age. She had about decided that every single one of them was nicer than Angel, a conclusion to which they all heartily agreed, even Angel's mother. A large portion of the flock were preparing to move to San Diego.

◀ *What conclusion did Lou Ann come to that Angel's entire family agrees with?*

"I can't believe it," she said, "first Manny and Ramona, you remember, the friends I told you about that saw the meteor shower? And now two of Angel's brothers and their wives and kids. You'd think they'd discovered gold out there. Angel used to always talk about moving to California too, but I'll tell you this right now, Mama would have had an apoplectic. She thinks in California they sell marijuana in the produce section of the grocery store."

"Maybe they do. Maybe that's why everybody wants to live there."

---

1. **bungalow.** One-story house with a low-pitched roof
2. **wainscoting.** Wood paneling

"Not me," Lou Ann said. "Not for a million, and I'll tell you why, too. In about another year they're due to have the biggest earthquake in history. I read about it someplace. They say all of San Diego might just end up in the ocean, like noodle soup."

"I guess the sharks will be happy," I said.

"Taylor, I swear! These are my relatives you're talking about."

"Angel's relatives," I said. "You're practically divorced."

"Not to hear them tell it," Lou Ann said.

Turtle was staring up at the wisteria flowers. "Beans," she said, pointing.

"Bees," I said. "Those things that go bzzzz are bees."

"They sting," Lou Ann pointed out.

▶ *What does Turtle point to on the wisteria vines?*

But Turtle shook her head. "Bean trees," she said, as plainly as if she had been thinking about it all day. We looked where she was pointing. Some of the wisteria flowers had gone to seed, and all these wonderful long green pods hung down from the branches. They looked as much like beans as anything you'd ever care to eat.

▶ *What does Taylor think is a miracle?*

"Will you look at that," I said. It was another miracle. The flower trees were turning into bean trees.

On the way home Lou Ann went to the corner to buy a newspaper. She was seriously job-hunting now, and had applied at a couple of nursery schools, though I could just hear how Lou Ann would ask for a job: "Really, ma'am, I could understand why you wouldn't want to hire a dumb old thing such as myself."

Turtle and I walked the other way, since we needed to stop in at the Lee Sing Market for eggs and milk. Lou Ann refused to set foot in there these days, saying that Lee Sing always gave her the evil eye. Lou Ann's theory was that she was mad at her for having had Dwayne Ray instead of a girl, going against some supposedly foolproof Chinese method of prediction. My theory was that Lou Ann suffered from the same disease as Snowboots: feeling guilty for things beyond your wildest imagination.

In any case, today Lee Sing was nowhere to be seen. She often went back to check on her famous century-old mother, the source of Mattie's purple beans, whom neither Lou Ann nor I had ever laid eyes on, though not for lack of curiosity. According to Mattie no one had sighted her for years, but you always had the feeling she was back there.

Lee Sing had left her usual sign by the cash register: BE BACK ONE MINUTE, PLEASE DO NOT STEAL ANYTHING. LEE SING. I spotted Edna Poppy in paper goods, the next aisle over from the dairy case. As best I could see, Edna was sniffing different brands of toilet tissue.

"Edna! Miss Poppy!" I called out. When I needed to call her by name I generally hedged my bets and used both first and last. Her head popped up and she seemed confused, looking all around.

"It's me, Taylor. Over here." I came around into the aisle where she had parked her cart. "Where's Mrs. Parsons today?" I stopped dead in my tracks. Edna had a white cane.

◀ *What does Edna have that stops Taylor dead in her tracks?*

"Virgie is ill in bed with a croup,[3] I'm sorry to say. She sent me out to get fresh lemons and a drop of whiskey. And of course a few other unmentionables." She smiled, dropping a package of orange toilet paper into the cart. "Can you tell me, dear, if these are lemons or limes I have?" She ran her hand over her goods and held up a lopsided plastic bag of yellow fruits.

Edna Poppy was blind. I stood for a minute staring, trying to reorganize things in my mind the way you would rearrange a roomful of furniture. Edna buying all her clothes in one color, ever since age sixteen. Virgie's grip on her elbow. I remembered the fantasy I'd constructed the day of our dinner party: Edna happily discovering red bobby pins in the drugstore. I'd had it completely wrong. It would have been Virgie Mae who found them, plucked them down off the rack of Oreo-cookie barrettes, and purchased them for her friend.

◀ *What does Taylor realize about Edna Poppy?*

"Are you with me, dear?"

"I'm sorry," I said. "Lemons. They're kind of small, but they look just fine."

When I got home I asked Lou Ann if she knew. She insisted I was making the whole thing up. "Is this a joke?" she kept asking. "Because if it is, it's a sick one."

"It's not a joke. She had a white cane. She asked me if what she had was lemons or limes. Think about it, the way she kind of looks over your head when she talks. The way Virgie leads her around. How Virgie always says everybody's name when the two of them come into a room."

Lou Ann was horrified. "Oh my God," she said. "Oh my merciful heavens, I feel about this big. When I think about all the times I've just bounced over there and said, 'See ya this! See ya that! Thanks for keeping an eye on Dwayne Ray.'"

"I don't think she'd mind. Her eyes are her hands. And Virgie. She has her own special ways of keeping an eye on

◀ *What two things does Taylor say function as eyes for Edna?*

3. **croup.** Illness marked by difficulty breathing and a hoarse cough

things," I told Lou Ann, and this seemed to make her feel better.

On Monday afternoon I asked if it would be okay if I went up to see Esperanza. I had never been upstairs at Mattie's and for some reason I felt it was off limits, but she said fine, to go on up. I went through the cramped study, which of course was still piled high with Mattie's dead husband's magazines (I knew by now that he had been dead many years, so it seemed unlikely that his mess would clear up any time soon) and on up the staircase into Mattie's living room.

It had the same crowded, higgledy-piggledy look as the office downstairs, though the stuff here had more to do with everyday living: junk mail, bills, pencils, magazines with color pictures of people like Tom Selleck[4] and the President (not Jesus), a folded newspaper with a half-worked crossword puzzle, the occasional pliers or screwdriver. It was the type of flotsam and jetsam[5] (a pair of words I had just learned from the dictionary) that washes up on your coffee table, lies around for a week or so, and then makes way for whatever comes in on the next tide.

▶ *What is hanging over Mattie's fireplace?*

Every surface was covered: tables, chairs, walls. Over the fireplace there was a big cross made up of hundreds of small, brightly glazed pieces of tile, each one shaped like something: a boy, a dog, a house, a palm tree, a bright blue fish. Together they all added up to a cross. I had never seen anything like it.

The wall across from the fireplace was covered with pictures of every imaginable size and shape. There were snapshots of people squinting into the sun, a few studio portraits of children, pictures of Mattie flanked by other people, all of them dark and shorter than herself. There were a number of children's drawings. I remembered Mattie telling me when we'd first met that she had "something like" grandchildren around, how that had struck me as such a peculiar thing to say.

▶ *What does Taylor notice about the children's drawings?*

I noticed that practically all the kids' drawings had guns in them somewhere, and huge bullets suspended in the air, hanging on the dotted lines that flowed like waterfalls out of the gun barrels. There were many men in turtle-shaped army helmets. One picture showed a helicopter streaming blood.

The living room had no windows, just doors opening off in four directions. An older woman came in with a cardboard box and looked at me with surprise, asking something

4. **Tom Selleck.** American television and film actor
5. **flotsam and jetsam.** Floating debris as of that from a shipwreck

in Spanish. I had never before seen anyone whose entire body looked sad. Her skin just seemed to hang from her, especially from her arms above the elbows, and her jaw.

◀ *How does Taylor describe the body of the older woman who comes into the room?*

"Esperanza," I said, and she nodded toward a door at the back.

That room seemed to belong in another house—it was empty. The walls were an antique-looking shade of light pink, completely bare except for a cross with two palm fronds stuck behind it, over one of the beds. The two beds were neatly made up with rough-looking blue blankets that surely no one would sleep under in this weather. Esperanza was not in either bed, but sitting up in a straight-backed chair by the window. She looked up when I knocked on the door casement.[6]

"Hi, I came to see how you are doing."

She got up from the chair and offered it to me. She sat on the bed. I don't believe she had been doing anything at all, just sitting with her hands in her lap.

We looked at each other for a second, then looked at other things in the room, of which there were painfully few. I didn't know why I'd thought I'd have the nerve to do this.

"How are you feeling now? Are you feeling better? Your stomach's okay?" I put my hand on my stomach. Esperanza nodded, then looked at her hands.

I had lost my directions somewhere when I came into the house. I looked out the window expecting to see Roosevelt Park, but this was not that window. We were at the back of the house. From here you got a terrific bird's-eye view of Lee Sing's back garden. I wondered if you might catch a peek at Lee Sing's old mother from up here, if you stayed at your post long enough.

"I've been meaning to tell you," I said, "I think Esperanza's a beautiful name. Estevan told me it means to wait, and also to hope. That in Spanish the same word means both things. But I thought it was pretty even before I knew it meant anything. It reminded me of, I don't know, a waterfall or something."

◀ *What does Esperanza's name mean in English?*

She nodded.

"Taylor doesn't mean anything that interesting. A tailor hems up people's pants and stuff like that."

Her mouth stretched a little bit in the direction of a smile. But her eyes looked blank. Dark, black holes.

◀ *How does Taylor describe Esperanza's eyes?*

"You understand basically everything I'm saying, right?"

She nodded again.

6. **casement.** Wood molding

"I think that's how Turtle is, too, but people always forget. They think she doesn't take in any more than she puts out, but I know better, I can tell she understands stuff. It's something about the way she looks at you."

Esperanza kept staring at her empty hands. I wished I had something to put in them, something that would be wonderful for her to look at.

▶ *How does Taylor describe Esperanza's eyes when Taylor asks her if it is okay to talk about Turtle?*

"I hope you don't mind me talking about Turtle."

Her eyes flew up at me like a pair of blackbirds scared out of safe hiding.

"Estevan told me about Ismene," I said. "I'm sorry. When I first found out you'd taken pills, I couldn't understand it, why you'd do such a thing to yourself. To Estevan. But when he told me that. God, how does a person live with something like that?"

She looked away. This conversation would have been hard enough even with two people talking. No matter what I said, it was sure to be the exact wrong thing to say to someone who recently swallowed a bottle of baby aspirin. But what would be right? Was there some book in the library where you could look up such things?

▶ *What is the main thing that Taylor came to tell Esperanza?*

"I guess the main thing I came up here to tell you is, I don't know how you go on, but I really hope you'll keep doing it. That you won't give up *esperanza*. I thought of that last night. *Esperanza* is all you get, no second chances. What you have to do is try and think of reasons to stick it out."

She had tears in her eyes, but that seemed better somehow than nothing at all. "It's terrible to lose somebody," I said, "I mean, I don't know firsthand, but I can imagine it must be. But it's also true that some people never have anybody to lose, and I think that's got to be so much worse."

After a long time I said, "He's crazy about you."

I went over and took one of the hands in her lap and held it for a second. Her skin felt cold and emptied-out, like there was nobody home.

As I left to go back to work I saw the woman with the cardboard box, still in the living room. She was sorting through a handful of possessions she had laid out on the sofa—a black skirt, a small book bound in red vinyl, a framed photograph, a pair of baby's sneakers tied together by the laces—and carefully putting them back into the box.

On Wednesday, just as I was finishing up the last patch of the day and getting ready to head for home, I spotted Lou Ann stepping off the bus at the Roosevelt stop. I yelled for her to wait up, and she came over and talked to me while I used the water hose to wash the black dust off my hands. One thing I can tell you right now about tires: they're dirty business.

Lou Ann had just been for a job interview at a convenience store on the north side. She'd left Turtle and Dwayne Ray with Edna and Mrs. Parsons.

"So the first thing the guy says to me is 'We get a lot of armed robberies in here, sweetheart.' He kept on calling me sweetheart and talking to my boobs instead of my face, this big flabby guy with greasy hair and you just know he reads every one of those porno magazines they keep behind the counter. 'Lots of stickups,[7] sweetheart, how do you hold up under pressure?' he says. Holdup, that was his idea of a big hilarious joke. Jeez, the whole thing gave me the creeps from the word go."

I could see that she had dressed up for this interview: a nice skirt, ironed blouse, stockings, pumps. In this heat. The humiliation of it made me furious. "Something better's bound to come along," I said. "You can hold out." I wiped my hands on a towel, hollered goodbye to Mattie, and we headed down the sidewalk.

"I hate that place," she said, nodding back over her shoulder at Fanny Heaven.

"Yeah," I said. "But on the bright side, Mattie says they don't do a whole lot of business. She thinks having a place called Jesus Is Lord right next door kind of puts a hex[8] on it."

Lou Ann shuddered. "That door's what gets me. The way they made that door handle. Like a woman is something you shove on and walk right through. I try to ignore it, but it still gets me."

◀ What does Lou Ann say bothers her about the door of Fanny Heaven?

"Don't ignore it, then," I said. "Talk back to it. Say, 'You can't do that number on me you shit-for-brains,' or something like that. Otherwise it kind of weasels its way into your head whether you like it or not. You know those hard-boiled eggs they keep around in jars of vinegar, in bars? It's like that. After a while they get to tasting awful, and it's not the egg's fault. What I'm saying is you can't just sit there, you got to get pissed off."

"You really think so?"

"I do."

"The thing about you, Taylor, is that you just don't let anybody put one over on you.[9] Where'd you ever learn to be like that?" Lou Ann wanted to know.

◀ What does Lou Ann say Taylor doesn't let anyone do to her? Where did Taylor learn to be that way?

"Nutter school."

7. **stickups.** Robberies at gunpoint, holdups
8. **hex.** Evil spell, jinx
9. **put one over on you.** Take advantage of you

Respond to the Selection

Taylor tells Estevan that he is wrong when he says, "I can see that it would be easier not to know." Do you think that individuals have a responsibility to stay informed about what is happening in the world around them? Why, or why not? Do you make an effort to educate yourself about current events? If so, how? If not, why not?

Investigate, Inquire, and Imagine

Recall: Gathering Facts

1a. When Taylor takes Turtle to the doctor, what do Turtle's x-rays show? What condition does the doctor say Turtle probably suffered from, and what caused it? How has this condition changed since Taylor took Turtle?

2a. When Taylor tells Estevan that she keeps finding out that life can be hard in ways she never knew about, how does Estevan respond?

3a. Who is Ismene, and what happened to her?

Interpret: Finding Meaning

1b. Why do you think Turtle's condition has changed?

2b. What does Taylor mean when she says that life can be hard in ways she never knew about? What does Estevan mean by his response?

3b. Why did the Guatemalan government take Ismene? Why didn't Estevan and Esperanza try to get her back?

Analyze: Taking Things Apart

4a. Look back to Chapter 10, and examine the image of the cross over Mattie's fireplace. Of what is the cross made? Identify the reference to the Bible that Taylor makes in Chapter 8. Consider the image of the cross above Mattie's fireplace, the biblical reference, and the name of Mattie's tire store. What kind of people run the sanctuary? Can you point to any other details in the novel that support this?

Synthesize: Bringing Things Together

4b. What does the image of the cross reveal about the way Mattie views what it means to be a religious person? What connection can you draw between the biblical reference and the events of *The Bean Trees?*

Perspective: LOOKING AT OTHER VIEWS

5a. In Chapter 8, Taylor apologizes to Estevan for Mrs. Parsons's remark that Salvadoran refugees who were shot upon returning to their country must have been drug dealers. Estevan says, "This is how Americans think....You believe that if something terrible happens to someone, they must have deserved it." Taylor replies, "I guess it makes us feel safe." Do you think it's true that Americans think this way? Why would this make Americans feel safe? How does someone who thinks like this view the world?

Empathy: SEEING FROM INSIDE

→ 5b. Taylor gets very angry that Esperanza tried to kill herself. Why does Taylor feel this way? How are her feelings an example of empathy? When Taylor realizes the sacrifice that Estevan and Esperanza have made, Estevan asks her what she would do, and Taylor answers, "I can't even begin to think about a world where people have to make choices like that." Estevan responds, "You live in that world." What does his statement mean?

Understanding Literature

IMAGE AND IMAGERY. An **image** is language that creates a concrete representation of an object or an experience. An image is also the vivid mental picture created in the reader's mind by that language. Taken together, the images of a work are referred to as its **imagery.**

Consider the following images: the muscly wisteria vines Taylor thought dead twisting their way up the trellis in the park; the garden Taylor sees "through the bones" when Dr. Pelinowsky places Turtle's x-rays on the window; the bird who builds her nest within the bushy-armed cactus and flies in and out among "the horrible spiny branches." Each of these images is part of the novel's imagery.

Taylor believed the wisteria vines were dead, but they bloomed again. What lesson can be gained from this? Can this lesson be applied to any of the characters in the story? Explain.

In the image of the garden beyond the bones, what are the bones a symbol of? What is the garden a symbol of? How does the image represent Turtle's life so far?

What amazes Taylor about the bird that makes her nest in the cactus, flying in and out of the spiny branches without hesitation? To which character might this natural image relate? Explain.

Consider what these images communicate about the characters. Taken together, what do these images communicate about life, making a home, or the nature of all living things? Discuss and refine your ideas with your classmates or other readers of the book. Keep in mind that different readers will have different ways of viewing and interpreting images.

Eleven

Dream Angels

▶ *What are the duties of Lou Ann's job?*

In the third week of May, Lou Ann got a job as a packer in the Red Hot Mama's salsa factory. This meant that she stood elbow to elbow with about a hundred other people in a sweaty packing line dicing chiles and tomatillos and crushing garlic cloves into moving vats, with so much salsa slopping onto the floor that by the end of the day it sloshed around their ankles. The few who hoped to preserve their footwear wore those clear, old-fashioned rainboots that button on over their shoes. Most people gave up the effort. On days when they were packing extra hot, their ankles burned as if they were standing on red ant hills.

The ones that handled the chiles grew accustomed to tingling fingertips, and learned never to touch their eyes or private parts (or anyone else's), not even on their days off. No matter how they scrubbed their hands, the residue of Red Hot Mama had a way of sticking around, as pesty and persistent as a chaperone at a high school dance.

Truly this was a sweatshop.[1] Half the time the air conditioner didn't work at all, and all the time the fumes made everyone's eyes water so furiously that contact lenses could not be worn on the premises. Lou Ann's vision was 20/20, so this wasn't a problem, nor was any of the rest of it for that matter. Lou Ann loved her job.

▶ *How does Lou Ann feel about her job? In what ways does Lou Ann go beyond the job responsibilities? About what does she lecture Taylor?*

If Red Hot Mama's had given out enthusiastic-employee awards Lou Ann would have needed a trophy case. She brought home samples and tried out recipes, some of which would eventually be printed on the jar labels, and some of which would not, God willing. She gave us lectures on how the tiniest amount of cilantro could make or break the perfect salsa. Six months ago I'd never heard of salsa. Now I was eating it on anything from avocados to pot roast.

It came in three speeds: the jars with green lids were "mild," whereas pink meant "hot." The red-lidded jars were so-called "firecracker style." The latter was not a big hit with the kids. Turtle would cry and pant at just the

1. **sweatshop.** Shop or factory in which workers are employed for long hours at low wages and under unhealthy conditions

words for everyday use

chap • er • one (sha′ pə rōn) *n.,* older person who accompanies young people at a social gathering to ensure proper behavior. *I nearly fainted when my father told me he was going to be a chaperone at the dance I was attending.*

slightest taste, fanning her tongue and eying Lou Ann like she was some spy that had tried to poison us. Dwayne Ray had better sense than to let the stuff enter his mouth.

"Enough already," I told Lou Ann. "How about we just put the jar on the table and use the honor system?" On my nights to cook I made the blandest things I could think of: broiled white fish and mashed potatoes and macaroni and cheese, to give our taste buds a chance to grow back.

But Lou Ann had bought the company propaganda, hook, line, and sinker. "It's good for you," she said. "Some doctors recommend a teaspoon a day to prevent ulcers.[2] Plus it clears your sinuses."

I informed Lou Ann that, thank you very much, my sinuses had just about vacated the premises.

Telling it this way it sounds like a lot of fights, but actually I was liking Lou Ann a great deal these days. In the few weeks since she'd started working, she had begun to cut her hair far less often and finally stopped comparing her figure to various farm animals. Having a job of her own seemed to even out some of Lou Ann's wrinkled edges.

◄ *What has Lou Ann stopped doing since she started working?*

She mostly worked swing shift, which meant that she left at three in the afternoon, leaving the kids with Edna Poppy and Mrs. Parsons until I came home a couple of hours later. For the longest time Lou Ann was scared to say two words to Edna, for fear she might let slip some reference to eyes. Finally I cleared the air, just stating right out to Edna that for a great while we hadn't realized she was blind, because she got on so well. Edna had just assumed we knew all along. She took it as a compliment, that it wasn't the first thing we noticed about her.

◄ *Why was Lou Ann afraid to speak to Edna? How does Taylor resolve the situation?*

Once she started swing shift Lou Ann's experimental family dinners, featuring Five-Alarm Casserole and so forth, were limited to her days off. Most of the time I fed the kids and put them to bed before Lou Ann came home at eleven. Then she and I would eat a late supper, or on nights when it was still too hot to look a plate of food in the eye, we'd sit at the kitchen table fanning ourselves in our underwear, reading the paper, and drinking iced coffee. Sleep was hopeless anyway. But mostly we'd talk. At first all she could ever talk

2. **ulcers.** Inflamed break in the skin or mucous membranes of the body due to injury, infection, or corrosive fluids such as stomach acids

words for everyday use

ex • per • i • men • tal (ik sper ə men′ təl) *adj.*, based on trying new procedures, ideas, or activities. *Leon takes a creative and experimental approach to color and fashion, and sometimes the combinations he tries are almost blinding.*

about was cilantro and tomatillos and the people at Red Hot Mama's, but after a time things got back to normal. She would leaf through the paper and read me all the disasters.

"Listen at this: 'Liberty, Kansas. The parents and doctor of severely deformed Siamese twins joined at the frontal lobe of the brain have been accused of attempting to murder the infants by withholding medical care.' Lord, you can't really blame them, can you? I mean, what would you do? Is it better to be totally retarded and deformed and miserable, or just plain old dead?"

"I honestly couldn't say," I said. "Not having been either one." Although, when I thought about it, being dead seemed a lot like not being born yet, and I hadn't especially minded that. But I didn't give it a lot of thought. I was interested in the weather forecast. We hadn't had a drop of rain since that double-rainbow hailstorm back in January, and the whole world was looking parched. When you walked by a tree or a bush it just looked like it ached, somehow. I had to drag the water hose around to the back every day for Mattie's squash and beans. The noise of the cicadas[3] was enough to drive you to homicide. Mattie said it was their love call, that they mated during the hottest, driest weeks of the year, but it was beyond belief that any creature—even another cicada—would be attracted by that sound. It was a high, screaming buzz, a sound that hurt your eyes and made your skin shrink, a sound in the same class with scratched-up phonograph records and squeaking chalk.

▶ *How do the trees and bushes look? Why?*

▶ *How does Taylor describe the sound of the cicadas?*

Lou Ann, who had lived here long enough to make the association, said the sound of the cicadas made her hot. For me it went way beyond that. I used the air hose to blast the accursed insects out of the low branches of the Palo Verde trees around Mattie's, sending them diving and screaming off through the air like bottle rockets. Every time I walked past the mural of Jesus Is Lord I begged Him for rain.

But every day the paper said: No precipitation expected.

"Remember that time at the zoo?" Lou Ann asked, still occupied with the Liberty, Kansas, horror. "About those Siamese twins born pregnant, or whatever it was?"

"I remember the giant turtles," I said.

3. **cicadas.** Family of insects that have stout bodies, wide blunt heads, and large transparent wings; the males produce a loud buzzing noise

words for everyday use

pre • cip • i • ta • tion (pri si pə tā′ shən) *n.,* something that falls, flows, or rushes with steep descent, such as rain, sleet, or snow. *We hoped there would be no precipitation during the weekend of our annual car wash fundraiser.*

Lou Ann laughed. "Now how's a turtle manage to be pregnant, I'd like to know. Do they get maternity shells? I almost feel like going back to see how she's doing."

"Do you know what Estevan told me?" I asked Lou Ann. "In Spanish, the way to say you have a baby is to say that you give it to the light. Isn't that nice?"

◀ *What is the meaning of "to have a baby" in Spanish?*

"You give the baby to the light?"

"Mmm-hmm." I was reading a piece about earthquakes under the ocean. They cause giant waves, but in a ship you can't feel it at all, it just rolls under you.

I twisted my hair into a knot to try and get it off my sweaty neck. I looked enviously at Lou Ann's blond head, cropped like a golf course.

"I was so sure Dwayne Ray was going to be a Siamese twin or something," she said. "Because I was so big. When he was born I had to ask the doctor about fifteen times if he was normal, before it sunk in. I just couldn't believe he was okay."

"And now you just can't believe he's going to get through a day without strangling or drowning in an ice chest," I said, but in a nice way. I put down the paper and gave Lou Ann my attention. "Why do you think you're such a worry wart,[4] if you don't mind my asking?"

◀ *What does Taylor ask Lou Ann?*

"Taylor, can I tell you something? Promise you won't tell anybody. Promise me you won't laugh."

"Cross my heart."

"I had this dream, one week after he was born. This angel came down, I guess from the sky—I didn't see that part. He was dressed kind of modern, in a suit, you know? With a brown tie? But he was an angel, I'm positive—he had wings. And he said: 'I was sent to you from the future of this planet.' Then he told me my son would not live to see the year two thousand."

◀ *What dream did Lou Ann have?*

"Lou Ann, please."

"But no, that's not even the scariest part. The next morning my horoscope said, 'Listen to the advice of a stranger.' Now don't you think that's got to mean something? That part's real, it's not a dream. I cut it out and saved it. And Dwayne Ray's said something about avoiding unnecessary travel, which I took to mean, you know, traveling through life. Not that you could avoid that. So what on earth was I supposed to do? It scared me to death."

"You were just looking for a disaster, that's all. You can't deny you hunt for them, Lou Ann, even in the paper. If you look hard enough you can always come up with what you want."

◀ *What does Taylor tell Lou Ann about disasters?*

4. **worry wart.** Person who is inclined to worry unnecessarily

"Am I just completely screwed up, Taylor, or what? I've always been this way. My brother and I used to play this game when we were little, with a cigar box. That box was our best toy. It had this slinky lady in a long red dress on the inside of the lid, with her dress slit way up to here. It's a wonder Granny Logan didn't confiscate it. She was holding out a cigar I think, I s'pose she was a Keno girl[5] or something, but we said she was a gypsy. We'd make believe that you could say to her, 'Myself at the age of fourteen.' Or whatever age, you know, and then we'd look in the box and pretend we could see what we looked like. My brother would go all the way up to ninety. He'd say, 'I see myself with a long beard. I live in a large white house with seventeen dogs' and on and on. He loved dogs, see, and Mama and Granny would only let him have just Buster. But me, I was such a chicken liver, I'd just go a couple of weeks into the future at the very most. I'd look at myself the day school was going to start in September, maybe, and say, 'I am wearing a new pink dress.' But I'd never, never go up even to twenty or twenty-five. I was scared."

▶ What scared Lou Ann about the game that she played with her brother when she was younger?

"Of what?"

"That I'd be dead. That I'd look in the box and see myself dead."

"But it was just pretend. You could have seen yourself any way you wanted to."

"I know it. But that's what I thought I'd see. Isn't that the most ridiculous thing?"

"Maybe it was because of your father. Maybe you got kind of hung up on death, because of him dying."

"I'm just totally screwed up, that's all there is to it."

▶ What does Taylor tell Lou Ann she has? How does Lou Ann respond to what Taylor tells her?

"No, Lou Ann. You have your good points too."

Usually Lou Ann spit out compliments you tried to feed her like some kind of nasty pill, but that night her blue eyes were practically pleading with me. "What good points?" she wanted to know.

"Oh gosh, tons of them," I faltered. It's not that it was a hard question, but I was caught off guard. I thought a minute.

"The flip side of worrying too much is just not caring, if you see what I mean," I explained. "Dwayne Ray will always

5. **Keno girl.** Woman who works in a casino

words for everyday use

con • fis • cate (kän′ fə skāt) *v.,* take possession of. *If security guards catch you sneaking food or beverages into the stadium, they will confiscate the items.*

know that, no matter what, you're never going to *neglect* him. You'll never just sit around and let him dehydrate, or grow up without a personality, or anything like that. And that would be ever so much worse. You read about it happening in the paper all the time." I meant it; she did. "Somebody forgetting a baby in a car and letting it roast, or some such thing. If anything, Lou Ann, you're just too good of a mother."

◀ What does Taylor say about the kind of mother Lou Ann is? What does Lou Ann say she is doing to Dwayne Ray?

She shook her head. "I'm just a total screwed-up person," she said. "And now I'm doing the same thing to poor Dwayne Ray. But I can't help it, Taylor, I can't. If I could see the future, if somebody offered to show me a picture of Dwayne Ray in the year 2001, I swear I wouldn't look."

"Well, nobody's going to," I said gently, "so you don't have to worry about it. There's no such thing as dream angels. Only in the Bible, and that was totally another story."

In June a package came from Montana, all cheery and colorful with stamps and purple postage marks. It contained, among other things, a pair of child-sized cowboy boots—still years too big for Dwayne Ray—and a beautiful calfskin belt for Lou Ann. It was carved or stamped somehow with acorns, oak leaves, and her name. There was also a red-and-black Indian-beaded hair clip, which was of course no use to Lou Ann at this particular point in the life of her hair.

◀ About what has Angel changed his mind? What does he want Lou Ann to do?

Angel had changed his mind about the divorce. He missed her. He wanted her to come up and live in Montana in something called a yurt. If that was not an acceptable option, then he would come back to Tucson to live with her.

"What in the heck is a yurt anyway?" Lou Ann asked. "It sounds like dirt."

"Beats me," I said. "Look it up."

She did. "A circular domed tent of skins stretched over a lattice framework," she read, pronouncing each word slowly without a Kentucky accent. She pronounced "a" like the letter "A." "Used by the Mongol nomads of Siberia."

As they say in the papers, I withheld comment.

"So what do you think, Taylor? Do you think it would have a floor, or plaster walls inside, anything like that? Think the bugs would get in?"

What popped into my head was: George eats old gray rutabagas and plasters his yurt.

▶ *What is the part that Lou Ann can't get over?*

▶ *With whom does Lou Ann argue? Why?*

▶ *What has happened to Lou Ann in three weeks' time at Red Hot Mama's? What does Lou Ann refuse to take it as proof of?*

▶ *Why won't Lou Ann allow Sal Monelli to touch any food that isn't sealed and crated?*

"The part I can't get over is that he asked for me," she said. "He actually says here that he misses me." She mulled it over and over, twisting her gold wedding band around her finger. She had stopped wearing it about the time she started working at the salsa factory, but now had put it on again, almost guiltily, as though Angel might have packed a spy into the box along with the belt and the boots.

"But I've got responsibilities now," she argued, with herself certainly because I was giving no advice one way or the other. "At Red Hot Mama's."

This was surely true. In just three weeks' time she had been promoted to floor manager, setting some kind of company record, but she refused to see this as proof that she was a good worker. "They just didn't have anybody else to do it," she insisted. "Practically everybody there's fifteen years old, or worse. Sometimes they send over retardeds from that Helpless program, or whatever the heck it's called."

"It's called the Help-Yourself program, and you know it, so don't try to change the subject. The word is handicapped, not retardeds."

"Right, that's what I meant."

"What about that woman you told me about that breeds Pekingeses and drives a baby-blue Trans Am? What's-her-name, that gave you the I Heart My Cat bumper stickers? And what about the guy that's building a hot-air blimp in his backyard? Are they fifteen?"

"No." She was flipping the dictionary open and closed, staring out the window.

"And Sal Monelli, how old's he?"

Lou Ann rolled her eyes. Sal Monelli was an unfortunate fellow whose name had struck such terror in her heart she forbade him to touch any food item that wasn't sealed and crated. Lou Ann's life was ruled by her fear of salmonella,[6] to the extent that she claimed the only safe way to eat potato salad was to stick your head in the refrigerator and eat it in there.

"He actually wants me to go," she kept repeating, and even though she said she wasn't going to make up her mind right away, I felt in my bones that sooner or later she'd go. If I knew Lou Ann, she would go.

It seemed like the world was coming apart at the gussets. Mattie was gone more than she was home these days, "birdwatching." Terry, the red-haired doctor, had moved

6. **salmonella.** Bacteria that causes food poisoning, gastrointestinal inflammation, typhoid fever, or blood poisoning in humans and other warm-blooded mammals

to the Navajo reservation up north (to work, not because he had head rights). Father William looked like he had what people in Pittman called a case of the nerves.

The last time I'd really had a chance to talk with Mattie, she'd said there was trouble in the air. Esperanza and Estevan were going to have to be moved to a safe house farther from the border. The two best possibilities were Oregon and Oklahoma.

◀ *What does Mattie say needs to happen to Estevan and Esperanza? Why?*

Flat, hopeless Oklahoma. "What would happen if they stayed here?" I asked.

"Immigration is making noises. They could come in and arrest them, and they'd be deported[7] before you even had time to sit down and think about it."

"Here?" I asked. "They would come into *your* house?"

Mattie said yes. She also said, as I knew very well, that in that case Estevan's and Esperanza's lives wouldn't be worth a plugged nickel.[8]

"That just can't be right," I said, "that they would do that to a person, knowing they'd be killed. There's got to be some other way."

"The only legal way a person from Guatemala can stay here is if they can prove in court that their life was in danger when they left."

◀ *What is the only legal way for a Guatemalan to stay in the United States? What kind of proof do they need?*

"But they were, Mattie, and you know it. You know what happened to them. To Esperanza's brother, and all." I didn't say, To their daughter. I wondered if Mattie knew, but of course she would have to.

"Their own say-so is no good; they have to have hard proof. Pictures and documents." She picked up a whitewall and I thought she was going to throw it across the lot, but she only hoisted it onto the top of a pile beside me. "When people run for their lives they frequently neglect to bring along their file cabinets of evidence," she said. Mattie wasn't often bitter but when she was, she was.

◀ *What does Mattie say people running for their lives frequently neglect to bring with them?*

I didn't want to believe the world could be so unjust. But of course it was right there in front of my nose. If the truth was a snake it would have bitten me a long time ago. It would have had me for dinner.

◀ *What doesn't Taylor want to believe?*

---

7. **deported.** Sent out of the country
8. **plugged nickel.** Coin with no monetary value

Twelve

Into The Terrible Night

▶ *What happened at 3 p.m.?*

At three o'clock in the afternoon all the cicadas stopped buzzing at once. They left such an emptiness in the air it hurt your ears. Around four o'clock we heard thunder. Mattie turned over the "Closed" sign in the window and said, "Come on. I want you to smell this."

She wanted Esperanza to come too, and surprisingly she agreed. I went upstairs to phone Edna and Mrs. Parsons, though I practically could have yelled to them across the park, to say I'd be home later than usual. Edna said that was fine, just fine, the kids were no trouble, and we prepared to leave. At the last minute it turned out that Estevan could come too; he had the night off. The restaurant was closed for some unexpected family celebration. We all piled into the cab of Mattie's truck with Esperanza on Estevan's lap and me straddling the stick shift. The three of us had no idea where we were headed, or why, but the air had sparks in it. I felt as though I had a blind date with destiny, and someone had heard a rumor that destiny looked like Christopher Reeve.[1]

▶ *What does Taylor say about the air? How does it make Taylor feel?*

Mattie said that for the Indians who lived in this desert, who had lived here long before Tucson ever came along, today was New Year's Day.

▶ *What is New Year's Day for the Indians of the desert? How do the Indians celebrate the day?*

"What, July the twelfth?" I asked, because that's what day it was, but Mattie said not necessarily. They celebrated it on whatever day the summer's first rain fell. That began the new year. Everything started over then, she said: they planted their crops, the kids ran naked through the puddles while their mothers washed their clothes and blankets and everything else they owned, and they all drank cactus-fruit wine until they fell over from happiness. Even the animals and plants came alive again when the drought finally broke.

"You'll see," Mattie said. "You'll feel the same way."

Mattie turned onto a gravel road. We bounced through several stream beds with dry, pebbled bottoms scorched white, and eventually pulled over on high ground about a mile or so out of town. We picked our way on foot through the brush to a spot near a grove of black-trunked mesquite trees[2] on the very top of the hill.

1. **Christopher Reeve.** American actor, well known for playing Superman in the movies
2. **mesquite trees.** Trees that are part of the legume, or bean, family

The whole Tucson Valley lay in front of us, resting in its cradle of mountains. The sloped desert plain that lay between us and the city was like a palm stretched out for a fortuneteller to read, with its mounds and hillocks, its life lines and heart lines of dry stream beds.

A storm was coming up from the south, moving slowly. It looked something like a huge blue-gray shower curtain being drawn along by the hand of God. You could just barely see through it, enough to make out the silhouette of the mountains on the other side. From time to time nervous white ribbons of lightning jumped between the mountain-tops and the clouds. A cool breeze came up behind us, sending shivers along the spines of the mesquite trees.

The birds were excited, flitting along the ground and perching on thin, wildly waving seed stalks.

What still amazed me about the desert was all the life it had in it. Hillbilly that I was, I had come to Arizona expecting an endless sea of sand dunes. I'd learned of deserts from old Westerns and Quickdraw McGraw cartoons. But this desert was nothing like that. There were bushes and trees and weeds here, exactly the same as anywhere else, except that the colors were different, and everything alive had thorns.

◀ What still amazes Taylor about the desert?

Mattie told us the names of things, but the foreign words rolled right back out of my ears. I only remembered a few. The saguaros were the great big spiny ones, as tall as normal trees but so skinny and personlike that you always had the feeling they were looking over your shoulder. Around their heads, at this time of year, they wore crowns of bright red fruits split open like mouths. And the ocotillos were the dead-looking thorny sticks that stuck up out of the ground in clusters, each one with a flaming orange spike of flower buds at its top. These looked to me like candles from hell.

Mattie said all the things that looked dead were just dormant. As soon as the rains came they would sprout leaves and grow. It happened so fast, she said, you could practically watch it.

◀ What does Mattie say about all the things that look dead? What will happen to them when the rains come?

As the storm moved closer it broke into hundreds of pieces so that the rain fell here and there from the high clouds in long, curving gray plumes. It looked like maybe fifty or sixty fires scattered over the city, except that the tall,

words for everyday use

dor • mant (dȯr′ mənt) *adj.*, marked by a suspension of growth or external activity. *Many plants go into a dormant state during winter, and then begin to grow again in the spring.*

smoky columns were flowing in reverse. And if you looked closely you could see that in some places the rain didn't make it all the way to the ground. Three-quarters of the way down from the sky it just vanished into the dry air.

Rays of sunlight streamed from between the clouds, like the Holy Ghost on the cover of one of Mattie's dead husband's magazines. Lightning hit somewhere nearby and the thunder made Esperanza and me jump. It wasn't all that close, really, about two miles according to Mattie. She counted the seconds between the lightning strike and the thunder. Five seconds equaled one mile, she told us.

One of the plumes of rain was moving toward us. We could see big drops spattering on the ground, and when it came closer we could hear them, as loud as pebbles on a window. Coming fast. One minute we were dry, then we were being pelted with cold raindrops, then our wet shirts were clinging to our shoulders and the rain was already on the other side of us. All four of us were jumping and gasping because of the way the sudden cold took our breath away. Mattie was counting out loud between the lightning and thunderclaps: six, seven, boom! . . . four, five, six, boom! Estevan danced with Esperanza, then with me, holding his handkerchief under his arm and then twirling it high in the air—it was a flirtatious, marvelous dance with thunder for music. I remembered how he and I had once jumped almost naked into an icy stream together, how long ago that seemed, and how innocent, and now I was madly in love with him, among other people. I couldn't stop laughing. I had never felt so happy.

▶ *With whom is Taylor madly in love?*

That was when we smelled the rain. It was so strong it seemed like more than just a smell. When we stretched out our hands we could practically feel it rising up from the ground. I don't know how a person could ever describe that scent. It certainly wasn't sour, but it wasn't sweet either, not like a flower. "Pungent" is the word Estevan used. I would have said "clean." To my mind it was like nothing so much as a wonderfully clean, scrubbed pine floor.

Mattie explained that it was caused by the greasewood bushes, which she said produced a certain chemical when it rained. I asked her if anybody had ever thought to bottle it, it was so wonderful. She said no, but that if you paid

▶ *How does Taylor describe the smell of the rain? What does Mattie explain causes the scent?*

words for everyday use

pun • gent (pən′ jənt) *adj.*, sharp; strong; harsh; spicy; vinegary. *Blue cheese has a pungent odor.*

attention you could even smell it in town. That you could always tell if it was raining in any part of the city.

I wondered if the smell was really so great, or if it just seemed that way to us. Because of what it meant.

It was after sunset when we made our way back to the truck. The clouds had turned pink, then blood red, and then suddenly it was dark. Fortunately Mattie, who was troubled by night-blindness, had thought to bring a flashlight. The night was full of sounds—bird calls, a high, quivery owl hoot, and something that sounded like sheep's baahs, only a hundred times louder. These would ring out from the distance and then startle us by answering right from under our feet. Mattie said they were spadefoot toads. All that noise came from something no bigger than a quarter. I would never have believed it, except that I had seen cicadas.

"So how does a toad get into the middle of the desert?" I wanted to know. "Does it rain toad frogs in Arizona?"

◀ How do the spadefoot toads get into the middle of the desert? What do they do when it rains?

"They're here all along, smarty. Burrowed in the ground. They wait out the dry months kind of deadlike, just like everything else, and when the rain comes they wake up and crawl out of the ground and start to holler."

I was amazed. There seemed to be no end to the things that could be hiding, waiting it out, right where you thought you could see it all.

"Jeez," I said, as one of them let out a squall next to my sneaker.

"Only two things are worth making so much noise about: death and sex," Estevan said. He had the devil in him tonight. I remembered a dream about him from a few nights before, one that I had not until that minute known I'd had. A very detailed dream. I felt a flush crawling up my neck and was glad for the dusk. We were following Mattie's voice to keep to the trail, concentrating on avoiding the embrace of spiny arms in the darkness.

"It's all one to a toad," Mattie said. "If it's not the one, it's the other. They don't have long to make hay[3] in weather like this. We might not get another good rain for weeks. By morning there'll be eggs in every one of these puddles. In two days' time, even less, you can see tadpoles. Before the puddles dry up they've sprouted legs and hit the high road."

◀ What does Mattie say will be in all the puddles by morning?

We were following behind Mattie in single file now, holding to one another's damp sleeves and arms in the darkness. All at once Esperanza's fingers closed hard around

3. **make hay.** Make the most of opportunities; in this context, reproduce

▶ Why will rattlesnakes climb?

▶ What does Mattie point out about the rattlesnake going after the bird's eggs?

▶ What can Taylor tell from Turtle's eyes?

▶ Why doesn't Taylor go to Turtle?

my wrist. The flashlight beam had found a snake, just at eye level, its muscular coils looped around a smooth tree trunk.

"Better step back easy, that's a rattler,"[4] Mattie said in a calm voice. With the flashlight she followed the coils to the end and pointed out the bulbs on the tail, as clear and fragile-looking as glass beads. The rattle was poised upright but did not shake.

"I didn't know they could get up in trees," I said.

"Sure, they'll climb. After birds' eggs."

A little noise came from my throat. I wasn't really afraid, but there is something about seeing a snake that makes your stomach tighten, no matter how you make up your mind to feel about it.

"Fair's fair," Mattie pointed out, as we skirted a wide path around the tree. "Everybody's got her own mouths to feed."

I knew right away that something had gone wrong. Lou Ann was standing on the front porch waiting and she looked terrible, not just because she was under a yellow light bulb. She had been crying, possibly screaming—her mouth looked stretched. She wasn't even supposed to be home yet.

I ran up the sidewalk, almost tripping twice on the steps. "What is it? Are you okay?"

"It's not me. Taylor, I'm so sorry to have to tell you this. I'm so sorry, Taylor. It's Turtle."

"Oh God, no." I went past her into the house.

Edna Poppy was sitting on the sofa with Turtle in her lap, all in one piece as far as I could see, but Turtle was changed. All these months we had spent together were gone for her. I knew it from her eyes: two cups of black coffee. I remembered exactly, exactly, how the whites of her eyes had been thin slivers of moon around the dark centers, how they had glowed orange, on and off, with the blinking neon sign from that Godforsaken bar.

I didn't go to her, because I couldn't. It is that simple. I didn't want any of this to be happening.

Mrs. Parsons was standing in the kitchen door with a broom. "A bird has got into the house," she explained, and disappeared into the kitchen again, and for a confused second I thought she meant that this was the terrible thing that had happened.

But Lou Ann was right behind me. "They were in the park, Edna and Turtle. It was so cool after the rain they

4. **rattler.** Rattlesnake

thought they'd enjoy the air for a little bit, and Virgie was to come tell them if it looked like another storm was coming. But Virgie didn't come, and Edna never realized it was getting dark."

◀ *What didn't Edna realize?*

"So what happened." I was sick to my stomach.

"We don't know, exactly. I've called the police and they're coming over with a medical examiner or a social worker or, Christ, I don't know, somebody that can talk to Turtle."

"But what happened? How much do you *know* happened?"

Edna's eyes looked more glassy than usual. I noticed, now that I looked at her, that her clothes were a little messed up. Just traces, the red sweater pulled down on one shoulder, a hole in her stocking.

"I heard a peculiar sound," Edna said. She seemed almost in another world, a hypnotized person speaking out of a trance. "It sounded just like a bag of flour hitting the dirt. Turtle had been talking, or singing I suppose would be more like it, and then she was quiet, just didn't make a peep, but I heard struggling sounds. I called out, and then I swung my cane. Oh, I swung it high, so I wouldn't hit the baby. I know how tall she is." She held her hand just where Turtle's head would be, if she had been standing on the floor in front of Edna.

◀ *What sounds did Edna hear?*

"Did you hit anything?"

"Oh, yes, dear. Yes. I don't know what, but something that had some—I'd say some *give* to it.[5] Do you understand what I mean? Oh, and I shouted too, some terrible things. The next thing I knew, I felt a great heavy weight on the hem of my skirt, and that was Turtle."

◀ *What did Edna feel her cane hit?*

"It took us twenty minutes to get her to turn loose," Lou Ann said. Now she was holding on to Edna's sleeve instead of her hem.

"Oh my dear, I feel terrible. If I had only thought to come in a little sooner."

"It could have happened to anybody, Edna," Lou Ann said. "You couldn't have known what was going to happen, I might have done the exact same thing. You saved her, is what you did. Anybody else might have been scared to swing at him."

Anybody else, I thought, might have seen he had a gun, or a knife.

5. **some *give* to it.** Some flexibility as opposed to something solid that doesn't move

▶ *Who is at the door?*

Someone knocked at the door and we all jumped. It was the police, of course, a small man who showed his detective badge and a woman who said she was a social worker,[6] both of them dressed in ordinary clothes. Edna told what there was of her story again. The social worker was a prim-looking strawberry blonde who was carrying two rag dolls with yarn hair, a boy and a pigtail-girl. She asked if I was the mother. I nodded, a dumb animal, not really a mother, and she took me into the hallway.

"Don't you think a doctor should look at her?" I asked.

▶ *What does the social worker tell Taylor? What does Taylor tell the social worker?*

"Yes, of course. If we find evidence that she's been molested we'll need to talk with the child about it."

"She won't talk," I said. "Not now. Maybe not ever."

The social worker put her hand on my arm. "Children do recover from this kind of thing," she said. "Eventually they want to talk about what's happened to them."

"No, you don't understand. She may not talk again at all. Period."

"I think you'll find that your daughter can be a surprisingly resilient little person. But it's very important that we let her say what she needs to say. Sometimes we use these dolls. They're anatomically accurate," she said, and showed me. They were. "A child generally doesn't have the vocabulary to talk about these things, so we encourage her to play with these dolls and show us what has happened."

"Excuse me," I said, and went to the bathroom.

But Mrs. Parsons was in there with the broom. "A bird is in the house," she repeated. "A song sparrow. It came down the chimney."

I took the broom out of her hands and chased the bird off its perch above the medicine cabinet. It swooped through the doorway into the kitchen, where it knocked against the window above the sink with an alarming crack, and fell back on the counter.

"It's dead!" Virgie cried, but it wasn't. It stood up, hopped to a sheltered place between a mixing bowl and Lou Ann's recipe file, and stood blinking. In the living room they were asking about medical records. I heard Lou Ann spelling out Dr. Pelinowsky's name.

6. **social worker.** One whose job is to provide service and material assistance to the underprivileged

words for everyday use

re • sil • ient (ri zil′ yənt) *adj.*, tending to recover from or adjust easily to misfortune or change. *The coach told his players that although losing the championship was difficult, they must be resilient and turn their attention to next season.*

Virgie moved toward the bird slowly, crooning, with her hand stretched out in front of her. But it took off again full tilt before she could reach it. I batted it gently with the broom, heading it off from the living room full of policemen and anatomically accurate dolls, and it veered down the hallway toward the back porch. Snowboots, at least, didn't seem to be anywhere around.

"Open the screen door," I commanded Virgie. "It's locked, you have to flip that little latch. Now hold it open."

Slowly I moved in on the terrified bird, which was clinging sideways to the screen. You could see its little heart beating through the feathers. I had heard of birds having heart attacks from fright.

"Easy does it," I said. "Easy, we're not going to hurt you, we just want to set you free."

The sparrow darted off the screen, made a loop back toward the hallway, then flew through the open screen door into the terrible night.

The medical examiner said that there was no evidence Turtle had been molested. She was shaken up, and there were finger-shaped bruises on her right shoulder, and that was all.

"All!" I said, over and over. "She's just been scared practically back into the womb is all." Turtle hadn't spoken once in the days since the incident, and was back to her old ways. Now I knew a word for this condition: catatonic.[7]

◀ *What effect has the incident had on Turtle?*

"She'll snap out of it," Lou Ann said.

◀ *What does Lou Ann say will happen?*

"Why should she?" I wanted to know. "Would you? I've just spent about the last eight or nine months trying to convince her that nobody would hurt her again. Why should she believe me now?"

"You can't promise a kid that. All you can promise is that you'll take care of them the best you can. Lord willing and the creeks don't rise, and you just hope for the best. And things work out, Taylor, they do. We all muddle through some way."

This from Lou Ann, who viewed most of life's activities as potential drownings, blindings, or asphyxiation;[8] who

7. **catatonic.** State that is characterized by lack of movement or expression
8. **asphyxiation.** Death caused by inadequate oxygen, the presence of toxic chemicals, or the obstruction of normal breathing

words for everyday use

croon (krün') *v.*, to sing or speak in a soft, murmuring manner. *It was sweet to watch the young mother croon to her new baby.*

▶ *Why is Lou Ann furious with Taylor?*

believed in dream angels that predicted her son would die in the year 2000. Lou Ann who had once said to me: "There's so many germs in the world it's a wonder we're not all dead already."

I didn't want to talk to her about it. And she was furious with me, anyway, saying that I had practically abandoned Turtle since that night. "Why didn't you go to her and pick her up? Why did you just leave her there, with the police and all, chasing that dumb bird around for heaven's sake? Chasing that bird like it was public enemy number one?"

"She was already good and attached to Edna," I said.

"That's the biggest bunch of baloney[9] and you know it. She would have turned loose of Edna for you. The poor kid was looking around the whole time, trying to see where you'd gone."

"I don't know what for. What makes anybody think I can do anything for her?"

I couldn't sleep nights. I went to work early and left late, even when Mattie kept telling me to go home. Lou Ann took off a week from Red Hot Mama's, putting her new promotion at risk, just to stay home with Turtle. The three of them—she, Edna, and Virgie—would sit together on the front porch with the kids, making sure we all understood it was nobody's fault.

And she stalked the neighborhood like a TV detective. "We're going to catch this jerk," she kept saying, and went knocking on every door that faced onto the park, insisting to skeptical housewives and elderly, hard-of-hearing ladies that they must have seen something or somebody suspicious. She called the police at least twice to try and get them to come take fingerprints off Edna's cane, on the off-chance that she'd whacked him on the hand.

"I know it was probably some pervert[10] that hangs out at that sick place by Mattie's," Lou Ann told me, meaning Fanny Heaven of course. "Those disgusting little movies they have, some of them with kids. Did you know that? Little girls! A guy at work told me. It had to have been somebody that saw those movies, don't you think? Why else would it even pop into a person's head?"

I told her I didn't know.

"If you ask me," Lou Ann said more than once, "that's like showing a baby how to put beans in its ears. I'm asking you, where else would somebody get the idea to hurt a child?"

9. **bunch of baloney.** Nonsense
10. **pervert.** One given to abnormal and socially unacceptable sexual behavior

I couldn't say. I sat on my bed for hours looking up words. Pedophilia.[11] Perpetrator.[12] Deviant.[13] Maleficent.[14] I checked books out of the library but there weren't any answers in there either, just more words. At night I lay listening to noises outside, listening to Turtle breathe, thinking: she could have been killed. So easily she could be dead now.

What is Taylor looking for in the books? What does she keep thinking about?

After dinner one night Lou Ann came into my room while the kids were listening to their "Snow White" record in the living room. I'd skipped dinner; I wasn't eating much these days. When I was young and growing a lot, and Mama couldn't feed me enough, she used to say I had a hollow leg. Now I felt like I had a hollow everything. Nothing in the world could have filled that space.

Lou Ann knocked softly at the door and then walked in, balancing a bowl of chicken-noodle soup on a tray.

"You're going to dry up and blow away, hon," she said. "You've got to eat something."

I took one look and started crying. The idea that you could remedy such evil with chicken-noodle soup.

"It's the best I can do," Lou Ann offered. "I just don't think you're going to change anything with your own personal hunger strike."

I put down my book and accepted her hug. I couldn't remember when I had felt so hopeless.

"I don't know where to start, Lou Ann," I told her. "There's just so damn much ugliness. Everywhere you look, some big guy kicking some little person when they're down—look what they do to those people at Mattie's. To hell with them, people say, let them die, it was their fault in the first place for being poor or in trouble, or for not being white, or whatever, how dare they try to come to this country."

"I thought you were upset about Turtle," Lou Ann said.

"About Turtle, sure." I looked out the window. "But it just goes on and on, there's no end to it." I didn't know how to explain the empty despair I felt. "How can I just be upset about Turtle, about a grown man hurting a baby, when the whole way of the world is to pick on people that can't fight back?"

What does Taylor say is the whole way of the world?

---

11. **Pedophilia.** Abnormal and socially unacceptable condition of an adult being sexually attracted to children

12. **Perpetrator.** One who acts, carries out, or commits; usually refers to a criminal act

13. **Deviant.** One who has turned away from normal, socially acceptable behavior

14. **Maleficent.** Evil, depraved, harmful

▶ *What does Taylor say should be punishment enough for the homeless families?*

▶ *What does Taylor say has become unpatriotic?*

"You fight back, Taylor. Nobody picks on you and lives to tell the tale."

I ignored this. "Look at those guys out in the park with no place to go," I said. "And women, too. I've seen whole families out there. While we're in here trying to keep the dry-cleaner bags out of the kids' reach, those mothers are using dry-cleaner bags for their children's *clothes,* for God's sake. For raincoats. And feeding them out of the McDonald's dumpster. You'd think that life alone would be punishment enough for those people, but then the cops come around waking them up mornings, knocking them around with their sticks. You've seen it. And everybody else saying hooray, way to go, I got mine, power to the toughest. Clean up the neighborhood and devil take the riffraff."[15]

Lou Ann just listened.

"What I'm saying is nobody feels sorry for anybody anymore, nobody even pretends they do. Not even the President.[16] It's like it's become unpatriotic." I unfolded my wad of handkerchief and blew my nose.

"What's that supposed to teach people?" I demanded. "It's no wonder kids get the hurting end of the stick. And she's so little, so many years ahead of her. I'm just not up to the job, Lou Ann."

Lou Ann sat with her knees folded under her, braiding and unbraiding the end of a strand of my hair.

"Well, don't feel like the Lone Ranger,"[17] she said. "Nobody is."

---

15. **riffraff.** Refers to people who are considered disreputable or of no use to society

16. **the President.** President Ronald Reagan, fortieth president of the United States, held office from 1981–1989.

17. **Lone Ranger.** Famous American television character of the 1950s; the Lone Ranger was a cowboy who fought outlaws with the help of his Indian companion Tonto.

Thirteen

Night-Blooming Cereus

Turtle turned out to be, as the social worker predicted, resilient. Within a few weeks she was talking again. She never did anything with the anatomical rag dolls except plant them under Cynthia's desk blotter, but she did talk some about the "bad man" and how Ma Poppy had "popped him one." I had no idea where Turtle had learned to talk like that, but then Edna and Virgie Mae did have TV. Cynthia was concerned about Turtle's tendency to bury the dollies, believing that it indicated a fixation with death, but I assured her that Turtle was only trying to grow dolly trees.

Cynthia was the strawberry blonde social worker. We went to see her on Mondays and Thursdays. Of the two of us, Turtle and me, I believe I was the tougher customer.

It was a miserable time. As wonderful as the summer's first rains had been, they soon wore out their welcome as it rained every day and soaked the air until it felt like a hot, stale dishcloth on your face. No matter how hard I tried to breathe, I felt like I couldn't get air. At night I'd lie on top of the damp sheets and think: breathe in, breathe out. It closed out every other thought, and it closed out the possibility of sleep, though sometimes I wondered what was the point of working so hard to stay alive, if that's what I was doing. I remembered my pep talk to Esperanza a few months before, and understood just how ridiculous it was. There is no point in treating a depressed person as though she were just feeling sad, saying, There now, hang on, you'll get over it. Sadness is more or less like a head cold—with patience, it passes. Depression is like cancer.

Cynthia had spent a lot of time talking with both of us about Turtle's earlier traumas, the things that had happened before I ever knew her. The story came out of me a little at a time.

But apparently it was no news to a social worker. Cynthia said that, as horrible as it was, this kind of thing happened often, not just on Indian reservations but in the most everyday-looking white frame houses and even places a whole lot fancier than that. She told me that maybe one out of every four little girls is sexually abused by a family member. Maybe more.

Surprisingly, hearing this wasn't really what upset me the most. Maybe by then I was already numb, or could only begin to think about the misfortunes of one little girl at a

▶ *What does Cynthia tell Taylor?*

▶ *What can't Taylor prove?*

▶ *What happens if a child has no legal guardian?*

time. But also, I reasoned, this meant that Turtle was not all alone. At least she would have other people to talk to about it when she grew up.

But there was other bad news. During the third week of sessions with Cynthia she informed me that it had recently come to the attention of the Child Protection Services Division of the Department of Economic Security,[1] in the course of the police investigation, that I had no legal claim to Turtle.

"No more legal claim than the city dump has on your garbage," I said. I think Cynthia found me a little shocking. "I told you how it was," I insisted. "Her aunt just told me to take her. If it hadn't been me, it would have been the next person to come down the road with an empty seat in the car. I guarantee you, Turtle's relatives don't want her."

"I understand that. But the problem is that you have no legitimate claim. A verbal agreement with a relative isn't good enough. You can't prove to the police that it happened that way. That you didn't kidnap her, for instance, or that the relatives weren't coerced."

"No, I can't prove anything. I don't understand what you're getting at. If I don't have a legal claim on Turtle, I don't see where anybody else does either."

Cynthia had these tawny gold eyes like some member of the cat family, as certain fair-haired people do. But unlike most people she could look you straight in the eye and stay there. I suppose that is part of a social worker's training.

"The state of Arizona has a claim," she said. "If a child has no legal guardian she becomes a ward of the state."[2]

"You mean, like orphan homes, that kind of thing?"

"That kind of thing, yes. There's a chance that you could adopt her eventually, depending on how long you've been a resident of the state, but you would have to qualify through the state agency. It would depend on a number of factors, including your income and stability."

---

1. **Child Protection Services Division of the Department of Economic Security.** The Child Protection Services Division is the division of the Department of Economic Security in Arizona responsible for managing services that seek to encourage the preservation and well-being of families, such as child-abuse prevention, and medical coverage for children under state, foster, or adoptive care.

2. **ward of the state.** Child who is under the care of the state; children who don't have legal guardians are placed into foster homes, and the state becomes their legal guardian.

words for everyday use

or • phan (ȯr′ fən) *n.*, child deprived by death of one, or usually both, parents. *Although Sandra is an orphan, she was adopted at a young age by a couple who have been loving parents to her.*

Income and stability. I stared at Cynthia's throat. In this hot weather, when everybody else was trying to wear as little as they could without getting arrested, Cynthia had on a pink-checked blouse with the collar pinned closed. I remembered hearing her say, at some point, that she was cool-blooded by nature.

"How soon would this have to happen?" I asked.

"It will take two or three weeks for the paperwork to get to a place where it's going to get noticed. After that, someone from Child Protection and Placement[3] will be in touch with you."

The pin at her throat was an ivory and flesh-colored cameo that looked antique. As Turtle and I were leaving I asked if it was something that had come down through her family.

Cynthia fingered the cameo and laughed. "I found it in the one-dollar bin at the Salvation Army."

"Figures," I said.

Lou Ann had a fit. I had never seen her so mad. The veins on her forehead stood out and her face turned pink, all the way up to her scalp.

◀ How does Lou Ann react to what the social worker told Taylor?

"Who in the hell do those people think they are? That they have the right to take her out of a perfectly good home and put her in some creepy orphanage where they probably make them sleep on burlap bags and feed them pig slop!"

"I don't think it's quite that bad," I said.

"I can't believe you," she said.

But I was ready to give in. "What else can I do? How can I fight the law?" I asked her. "What am I going to do, get a gun and hold Turtle hostage in here while the cops circle the house?"

"Taylor, don't. Just don't. You're acting like it's a lost cause, and that I'm telling you to do something stupid. All I'm saying is, there's got to be some way around them taking her, and you're not even trying to think of it."

"Why should I, Lou Ann? Why should I think Turtle's better off with me than in a state home?[4] At least there they know how to take care of kids. They won't let anything happen to her."

◀ What does Taylor say about a state home?

"Well, that's sure a chickenshit thing to say."

---

3. **Child Protection and Placement.** Also a division of the Department of Economic Security that manages issues relating to the placement of children into foster or adoptive care

4. **state home.** Foster home into which children who do not have parents or legal guardians are placed temporarily

"Maybe it is."

She stared at me. "I cannot believe you're just ready to roll over and play dead about this, Taylor. I thought I knew you. I thought we were best friends, but now I don't hardly know who in the heck you are."

I told her that I didn't know either, but that didn't satisfy Lou Ann in the slightest.

"Do you know," she told me, "in high school there was this girl, Bonita Jankenhorn, that I thought was the smartest and the gutsiest person that ever walked. In English when we had to work these special crossword puzzles about *Silas Marner*[5] and I don't know what all, the rest of us would start to try out different words and then erase everything over and over again, but Bonita worked hers with an *ink pen*. She was that sure of herself, she'd just screw off the cap and start going. The first time it happened, the teacher started to tell her off and Bonita said, 'Miss Myers, if I turn in a poor assignment then you'll have every right to punish me, but not until then.' Can you even imagine? We all thought that girl was made out of gristle.[6]

▶ *What did Lou Ann think about Taylor when she met her?*

"But when I met you, that day you first came over here, I thought to myself, 'Bonita Jankenhorn, roll over. This one is worth half a dozen of you, packed up in a box and gift-wrapped.'"

"I guess you were wrong," I said.

"I was *not* wrong! You really were like that. Where in the world did it all go to?"

"Same place as your meteor shower," I said. I hadn't intended to hurt Lou Ann's feelings, but I did. She let me be for a while after that.

▶ *What does Taylor keep saying? How does Lou Ann keep answering her?*

But only for a while. Then she started up again. Really, I don't think the argument stopped for weeks, it would just take a breather from time to time. Although it wasn't an argument, strictly speaking. I couldn't really disagree with Lou Ann—what Cynthia and the so-called Child Protectors wanted to do was wrong. But I didn't know what was right. I just kept saying how this world was a terrible place to try and bring up a child in. And Lou Ann kept saying, For God's sake, what other world have we got?

▶ *What hasn't Mattie been able to work out?*

Mattie had her own kettle of fish to worry about.[7] She hadn't been able to work out a way to get Esperanza and Estevan out of Tucson, much less all the way to a sanctuary

5. ***Silas Marner.*** Novel by George Eliot
6. **gristle.** Cartilage; tough, fibrous matter
7. **her own kettle of fish to worry about.** Her own problems to worry about

church in some other state. Apparently several people had offered, but each time it didn't work out. Terry the doctor had made plans to drive them to San Francisco, where they would meet up with another group going to Seattle. But because of this new job on the Indian reservation the government liked to keep track of his comings and goings. Mattie always said she trusted her nose. "If I don't like the smell of something," she said, "then it's not worth the risk."

Even with this on her mind, she spent a lot of time talking with me about Turtle. She told me some things I didn't know. Obviously Mattie knew what there was to know about loopholes.[8] She was pretty sure that there were ways a person could adopt a child without going through the state.

But I confessed to Mattie that even if I could find a way I wasn't sure it would be the best thing for Turtle.

◄ What does Taylor confess to Mattie?

"Remember when I first drove up here that day in January?" I asked her one morning. We were sitting in the back in the same two chairs, drinking coffee out of the same two mugs, though this time I had the copulating rabbits. "Tell me the honest truth. Did you think I seemed like any kind of a decent parent?"

"I thought you seemed like a bewildered parent. Which is perfectly ordinary. Usually the bewilderment wears off by the time the kid gets big enough to eat peanut butter and crackers, but knowing what I do now, I can see you were still in the stage most mothers are in when they first bring them home from the hospital."

I was embarrassed to think of how Mattie must have seen straight through my act. Driving up here like the original tough cookie in jeans and a red sweater, with my noncommital answers and smart remarks, acting like two flat tires were all in a day's work and I just happened to have been born with this kid growing out of my hip, that's how cool I was. I hadn't felt all that tough on the inside. The difference was, now I felt twice that old, and too tired to put on the show.

8. **loopholes.** Means of escape, especially an ambiguity or omission in the legal text through which the intent of a statute or contract may be evaded

words for everyday use

be • wil • der (bi wil′ dər) *v.*, to perplex or confuse by a complexity, variety, or multitude of objects or considerations; to cause to lose one's bearings. *The multitude of one-way streets, dead ends, and no u-turn signs were enough to bewilder even the most confident driver.*

non • com • mit • tal (nän kə mi′ təl) *adj.*, giving no clear indication of attitude or feeling. *I tried to play it cool by giving Eli a noncommittal "maybe" when he asked me if I wanted to see a movie on Saturday night.*

"You knew, didn't you? I didn't know the first thing about how to take care of her. When you told me that about babies getting dehydrated it scared the living daylights out of me. I realized I had no business just assuming I could take the responsibility for a child's life."

"There's not a decent mother in the world that hasn't realized that."

"I'm serious, Mattie."

She smiled and sipped her coffee. "So am I."

"So how does a person make a decision that important? Whether or not they're going to do it?"

"Most people don't decide. They just don't have any choice. I've heard you say yourself that you think the reason most people have kids is because they get pregnant."

I stared at the coffee grounds that made a ring in the bottom of the white mug. Back in Pittman I'd heard of a fairly well-to-do woman who made her fortune reading tea leaves and chicken bones, which she kept in a bag and would scatter across her kitchen floor like jacks. On the basis of leaves and bones, she would advise people on what to do with their lives. No wonder she was rich. It seems like almost anything is better than having only yourself to blame when you screw things up.

"Taylor, honey, if you don't mind my saying so I think you're asking the wrong question."

"How do you mean?"

▶ *What question does Mattie say Taylor is asking herself? What does Mattie say is the answer to that question?*

"You're asking yourself, Can I give this child the best possible upbringing and keep her out of harm's way her whole life long? The answer is no, you can't. But nobody else can either. Not a state home, that's for sure. For heaven's sake, the best they can do is turn their heads while the kids learn to pick locks and snort hootch, and then try to keep them out of jail. Nobody can protect a child from the world. That's why it's the wrong thing to ask, if you're really trying to make a decision."

"So what's the right thing to ask?"

▶ *What does Mattie say is the right question to ask?*

"Do I want to try? Do I think it would be interesting, maybe even enjoyable in the long run, to share my life with this kid and give her my best effort and maybe, when all's said and done, end up with a good friend."

"I don't think the state of Arizona's looking at it that way."

"I guarantee you they're not."

It occurred to me to wonder whether Mattie had ever raised kids of her own, but I was afraid to ask. Lately whenever I'd scratched somebody's surface I'd turned up a ghost story. I made up my mind not to bring it up.

I called for an appointment to meet with Cynthia alone, without Turtle. In past appointments she had talked about legal claim and state homes and so forth in Turtle's presence. Granted Turtle had been occupied with the new selection of toys offered by the Department of Economic Security, but in my experience she usually got the drift of what was going on, whether or not she appeared to be paying attention. If either I or the state of Arizona was going to instill in this child a sense of security, discussing her future and ownership as though she were an item of commerce wasn't the way to do it. The more I thought about this, the madder I got. But that wasn't what I intended to discuss with Cynthia.

◀ *Why does Taylor make an appointment to meet with Cynthia alone?*

The appointment was on a Friday afternoon. I started to lose my nerve again when I saw her in her office, her eyes made up with pale green shadows and her hair pulled back in a gold barrette. I don't believe Cynthia was much older than I was, but you put somebody in high-heeled pumps and sit her behind a big desk and age is no longer an issue—she is more important than you are, period.

"Proof of abandonment is very, very difficult," she was explaining to me. "In this case, probably impossible. But you're right, there are legal alternatives. The cornerstone of an adoption of this type would have to be the written consent of the child's natural parents. And you would need to be named in the document."

◀ *What does Cynthia say about proving that Turtle was abandoned?*

"What if there were no natural parents? If they were to be dead, for instance."

"Then it would have to come from the nearest living relative, the person who would normally have custody, and a death certificate would have to be presented as well. But the most important thing, as I said, is that the document would name you, specifically, as the new guardian."

◀ *What does Taylor need to adopt Turtle?*

"What kind of document exactly?"

words for everyday use

in • still (in stil′) *v.,* to impart gradually; initiate; sow the seeds of. *My parents believe the best way to instill good values in their children is to lead by example.*

com • merce (kä′ mərs) *n.,* trade; buying and selling; business. *Commerce between countries has always been an important part of international politics.*

a • ban • don • ment (ə ban′ dən mənt) *n.,* desertion; the act of leaving without return; the act of leaving a person helpless and without protection. *When the toddler was left with a babysitter, he wailed as if his mother had committed an act of abandonment.*

cor • ner • stone (kȯr′ nər stōn) *n.,* foundation; basic element. *Paying attention in class is the cornerstone of a successful academic career.*

cus • to • dy (kəs′ tə dē) *n.,* immediate charge and control exercised by a person or authority; guardianship; care. *The judge must decide who will have legal custody of the child.*

"The law varies. In some states the mother would have to acknowledge her consent before a judge or a representative of the Department of Economic Security. In others, a simple written statement, notarized and signed before witnesses, is sufficient."

"What about on an Indian reservation? Do you know that sometimes on Indian reservations they don't give birth or death certificates?"

Cynthia wasn't the type that liked to be told anything. "I'm aware of that," she said. "In certain cases, exceptions are made."

Cynthia's office was tiny, really, and her desk wasn't actually all that big. She didn't even have a window in there.

"Don't you miss knowing what the weather's like?" I asked her.

"I beg your pardon?"

"You don't have a window. I just wondered if you ever kind of lost touch with what was going on outside, being cooped up in here all day with the air conditioning and the fluorescent lighting." It was the first time in my life I'd ever said anything like "fluorescent lighting" out loud.

"As you recall, I came to your house on the evening that your, that April was assaulted." Cynthia always called Turtle by her more conventional name. "I do my share of field work,"[9] she said.

"Of course."

"Have I answered your questions, Taylor?"

"Mostly. Not completely. I'd like to know how a person would go about finding the information you mentioned. About the laws in different states. Like Oklahoma, for instance."

▶ *What does Cynthia say she can do for Taylor?*

"I can look that up and get back to you. If you like, I can get you the name of someone in Oklahoma City who could help you formalize the papers."

This took me by surprise. "You'd be willing to help me out?"

"Certainly. I'm on your side here, Taylor." She leaned forward and folded her hands on her desk blotter, and I noticed her fingernails were in bad shape. It's possible that Cynthia was a nailbiter.

9. **field work.** Work conducted outside the office

words for everyday use

con • ven • tion • al (kən ven′ shə nəl) *adj.*, ordinary; customary; normal; lacking originality. *Rather than painting rooms the conventional off-white, people are using colors like red, gold, and plum.*

"Are you saying that you'd rather see Turtle stay with me than go into a state home?"

"There has never been any doubt in my mind about that."

I stood up, walked around the chair, and sat down again. "Excuse my French, but why in hell didn't you say so before now?"

She blinked her gold-coin eyes. "I thought that ought to be your decision."

At the end of my hour I was halfway out the door, but then stopped and came back, closing the door behind me. "Thank you," I said.

"You're welcome."

"Can I ask you a kind of personal question? It's about the cameo brooch."

She looked amused. "You can ask," she said.

"Do you have to shop at the Salvation Army? I mean, is it because of your pay, or do you just like rummaging through other people's family heirlooms?"

"I'm a trained therapist," Cynthia said, smiling. "I don't answer questions like that."

Out in the lobby I stopped to chat with one of the secretaries, who asked where my little girl was today. The secretary's name was Jewel. I had spoken with her several times before. She had a son with dyslexia, which she explained was a disease that caused people to see things backwards. "Like the American flag, for instance," she said. "The way he would see it would be that the stars are up in the right-hand corner, instead of the left. But then there's other things where it doesn't matter. Like you take the word WOW, for instance. That's his favorite word, he writes it all over everything. And the word MOM, too."

Before I had gotten around to leaving the building, another secretary came hustling over and handed me a note, which she said was from Cynthia. It said, "I appreciate your sensitivity in not wishing to discuss April's custody in her presence. I'm sorry if I have been careless."

◀ *What does the note from Cynthia say?*

There was also a name: Mr. Jonas Wilford Armistead—along with an Oklahoma City address—and underneath, the words "Good luck!"

words for everyday use

heir • loom (ār' lüm) *n.,* something of special value passed on from one generation to the next. *The silver tray is a family heirloom handed down from my great-grandmother.*

All evening, after I'd fed the kids and put them to bed, I paced the house. I couldn't wait for Lou Ann to get home, but then when she did I wasn't sure I wanted to tell her anything yet. I hadn't completely made up my mind.

"For heaven's sake," Lou Ann said, "you're making me nervous. Either sit down or wash the dishes." I washed the dishes.

"Whatever's on your mind, I hope you get it settled," she said, and went to the living room to read. She had been reading a novel called *Daughter of the Cheyenne Winds,* which she claimed she had found in her locker at Red Hot Mama's, and had nothing whatever to do with Angel being on the Montana-Colorado Circuit.

I followed her into the living room. "You're not mad are you? Because I don't want to talk about it?"

"Nope."

"I'll tell you tomorrow. I just have to think some more."

She didn't look up. "Go think," she said. "Think, and wash the dishes."

I didn't sleep at all that night. I was getting used to it. I watched Turtle roll from her side to her stomach and back again. Her eyes rolled back and forth under her eyelids, and sometimes her mouth worked too. Whoever she was talking to in her dream, she told them a whole lot more than she'd ever told me. I would have paid good money to be in that dream.

In the morning I left her asleep and went to Mattie's to finish an alignment and front-and-rear rotation I'd left undone the previous afternoon. The guy was coming in sometime that day to pick it up. I didn't look at a clock but it must have been early when I went in because I was already finished and ready to go home before Mattie came downstairs. I hung around a while longer, making coffee and dusting the shelves and changing the calendar (it was still on May, and this was August). I stared for a long time at the picture of the Aztec man carrying the passed-out woman, thinking about whatever Latin American tragedy it stood for. Thinking, naturally, of Esperanza and Estevan. Though I knew that more often than not it was the other way around, the woman carried the man through the tragedy. The man and the grandma and all the kids.

Finally Mattie came down. We had a cup of coffee, and we talked.

Afterward I found Lou Ann and the kids in the park. Turtle was amusing herself by sweeping a patch of dirt with an old hairbrush, presumably Edna's since it was red, and Lou Ann had momentarily put aside *Daughter of the Cheyenne Winds* to engage in a contest of will with Dwayne Ray. Lou Ann was bound to win, of course.

"I said no! Give it to me right now. Where'd you get that from?" She grabbed his fist, which was headed on an automatic-pilot course for his mouth, and extracted a dirt-covered purple jelly bean. "Where in the heck do you think he got that? My God, Taylor, just imagine if he'd eaten it!"

Dwayne Ray's mouth remained in the shape of an O for several seconds, still expecting the intercepted jelly bean, and then he started to scream.

"I used to know this old farm woman that said you've got to eat a peck of dirt before you die," I said.

Lou Ann picked up Dwayne Ray and bounced him. "Well, maybe if you don't eat a peck of dirt before your first birthday then you won't die so quick, is what I say."

I sat down on the bench. "Listen, I've made up my mind about something. I'm going to drive Esperanza and Estevan to a safe house[10] in Oklahoma. And while I'm there I'm going to see if I can find any of Turtle's relatives."

◀ *What has Taylor made up her mind to do?*

She stared at me. Dwayne Ray came down on her knee with a bump, and was stunned into being quiet.

"What for?"

"So they can sign her over to me."

"Well, what if they won't? What if they see how good she's turning out and decide they want her back?"

"I don't think they will."

"But what if they do?"

"Damn it, Lou Ann, you've been telling me till you were blue in the face to do something, take action, think positive, blah, blah, blah. I'm trying to think positive here."

"Sorry."

"What other choice have I got than to go? If I just sit here on my hands, then they take her."

"I know. You're right."

"If her relatives want her back, then I'll think of something. We'll cut that fence when we come to it."

"What if you can't find them? Sorry."

"I'll find them."

---

10. **safe house.** Place where one may take refuge

words for everyday use

ex • tract (ik strakt') *v.,* to pull or take out forcibly. *Mama used tweezers to extract the splinter from my hand.*

in • ter • cept (in tər sept') *v.,* stop, seize, or interrupt in progress or course before arrival. *Our teacher was sharp and managed to intercept the note that was being passed from one side of the classroom to the other.*

▶ *What is the possible penalty if Taylor gets caught aiding Estevan and Esperanza?*

▶ *What does Taylor point out to Mattie about getting caught?*

▶ *Why does Taylor think Mattie is mad at her?*

Lou Ann, uncharacteristically, had overlooked the number-one thing I ought to be worried about. Over the next few days Mattie asked me about fifty times if I was sure I knew what I was doing. She told me that if I got caught I could get five years in prison and a $2,000 fine for each illegal person I was assisting, which in this case would be two. To tell the truth, I couldn't even let these things enter my head.

But Mattie persisted. "This isn't just hypothetical. It's actually happened before that people got caught."

"I don't know why you're worried about me," I told her. "Esperanza and Estevan would get a whole lot worse than prison and a fine."

I did suggest to Mattie, though, that it might be a good idea to fix the ignition on Two-Two, my VW, now that we were setting out across the country again. She looked at me as though I had suggested shooting an elected official.

"You are *not* taking that old thing," she said. "You'll take the Lincoln.[11] It's got a lot of room, and it's reliable."

I was offended. "What's wrong with my car?" I wanted to know.

"What's wrong with it, child, I could stand here telling you till the sun went down. And just about any one of those things could get you pulled over by a cop. If you think you care so much about Esperanza and Estevan, you'd better start using that head of yours for something besides thinking up smart remarks." Mattie walked off. I'd seen her bordering on mad before, but never at me. Clearly she did not want me to go.

The night before I was to leave, Virgie Mae Parsons came knocking on the door. It was late but Lou Ann and I were still up, going round and round about what I ought to pack. She thought I should take my very best clothes in case I might have to impress someone with my financial security. She was sure that at the very least I ought to take a pair of stockings, which I would have to borrow from Lou Ann, not being in the habit of owning such things myself. I pointed out to her that it was the middle of summer and I didn't think I'd need to impress anyone that much. We didn't notice a timid little peck at the door until it grew considerably louder. Then Lou Ann was afraid to answer it.

I looked out the window. "It's Virgie Mae, for heaven's sake," I said, and let her in.

11. **Lincoln.** Brand of luxury automobile

She stood looking befuddled for a second or two, then pulled herself together and said, "Edna said I ought to come over and get you. We have something the children might like to see, if you don't think it would do too much harm to wake them."

"What, a surprise?" Lou Ann asked. She was back in less than a minute with Dwayne Ray in one arm and Turtle by the other hand. Turtle trailed grumpily behind, whereas Dwayne Ray chose to remain asleep, his head bobbing like an old stuffed animal's. In the intervening minute I had not extracted any further information from Virgie.

We followed her out our front door and up the walk to their porch. I could make out Edna sitting in the glider, and in the corner of the porch we saw what looked like a bouquet of silvery-white balloons hanging in the air.

Flowers.

A night-blooming cereus, Virgie Mae explained. The flowers open for only one night of the year, and then they are gone.

◀ What does Virgie Mae show Taylor, Lou Ann, and the children? What is special about it?

It was a huge, sprawling plant with branches that flopped over the porch railing and others that reached nearly as high as the eaves. I had certainly noticed it before, standing in the corner in its crumbling pot, flattened and spiny and frankly extremely homely, and it had crossed my mind to wonder why Virgie Mae didn't throw the thing out.

"I've never seen anything so heavenly," Lou Ann said.

Enormous blossoms covered the plant from knee level to high above our heads. Turtle advanced on it slowly, walking right up to one of the flowers, which was larger than her face. It hung in the dark air like a magic mirror just inches from her eyes. It occurred to me that she should be warned of the prickles, but if Lou Ann wasn't going to say anything I certainly wasn't. I knelt beside Turtle.

There was hardly any moon that night, but gradually our eyes were able to take in more and more detail. The flowers themselves were not spiny, but made of some nearly transparent material that looked as though it would shrivel and bruise if you touched it. The petals stood out in starry rays, and in the center of each flower there was a complicated construction of silvery threads shaped like a

words for everyday use

be • fud • dle (bi fə' dəl) *v.*, daze; confuse; fluster. *It seemed to befuddle Jane when we all yelled "Surprise," but a moment later, her face broke into a huge smile.*

in • ter • vene (in tər vēn') *v.*, to occur between points of time or events. *Intermissions are short breaks of ten to fifteen minutes that intervene between the first and second halves of a play or concert.*

pair of cupped hands catching moonlight. A fairy boat, ready to be launched into the darkness.

"Is that?" Turtle wanted to know. She touched it, and it did not shrivel, but only swayed a little on the end of its long green branch.

"It's a flower, dear," Virgie said.

Lou Ann said, "She knows that much. She can tell you the name of practically every flower in the Burpee's catalogue, even things that only grow in Florida and Nova Scotia."

"Cereus," I said. Even its name sounded silvery and mysterious.

"See us," Turtle repeated.

Lou Ann nosed into a flower at eye level and reported that it had a smell. She held Dwayne Ray up to it, but he didn't seem especially awake. "I can just barely make it out," she said, "but it's so sweet. Tart, almost, like that lemon candy in a straw that I used to die for when I was a kid. It's just ever so faint."

▶ *Why is Edna the one to notice when the cereus blooms?*

"I can smell it from here." Edna spoke from the porch swing.

"Edna's the one who spots it," Virgie said. "If it was up to me I would never notice to save my life. Because they come out after dark, you see, and I forget to watch for the buds. One year Edna had a head cold and we missed it altogether."

Lou Ann's eyes were as wide and starry as the flower she stared into. She was as captivated as Turtle.

"It's a sign," she said.

▶ *What does Lou Ann say the cereus is a sign of?*

"Of what?" I wanted to know.

"I don't know," she said quietly. "Something good."

"I can get the pruning shears and cut one off for you, if you like," Virgie Mae offered. "If you put it in the icebox it will last until tomorrow."

But Lou Ann shook her head. "No thanks. I want to remember them like this, in the dark."

"After you pluck them they lose their fragrance," Edna told us. "I don't know why, but it just goes right away."

If the night-blooming cereus was an omen of anything, it was of good weather for traveling. The morning was overcast and cool. Once again we rolled the children out of

words for everyday use

o • men (ō′ mən) *n.,* occurrence believed to foreshadow a future event; sign; premonition. *To those who are superstitious, a black cat crossing one's path is an omen of bad things to come.*

bed, and Lou Ann and Dwayne Ray came with us over to Mattie's. Turtle wanted to be carried, like Dwayne Ray, but we had the bags to deal with.

"We'll just walk this little way," I told her. "Then you can sleep in the car for a long time."

Estevan and Esperanza had one suitcase between them and it was smaller than mine, which did not even include Turtle's stuff. I had packed for a week, ten days at the outside, and they were packed for the rest of their lives.

Several people had come to see them off, including the elderly woman I had once seen upstairs at Mattie's and a very young woman with a small child, who could have been her daughter or her sister, or no relation for that matter. There was lots of hugging and kissing and talking in Spanish. Mattie moved around quickly, introducing people and putting our things in the car and giving me hundreds of last-minute instructions.

"You might have to choke her good and hard to get her going in the mornings," Mattie told me, and in my groggy state it took me a while to understand whom or what I was supposed to be choking. "She's tuned for Arizona. I don't know how she'll do in Oklahoma."

"She'll do fine," I said. "Remember, I'm used to cantankerous cars."

"I know. You'll do fine," she said, but didn't seem convinced.

After we had gotten in and fastened our seat belts, on Mattie's orders, she leaned in the window and slipped something into my hand. It was money. Esperanza and Estevan were leaning out the windows on the other side, spelling out something—surely not an address—very slowly to the elderly woman, who was writing it down on the back of a window envelope.

"Where did this come from?" I asked Mattie quietly. "We can get by."

"Take it, you thick-headed youngun. Not for your sake, for theirs." She squeezed my hand over the money. "Poverty-stricken isn't the safest way to go."

"You didn't answer my question."

words for everyday use

can • tan • ker • ous (kan taŋ ′ kə rəs) *adj.*, difficult or irritating to deal with; crabby; quarrelsome. *Vanda stayed up all night to finish her project, so the next day she was cantankerous, snapping at anyone who spoke to her.*

▶ *Where does Mattie say the money comes from? What does Mattie say about some folks and other folks?*

▶ *What reasons does Taylor give for what she is doing? What does Taylor say about being a hero?*

"It comes from people, Taylor, and let's just leave it. Some folks are the heroes and take the risks, and other folks do what they can from behind the scenes."

"Mattie, would you please shut up about heroes and prison and all."

"I didn't say prison."

"Just stop it, okay? Estevan and Esperanza are my friends. And, even if they weren't, I can't see why I shouldn't do this. If I saw somebody was going to get hit by a truck I'd push them out of the way. Wouldn't anybody? It's a sad day for us all if I'm being a hero here."

She looked at me the way Mama would have.

"Stop it," I said again. "You're going to make me cry." I started the engine and it turned over with an astonishing purr, like a lioness waking up from her nap. "This is the good life, cars that start by themselves," I said.

"When I hired you, it was for fixing tires. Just fixing tires, do you understand that?"

"I know."

"As long as you know."

"I do."

She reached in the window and gave me a hug, and I actually did start crying. She put kisses on her hand and reached across and put them on Esperanza's and Estevan's cheeks, and then Turtle's.

"Bless your all's hearts," she said. "Take good care."

"Be careful," Lou Ann said.

Mattie and Lou Ann and the others stood in the early-morning light holding kids and waving. It could have been the most ordinary family picture, except for the backdrop of whitewall tires. Esperanza and Turtle waved until they were out of sight. I kept blinking my eyelids like windshield wipers, trying to keep a clear view of the road.

On Mattie's advice we took one of the city roads out of town, and would join up with the freeway just south of the city limits.

Outside of town we passed a run-over blackbird in the road, flattened on the center line. As the cars and trucks rolled by, the gusts of wind caused one stiff wing to flap up and down in a pitiful little flagging-down gesture. My instinct was to step on the brakes, but of course there was no earthly reason to stop for a dead bird.

Respond to the Selection

Taylor is willing to risk going to prison to help Estevan and Esperanza. Do you think her actions are heroic? Have you ever risked getting into trouble to help a friend?

Investigate, Inquire, and Imagine

Recall: Gathering Facts

Interpret: Finding Meaning

1a. How does Lou Ann react to Angel's request that she join him Montana? How does Lou Ann react to what happens to Turtle at the park? How does Lou Ann react to the news that Taylor receives from the social worker? What does she want to Taylor to do?

→ 1b. In what ways has Lou Ann changed?

2a. How do the Indians of the desert look upon the first summer rain?

→ 2b. The first summer rain is a time of renewal and starting over for the Indians of the desert. In what ways are the lives of Lou Ann, Taylor, Turtle, Estevan, and Esperanza changing or about to change?

3a. Why does Virgie Mae summon Taylor, Lou Ann, and the children to see the night-blooming cereus? As Turtle walks up and stands face to face with it, how does the author describe it? What does it seem would happen if you touched the flowers? Does that happen when Turtle touches a flower?

→ 3b. Amid Lou Ann's fears of freak accidents and death, and the experiences that Estevan, Esperanza, and Turtle have endured, what is so special and significant about the night-blooming cereus? What is particularly significant about the image of Turtle staring into the flower and what the author compares the flower to? How is Turtle like the night-blooming cereus?

Analyze: TAKING THINGS APART

4a. As a result of what happened to Turtle in the park, what fears and doubts does Taylor develop regarding her ability to care for Turtle? As a result of finding out what has happened and what is happening to Estevan and Esperanza, what aspects of society does Taylor begin to criticize? Provide evidence from the story to support your answer.

Synthesize: BRINGING THINGS TOGETHER

→ 4b. How have the incident that happened to Turtle and learning the details of Estevan and Esperanza's story changed Taylor and the way she views the world?

Perspective: LOOKING AT OTHER VIEWS

5a. Consider how "having proof" is addressed in the story. What does "having proof" have to do with the story of Estevan and Esperanza and the situation Taylor finds herself in? What are the likely consequences in each situation if that proof cannot be provided? In your opinion, are Taylor, Estevan, and Esperanza justified in doing whatever is necessary to avoid the consequences of their lack of proof? Explain.

Empathy: SEEING FROM INSIDE

→ 5b. Consider the decision that Taylor makes to drive Estevan and Esperanza to a safe church in Oklahoma and to search for Turtle's relatives in the Cherokee Nation. What risks does Taylor assume when she makes this decision? What are the motivations behind her decision? If you were in Taylor's situation, do you think you would make the same decision? Why, or why not?

Understanding Literature

PLOT, SUBPLOT, AND CONFLICT. A **plot** is a series of events related to a central conflict or struggle. A plot usually involves the introduction of a conflict, its development, and its eventual resolution. The main plot of *The Bean Trees* is the story of Taylor and Turtle. A **subplot** is a subordinate story told in addition to the major story in a work of fiction. Often a subplot mirrors or contrasts with the primary plot. The story of Estevan and Esperanza is one subplot. The story of Lou Ann and Angel is another subplot. A **conflict** is a struggle between two people or things in a literary work. A conflict can be internal or external. A struggle that takes place between a character and some outside force such as another character, society, or nature is called an *external conflict.* A struggle that takes place within a character is called an *internal conflict.*

Plot/Subplots	Central Conflict	Internal/External
Main plot: Taylor and Turtle		
Subplot: Estevan and Esperanza		
Subplot: Lou Ann and Angel		

Use the chart above as a model for recording your answers to the following questions.

In Chapter 13, Cynthia, the social worker, presents Taylor with information that makes clear the central conflict of the main plot. What is the central conflict of the novel? Is it an internal or external conflict? Explain. Mattie provides Taylor with the information that makes apparent the central conflict of Estevan and Esperanza's subplot. What is the central conflict of this subplot? Is it an internal or external conflict? Explain.

The central conflict of Lou Ann's subplot is not as easy to identify because it does not get as much attention. However, it comes into focus in Chapter 11 when Angel sends Lou Ann a package and asks her to get back together. What is the central conflict of this subplot? Is it an internal or external conflict? Explain.

Mood. Mood, or *atmosphere,* is the emotion created in the reader by all or part of a literary work. By working carefully with descriptive language and sensory details, the writer can evoke in the reader an emotional response. What images from the natural world help to create a mood of anticipation before the storm? What does Mattie say about all the things that looked dead before the storm? How do images from the natural world create a mood of purification and renewal after the storm?

Foreshadowing. Foreshadowing presents materials that hint at events to occur later in the story. In Chapter 12, the storm and the renewal and purification that follow it foreshadow events that will occur in the rest of the novel. What other examples of foreshadowing can you find in the novel so far?

Fourteen

Guardian Saints

We were stopped by Immigration about a hundred miles this side of the New Mexico border. Mattie had warned me of this possibility and we had all prepared for it as best we could. Esperanza and Estevan were dressed about as American as you could get without looking plain obnoxious: he had on jeans and an alligator shirt donated from some church on the east side where people gave away stuff that was entirely a cut above New To You. Esperanza was wearing purple culottes,[1] a yellow T-shirt, and sunglasses with pink frames. She sat in the back seat with Turtle. Her long hair was loose, not braided, and as we sped down the highway it whipped around her shoulders and out the window, putting on a brave show of freedom that had nothing to do with Esperanza's life. Twice I asked if it was too much wind on her, and each time she shook her head no.

Every eastbound car on the highway was being stopped by the Border Patrol. The traffic was bottled up, which gave us time to get good and nervous. This kind of check was routine; it had not been set up for the express purpose of catching us, but it still felt that way. To all of us, I believe. I was frantic. I rattled my teeth, as Mama would say.

"There's this great place up ahead called Texas Canyon," I told them, knowing full well that none of us might make it to Texas Canyon. Esperanza and Estevan might not make it to their next birthday. "Wait till you see it. It's got all these puffy-looking rocks," I chattered on. "Turtle and I loved it."

They nodded quietly.

When our turn came I threw back my head like a wealthy person, yanked that Lincoln into gear and pulled up to the corrugated tin booth. A young officer poked his head in the car. I could smell his aftershave.

"All U.S. citizens?" he asked.

"Yes," I said. I showed my driver's license. "This is my brother Steve, and my sister-in-law."

▶ Why did Estevan say that Turtle is his and Esperanza's daughter?

The officer nodded politely. "The kid yours or theirs?"

I looked at Estevan, which was a stupid thing to do.

"She's ours," Estevan said, without a trace of an accent.

The officer waved us through. "Have a nice day," he said.

After we had passed well beyond the checkpoint Estevan started apologizing. "I thought it would be the most believable thing. Since you hesitated."

1. **culottes.** Shorts

"Yeah, I did."

"You looked at me. I thought it might seem suspicious if I said she was yours. He might wonder why you didn't say it."

"I know, I know, I know. You're right. It's no problem. The only thing that matters is we made it through." It did bother me though, just as it bothered me that Turtle was calling Esperanza "Ma." Which was a completely unreasonable thing to resent, I know, since Turtle called every woman Ma something. There's no way she could have managed "Esperanza."

We got out at the rest station in Texas Canyon. It turned out there weren't rest rooms there, just picnic tables, so I took Turtle behind a giant marshmallow-shaped boulder. Ever since I'd found out she was three years old, we'd gotten very serious about potty training.

When we came back Estevan and Esperanza were standing by the guard rail looking out over an endless valley of boulders. A large wooden sign, which showed dinosaurs and giant ferny trees and mountains exploding in the background, explained that this was the lava flow from a volcanic explosion long ago. Along with the initials and hearts scratched into the sign with pocket knives, someone had carved "Repent."

The setting did more or less put you in that frame of mind. There wasn't a bush or tree in sight, just rocks and rocks, sky and more sky. Estevan said this is what the world would have looked like if God had gone on strike after the second day.

It was a peculiar notion, but then you had to consider Estevan's background with the teachers' union. He would think in those terms.

They seemed uncomfortable out of the car so we stayed on the move after that, driving down an endless river of highway. After my VW, driving Mattie's wide white car felt like steering a boat, not that I had ever actually steered anything of the kind. Estevan and Esperanza didn't have proper drivers' licenses, of course—that was the very least of what they didn't have—so to be on the safe side I did all the driving. The first night we would try to go straight through, pulling over for naps when I needed to. Lou Ann had made us a Thermos of iced coffee. For the second night, I told them, I knew of a nice motor lodge in Oklahoma where we could most likely stay for free.

Estevan and I talked about everything you can think of. He asked me if the alligator was a national symbol of the

◀ *What does Estevan ask Taylor about the alligator? Why?*

▶ *What is the national symbol of Guatemalan Indians? What happens if the bird is caged?*

▶ *Why do Estevan and Esperanza speak Spanish to each other?*

▶ *What does Estevan tell Taylor about Mayans?*

United States, because you saw them everywhere on people's shirts, just above the heart.

"Not that I know of," I told him. It occurred to me, though, that it might be kind of appropriate.

He told me that the national symbol of the Indian people in Guatemala was the quetzal, a beautiful green bird with a long, long tail. I told him I had seen military macaws at the zoo, and wondered if the quetzal was anything like those. He said no. If you tried to keep this bird in a cage, it died.

Shortly after sunset we left the interstate to take a two-lane road that cut through the mountains and would take about two hundred miles of New Mexico off our trip. I wished we could keep New Mexico in and cut out two hundred miles of Oklahoma instead, but of course Oklahoma was where we were going. I had to keep reminding myself of that. For some reason I had in the back of my mind that we were headed for Kentucky. I kept picturing Mama's face when we all pulled up in the driveway.

I squinted and flashed my lights at a car coming toward us with its brights on. They dimmed.

"Do you miss your home a lot?" I asked Estevan. "I know that's a stupid question. But does it make you tired, being so far away from what you know? That's how I feel sometimes that I would just like to crawl in a hole somewhere and rest. Go dormant, like those toad frogs Mattie told us about. And for you it's just that much worse; you're not even speaking your own language."

He let out a long breath. "I don't even know anymore which home I miss. Which level of home. In Guatemala City I missed the mountains. My own language is not Spanish, did you know that?"

I told him no, that I didn't.

"We are Mayan people, we speak twenty-two different Mayan languages. Esperanza and I speak to each other in Spanish because we come from different parts of the highlands."

"What's Mayan, exactly?"

"Mayans lived here in the so-called New World before the Europeans discovered it. We're very old people. In those days we had astronomical observatories, and performed brain surgery."

I thought of the color pictures in my grade-school history books: Columbus striding up the beach in his leotards and feathered hat, a gang of wild-haired red men in loin cloths scattering in front of him like rabbits. What a joke.

"Our true first names are Indian names," Estevan said. "You couldn't even pronounce them. We chose Spanish names when we moved to the city."

I was amazed. "So Esperanza is bilingual. You're, what do you call it? Trilingual."

I knew that Esperanza spoke some English too, but it was hard to say how much since she spoke it so rarely. One time I had admired a little gold medallion she always wore around her neck and she said, with an accent, but plainly enough: "That is St. Christopher, guardian saint of refugees." I would have been no more surprised if St. Christopher himself had spoken.

Christopher was a sweet-faced saint. He looked a lot like Stephen Foster, who I suppose you could say was the guardian saint of Kentucky. At least he wrote the state song.

"I chose a new name for myself too, when I left home," I said to Estevan. "We all have that in common."

"You did? What was it before?"

I made a face. "Marietta."

He laughed. "It's not so bad."

"It's a town in Georgia where Mama's and my father's car broke down once, I guess, when they were on their way to Florida. They never made it. They stayed in a motel and made me instead."

"What a romantic story."

"Not really. I was a mistake. Well, not really a mistake, according to Mama, but an accident. A mistake I guess is when you regret it later."

"And they didn't?"

"Mama didn't. That's all that counts, in my case."

"So Papa went on to Florida?"

"Or wherever."

"Esperanza also grew up without her father. The circumstances were different, of course."

In the back seat Esperanza was stroking Turtle's hair and singing to her quietly in a high, unearthly voice. I had heard enough Spanish to understand that the way her voice was dipping and gliding through the words was more foreign than that. I remembered Estevan's yodely songs the day of our first picnic. They had to have been Mayan songs, not Spanish. Songs older than Christopher Columbus, maybe even older than Christopher the saint. I wondered if, when they still had Ismene, they had sung to her in both their own languages. To think how languages could accumulate in a family, in a country like that. When I thought of Guatemala I imagined a storybook place: jungles full of

◀ *What does Taylor picture when she thinks of Guatemala?*

long-tailed birds, women wearing rainbow-threaded dresses.

▶ *What other things does Taylor know are also part of the picture?*

But of course there was more to the picture. Police everywhere, always. Whole villages of Indians forced to move again and again. As soon as they planted their crops, Estevan said, the police would come and set their houses and fields on fire and make them move again. The strategy was to wear them down so they'd be too tired or too hungry to fight back.

Turtle had fallen asleep with her head in Esperanza's lap.

▶ *What does Taylor want to know about Indians?*

"What's with everybody always trying to get rid of the Indians?" I said, not really asking for an answer. I thought again of the history-book pictures. Astronomers and brain surgeons. They should have done brain surgery on Columbus while they had the chance.

▶ *What does Estevan hate?*

After a while Estevan said, "What I really hate is not belonging in any place. To be unwanted everywhere."

I thought of my Cherokee great-grandfather, his people who believed God lived in trees, and that empty Oklahoma plain they were driven to like livestock. But then, even the Cherokee Nation was *someplace.*

▶ *What does Taylor say you can't say about a person?*

"You know what really gets me?" I asked him. "How people call you 'illegals.' That just pisses me off, I don't know how you can stand it. A human being can be good or bad or right or wrong, maybe. But how can you say a person is illegal?"

"I don't know. You tell me."

"You just can't," I said. "That's all there is to it."

On the second day we got into flatlands. The Texas panhandle, and then western Oklahoma, stretched out all around us like a colossal pancake. There was no way of judging where you were against where you were going, and as a consequence you tended to start feeling you were stuck out there, rolling your wheels on some trick prairie treadmill.

Estevan, who had apparently spent some time on a ship, said it reminded him of the ocean. He knew a Spanish word for the kind of mental illness you get from seeing too much horizon. Esperanza seemed stunned at first, then a little scared. She asked Estevan, who translated for me, whether or not we were near Washington. I assured her we weren't, and asked what made her think so. She said she thought they might build the President's palace in a place like this, so that if anyone came after him his guards could spot them a long way off.

To keep ourselves from going crazy with boredom we tried to think of word games. I told about the secretary named Jewel with the son who sees things backwards, and we tried to think of words he would like. Esperanza thought of *ala,* which means wing. Estevan knew whole sentences, some in Spanish and some in English. The English ones were "A man, a plan, a canal: Panama!" (which he said was a typical gringo way of looking at that endeavor), and "Able was I ere I saw Elba," which was what Napoleon[2] supposedly said when he was sent into exile. I hadn't known, before then, where or what Elba was. I'd had a vague idea that it was a kind of toast.

Turtle was the only one of us who didn't seem perturbed by the landscape. She told Esperanza a kind of ongoing story, which lasted for hundreds of miles and sounded like a vegetarian version of Aesop's Fables, and when she ran out of story she played with her baby doll. The doll was a hand-me-down from Mattie's. It came with a pair of red-checked pajamas, complete with regular-sized shirt buttons, that someone had apparently sewn by hand. Turtle adored the doll and had named it, with no help from anyone, Shirley Poppy.

We bypassed Oklahoma City and headed north on I-35, reversing the route I had taken through Oklahoma the first time. We reached the Broken Arrow Motor Lodge by late afternoon. At first I thought the place had changed hands. Which it had, in a way: Mrs. Hoge had died, and Irene was a different person, a slipcover of her former self. She had lost 106 pounds in 24 weeks by eating one Weight Watchers frozen dinner per day and nothing else but chamomile tea, unsweetened.

"I told Boyd if he wanted something different he could learn to cook it himself. Anybody that can butcher a side of beef can learn to cook," she explained. She had started the diet on her doctor's advice, when she decided she wanted to have a baby.

Irene seemed thrilled to see Turtle and me again and insisted on feeding the whole bunch of us. She made a pot roast with onions and potatoes even though she couldn't

2. **Napoleon.** The Emperor of France from 1804–1815

words for everyday use

ex • ile (eg′ zīl) *n.,* the state or period of forced absence from one's country or home. *Refugees in exile from their homeland hope to return when the political situation becomes stable.*

per • turb (pər tərb′) *v.,* disturb; agitate; distract. *The loud buzzing of the weed trimmer next door began to perturb me.*

touch it herself. She told us Mrs. Hoge had passed away in January, just a few weeks after I left.

"We knew it was coming, of course," she said to Esperanza and Estevan. "She had the disease where you shake all the time."

"That was a disease?" I asked. "I had no idea it was something you could die from. I thought it was just old age."

"No," Irene shook her head gravely. "Parkerson's."[3]

"Who?" I asked.

"That's the disease," she said. "I notice she's talking now." She meant Turtle, who was busily naming every vegetable on Esperanza's plate. She named them individually so it went like this: "Tato, carrot, carrot, carrot, carrot, tato, onion," et cetera. Toward the end of the meal she also said "car," because underneath all the food the plates had pictures of old-timey cars on them.

After the others went to bed I stayed up with Irene, who was expecting her husband in from Ponca City after midnight. We sat on high stools behind the desk in the bright front office, looking out through the plate glass at the highway and the long, flat plain behind it. She told me she missed Mrs. Hoge something fierce.

"Oh, I know she wasn't *kind,*" Irene said, her thinned-down bosom heaving with a long, sad sigh. "It was always 'Here's my daughter-in-law Irene that can't make up a bed with hospital corners and is proud of it.' But really I think she meant well."

▶ *What decision do Estevan and Esperanza make in the morning?*

The next morning we had to make a decision. Either we would go straight to the sanctuary church, which was a little to the east of Oklahoma City, or we could all stay together for another day. They could come with me to the bar where I'd been presented with Turtle, to help me look for whatever I thought I was going to find in the way of Turtle's relatives. I admitted to them that I could use the moral support, but on the other hand I would understand if they didn't want to risk being on the road any more than they had to be. Without hesitation, they said they wanted to go with me.

Retracing my original route became a little more complicated. I had left the interstate highway when my steering column set itself free, that much I knew, and I'd stayed on a side road for several hours before joining back up with the main highway. I could remember hardly any

3. **Parkerson's.** Parkinson's, a disease marked by tremors and weakness of the muscles

exact details from that night, in the way of landmarks, and of course there were precious few there to begin with.

The clue that tipped me off was a sign to the Pioneer Woman Museum. I remembered that. We found a two-lane road that I was pretty sure was the right one.

As soon as we left the interstate, trading the fast out-of-state tourist cars for the companionship of station wagons and pickup trucks packed with families, we were on the Cherokee Nation. You could feel it. We began to understand that Oklahoma had been a good choice: Estevan and Esperanza could blend in here. Practically half the people we saw were Indians.

◀ *What becomes clear about Oklahoma? Why?*

"Do Cherokees look like Mayans?" I asked Estevan.

"No," he said.

"Would a white person know that?"

"No."

After a little bit I asked him, "Would a Cherokee?"

"Maybe, maybe not." He was smiling his perfect smile.

I asked Turtle if anything looked familiar. When I looked in the rear-view mirror I caught sight of her on Esperanza's lap, playing with Esperanza's hair and trying on Esperanza's sunglasses. Later I saw them playing a clapping-hands game. The two of them looked perfectly content: "Madonna and Child with Pink Sunglasses." Nobody, not even a Mayan, could say they weren't. One time I thought—though I couldn't swear it—I heard her call Turtle Ismene. I was getting a cold feeling in the bottom of my stomach.

◀ *What does Taylor think she heard Esperanza call Turtle? How does it make her feel?*

I tried to keep myself cheerful. "I always tell Turtle she's as good as the ones that came over on the *Mayflower,*" I told Estevan. "They landed at Plymouth Rock. She just landed in a Plymouth."

Estevan didn't laugh. In all fairness, I might not have told him before that she was born in a car, but also he was preoccupied, going over and over the life history he had invented for himself and his Cherokee bride. He was quite imaginative. He had a whole little side plot about how his parents had disapproved of the marriage, but had softened their hearts when they saw what a lovely woman Hope was.

"Steven and Hope," he said. "But we need a last name."

"How about Two Two?" I said. "That's a good solid Cherokee name. It's been in my family for months."

"Two Two," he repeated solemnly.

I missed my own car. I missed Lou Ann, who always laughed at my jokes.

I was positive I wouldn't recognize the place, if it was even still there, but as soon as I laid eyes on it I knew. A little brick building with a Budweiser sign, and across the parking lot a garage. The garage looked closed.

"That's it," I said. I slowed down. "What do I do?"

"Stop the car," Estevan suggested, but I kept going. My heart was pounding like a piston. A quarter of a mile down the road I stopped.

"I'm sorry, but I can't do this," I said.

We all sat quietly for a minute.

▶ *What does Taylor say is the worst thing that could happen if she goes looking for Turtle's relatives?*

"What is the worst thing that can happen?" Estevan asked.

"I don't know. That I won't find anybody that knows Turtle. Or that I will, and they'll want her back." I thought for a minute. "The worst thing would be that we lose her, some way," I said finally.

"What if you don't go in?"

"We lose her."

Estevan gave me a hug. "For courage," he said. Then Esperanza gave me a hug. Then Turtle did. I turned the car around and drove back to the bar.

"First let me go in alone," I said.

It looked like a different place. I remembered all the signs—IN CASE OF FIRE YELL FIRE. They were gone. Blue gingham curtains hung in the windows and there were glasses of plastic roses and bachelor buttons on all the tables. I would have walked right out again, but I recognized the TV. Good picture, but no sound. And there was the same postcard rack too, although it seemed to have changed its focus, placing more emphasis on scenic lakes and less on Oral Roberts University.

A teenaged girl in jeans and an apron came through a door from the kitchen. She had a round Indian face behind large, blue-rimmed glasses.

"Get you some coffee?" she asked cheerfully.

"Okay," I said, and sat down at the counter.

"Now, what else can I do for you?"

"I'm not sure. I'm looking for somebody."

"Oh, who? Were you meeting them here for lunch?"

"No, it's not like that. It's kind of complicated. I was in here last December and met some people I have to find again. I think they might live around here. It's very important."

She leaned on her elbows on the counter. "What was their names?"

"I don't know. There was a woman, and two men in cowboy hats. I think one of them might have been her husband, or her boyfriend. I know, this isn't getting anywhere. Ed knew their names."

"Ed?"

"Isn't that who runs this place?"

"No. My parents own it. We bought it in March, I think. Or April."

"Well, would your parents know Ed? Would he be around here?"

She shrugged. "The place was just up for sale. I think whoever owned it before musta died. It was gross in here."

"You mean he died *in here?"*

She laughed. "No, I just mean all the dirt and stuff. I had to scrub the grease off the back of the stove. It was *black.* I was thinking about running away and going back home. We're not from here, we're from over on tribal land.[4] But I like some kids here now."

"Do any of the same people come in here that always did? Like men, drinking after work and that kind of thing."

She shrugged.

"Right. How would you know."

I stared at my cup of coffee as though I might find the future in it, like the chickenbone lady back home. "I don't know what to do," I finally said.

She nodded out the window. "Maybe you should bring your friends in for lunch."

I did. We sat at one of the spick-and-span tables with plastic flowers and had grilled-cheese sandwiches. Turtle bounced in her seat and fed tiny pieces of grilled cheese to Shirley Poppy. Estevan and Esperanza were quiet. Of course. You couldn't speak Spanish in this part of the country—it would be noticed.

◀ *Why do Estevan and Esperanza stay quiet?*

After lunch I went up to the register to pay. No other member of the family had materialized from the kitchen, so I asked the girl if there was anyone else around that might help me. "Do you know the guy that runs the garage next door? Bob Two Two?"

She shook her head. "He never came over here, because we serve beer. He was some religion, I forget what."

"Are you telling me he's dead now too? Give me a break."

"Nah, he just closed. I think Pop said he was getting a place closer to Okie City."[5]

"It wasn't even a year ago that I was here."

4. **tribal land.** Land owned by the Cherokee Nation
5. **Okie City.** Oklahoma City

words for everyday use

ma • te • ri • al • ize (mə tir′ ē ə līz) *v.,* to cause to appear in bodily form; to come into existence. *If the invisible man in the movie wanted to materialize so that others could see him, he had to paint his face.*

She shrugged. "Nobody ever comes out here anyway. I never could see who would go to that garage in the first place."

I put the change in my pocket. "Well, thanks anyway," I told her. "Thanks for trying to help. I hope your family does all right by this place. You've fixed it up real nice."

She made a small gesture with her shoulders. "Thanks."

"What did you mean when you said you came from tribal land? Isn't this the Cherokee Nation?"

"*This!* No, this is nothing. This is kind of the edge of it I guess, they do have that sign up the road that says maintained by the Cherokee tribe. But the main part's over east, toward the mountains."

"Oklahoma has mountains?"

She looked at me as though I might be retarded. "Of course. The Ozark Mountains. Come here, look." She went over to the postcard rack and picked out some of the scenery cards. "See how pretty? That's Lake o' the Cherokees; we used to go there every summer. My brothers like to fish, but I hate the worms. And this is another place on the same lake, and this is Oologah Lake."

"That looks beautiful," I said. "That's the Cherokee Nation?"

▶ *What does the girl tell Taylor the Cherokee Nation is?*

"Part of it," she said. "It's real big. The Cherokee Nation isn't any one place exactly. It's people. We have our own government and all."

"I had no idea," I said. I bought the postcards. I would send one to Mama, although she was married now of course and didn't have any use for our old ace in the hole, the head rights. But even so I owed an apology to great grandpa, dead though he was.

As we were leaving I asked her about the TV. "That's the one thing that's still the same. What's with it anyway? Doesn't anybody ever turn the sound up?"

"The stupid thing is broke. You get the sound on one station and the picture on the other. See?" She flipped to the next channel, which showed blue static but played the sound perfectly. It was a commercial for diet Coke. "My gramma likes to leave it on 9, she's just about blind anyway, but the rest of us like it on 8."

"Do you ever get the Oral Roberts shows?"

She shrugged. "I guess. I like Magnum P.I."

Somehow I had been thinking that once we got back in the car and on the road again, everything would make sense and I would know what to do. I didn't. This time I didn't even know which way to head the car. If only Lou Ann were here, I thought. Lou Ann with her passion for playing Mrs. Neighborhood Detective. I knew she would say I was giving up too easily. But what was I supposed to do? Stake out the bar for a week or two and see if the woman ever showed up again? Would I recognize her if she did? Would she be willing to go to Oklahoma City with me to sign papers?

◀ What does Taylor wish? Why?

There had never been the remotest possibility of finding any relative of Turtle's. I had driven across the country on a snipe hunt. A snipe hunt is a joke on somebody, most likely some city cousin. You send him out in the woods with a paper bag and see how long it takes for him to figure out what a fool he is.

But it also occurred to me to wonder why I had come this far. Generally speaking, I am not a fool. I must have wanted something, and wanted it badly, to believe that hard in snipes.

"I can't give up," I said as I turned the car around. I smacked my palms on the steering wheel again and again. "I just can't. I want to go to Lake o' the Cherokees. Don't even ask me why."

◀ What does Taylor decide she can't do?

They didn't ask.

"So do you want to come with me, or should we take you to your church now? Really, I can go either way."

They wanted to come with me. I can see, looking back on it, that we were getting attached.

"We'll have a picnic by the lake, and stay in a cabin, and maybe find a boat somewhere and go out on the water. We'll have a vacation," I told them. "When's the last time you two had a vacation?"

Estevan thought for a while. "Never."

"Me too," I said.

Fifteen

Lake o' the Cherokees

▶ *What happens to Estevan and Esperanza over the next two hours?*

Esperanza and Estevan were transformed in an unexplainable way over the next two hours. They showed a new side, like the Holy Cards we used to win for attendance in summer Bible school: mainly there was a picture of Jesus on the cross, a blurred, shimmering picture with flecks of pink and blue scattered through it, but tip it just so and you could see a dove flying up out of His chest. That was the Holy Ghost.

We must have been getting closer to the heart of the Cherokee Nation, whatever or wherever it was, because as we drove east we saw fewer and fewer white people. Everybody and his mother-in-law was an Indian. All the children were Indian children, and the dogs looked like Indian dogs. At one point a police car came up behind us and we all got quiet and kept an eye out, as we had grown accustomed to doing, but when he passed us we just had to laugh. The cop was an Indian.

▶ *What does Taylor say shows in the bodies of Estevan and Esperanza? Why?*

It must have been a very long time since Esperanza and Estevan had been in a place where they looked just like everybody else, including cops. The relief showed in their bodies. I believe they actually grew taller. And Turtle fit right in too; this was her original home. I was the odd woman out.

Although, of course, I supposedly had enough Cherokee in me that it counted. I knew I would never really claim my head rights, and probably couldn't even if I wanted to—they surely had a statute of limitations or some such thing. But it was a relief to know the Cherokee Nation wasn't a complete bust.[1] I read a story once, I might have this confused but I think the way it went was that this lady had a diamond necklace put away in a safe-deposit box[2] all her life, thinking that if she ever got desperate she could sell it, only to find out on her deathbed that it was rhinestones. That was more or less the way I felt on that first terrible trip through Oklahoma.

▶ *What does Taylor compare to diamonds?*

It was nice to find out, after all, that Mama's and my ace in the hole for all those years really did have a few diamonds in it: Lake Oolagah, Lake o' the Cherokees.

"The Cherokee Nation has its own Congress and its own President," I reported to Esperanza and Estevan. "Did you

1. **complete bust.** Complete disappointment
2. **safe-deposit box.** Locking box for the safe storage of valuable items

know that?" I wasn't sure if I actually knew this or was just elaborating on what the girl in the restaurant had told me.

The scenery grew more interesting by the mile. At first it was still basically flat but it kind of rolled along, like a great green, rumpled bedsheet. Then there were definite hills. We passed through little towns with Indian names that reminded me in some ways of Kentucky. Here and there we saw trees.

Once, all of a sudden, Turtle shouted, "Mama!" She was pointing out the window.

◀ *What word does Turtle shout as she points out the window?*

My heart lost its beat for a second. To my knowledge she had never referred to anyone as Mama. We looked, but couldn't see anybody at all along the road. There was only a gas station and a cemetery.

Turtle and Esperanza were becoming inseparable. Turtle sat on her lap, played with her, and whined at the rest stops when Esperanza wanted to go to the bathroom by herself. I suppose I should have been grateful for the babysitting. I couldn't quite imagine how I would have kept Turtle entertained by myself, while I was driving. We'd managed a long trip before, of course, but that was in Turtle's catatonic period. At that stage of her life, I don't think she would have minded much if you'd put her in a box and shipped her to Arizona. Now everything was different.

Lake o' the Cherokees was a place where you could imagine God might live. There were enough trees.

◀ *What does Taylor say about Lake o' the Cherokees?*

I still would have to say it's stretching the issue to call the Ozarks mountains, but they served. I felt secure again, with my hopes for something better tucked just out of sight behind the next hill.

We found a cottage right off the bat. It was perfect: there were two bedrooms, a fireplace with a long-tailed bird (stuffed) on the mantel, and a bathroom with an old claw-foot tub (one leg poked down through the floor, but the remaining three looked steadfast). It was one of a meandering row of mossy, green-roofed cottages lined up along a stream bank in a place called Saw Paw Grove.

words for everyday use

elab • o • rate (i la′ bə rāt) *v.*, to expand something in detail. *The teacher asked the student to elaborate on her basic theory by providing supporting evidence.*

in • sep • a • ra • ble (in se′ pə rə bəl) *adj.*, incapable of being separated; indivisible. *The two young girls quickly became inseparable best friends who did everything together.*

me • an • der (mē an′ dər) *v.*, to follow a winding course; to wander aimlessly without destination. *Some people like to plan where they will go when on vacation in a new city; others prefer to meander.*

They didn't want to take it for the night, but I insisted. We had the money from Mattie, and besides, it wasn't that expensive. No more than we would have spent the night before if I hadn't had connections at the Broken Arrow. It took some doing, but I convinced Estevan and Esperanza that we weren't doing anything wrong. We deserved to have a good time, just for this one day.

▶ *How does Taylor tell Estevan and Esperanza to think of the one-day vacation? What does she say it will be if they don't accept?*

I told them to think of it as a gift. "As an ambassador of my country I'm presenting you with an expenses-paid one-day vacation for four at Lake o' the Cherokees. If you don't accept, it will be an international incident."

They accepted. We sat on the cottage's little back porch, watching out for Turtle and the holes where the floor-boards were rotted out, and stared at the white stream as it went shooting by. No water in Arizona was ever in that much of a hurry. The moss and the ferns looked so good I just drank up all that green. Even the rotten floor planks looked wonderful. In Arizona things didn't rot, not even apples. They just mummified. I realized that I had come to my own terms with the desert, but my soul was thirsty.

Growing all along the creek there were starry red-and-yellow flowers that bobbed on the ends of long, slender stems. Turtle informed us they were "combines,"[3] and we accepted her authority. Estevan climbed down the slick bank to pick them. I thought to myself, Where in the universe will I find another man who would risk his neck for a flower? He fell partway into the creek, soaking one leg up to the knee—mainly, I think, for our benefit. Even Esperanza laughed.

▶ *What does Taylor say is happening to Esperanza? To what does Taylor compare it?*

Something was going on inside of Esperanza. Something was thawing. Once I saw a TV program about how spring comes to Alaska. They made a big deal about the rivers starting to run again, showing huge chunks of ice rumbling and shivering and bashing against each other and breaking up. This is how it was with Esperanza. Behind her eyes, or deeper, in the arteries around her heart, something was starting to move. When she held Turtle on her lap she seemed honestly happy. Her eyes were clear and she spoke to Estevan and me directly, looking at our eyes.

Estevan survived his efforts and handed a flower to each of us. He kissed Esperanza and said something in Spanish

3. **combines.** Columbines, a type of flower

words for everyday use

am • bas • sa • dor (am bas′ ə dər) *n.*, diplomat; representative, a person chosen to represent one government in its dealings with another. *If you are an ambassador to a foreign country, you must reside in that country.*

that included "mi amor,"[4] and fixed the flower in her buttonhole so that it sprang out from her chest like one of those snake-in-the-can tricks. I could imagine them as a young couple, shy with each other, doing joky things like that. I braided the stem of my flower into my hair. Turtle waved hers up and down like a drum major's baton, shouting, "Combine, combine, combine!" None of us, apparently, was able to think of any appropriate way of following this command.

I was supposed to be calling them Steven and Hope now so they could begin getting used to it. I couldn't. I had changed my own name like a dirty shirt, but I couldn't help them change theirs.

"I love your names," I said. "They're about the only thing you came here with that you've still got left. I think you should only be Steven and Hope when you need to pull the wool over somebody's eyes, but keep your own names with your friends."

◀ *What does Taylor say about Estevan and Esperanza's names?*

Neither of them said anything, but they didn't urge me again to call them by false names.

Later we found a place that rented boats by the half hour and Estevan and I took one out onto the lake. Esperanza didn't want to go. She didn't know how to swim, and I wasn't sure about Turtle, so the two of them stayed on the shore feeding ducks.

Estevan and I took turns rowing and waving at the shore until Turtle was a tiny bouncing dot. By then we were in the very middle of the lake, and we let ourselves drift. The sun bounced off the water, making bright spangles and upside-down shadows on our faces. I rolled my jeans up to my knees and dangled my bare feet over the side. There was a fishy-smelling assortment of things in the bottom of the boat, including a red-and-white line floater and a collection of pop-top rings from beer cans.

Estevan took off his shirt and lay back against the front of the boat, his hands clasped behind his head, exposing his smooth Mayan chest to the sun. And to me. How could he possibly have done this, if he had any idea how I felt? I knew that Estevan had walked a long, hard road beyond innocence, but still he sometimes did the most simple, innocent, heart-breaking things. As much as I have wanted anything, ever, I wanted to know how that chest would feel against my face. I looked toward the shore so he wouldn't see the water in my eyes.

4. **"mi amor."** "My love" in Spanish

I pulled the wilted flower out of my braid and twisted the stem in my fingers. "I'm going to miss you a lot," I said. "All of you. Both, I mean."

Estevan didn't say he was going to miss all of me. We knew this was a conversation we couldn't afford to get into. In more ways than one, since we were renting by the half-hour.

After a while he said, "Throw a penny and make a wish."

"That's wasteful," I said, kicking my toes in the water. "My mother always said a person that throws away money deserves to be poor. I'd rather be one of the undeserving poor."

"Undeservedly," he corrected me, smiling.

"One of the undeservedly poor." Even my English was going to fall apart without him.

"Then we can wish on these." He picked up one of the pop-top rings. "These are appropriate for American wishes."

I made two American wishes on pop tops in Lake o' the Cherokees. Only one of them had the remotest possibility of coming true.

At dusk we found picnic tables in a little pine forest near the water's edge. Both Mattie and Irene had packed us fruit and sandwiches for the road, most of which were still in the Igloo[5] cooler in the trunk. We threw an old canvas poncho[6] over the table and spread out the pickle jars and bananas and apples and goose-liver sandwiches and everything else. Other picnickers here and there were working on modest little balanced meals of things that all went together, keeping the four food groups in mind, but we weren't proud. Our party was in the mood for a banquet.

▶ *How does Taylor feel if she doesn't think about the future?*

The sun was setting behind us but it lit up the clouds in the east, making one of those wraparound sunsets. Reflections of pink clouds floated across the surface of the lake. It looked like a corny painting. If I didn't let my mind run too far ahead, I felt completely happy.

Turtle still had a good deal of energy, and was less interested in eating than in bouncing and jumping and running

5. **Igloo.** Brand name

6. **poncho.** Blanket with a slit in the middle so that it can be slipped over the head and worn as a sleeveless garment

words for everyday use

un • de • serv • ed • ly (ən di zər′ vəd lē) *adv.*, not deserved. *She accepted the blame, but felt she was undeservedly accused.*

in circles around the trees. Every so often she found a pine cone, which she would bring back and give to me or to Esperanza. I tried very hard not to keep count of whose pile of pine cones was bigger. Turtle looked like a whirling dervish[7] in overalls and a green-striped T-shirt. We hadn't realized how cooped up she must have felt in the car, because she was so good. It's funny how people don't give that much thought to what kids want, as long as they're being quiet.

◀ What does Taylor try hard not to keep count of?

It's also interesting how it's hard to be depressed around a three-year-old, if you're paying attention. After a while, whatever you're mooning[8] about begins to seem like some elaborate adult invention.

Estevan asked us which we liked better, sunrise or sunset. We were all speaking in English now, because Esperanza had to get into practice. I couldn't object to this—it was a matter of survival.

"Sun set, because sun rise comes too early," Esperanza said, and giggled. She was very self-conscious in English, and seemed to have a whole different personality.

I told them that I liked sunrise better. "Sunset always makes me feel a little sad."

"Why?"

I peeled a banana and considered this. "I think because of the way I was raised. There was always so damn much work to do. At sunrise it always seems like you've got a good crack at getting everything done, but at sunset you know that you didn't."

Esperanza directed our attention to Turtle, who was hard at work burying Shirley Poppy in the soft dirt at the base of a pine tree. I had to laugh.

I went over and squatted beside her at the foot of the tree. "I've got to explain something to you, sweet pea. Some things grow into bushes or trees when you plant them, but other things don't. Beans do, doll babies don't."

"Yes," Turtle said, patting the mound of dirt. "Mama."

It was the second time that day she had brought up a person named Mama. I registered this with something like an electric shock. It started in my hands and feet and moved in toward the gut.

◀ What effect does Turtle saying Mama have on Taylor? What does she ask Turtle about her mama?

7. **whirling dervish.** One that whirls or dances with abandon
8. **mooning.** Daydreaming, pouting

words for everyday use

e • lab • o • rate (i la′ bə rət) *adj.*, intricate; complete; detailed. *The elaborate frame overpowered the simple painting.*

I kneeled down and pulled Turtle into my lap. "Did you see your mama get buried like that?" I asked her.

"Yes."

It was one of the many times in Turtle's and my life together that I was to have no notion of what to do. I remembered Mattie saying how it was pointless to think you could protect a child from the world. If that had once been my intention, it should have been clear that with Turtle I'd never had a chance.

I held her in my arms and we rocked for a long time at the foot of the pine tree.

"I'm sorry," I said. "It's awful, awful sad when people die. You don't ever get to see them again. You understand that she's gone now, don't you?"

Turtle said, "Try?" She poked my cheek with her finger.

"Yeah, I'm crying." I leaned forward on my knees and pulled a handkerchief out of my back pocket.

"I know she must have loved you very much," I said, "but she had to go away and leave you with other people. The way things turned out is that she left you with me."

Out on the lake people in boats were quietly casting their lines into the shadows. I remembered fishing on my own as a kid, and even younger going out with Mama, probably not being much help. I had a very clear memory of throwing a handful of rocks in the water and watching the fish dart away. And screaming my heart out. I wanted them, and knew of no reason why I shouldn't have them. When I was Turtle's age I had never had anyone or anything important taken from me.

I still hadn't. Maybe I hadn't started out with a whole lot, but pretty nearly all of it was still with me.

▶ *What does Taylor tell Turtle she'll try as hard as she can to do?*

After a while I told Turtle, "You already know there's no such thing as promises. But I'll try as hard as I can to stay with you."

"Yes," Turtle said. She wiggled off my lap and returned to her dirt pile. She patted a handful of pine needles onto the mound. "Grow beans," she said.

"Do you want to leave your dolly here?" I asked.

"Yes."

words for everyday use

in • ten • tion (in ten′ shən) *n.*, purpose; aim; objective. *Even though Matthew made a mess out of the kitchen, his intention was kind—to surprise his family with a delicious dinner.*

Later that night I asked Esperanza and Estevan if they would be willing to do one more thing with me. For me, really. I explained that it was a favor, a very big one, and then I explained what it was.

"You don't have to say yes," I said. "I know it involves some risk for you, and if you don't feel like you can go through with it I'll understand. Don't answer now, because I want to be sure you've really thought about it. You can tell me in the morning."

Esperanza and Estevan didn't want to think about it. They told me, then and there, they wanted to do it.

Sixteen

Soundness of Mind and Freedom of Will

Mr. Jonas Wilford Armistead was a tall, white-haired man who seemed more comfortable with the notarizing[1] part of his job than with the public. Even though he had been forewarned, when all of us came trooping into his office he seemed overwhelmed and showed a tendency to dither. He moved papers and pens and framed pictures from one side of his desk to the other and wouldn't sit down until all of us could be seated, which unfortunately didn't happen for quite a while because there weren't enough chairs. Mr. Armistead sent his secretary, Mrs. Cleary, next door to borrow a chair from the real-estate office of Mr. Wenn.

Mr. Armistead wore a complicated hearing aid that had ear parts, and black-and-white wires and a little silver box that had to be placed for maximum effectiveness on exactly the right spot on his desk, which he seemed unable to find. If he ever did, I thought I might suggest to him that he mark this special zone with paint as they do on a basketball court.

The silver box had tiny controls along one side, and Mr. Armistead also fiddled with these almost constantly, apparently without much success. Mrs. Cleary seemed during their working coexistence to have adjusted her volume accordingly. Even when she was talking to us, she practically shouted. It had an intimidating effect, especially on Esperanza.

But we all managed small talk while we waited. Which was all the more admirable when you consider that not one word any of us was saying was true, so far as I know. Estevan was an astonishingly good liar, going into great detail about the Oklahoma town where he and his wife had been living, and the various jobs he'd had. I talked about my plans to move to Arizona to live with my sister and her little boy. I think we were all amazed by the things that were popping out of our heads like corn.

---

1. **notarizing.** Authorizing, as a public officer, the authenticity of a document

words for everyday use

co • ex • is • tence (kō ig zis′ təns) *n.*, state of living peacefully together. *Often, people who get along well as friends are not compatible enough to achieve a peaceful coexistence as roommates.*

in • tim • i • date (in tim′ ə dāt) *v.*, to make timid or fearful; to frighten. *My brother tried to intimidate me by raising his voice and shaking his fist in my face.*

Sister, indeed. I remembered begging my mother for a sister when I was very young. She'd said she was all for it, but that if I got one it would have to be arranged by means of a miracle. At the time I'd had no idea what she meant. Now I knew about celibacy.[2]

Mrs. Cleary returned in due time, rolling a chair on its little wheels, and asked several questions about what forms would need to be typed up. We shuffled around again as we made room for Estevan and the new chair, and Mr. Armistead finally agreed to come down from his great height and roost like a long-legged stork on the chair behind his desk.

"It became necessary to make formal arrangements," Estevan explained, "because our friend is leaving the state."

Esperanza nodded.

"Mr. and Mrs. Two Two, do you understand that this is a permanent agreement?" He spoke very slowly, the way people often speak to not-very-bright children and foreigners, although I'm positive that Mr. Armistead had no inkling that the Two Two family came from any farther away than the Cherokee Nation.

◀ *By what names does Mr. Armistead call Estevan and Esperanza? Where does he think they live?*

They nodded again. Esperanza was holding Turtle tightly in her arms and beginning to get tears in her eyes. Already it was clear that, of the three of us, she was first in line for the Oscar nomination.

He went on, "After about six months a new birth certificate will be issued, and the old one destroyed. After that you cannot change your minds for any reason. This is a very serious decision."

"There wasn't any birth certificate issued," Mrs. Cleary shouted. "It was born on tribal lands."

"She," I said. "In a Plymouth," I added.

"We understand," Estevan said.

"I just want to make absolutely certain."

"We know Taylor very well," Estevan replied. "We know she will make a good mother to this child."

◀ *What does Estevan say about Taylor?*

Even though they were practically standing on it, Mr. Armistead and Mrs. Cleary seemed to think of "tribal land" as some distant, vaguely civilized country. This, to them, explained everything including the fact that Hope, Steven,

2. **celibacy.** Abstinence from sexual intercourse

words for everyday use

civ • i • lized (si' və lizd) *adj.*, characterized by taste or refinement; domesticated; tamed. *The museum opening was quite the civilized affair, with fancy food and people and beautiful art.*

▶ *What does Esperanza say about Turtle?*

▶ *As Taylor and the others watch Esperanza saying goodbye to Turtle, what does Taylor say Esperanza and Turtle are?*

and Turtle had no identification other than a set of black-and-white souvenir pictures taken of the three of them at Lake o' the Cherokees. It was enough that I, a proven citizen with a Social Security card,[3] was willing to swear on pain of I-don't-know-what (and sign documents to that effect) that they were all who they said they were.

By this point we had run out of small talk. I was over my initial nervousness, but without it I felt drained. Just sitting in that small, crowded office, trying to look the right way and say the right thing, seemed to take a great deal of energy. I couldn't imagine how we were all going to get through this.

"We love her, but we cannot take care for her," Esperanza said suddenly. Her accent was complicated by the fact that she was crying, but it didn't faze Mr. Armistead or Mrs. Cleary. Possibly they thought it was a Cherokee accent.

"We've talked it over," I said. I began to worry a little about what was going on here.

"We love her. Maybe someday we will have more children, but not now. Now is so hard. We move around so much, we have nothing, no home." Esperanza was sobbing. This was no act. Estevan handed her a handkerchief, and she held it to her face.

"Try, Ma?" Turtle said.

"That's right, Turtle," I said quietly. "She's crying."

Estevan reached over and lifted Turtle out of her arms. He stood her up, her small blue sneakers set firmly on his knees, and held her gently by the shoulders and looked into her eyes. "You must be a good girl. Remember. Good and strong, like your mother." I wondered which mother he meant, there were so many possibilities. I was touched to think he might mean me.

"Okay," Turtle said.

He handed her carefully back to Esperanza, who folded her arms around Turtle and held her against her chest, rocking back and forth for a very long time with her eyes squeezed shut. Tears drained down the shallow creases in her cheeks.

The rest of us watched. Mr. Armistead stopped fidgeting and Mrs. Cleary's hands on her papers went still. Here were a mother and her daughter, nothing less. A mother and child—in a world that could barely be bothered with mothers and children—who were going to be taken apart. Everybody believed it. Possibly Turtle believed it. I did.

3. **Social Security card.** Form of personal identification indicated by a number issued by the U.S. government

Of all the many times when it seemed to be so, that was the only moment in which I really came close to losing Turtle. I couldn't have taken her from Esperanza. If she had asked, I couldn't have said no.

When she let go, letting Turtle sit gently back on her lap, Turtle had the sniffles.

Esperanza wiped Turtle's nose with Estevan's big handkerchief and kissed her on both cheeks. Then she unclasped the gold medallion of St. Christopher, guardian saint of refugees, and put it around Turtle's neck. Then she gave Turtle to me.

Esperanza told me, "We will know she is happy and growing with a good heart."

"Thank you," I said. There was nothing else I could say.

It took what seemed like an extremely long time to draw up a statement, which Mrs. Cleary shuttled off to type. She came back and was sent off twice more to make repairs. After several rounds of White-out we had managed to create an official document:

> We, the undersigned, Mr. Steven Tilpec Two Two and Mrs. Hope Roberta Two Two, being the sworn natural parents of April Turtle Two Two, do hereby grant custody of our only daughter to Ms. Taylor Marietta Greer, who will from this day forward become her sole guardian and parent.
>
> We do solemnly swear and testify to our soundness of mind and freedom of will.
>
> Signed before witnesses on this ——— day of ———, in the office of Jonas Wilford Armistead, Oklahoma City, Oklahoma.

Mrs. Cleary went off once again to Mr. Wenn's office, this time to borrow his secretary Miss Brindo to be a second witness to the signing. Miss Brindo, who appeared to have at least enough Cherokee in her to claim head rights, had on tight jeans and shiny red high heels, and snapped her gum. She had a complicated haircut that stood straight up on top, and something told me she led a life that was way too boring for her potential. I wished she could have known what she was really witnessing that morning.

In a way, I wish all of them could know, maybe twenty years later or so when it's long past doing anything about it. Mrs. Cleary's and Mr. Armistead's hair would have stood straight up too, to think what astonishing things could be made legal in a modest little office in the state of Oklahoma.

◀ *Why does Taylor say that was the only moment in which she could have lost Turtle?*

◀ *What does Esperanza put around Turtle's neck? What does she say to Taylor as she hands Turtle to her?*

◀ *What does the document that Mrs. Cleary types up say about Estevan and Esperanza? What does it say they are doing?*

▶ *As they exit, how does Taylor say Esperanza's face looks?*

We shook hands all around, I got the rest of the adoption arrangements straightened out with Mr. Armistead, and we filed out, a strange new combination of friends and family. I could see the relief across Estevan's back and shoulders. He held Esperanza's hand. She was still drying tears but her face was changed. It shone like a polished thing, something old made new.

They both wore clean work shirts, light blue with faded elbows. Esperanza had on a worn denim skirt and flat loafers. I had asked them please not to wear their very best for this occasion, not their Immigration-fooling-clothes. It had to look like Turtle was going to be better off with me. When they came out that morning dressed as refugees I had wanted to cry out, No! I was wrong. Don't sacrifice your pride for me. But this is how badly they wanted to make it work.

Seventeen

Rhizobia

It had crossed my mind that Turtle might actually have recognized the cemetery her mother was buried in, and if so, I wondered whether I ought to take her back there to see it. But my concerns were soon laid to rest. We passed four cemeteries on the way to the Pottawatomie Presbyterian Church of St. Michael and All Angels, future home of Steven and Hope Two Two, and at each one of them Turtle called out, "Mama!"

◀ *What does Turtle call out at each cemetery they pass?*

There would come a time when she would just wave at the sight of passing gravestones and quietly say, "Bye bye."

Finding the church turned out to be a chase around Robin Hood's barn. Mattie's directions were to the old church. The congregation[1] had since moved its home of worship plus its pastor and presumably its refugees into a new set of buildings several miles down the road. I was beginning to form the opinion that Oklahomans were as transient a bunch as the people back home who slept on grass-flecked bedrolls in Roosevelt Park.

The church was a cheery-looking place, freshly painted white with a purple front door and purple gutters. When Mattie used to talk about the Underground Railroad, by which she meant these churches and the people who carried refugees between them, it had always sounded like the dark of night. I'd never pictured old white Lincolns with soda pop spilled on the seats, and certainly not white clapboard churches with purple gutters.

◀ *What did Mattie mean by the Underground Railroad?*

Reverend and Mrs. Stone seemed greatly relieved to see us, since they had apparently expected us a day or two earlier, but no one made an issue of it. They helped carry things up a sidewalk bordered with a purple fringe of ageratums[2] into the small house behind the parsonage[3]. Meanwhile Estevan and I worked on getting possessions sorted out. Things had gotten greatly jumbled during the trip, and Turtle's stuff was everywhere. She was like a pack rat, taking possession of any item that struck her fancy (like Esperanza's hairbrush) and tucking another one into its place (like a nibbled cracker). Turtle herself was exhausted with the events of the day, or days, and was in the back seat sleeping the sleep of the dead, as Lou Ann would put it. Esperanza and Estevan

1. **congregation.** Gathering; religious community
2. **ageratums.** Type of flower
3. **parsonage.** House provided by a church for its pastor

▶ *Why does Taylor insist that Estevan and Esperanza say goodbye again to Turtle?*

had already said goodbye to her in a very real way back in Mr. Armistead's office, and didn't think there was any need to wake her up again. But I stood firm.

"It's happened too many times that people she loved were whisked away from her without any explanation. I want her to see you, and see this place, so she'll know we're leaving you here."

She woke reluctantly, and groggily accepted my explanation of what was happening. "Bye bye," she said, standing up on the seat and waving through the open back window.

I think we all felt the same exhaustion. There are times when it just isn't possible to say goodbye. I hugged Esperanza and shook hands with Reverend and Mrs. Stone in a kind of daze. The day seemed too bright, too full of white clapboard and cheerful purple flowers, for me to be losing two good friends forever.

I was left with Estevan, who was checking under the back seat for the last time. I checked the trunk. "You ought to take some of this food," I said. "Turtle and I will never eat it all; it will just go to waste. At least the things there are whole jars of, like mustard and pickles." I bent over the cooler, stacking and unstacking the things that were swimming in melted ice in the bottom.

Estevan put his hand on my arm. "Taylor."

▶ *What does Estevan say he and Esperanza plan to do?*

I straightened up. "What's going to happen to you here? What will you do?"

"Survive. That has always been our intention."

"But what kind of work will you find around here? I can't imagine they have Chinese restaurants, which is probably a good thing. Oh God," I put my knuckle in my mouth. "Shut me up."

Estevan smiled. "I would never pray for that."

"I'm just afraid for you. And for Esperanza. I'm sorry for saying this, it's probably a very nice place, but I can't stand to think of you stuck here forever."

▶ *How does Estevan tell Taylor to think of Esperanza and him?*

"Don't think of us here forever. Think of us back in Guatemala with our families. Having another baby. When the world is different from now."

"When will that ever be," I said. "Never."

"Don't say that." He touched my cheek. I was afraid I was going to cry, or worse. That I would throw my arms

words for everyday use

whisk (hwisk') *v.*, to move briskly. *My mom passed her hand lightly over the back of my coat to whisk away some crumbs.*

re • luc • tant • ly (ri lək' tənt lē) *adv.*, unwilling; hesitant. *She waited until the last possible moment and left reluctantly for the first day of school.*

grog • gi • ly (grä' gə lē) *adv.*, in a sleepy or dazed way. *Keith rubbed his eyes groggily as he tried to wake up.*

around his ankles like some lady in a ridiculous old movie and refuse to let him go.

When tears did come to me it was a relief. That it was only tears. "Estevan, I know it doesn't do any good to say things like this, but I don't want to lose you. I've never lost anybody I loved, and I don't think I know how to." I looked away, down the flat, paved street. "I've never known anybody like you."

◀ What does Taylor say she doesn't know how to do?

He took both my hands in his. "Nor I you, Taylor."

"Can you write? Would it be safe, I mean? You could use a fake return address or something."

"We can send word by way of Mattie. So you will know where we are and what happens to us."

"I wish that didn't have to be all."

"I know." His black pupils moved back and forth between my eyes.

"But it does, doesn't it? There's no way around the hurt, is there? You just have to live with it."

◀ What does Taylor say about the hurt she feels?

"Yes, I'm sorry."

"Estevan, do you understand what happened back there in that office, with Esperanza?"

"Yes."

"I keep thinking it was a kind of, what would you call it?"

"A catharsis."[4]

"A catharsis," I said. "And she seems happy, honest to God, as happy as if she'd really found a safe place to leave Ismene behind. But she's believing in something that isn't true. Do you understand what I'm saying? It seems wrong, somehow."

◀ What does Taylor say Esperanza believes she has done?

"Mi'ija, in a world as wrong as this one, all we can do is to make things as right as we can." He put his hands on my shoulders and kissed me very, very sweetly, and then he turned around and walked into the house.

All four of us had buried someone we loved in Oklahoma.

◀ What does Taylor say all four of them have done?

I called Mama from a pay phone at a Shell station. I dug two handfuls of coins out of my jeans pockets, splayed them out on the metal shelf, and dialed. I was scared to death she would hang up on me. She had every right. I hadn't said boo to her for almost two months, not even to congratulate her on getting married. She'd written to say they'd had a real nice time at the wedding and that Harland was moving into our house. Up until the wedding he'd always lived in a so-called bachelor apartment, which means a bed plus hot

4. **catharsis.** A purification or purging of emotions that brings about spiritual renewal or release from tension

plate plus roach motel[5] in his sock drawer, in back of El-Jay's Paint and Body.

There was static in the line. "Mama, I'm sorry to bother you," I said. "I'm just outside of Oklahoma City so I thought I'd give you a ring. It's a lot closer than Arizona."

"Is that you? Bless your heart, it is you! I'll swan. Now weren't you sweet to call." She sounded so far away.

"So how's it going, Mama? How's married life treating you?"

She lowered her voice. "Something's wrong, isn't it?"

"Why would you think that?"

"Either you've got a bad cold or you've been crying. Your sound's all up in your head."

The tears started coming again, and I asked Mama to hang on just a minute. I had to put down the receiver to blow my nose. The one thing Lou Ann hadn't thought of was that I should have packed two dozen hankies.

When I got on the line again the operator was asking for more coins, so I dropped them in. Mama and I listened to the weird bonging song and didn't say anything to each other for a little bit.

▶ *What does Taylor tell her mother about saying goodbye to Estevan? What does Mama want to know? How does Taylor answer?*

"I just lost somebody I was in love with," I finally told her. "I just told him goodbye, and I'm never going to see him again."

"Well, what did you turn him loose for?" Mama wanted to know. "I never saw you turn loose of nothing you wanted."

"This is different, Mama. He wasn't mine to have."

She was quiet for a minute. We listened to the static playing up and down. It sounded like music from Mars.

"Mama, I feel like, I don't know what. Like I've died."

"I know. You feel like you'll never run into another one that's worth turning your head around for, but you will. You'll see."

"No, it's worse than that. I don't even care if I ever run into anybody else. I don't know if I even want to."

"Well, Taylor honey, that's the best way to be, is not on the lookout. That way you don't have to waste your time. Just let it slip up on you while you're going about your business."

"I don't think it will. I feel like I'm too old."

"Old my foot! Lordy, child, look at me. I'm so far over the hill I can't call the hogs to follow, and here I am running around getting married like a teenager. It's just as well you're not here, you'd have to tell everybody, Don't pay no mind

5. **roach motel.** Poisonous trap used to kill roaches

that old fool, that's just my mother done got bit by the love bug at a elderly age."

I laughed. "You're not elderly," I said.

"It won't be as long as it has been."

"Mama, shush, don't even say that."

"Oh, don't you worry about me, I don't care if I drop over tomorrow. I'm having me a time."

"That's good, Mama. I'm glad. I really am."

"I've done quit cleaning houses. I take in some washing now and again to keep me out of trouble, but I'm getting about ready to join the Women's Garden Club instead. The only dirt I feel like scratching in nowdays is my own. They meet of a Thursday."

I couldn't believe it. Mama retired. "You know what's funny?" I said. "I just can't picture you without an iron or a mop or something like that in your hand."

"Oh, picture it, girl, it's a pretty sight. You remember Mrs. Wickentot? The one always wore high heels to the grocery and thought she was the cat's meow?"

"Yeah, I remember. Her kids never would give me the time of day. They called me the Cleaning Lady's Girl."

"Well you can put it to rest now, because I told her off good when I quit. I told her if I had the kind of trash she has in her closets, and the way she lets those boys run wild, what I found under their beds, I just wouldn't act so high and mighty, is what I told her."

"You told her that?"

"I did. And then some. All these years, you know, these ladies get to thinking they own you. That you wouldn't dare breathe a word for fear of getting fired. Now I think they're all scared to death I'm going to take out an ad in the paper."

I could just see it, right on the back page under the obituaries[6] and deed-of-trust announcements. Or better yet, on the society page:

"Alice Jean Greer Elleston wishes to announce that Irma Ruebecker has fifty-two pints of molded elderberry jelly in her basement; Mae Richey's dishes would be carried off by the roaches if she didn't have hired help; and Minerva Wickentot's boys read porno magazines."

I couldn't stop laughing. "You ought to do it," I said. "It would be worth the thirty-five cents a word."

"Well, I probably won't. But it's good for a gal to have something like that up her sleeve, don't you think?" She chuckled. "It makes people respect you."

6. **obituaries.** Notices of people's deaths with short biographical accounts

"Mama, you're really something. I don't know how the good Lord packed so much guts into one little person." The words were no sooner out of my mouth before I realized this was something she used to say to me. In high school, when I was having a rough time of it, she said it practically every other day.

"How's that youngun of yours?" Mama wanted to know. She never failed to ask.

"She's fine. She's asleep in the car right now or I'd put her on to say hi. Or peas and carrots, more likely. You never know what she's going to say."

"Well, she comes by that honest."

"Don't say that, Mama. That means it proves a baby's not a bastard.[7] If it acts like you, it proves it's legitimate."

"I never thought about it that way."

"It's okay. I guess I'm just sensitive, you know, since she's not blood kin."[8]

▶ *What does Mama say is the main way kids come by things honest? What does Mama say about Newt Hardbine?*

"I don't think blood's the only way kids come by things honest. Not even the main way. It's what you tell them, Taylor. If a person is bad, say, then it makes them feel better to tell their kids that they're even worse. And then that's just exactly what they'll grow up to be. You remember those Hardbines?"

"Yeah. Newt. I especially remember Newt."

"That boy never had a chance. He was just doing his best to be what everybody in Pittman said he was."

"Mama, you were always so good to me. I've been meaning to tell you that. You acted like I'd hung up the moon. Sometimes I couldn't believe you thought I was that good."

"But most of the time you believed it."

"Yeah. I guess most of the time I thought you were right."

The operator came on and asked for more money. My pile of change was thinning out. "We're just about done," I told her, but she said this was for the minutes that we'd already talked. I was out of quarters and had to use a whole slew of nickels.

"Guess what?" I said to Mama after the coins had dropped. "Here's the big news, Turtle's my real daughter. I adopted her."

"Did you? Now aren't you smart. How'd you do that?"

---

7. **bastard.** Derogatory term used to refer to a child born to two parents not married to each other

8. **blood kin.** Blood relation

"Kind of by hook or crook.[9] I'll tell you about it in a letter, it's too complicated for long distance. But it's all legal. I've got the papers to prove it."

"Lord have mercy. Married and a legal grandma all in the same summer. I can't wait to see her."

"We'll get back there one of these days," I said. "Not this trip, but we will. I promise."

"You better watch out, one of these days me and old Harland might just up and head for Arizona."

"I wish you would."

Neither of us wanted to hang up. We both said, "Bye," about three times.

"Mama," I said, "this is the last one. I'm hanging up now, okay? Bye. And say hi to Harland for me too, okay? Tell him I said be good to you or I'll come whip his butt."

"I'll tell him."

Turtle and I had a whole afternoon to kill in Oklahoma City while we waited for some paperwork on the adoption to clear. After her nap she was raring to go. She talked up a storm, and wanted to play with Esperanza's medallion. I let her look at it in the side-view mirror.

"You have to keep it on," I told her. "That's St. Christopher, the guardian saint of refugees. I think you'd count. You're about as tempest-tossed as they come."

A tempest was a bad storm where things got banged around a lot. "Tempest-tossed" was from the poem on the Statue of Liberty that started out, "Give me your tired, your poor." Estevan could recite the whole poem. Considering how America had treated his kind, he must have thought this was the biggest joke ever to be carved in giant letters on stone.

◀ *What does Taylor say Estevan must think about the poem on the Statue of Liberty? Why?*

I tried not to think about Estevan, but after a while decided it felt better to think about him than not to. And Turtle was good company. We cruised around in Mattie's Lincoln, a couple of free-wheeling females out on the town. Her favorite part was driving over the speed bumps at the Burger King.

During this time we had what I consider our second real conversation, the first having taken place at the foot of a pine tree at Lake o' the Cherokees. It went something like this:

"What do you want to do?"

"Okay."

9. **hook or crook.** Whatever means are necessary

"Are you hungry?"

"No."

"Well, where should we go, do you think? Anything in particular you want to see, as long as we're here in the big city?"

"Ma Woo-Ahn."

"Lou Ann's at home. We'll see her when we get home. And Edna and Virgie and Dwayne Ray and everybody."

"Waneway?"

"That's right."

"Ma Woo-Ahn?"

▶ *What does Taylor tell Turtle she has only one of?*

"That's right. Only let me tell you something. Starting right now, you've only got one Ma in the whole world. You know who that is?"

"Yes."

"Who?"

"Ma."

▶ *What does Taylor tell Turtle about Lou Ann, Edna, Mattie, Estevan, and Esperanza?*

"That's right. That's me. You've got loads of friends. Lou Ann's your friend, and Edna and Mattie and all the others, and they all love you and take care of you sometimes. And Estevan and Esperanza were good friends too. I want you to remember them, okay?"

"Steban and Mespanza," she nodded gravely.

"Close enough," I said. "I know it's been confusing, there's been a lot of changes in the management. But from here on in I'm your Ma, and that means I love you the most. Forever. Do you understand what that means?"

"That beans?" She looked doubtful.

"You and me, we're sticking together. You're my Turtle."

"Urdle," she declared, pointing to herself.

"That's right. April Turtle Greer."

"Ableurdledear."

"Exactly."

On an impulse I called 1-800-THE LORD, from a public phone in the City Library where we'd come after Turtle decided she'd like to look at some books. I don't know what possessed me to do it. I'd been saving it up all this time, like Mama and our head rights, and now that I'd hit bottom and survived, I suppose I knew that I didn't really need any ace in the hole.

The line rang twice, three times, and then a recording came on. It told me that the Lord helps those that help themselves. Then it said that this was my golden opportunity to help myself and the entire Spiritual Body by making my generous contribution today to the Fountain of Faith missionary fund. If I would please hold the line an operator would be available momentarily to take my pledge.[10] I held the line.

"Thank you for calling," she said. "Would you like to state your name and address and the amount of your pledge?"

"No pledge," I said. "I just wanted to let you know you've gotten me through some rough times. I always thought, 'If I really get desperate I can call 1-800-THE LORD.' I just wanted to tell you, you have been a Fountain of Faith."

She didn't know what to make of this. "So you don't wish to make a pledge at this time?"

"No," I said. "Do you wish to make a pledge to me at this time? Would you like to send me a hundred dollars, or a hot meal?"

She sounded irritated. "I can't do that, ma'am," she said.

"Okay, no problem," I said. "I don't need it, anyway. Especially now. I've got a whole trunkful of pickles and baloney."

"Ma'am, this is a very busy line. If you don't wish to make a pledge at this time."

"Look at it this way," I said. "We're even."

After I hung up I felt like singing and dancing through the wide, carpeted halls of the Oklahoma City Main Library. I once saw a movie where kids did cartwheels all over the library tables while Marian the librarian chased them around saying "Shhhh!" I felt just like one of those kids.

But instead Turtle and I snooped politely through the stacks. They didn't have *Old MacDonald Had an Apartment,* and as a matter of fact we soon became bored with the juvenile section and moved on to Reference. Some of these had good pictures. Turtle's favorite was the *Horticultural*[11] *Encyclopedia.* It had pictures of vegetables and flowers that were far beyond both her vocabulary and mine. She sat on my lap and together we turned the big, shiny pages. She pointed out pictures of plants she liked, and I read about them. She even found a picture of bean trees.

"Well, you smart thing, I would have missed it altogether," I said. I would have, too. The picture was in black and white, and didn't look all that much like the ones back home in Roosevelt Park, but the caption said it was wisteria. I gave Turtle a squeeze. "What you are," I told her, "is a horticultural genius." I wouldn't have put it past her to

---

10. **pledge.** Verbal agreement to donate a specified amount of money
11. **Horticultural.** Related to gardening

say "horticulture" one of these days, a word I hadn't uttered myself until a few months ago.

Turtle was thrilled. She slapped the picture enthusiastically, causing the young man at the reference desk to look over his glasses at us. The book had to have been worth a hundred dollars at least, and it was very clean.

"Here, let's don't hit the book," I said. "I know it's exciting. Why don't you hit the table instead?"

She smacked the table while I read to her in a whisper about the life cycle of wisteria. It is a climbing ornamental vine found in temperate latitudes, and came originally from the Orient. It blooms in early spring, is pollinated by bees, and forms beanlike pods. Most of that we knew already. It actually is in the bean family, it turns out. Everything related to beans is called a legume.

▶ In what kind of soil do wisteria often thrive? What is their secret?

But this is the most interesting part: wisteria vines, like other legumes, often thrive in poor soil, the book said. Their secret is something called rhizobia. These are microscopic bugs that live underground in little knots on the roots. They suck nitrogen gas right out of the soil and turn it into fertilizer for the plant.

▶ To what does Taylor compare the rhizobia?

The rhizobia are not actually part of the plant, they are separate creatures, but they always live with legumes: a kind of underground railroad moving secretly up and down the roots.

"It's like this," I told Turtle. "There's a whole invisible system for helping out the plant that you'd never guess was there." I loved this idea. "It's just the same as with people. The way Edna has Virgie, and Virgie has Edna, and Sandi has Kid Central Station, and everybody has Mattie. And on and on."

The wisteria vines on their own would just barely get by, is how I explained it to Turtle, but put them together with rhizobia and they make miracles.

At four o'clock we went to the Oklahoma County Courthouse to pick up the adoption papers. On Mr. Armistead's directions we found a big bright office where about twenty women sat typing out forms. All together they made quite a racket. The one who came to the front counter had round-muscled shoulders bulging under her pink cotton blazer and a half grown-out permanent in her straight Cherokee hair—a body trying to return to its natural state. She took our names and told us to have a seat, that it would be awhile. The waiting made me nervous, even though no one here looked important enough to stop what had already been set in motion. It was only a roomful of women with typewriters and African violets and pictures of their kids on their desks, doing as they were told. Still, I was afraid of sitting around looking anxious, as if one of them might catch sight of me fidgeting and cry out, "That's no adoptive mother, that's an impostor!" I could imagine them all then, scooting back their chairs and scurrying after me in their high-heeled pumps and tight skirts.

I needed to find something to do with myself. I asked if there was a telephone I could use for long distance. The muscular woman directed me to a pay phone out in the hall.

I dialed Lou Ann. It seemed to take an eternity for all the right wires to connect, and when she finally did take the call she sounded even more nervous than I was, which was no help.

"It's okay, Lou Ann, everything's fine, I just called collect because I'm about out of quarters. But we'll have to keep it short or we'll run up the phone bill."

"Oh, hell's bells, Taylor, I don't even care." Lou Ann relaxed immediately once she knew we hadn't been mangled in a car crash. "I don't know how many times this week I've said I'd give a million dollars to talk to Taylor, so here's my chance. It just seems like everything in the world has happened. Where in the tarnation are you, anyway?"

"Oklahoma City. Headed home." I hesitated. "So what all's happened? You've decided to take Angel back? Or go up there and live in his yurdle, or whatever?"

"Angel? Heck no, not if you paid me. Listen, do you know what his mother told me? She said Angel just wants what he can't have. That I'd no sooner get up to Montana before he'd decide he'd had enough of me again. She said I was worth five or six of Angel."

◀ *What did Angel's mother tell Lou Ann about Angel?*

"His own mother said that?"

"Can you believe it? Of course it was all in Spanish, I had to get it secondhand, but that was the general gist. And it makes sense, don't you think? Isn't there some saying about not throwing good loving after bad?"

"I think it's money they say that about. Good money after bad."

words for everyday use

im • pos • tor (im päs′ tər) *n.*, one who assumes a false identity for the purpose of deception. *The character we thought was the cop in the movie was actually an impostor who turned out to be the bad guy.*

scur • ry (skər′ ē) *v.*, scamper; move around in an agitated or confused way. *The dog began to scurry around the room to get away from the vacuum.*

man • gle (măŋ ′ gəl) *v.*, crush; cut; tear. *I quickly turned off the garbage disposal before it could mangle the spoon I'd accidentally dropped into it.*

"Well, the same goes, is what I say. Oh shoot, can you hang on a second? Dwayne Ray's got something about ready to put in his mouth." I waited while she saved Dwayne Ray from his probably nineteen-thousandth brush with death. I loved Lou Ann.

Turtle was playing the game where you see how far you can get without touching the floor, walking only on the furniture. She was doing pretty well. There was a long row of old-fashioned wooden benches with spindle backs and armrests, lined up side by side down one wall of the hallway. For some reason it made me think of a chain gang[12]—a hundred guys could sit on those benches, all handcuffed together. Or a huge family, I suppose, waiting for some important news. They could all hold hands.

▶ *What did Lou Ann find out about the meteor shower? What occurs to Taylor when Lou Ann tells her this?*

"Okay, I'm back. So there's one more thing I have to tell you. Remember about the meteors? I called up Ramona Quiroz in San Diego, long distance. There wasn't any meteor shower. Not at all! Can you believe it? That was just the absolute last straw."

"Well, thank heavens," I said. It occurred to me that nobody else on earth could have understood what Lou Ann had just said.

"So that's the scoop, Angel's history. Now I'm seeing this guy from Red Hot Mama's by the name of Cameron John. Cameron's his first name and John's his last. Can you believe it?"

"I had a science teacher like that once," I said. "So does Red Hot Mama's give out a sex manual for the chile packers—how to do it without touching anything?"

"Taylor, I swear. He does tomatillos, and I just boss people now, as you very well know. Anyway I can't wait till you meet him, to see what you think. I know Mama would take one look and keel over dead—he's about seven feet tall and black as the ace of spades. But, Taylor, he is so sweet. My biggest problem is I keep feeling like I don't deserve anybody to be that nice to me. He invited me over for dinner and made this great something or other with rice and peanuts and I don't know what all. He used to be a Rastafarian."

"A what?"

▶ *How does Lou Ann say she has changed from hanging around Taylor?*

"Rastafarian. It's a type of religion. And he's got this dog, a Doberman pinscher? Named Mister T, only Cameron didn't name it that, somebody gave it to him. It's got pierced ears, Taylor, I swear to God, with all these little gold rings. I can't believe I actually went out with this guy. I've gotten so brave hanging around you. Six months ago it would

12. **chain gang.** Gang of convicts chained together

have scared the living daylights out of me just to have to walk by him on the street."

"Which, Cameron or Mister T?"

"Either one. And oh, I can't tell you, he was so good with Dwayne Ray. It just made me want to cry, or take a picture or something, to see this great big man playing with a little teeny pale white baby."

"So are you moving in with him, or what?" I tried my best to sound happy for her.

"What, me? No! Cameron's sweet as can be, but I'm real content with things the way they are now. To tell you the truth, I'm sure you're a lot easier to live with than him and Mister T."

"Oh. Well, I'm glad."

"Taylor, remember that time you were mad at me because you didn't want us to act like a family? That all we needed was a little dog named Spot? Well, don't get mad, but I told somebody that you and Turtle and Dwayne Ray were my family. Somebody at work said, 'Do you have family at home?' And I said, 'Sure,' without even thinking. I meant you all. Mainly I guess because we've been through hell and high water[13] together. We know each other's good and bad sides, stuff nobody else knows."

◀ *Why does Lou Ann think of Taylor and Turtle as a family?*

It was hard for me to decide what to say.

"I don't mean till death do us part, or anything," she said. "But nothing on this earth's guaranteed, when you get right down to it, you know? I've been thinking about that. About how your kids aren't really *yours,* they're just these people that you try to keep an eye on, and hope you'll all grow up someday to like each other and still be in one piece. What I mean is, everything you ever get is really just on loan. Does that make sense?"

"Sure," I said. "Like library books. Sooner or later they've all got to go back into the night drop."

"Exactly. So what's the point worrying yourself sick about it. You'd just as well enjoy it while you've got it."

"I guess you could say we're family," I said. I watched Turtle climb over the armrests onto the last bench by the front door, which stood wide open to the street. She turned around and looked for me, and started making her way back.

There was silence on the other end of the line. "Lou Ann? You still there?" I asked.

"I can't stand the suspense, Taylor. Do you still have her?"

"Have who?"

"Turtle, for heaven's sake."

13. **hell and high water.** Worst that could happen

"Oh, sure. She's my legal daughter now."

"What!" Lou Ann shrieked. "You're kidding!"

"Nope. It's done, for all practical purposes. There's still some rigamarole in court for getting a birth certificate that takes about six months, but that's not too bad. It takes longer than that to make a kid from scratch, is how I look at it."

"I can't believe it. You found her mother? Or her aunt, or whatever it was?"

I looked down the hall. "I can't really talk here. We'll be home in two days at the outside, and I'll tell you everything then, okay? But it's going to take all night and a lot of junk food. Do you know what? I missed your salsa. The medium, though, not the firecracker style."

▶ *What was Lou Ann scared of?*

Lou Ann's breath came out like a slow leak in a tire. "Taylor, I was scared to death you'd come back without her."

We had cleared Oklahoma City and were out on the plain before sundown. It felt like old times, heading into the low western horizon. I let Turtle see the adoption certificate and she looked at it for a very long time, considering that there were no pictures on it.

"That means you're my kid," I explained, "and I'm your mother, and nobody can say it isn't so. I'll keep that paper for you till you're older, but it's yours. So you'll always know who you are."

She bobbed her head up and down like a hen, with her eyes fixed on something out the window that only she could see.

"You know where we're going now? We're going home."

She swung her heels against the seat. "Home, home, home, home," she sang.

▶ *What doesn't seem to matter to Turtle? Why?*

The poor kid had spent so much of her life in a car, she probably felt more at home on the highway than anywhere else. "Do you remember home?" I asked her. "That house where we live with Lou Ann and Dwayne Ray? We'll be there before you know it."

But it didn't seem to matter to Turtle, she was happy where she was. The sky went from dust-color to gray and then cool black sparked with stars, and she was still wide awake. She watched the dark highway and entertained me with her vegetable-soup song, except that now there were people mixed in with the beans and potatoes: Dwayne Ray, Mattie, Esperanza, Lou Ann and all the rest.

And me. I was the main ingredient.

◆ ◆ ◆

Respond to the Selection

Barbara Kingsolver's sequel to *The Bean Trees* is *Pigs in Heaven.* Based on what you have read, what would you like to see happen next for Taylor and Turtle?

Investigate, Inquire, and Imagine

Recall: GATHERING FACTS

1a. In Chapter 14, why does Taylor begin to recognize that Oklahoma is a good choice for Estevan and Esperanza? What does she ask Estevan about Cherokees and Mayans? What does she ask Estevan if a white person would be able to tell?

2a. As Taylor, Estevan, Esperanza, and Turtle sit beside the stream in Saw Paw Grove, Taylor notices that there is "something going on inside of Esperanza." To what does Taylor compare this something that is happening?

3a. How does Taylor say that Mr. Armistead talks to Estevan and Esperanza? What does she say Mr. Armistead has no inkling of? How does Taylor say that Mr. Armistead and Mrs. Cleary think of "tribal land"?

Interpret: FINDING MEANING

➛ 1b. Why do you think Taylor asks Estevan what she does about the physical appearance of Cherokees and Mayans?

➛ 2b. What do you think is happening to Esperanza, and what are the causes of it? Explain, citing evidence from the story to support your answer.

➛ 3b. What opinions does Mr. Armistead seem to have of the Cherokee people? How does Mr. Armistead's attitude toward Native Americans make it possible for Taylor to gain custody of Turtle?

Analyze: TAKING THINGS APART

4a. As Taylor watches Esperanza embrace Turtle in Mr. Armistead's office, she observes, "Here were a mother and her daughter, nothing less. A mother and child—in a world that could barely be bothered with mothers and children…" Consider Taylor's observation, then think back through the novel, and identify ways in which the story comments on how the "world" treats mothers and their children.

Synthesize: BRINGING THINGS TOGETHER

→ 4b. Based on your answer to question 4a., in your own words, explain the various ways in which the world can barely be bothered with mothers and children.

Evaluate: MAKING JUDGMENTS

5a. Taylor and Turtle discover in the *Horticultural Encyclopedia* that rhizobia enable wisteria to thrive in poor soil. The relationship between rhizobia and wisteria is known as symbiosis, the intimate living together of two dissimilar organisms in a mutually beneficial relationship. As Taylor points out, symbiosis also applies to relationships between people. How effectively does *The Bean Trees* show symbiosis at work in human relationships? You may want to use the relationship between Taylor and Turtle, Edna and Virgie Mae, or Mattie and other characters to support your answer.

Extend: CONNECTING IDEAS

→ 5b. Apply this idea of symbiosis to the people in heaven and hell in Estevan's story in Chapter 7. Which people take roles similar to those of rhizobia and wisteria? What do Estevan's story and symbiosis in the natural world suggest about the importance of community and cooperation?

Understanding Literature

CATHARSIS. The ancient Greek philosopher Aristotle described tragedy as bringing about a **catharsis**, or purging, of the emotions of fear and pity. In Aristotle's view, a tragedy causes the audience to feel emotions of fear and pity, which are then released at the end of the play, leaving audience members calmer, wiser, and perhaps more thoughtful. A catharsis can also be described as a purification or purgation that brings about spiritual renewal or release from tension.

In Chapter 17, Taylor and Estevan both refer to Esperanza's experience in Mr. Armistead's office as a catharsis. In this scene, Esperanza is physically saying goodbye to Turtle, but emotionally she is saying goodbye to Ismene, the daughter taken from her in Guatemala. Esperanza chooses to believe that the child she is leaving behind will be cared for by someone who will make sure she is "happy and growing with a good heart." After Esperanza undergoes this emotional experience, or catharsis, her face shines like "a polished thing, something old made new," and she regains her will to live.

Examine both descriptions of catharsis. In Aristotle's view, who undergoes a cathartic experience? How does the catharsis described in the novel differ from Aristotle's view? In what ways are both descriptions of cathartic experiences similar?

THEME. A **theme** is a central idea in a literary work. Themes commonly address universal topics—things like love, death, family, and friendship—and communicate a message about that topic. For example, one theme of *The Bean Trees* is that it is important for people to take risks and change even if it means leaving behind what is comfortable. What are other themes in this novel? What messages do you think Kingsolver is trying to convey about family, individual freedom, the power of community, and the relationship between people and the natural world?

Plot Analysis of *The Bean Trees*

A **plot** is a series of events related to a **central conflict**, or struggle. The following plot pyramid illustrates the main parts of a plot.

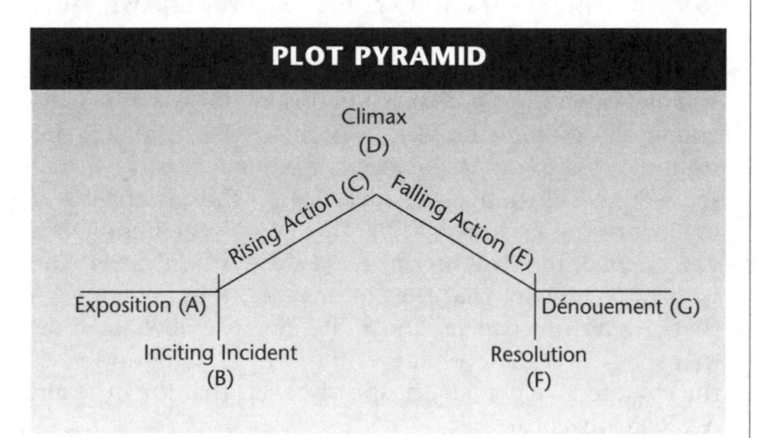

The parts of a plot are as follows:

The **exposition** is the part of a plot that provides background information about the characters, setting, or conflict.

The **inciting incident** is the event that introduces the central conflict.

The **rising action**, or complication, develops the conflict to a high point of intensity.

The **climax** is the high point of interest or suspense in the story.

The **falling action** is all the events that follow the climax.

The **resolution** is the point at which the central conflict is ended or resolved.

The **dénouement** is any material that follows the resolution and that ties up loose ends.

Exposition (A)

As the novel opens, the reader is introduced to Taylor Greer (Marietta or Missy, as she is called until she changes her name to Taylor later in Chapter 1), who confesses in the first sentence her greatest fear, exploding tractor tires. Taylor, the narrator of Chapter 1, describes life in her hometown of Pittman, Kentucky, her relationship with her mother, and her plan to get out of Pittman.

Taylor saves enough money to buy a 1955 Volkswagen and heads west. When her car breaks down within the boundaries of the Cherokee Nation in Oklahoma, Taylor stops to eat at a bar. As she leaves, a woman outside the bar sets a "bundle" wrapped in a blanket on the passenger seat of Taylor's car, and says, "Take this baby." The bundle is a young child, the daughter of the woman's dead sister. The woman tells Taylor that the child was born in a Plymouth, that she has no papers, and that nobody knows or cares that she is alive. Later that evening, when Taylor undresses the child to give her a bath, she discovers that the little girl was sexually abused.

The narration changes to a third-person point of view in Chapter 2, when the reader is introduced to Lou Ann Ruiz. Lou Ann lives in Tucson, but thinks of herself as a Kentuckian who is a long way from home. The reader learns about the character of Angel, Lou Ann's husband, and the details of their failing marriage. The reader also learns that Lou Ann is pregnant. Details of the setting of the Tucson neighborhood in which Lou Ann lives are also provided.

In Chapter 3, Taylor again takes up the narration. Talor has named the child Turtle for the way she "holds on." The reader is introduced to the character of Mattie when she meets Taylor and Turtle. Mattie runs a tire shop called Jesus Is Lord Used Tires that was started by her husband, who was very religious and who has died.

In Chapter 7, the reader is introduced to the characters of Estevan and Esperanza. The reader learns that both Estevan and Esperanza are Indians from Guatemala, and that Estevan was an English teacher in Guatemala City. The characters of Edna Poppy and Virgie Mae Parsons are also introduced in this chapter.

Inciting Incident (B)

The inciting incident of the novel takes place in Chapter 1 when Turtle is given to Taylor. Taylor sits in her car in the parking lot of the bar with Turtle in the passenger's seat, trying to decide whether to return Turtle to one of the people in the bar, or drive off with her, get some sleep, and think things over. While she is deciding, all the lights in the bar go out, and the few people left in the bar drive off. From this point on, Taylor accepts responsibility for Turtle.

Rising Action (C)

In Chapter 12, the arrival of the first summer rain foreshadows the rising action about to take place in the plot. Taylor returns home from the desert, where she, Mattie, Estevan, and Esperanza have been reveling in the first summer storm, and knows instantly that something bad has happened. Taylor finds out that someone tried to harm Turtle while she was at the park with Edna.

In the days following the incident at the park, Turtle is disturbed by what has happened, and she withdraws. The police and Cynthia, a social worker, visit Taylor. The social worker informs her that she has no legal claim to Turtle, and that unless she can provide one, Turtle will become a ward of the state. As Taylor experiences guilt about what has happened to Turtle, she struggles over whether she can provide good care for Turtle or whether she should allow the state of Arizona to put the little girl into foster care.

Simultaneously, action is rising in the subplot that tells the story of Estevan and Esperanza. Mattie tells Taylor that Immigration is beginning to investigate and that it is necessary to move Estevan and Esperanza to another safe house. Taylor's inner struggle continues as she experiences anger and depression over the way society deals with people like Turtle, Estevan, and Esperanza.

The rising action reaches its peak when Taylor decides to drive Estevan and Esperanza to a safe house in Oklahoma and to search for relatives of Turtle who might be able to provide her with a legal claim to Turtle. By making this decision, Taylor assumes the risk of going to prison for helping Estevan and Esperanza and the risk of finding a relative of Turtle who will want to take Turtle back.

Climax (D)

The climax of the main plot takes place in Chapter 16 in Mr. Armistead's office. Estevan and Esperanza pose as Steven and Hope Two Two and claim that Turtle is their daughter. They sign legal documentation that grants custody of Turtle to Taylor.

The climax of the subplot of the story of Estevan and Esperanza also takes place in Chapter 16 in Mr. Armistead's office when Esperanza embraces Turtle and hands her over to Taylor. Mr. Armistead believes that Esperanza's emotion comes from saying goodbye to Turtle, her daughter, as she gives her to Taylor. But Esperanza is symbolically saying goodbye to her daughter—her real daughter, Ismene—who was kidnapped by the Guatemalan government. Through the actions that take place in Mr. Armistead's office, Esperanza experiences the emotional release of saying goodbye to Ismene and placing her in the hands of someone who will take good care of her. She never had the opportunity to do either of these things with Ismene.

Falling Action (E)

Taylor takes Estevan and Esperanza to their new safe house. Estevan and Esperanza say goodbye to Turtle, and Estevan and Taylor share a tender and emotional goodbye. Taylor reveals to Estevan that she loves him, and he reveals the same to her without saying it. Taylor calls Mama to tell her of the events that have transpired. Taylor and Turtle visit the Oklahoma City library, where Taylor reads to Turtle about wisteria plants and their symbiotic relationship with rhizobia. Taylor picks up the official adoption papers for Turtle, and calls Lou Ann to tell her what has happened. Lou Ann is relieved, and she tells Taylor that she thinks of Taylor and Turtle as family. Taylor and Turtle head home to Arizona.

Resolution (F)

Resolution of the main plot is achieved as Taylor, Turtle, Estevan, and Esperanza leave Mr. Armistead's office with a notarized document declaring Taylor the legal guardian of Turtle. Resolution of the story of Estevan and Esperanza is achieved when Taylor safely delivers them to the safe house in Oklahoma.

Dénouement (G)

Taylor and Turtle spend the afternoon in Oklahoma, and begin their trip back to Arizona.

from *The Cherokee Lottery: A Sequence of Poems*

by William Jay Smith

William Jay Smith

ABOUT THE RELATED READING

William Jay Smith has written more than fifty books, including poetry, literary criticism, and memoirs. Former poet laureate to the Library of Congress, poet-in-residence at Williams College, and chairman of the Writing Division of the School of the Arts at Columbia University, Smith is professor emeritus of English at Hollins College. He became interested in the forced removal of Indian tribes of the Southeast while researching his own Chocktaw heritage. His research inspired *The Cherokee Lottery.*

The introductory paragraph, "A Sequence of Poems," and "II. Cherokee Lottery" precede two poems by Smith, and provide historical context for the events leading up to the lottery of Cherokee lands and the Trail of Tears. *"Georgia 1838"* depicts the lottery held to give away Cherokee lands. "VII. The Pumpkin Field" tells of events, as seen through the eyes of a lieutenant in the U.S. Army, on the forced march of the Cherokee—what became known as the Trail of Tears—from their land in Georgia to Indian Territory in Oklahoma. The events of the poem take place in Arkansas in 1838. (Before reading, you may wish to refer back to page xii.)

A Sequence of Poems

In 1828 gold was discovered on Cherokee land at Dahlonega, in northern Georgia. Where the Cherokees for centuries had hunted, now they grew corn, cotton, squash, and beans, and tended lush peach orchards and rich cattle farms. But still they did not own Dahlonega "just because they had seen it from the mountain or passed it in the chase," so President Andrew Jackson, former Indian fighter, then decreed. In May 1830, at

words for everyday use

de • cree (di krē′) *v.,* command; order judicially. *The judge is expected to decree that the defendants be held without bail.*

Jackson's prodding, Congress passed the Removal Act, which set aside, in territory west of the Mississippi, districts "for the reception of such tribes or nations of Indians as may choose to exchange the lands where they now reside and remove there." But the Indians had no choice: eight years later, when all resistance had failed, most of the eighteen thousand Cherokees joined the other southern tribes—Choctaws, Chickasaws, Creeks, and Seminoles—in forced exile, where thousands died on what became known as the Trail of Tears.

II The Cherokee Lottery

"The Cherokee Nation . . . is a distinct community, occupying its own territory . . . which the citizens of Georgia have no right to enter, but with the assent of the Cherokees themselves, or in conformity with treaties and with the acts of Congress."

—Chief Justice John Marshall
The United States Supreme Court, 1832

"John Marshall has made his decision: now let him enforce it."

—Andrew Jackson
President of the United States, 1832

Georgia 1838

When the Cherokees refused to leave,
the state set up a lottery[1]
to rid them of their land:
a clumsy wooden wheel
sat poised above great black
numbers painted on bright squares—
woodpecker red and watermelon green,

1. **lottery.** Drawing in which prizes are distributed to the winners among persons buying a chance

words for everyday use

prod (präd') *v.,* urge someone on; incite to action. *My younger brother likes to prod my sister to do things that will get her in trouble.*

as • sent (ə sent') *v.,* to agree to something after careful consideration; consent. *I think that once Mom finds out who is chaperoning, she will assent to let me go to the party.*

poise (pȯiz') *v.,* balance; to hold suspended without motion in a steady position. *The gymnast was poised on the balance beam ready to begin her routine.*

wild azalea[2] orange
and morningglory[3] blue—
to designate the farms
that now were up for grabs[4]:
and while the wheel creaked
slowly round, the Georgians
danced and sang:
"All we want in this creation
is a pretty little girl
and a big plantation
way down yonder
in the Cherokee Nation!"
and laughed until they cried.

◀ What do the brightly painted squares designate?

General Winfield Scott,[5]
blue-uniformed, bushy-browed, six-foot-three,
arrived from Washington
and addressed the Cherokees:
"May's full moon
is already on the wane,[6]
and before another
passes, every Cherokee,
man, woman, and child,
must move along to join
their brothers in the West."

◀ Where does General Scott tell the Cherokees they must go?

And when his troops swept in
from every quarter,
fixed bayonets[7] flashing in the sun
to roust[8] them from their tables
and their beds,

---

2. **azalea.** Flowering shrub
3. **morningglory.** Morning glory, a viny plant with trumpet-shaped flowers that are often a bright sky-blue
4. **up for grabs.** Free for the taking, offered to anyone who wants it
5. **General Winfield Scott.** Scott fought in the War of 1812, the Mexican-American War, the American Civil War, and several Indian Wars; in 1832 he was made commander of the federal troops in charge of removing the Cherokee from their land in Georgia.
6. **wane.** Period from the full phase of the moon to the new moon when the fullness of the moon decreases
7. **bayonets.** Steel blades attached to rifles and used in hand-to-hand combat
8. **roust.** To drive, roughly or unceremoniously, out or away

words for everyday use

des • ig • nate (de' zig nāt) *v.,* indicate and set apart; point out; make known; specify. *The saleswoman told us that the orange stickers designate sale items.*

What do the Cherokee do when General Scott's troops roust them from their homes?

▶ As the Cherokee assemble behind White-haired Going Snake, who voices the nation's grief?

the Cherokees, stripped
of everything they owned,
at last lined up to go.

White-haired Going Snake,
the eighty-year-old chief,
on his pony led the way,
followed by young men on horseback.
Then the women and children,
with the rustling sound
wind makes in tall dry grass
came on, and no one spoke,
no one cried: only the dogs
howled as if they alone
could voice the nation's grief
while the procession slowly wound its way
off through the tall pines
over the red clay.

At the moment they began to move,
a low rumble of distant thunder
broke directly westward
and a dark spiral cloud rose
above the horizon,
but the sun was unclouded,
the thunder rolled away,
and no rain fell.

VII The Pumpkin Field

An Army Lieutenant observes the Cherokees he guards on their passage to the west, Arkansas 1838

What a grand lot they were,
the Cherokees I first saw in June,
lined up in their Georgian camp
to greet the chief on their departure,
elegant blankets hanging loose
about their shoulders, ramrod-straight,
dark eyes darting from high-boned
copper faces under bright turbans
and striped caps pulled down at an angle,
some in long robes, some in tunics,[1]

1. **tunics.** Slip-on garments

all with sashes or wondrous drapery,
they stood, framed by bearded oaks,
Old Testament patriarchs[2]
pausing on their way to the Promised Land.[3]

Then in October, where I'd been sent ahead
to patrol their passage here in Arkansas,
they came from a cold and threadbare wood,
thin pines bent and tipped with sleet,
eyes glazed and blank,
half-naked, barefoot,
bones poking through
their scarecrow shredded clothing,
and stumbled through layers of mist
onto a scraggly open field
where in wet and tangled grass
fat pumpkins lay in rows
like painted severed heads.

Oblivious to all around them,
skeletal automatons,[4]
the Cherokees plunged ahead
until a farmer on the edge
bade[5] them halt
and, breaking off a pumpkin,
invited them to take
whatever his poor field could offer.

Flies swarming to their target,
they darted up and down the rows,
black hair flying,
long-nailed tentacles[6]
protruding, they ripped apart
the pumpkin flesh

◀ *How do the Cherokee look when the lieutenant first sees them in June in Georgia?*

◀ *How do the Cherokee look when the lieutenant sees them in October in Arkansas?*

◀ *What does the poor farmer offer to the Cherokee?*

2. **Old Testament patriarchs.** Refers to early male leaders in the Bible, from Adam to Abraham and Moses, considered to be fathers of the human race
3. **Promised Land.** Biblical land of Canaan; today, the country of Israel; the land promised to Abraham by the Lord, according to the Bible
4. **automatons.** Robots; individuals who act in a mechanical fashion
5. **bade.** Offered; invited
6. **tentacles.** Long, flexible, finger-like growths capable of grasping, usually borne by invertebrate animals on the head or about the mouth

words for everyday use

pro • trud • ing (prō trüd″ iŋ) *v.*, jutting out; sticking out. *I knew my brother was hiding behind the drapes because I saw his feet protruding.*

until their brown and vacant
faces merged with jagged pulp,
seeds foaming from
their hungry mouths, and all I could see,
as on some battlefield, was
everywhere a wasted mass of orange flesh.

A light rain then began to fall
as if the shredded pumpkin fiber
drifted down around us:
I felt ill
and sensed that cholera[7]
had set in. The farmer guided
me inside his cabin
and put me down in a dark corner
where between the logs
I could empty my stomach.

All night long I lay there
while wind roared
and rain beat down
and through it I could hear the sloshing
of the weary feet,
the creak and rattle of ox-carts,
the cursing of the drivers,
cracking their long whips to urge the oxen on,
the whinnying of horses
as they struggled through the mud.

▶ As the lieutenant lies sick in the farmer's cabin all night, what can he hear?

"What have we done to these people?"
I cried out . . . And then a silence fell;
across the dark I saw
row after row of pumpkins carved and slit,
their crooked eyes
and pointed teeth all candle-lit within,
not pumpkins but death's-heads they were
with features of the vacant
hungry faces I had seen,
stretching to infinity
and glowing in the dark—
and glowing still when I awoke—

as they do now, and as they always will.

7. **cholera.** Any of several diseases of humans and domestic animals marked by severe stomach and intestinal symptoms

Critical Thinking Questions

1. According to the first reading, "A Sequence of Poems," what does President Andrew Jackson say about the Cherokee's claim to the land of Dahlonega, Georgia? What does Jackson encourage Congress to do? What do Jackson's actions reveal about his attitude toward the Cherokee?

2. According to the second reading, "II. Cherokee Lottery," when the state of Georgia tried to force the Cherokee off their land, the Cherokee sued the state. In whose favor did Chief Justice John Marshall rule? What does President Andrew Jackson's comment in response to Justice Marshall's ruling reveal about Jackson?

3. A **stanza** is a group of lines in a poem. Stanzas are usually separated from each other by spaces. In "VII. The Pumpkin Field," compare the description in the first stanza of the Cherokees in June with the description in the second stanza of the Cherokees in October. Why have they changed so dramatically?

4. Read again the last stanza and the last line of the poem. How do you think the army lieutenant feels about what has been done to the Cherokee? How do you know this?

RELATED READING

from *The Desert Smells Like Rain: A Naturalist in O'odham Country*

by Gary Paul Nabhan

ABOUT THE RELATED READING

"An Overture" is taken from the book *The Desert Smells Like Rain: A Naturalist in O'odham Country* by Gary Paul Nabhan. Nabhan is a natural history writer and director of the Center for Sustainable Environments at Northern Arizona University in Flagstaff, Arizona. An ethnobiologist who studies how people interact with living organisms, he has worked with native farmers throughout the southwestern United States to conserve traditional food plants. In *The Desert Smells Like Rain*, Nabhan writes about the Tohono O'odham people, also called the Papago Indians, who have spent hundreds of years living off the land in the south-central part of the Sonoran Desert. In "An Overture," Nabhan writes poetically of the first summer rains of the desert, and what they mean to the plants, the animals, and the Papago Indians.

from *The Desert Smells Like Rain: A Nationalist in O'odham Country*

An Overture

With many dust storms, with many lightnings,
with many thunders, with many rainbows, it started to go.
From within wet mountains, more clouds came out
and joined it.

Joseph Pancho, *Mockingbird Speech*

Last Saturday before dusk, the summer's 114-degree heat broke to 79 within an hour. A fury of wind whipped up, pelting houses with dust, debris, and gravel. Then a scatter of rain came, as a froth of purplish clouds charged across the skies. As the last of the sun's light dissipated, we could see Baboquivari Peak silhouetted on a red horizon, lightning dancing around its head.

words for everyday use

de • bris (də brē′) *n.,* remains of something broken down or destroyed; accumulation of fragments of rock; something discarded; trash. *The parking lot was covered with paper, cans, and other debris.*

dis • si • pate (di′ sə pāt) *v.,* scatter; disperse; grow thin and gradually vanish. *After the musical festival ended, it took hours for the crowd of fans to dissipate.*

The rains came that night—they changed the world.

Crusty dry since April, the desert floor softened under the rain's dance. Near the rain-pocked surface, hundreds of thousands of wild sprouts of bloodroot amaranth are popping off their seedcoats[1] and diving toward light. Barren places will soon be shrouded in a veil of green.

Desert arroyos[2] are running again, muddy water swirling after a head of suds, dung,[3] and detritus.[4] Where sheetfloods[5] pool, buried animals awake, or new broods[6] hatch. At dawn, dark egg-shaped clouds of flying ants hover over ground, excited in the early morning light.

In newly filled waterholes, spadefoot toads[7] suddenly congregate. The males bellow. They seek out mates, then latch onto them with their special nuptial[8] pads. The females spew out egg masses into the hot murky water. For two nights, the toad ponds are wild with chanting while the Western spadefoot's burnt-peanut-like smell looms thick in the air.

A yellow mud turtle crawls out of the drenched bottom of an old adobe borrow pit where he had been buried through the hot dry spell. He plods a hundred yards over to a floodwater reservoir and dives in. He has no memory of how many days it's been since his last swim, but the pull of the water—*that* is somehow familiar.

◀ *What does the author say the rains did?*

◀ *What does the author say about barren places?*

◀ *What does a yellow mud turtle do? Of what does he have no memory? What is familiar to the turtle?*

This is the time when the Papago Indians of the Sonoran Desert celebrate the coming of the rainy season moons, the *Jujkiabig Mamsad,* and the beginning of a new year.

---

1. **seedcoats.** Outer protective covering of a seed
2. **arroyos.** Water-carved gully or channel
3. **dung.** Excrement of an animal, manure
4. **detritus.** Loose material, such as rock fragments, that results from disintegration; debris
5. **sheetfloods.** Tremendous discharges of rain water that travel downhill, such as down a mountain slope, and wash over a flat area all at once
6. **broods.** Young of an animal
7. **spadefoot toads.** Any of a family of burrowing toads
8. **nuptial.** Characteristic of or occurring in the breeding season

words for everyday use

shroud (shroud') *v.,* covered; concealed. *As dark clouds moved in to shroud the sun, the people on the beach gathered their belongings and left.*

con • gre • gate (käŋ' grə gāt) *v.,* gather, assemble, come together in a group. *People began to congregate around the band until the dance floor was crowded.*

bel • low (be' lō) *v.,* make a loud, deep sound. *The cows in the pasture bellow so loudly people a mile away can hear them.*

▶ *When the author stops by the Madrugada home, what is the family eagerly talking about? Earlier, what hadn't the family been sure about? Why?*

▶ *What did the author once ask a Papago boy? How did the boy answer?*

▶ *How does the author say most people would react to the boy's answer to the question? Why does the author say the boy answered the question as he did?*

Fields lying fallow[9] since the harvest of the winter crop are now ready for another planting. If sown within a month after summer solstice,[10] they can produce a crop quick enough for harvest by the Feast of San Francisco, October 4.

When I went by the Madrugada home in Little Tucson on Monday, the family was eagerly talking about planting the flashflood field again. At the end of June, Julian wasn't even sure if he would plant this year—no rain yet, too hot to prepare the field, and hardly any water left in their *charco* catchment basin.[11]

Now, a fortnight later, the pond is nearly filled up to the brim. Runoff has fed into it through four small washes. Sheetfloods have swept across the field surface. Julian imagines big yellow squash blossoms in his field, just another month or so away. It makes his mouth water.

Once I asked a Papago youngster what the desert smelled like to him. He answered with little hesitation:

"The desert smells like rain."

His reply is a contradiction in the minds of most people. How could the desert smell like rain, when deserts are, by definition, places which lack substantial rainfall?

The boy's response was a sort of Papago shorthand. Hearing Papago can be like tasting a delicious fruit, while sensing that the taste comes from a tree with roots too deep to fathom.

The question had triggered a scent—creosote bushes after a storm—their aromatic oils released by the rains. His nose remembered being out in the desert, overtaken: *the desert smells like rain.*

Most outsiders are struck by the apparent absence of rain in deserts, feeling that such places lack something vital. Papago, on the other hand, are intrigued by the unpredictability rather than the paucity of rainfall—theirs

9. **fallow.** Dormant, inactive; left untilled or unsown after plowing
10. **summer solstice.** June 21, the longest day of the year
11. ***charco* catchment basin.** *Charco* is a Spanish word meaning *pool* or *watering hole;* a catchment basin is a large bowl-shaped depression in the earth used to catch water.

words for everyday use

pau • ci • ty (po' sə tē) *n.,* smallness of quantity; scarcity; small amount. *The paucity of food on the buffet meant that half the people at the party didn't get anything to eat.*

is a dynamic, lively world, responsive to stormy forces that may come at any time.

A Sonoran Desert village may receive five inches of rain one year and fifteen the next. A single storm may dump an inch and a half in the matter of an hour on one field and entirely skip another a few miles away. Dry spells lasting four months may be broken by a single torrential cloudburst, then resume again for several more months. Unseasonal storms, and droughts during the customary rainy seasons, are frequent enough to reduce patterns to chaos.

The Papago have become so finely tuned to this unpredictability that it shapes the way they speak of rain. It has also ingrained itself deeply in the structure of their language.

◀ *To what does the author say the Papago have become finely attuned?*

Linguist William Pilcher has observed that the Papago discuss events in terms of their probability of occurrence, avoiding any assumption that an event will happen for sure:

> . . . . it is my impression that the Papago abhor the idea of making definite statements. I am still in doubt as to how close a rain storm must be before one may properly say *t'o tji:* (It is going to rain on us), rather than *tki'o tju:ks* (something like: It looks like it may be going to rain on us).

Since few Papago are willing to confirm that something will happen until it does, an element of surprise becomes part of almost everything. Nothing is ever really cut and dried. When rains do come, they're a gift, a windfall, a lucky break.

Elderly Papago have explained to me that rain is more than just water. There are different ways that water comes to living things, and what it brings with it affects how things grow.

◀ *What have elderly Papago explained to the author?*

Remedio Cruz was once explaining to me why he plants the old White Sonora variety of wheat when he does. He had waited for some early January rains to gently moisten his field before he planted.

words for everyday use

dy • nam • ic (dī na′ mik) *adj.*, marked by continuous change. *The weather this spring was dynamic, hot and sunny one day and cold and rainy the next.*

ab • hor (əb hȯr′) *v.*, loathe; hate. *I abhor it when people are intentionally cruel to others.*

"That Pap'go wheat—it's good to plant just in January or early February. It grows good on just the *rain*water from the sky. It would not do good with water from the *ground,* so that's why we plant it when those soft winter rains come to take care of it."

▶ *In the 1950s, what did ecologist Lloyd Tevis try to do?*

In the late 1950s, a Sonoran Desert ecologist tried to simulate the gentle winter rains in an attempt to make the desert bloom. Lloyd Tevis used untreated groundwater from a well, sprayed up through a sprinkler, to encourage wildflower germination[12] on an apparently lifeless patch of desert. While Tevis did trigger germination of one kind of desert wildflower with a little less than two inches of fake rain, none germinated with less than an inch. In general, production of other wildflowers required more than three or four inches of fake rain.

Tevis was then surprised to see what happened when less than an inch of real rain fell on his experimental site in January. He noticed in the previously sparse vegetation "a tremendous emergence of seedlings. Real rain demonstrated an extraordinary superiority over the artificial variety to bring about a high rate of germination." With one particular kind of desert wildflower, seedlings were fifty-six times more numerous after nearly an inch of real rain than they were after the more intense artificial watering.

The stimulating power of rain in the desert is simply more than moisture. Be it the nutrients released in a rainstorm, or the physical force of the water, there are other releasing mechanisms associated with rainwater. But even if someone worked up a better simulation of rain using *fortified* groundwater, would it be very useful in making the desert bloom?

Doubtful. Remedio himself wonders about the value of groundwater pumping for farming, for water is something he *sings* rather than pumps into his field. Every summer, Remedio and a few elderly companions sing to bring the waters from the earth and sky to meet each other. Remedio senses that only with this meeting will his summer beans, corn, and squash grow. A field relying solely on groundwater would not have what it takes. He has heard that well

12. **germination.** Act of or condition of seeds beginning to sprout and develop into plants

words for everyday use

sim • u • late (sim' yə latē) *v.,* to copy, represent, feign. *He designed a game to simulate a real estate sale.*

water has some kind of "medicine" (chemical) in it that is no good for crops. In addition, he believes that groundwater pumping as much as twenty miles away adversely affects the availability of moisture to his field.

I joined in a study with other scientists to compare the nutritive[13] value of tepary beans[14] grown in Papago flashflood fields with those grown in modern Anglo-American[15]-style groundwater-irrigated fields nearby. The protein content of the teparies grown in the traditional flashflood environments tended to be higher than that of the same tepary bean varieties grown with water pumped from the ground. Production appeared to be more efficient in the Papago fields—more food energy was gained with less energy in labor and fuel spent. No wonder—it is a way of agriculture that has fine-tuned itself to local conditions over generations.

◀ *What does the author say of Papago agriculture?*

There they are, Julian and Remedio—growing food in a desert too harsh for most kinds of agriculture—using cues that few of us would ever notice. Their sense of how the desert works comes from decades of day-to-day observations. These perceptions have been filtered through a cultural tradition that has been refined, honed, and handed down over centuries of living in arid places.

◀ *How do the Papago gain their sense of how the desert works?*

If others wish to adapt to the Sonoran Desert's peculiarities, this ancient knowledge can serve as a guide. Yet the best guide will tell you: there are certain things you must learn on your own. The desert is unpredictable, enigmatic. One minute you will be smelling dust. The next, the desert can smell just like rain.

---

13. **nutritive.** Nourishing
14. **tepary beans.** Annual twining bean that is native to the southwestern United States and Mexico and is cultivated for its edible seeds
15. **Anglo-American.** Relating to English-speaking North Americans of English descent

words for everyday use

enig • mat • ic (enig ma' tik) *adj.*, mysterious; unexplainable; mystifying. *The psychic created an enigmatic atmosphere to camouflage the fact that she was a fake.*

Critical Thinking Questions

1. The author writes, "The rains came that night—they changed the world." How do the rains "change the world"? Provide several specific examples from the essay.

2. An **image** is language that creates a concrete representation of an object or an experience. An image is also the vivid mental picture created in the reader's mind by that language. The author creates several images in the first six paragraphs. Identify an image you find particularly effective and explain why.

3. Why do you think the author chose to title his book *The Desert Smells Like Rain?*

from *Children of the Maya: A Guatemalan Indian Odyssey*

by Brent Ashabranner
photographs by Paul Conklin

ABOUT THE RELATED READING

Brent Ashabranner has written widely on American social history and issues. Former director of the Peace Corps in India and deputy director of the Peace Corps in Washington, D.C., he worked in Ethiopia, Libya, and Nigeria for U.S. foreign assistance programs and for the Ford Foundation in the Philippines and Indonesia.

"An Uncertain Future," an excerpt from *Children of the Maya,* a book published in 1986, tells the story of Indiantown, Florida. In the 1980s, during the most violent part of the Guatemalan Civil War, many Mayan Indians fleeing Guatemala settled in Indiantown, a small community thirty miles west of West Palm Beach, Florida. The excerpt offers insight into the impact of the civil war on Guatemalan children, and describes how Father Frank O'Loughlin and Peter Upton of the American Friends Service Community fought to keep refugees from being sent back to Guatemala.

from *Children of the Maya: A Guatemalan Indian Odyssey*

An Uncertain Future

THE THREAT of being sent back to Guatemala is the darkest cloud hovering over the Mayan Indians in Indiantown and for others who have sought refuge in Arizona and California. Just a few days after their arrival in Indiantown, six Guatemalans were picked up by the border patrol[1] and taken to the Krome Detention Center for illegal aliens[2] in Miami. They were separated from their children, who were cared for by other Mayan families.

◀ *What was the darkest cloud hovering over the Mayan Indians? Just a few days after their arrival in Florida, what happened to six Guatemalan refugees?*

Father Frank O'Loughlin, the parish[3] priest at Holy Cross Catholic Church in Indiantown, spends a great deal

1. **border patrol.** Mobile, uniformed law enforcement arm of the U.S. government responsible for detecting and apprehending people who enter the country illegally
2. **illegal aliens.** People from other countries who enter the United States without legal permission
3. **parish.** Local church community

of his time fighting for a better life for migrant[4] farmworkers. He quickly took to heart the plight of the Mayan Indians and led the community efforts to help them. When word reached him that some of the Guatemalans had been taken to the detention center,[5] he went immediately to Miami to get them out.

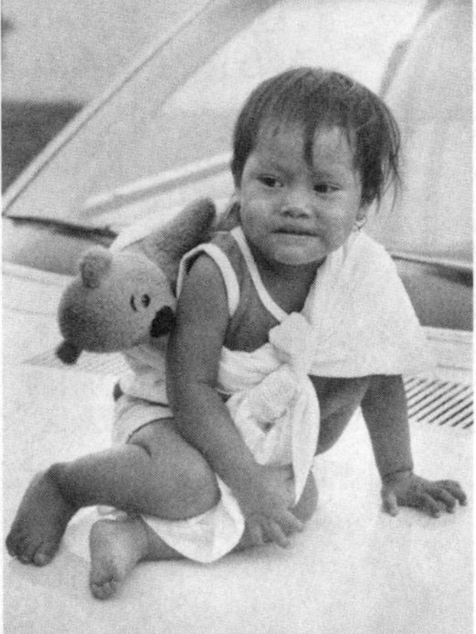

This Guatemalan child carries a stuffed toy in the type of Mayan wrap traditionally used to carry babies and young children.

Few things are harder than battling the immigration bureaucracy, but Father Frank is a battler. He is also an Irish immigrant and naturalized U.S. citizen[6] that one newspaper reporter admiringly described as a street fighter. The priest sought the help of civil rights lawyers with the American Friends Service Committee[7] and Florida Rural Legal Services.[8] It took them almost two months, but they finally got a federal judge to release the Guatemalans. But the release was only temporary while they waited for the immigration court to rule on their applications for asylum as refugees.

▶ *Whose help did Father O'Loughlin seek, and what did they accomplish?*

The Maya in Indiantown have put their hopes of staying legally in the country entirely in the hands of the civil rights lawyers, who must present each case to the court

4. **migrant.** Person who moves regularly in order to find work, especially harvesting crops

5. **detention center.** Building or place in which people are held in temporary custody; refugees seeking asylum in the United States may be held for indefinite periods of time in detention centers while the federal government processes their applications for asylum.

6. **naturalized U.S. citizen.** Person who was not born a U.S. citizen, but who came legally to the United States and fulfilled government requirements for becoming a citizen

7. **American Friends Service Committee.** Organization based on the beliefs of the Religious Society of Friends, or Quakers, that is committed to resolving conflict and seeking justice around the world through nonviolent methods

8. **Florida Rural Legal Services.** Organization offering legal help to moderate- and low-income people in rural Florida

words for everyday use

a • sy • lum (ə sī′ ləm) *n.*, protection from arrest and being sent back to the country from which one flees, given especially to political refugees by a nation, an embassy, or other agency. *In many places around the world, war and forces thousands of people to flee their native countries and seek asylum in other countries.*

individually. Immigration laws are meaningless to the Guatemalans, although they know only too well the dangers they face if they are returned to their country. Some have heard from relatives and friends in Guatemala that others who have returned to their homes have been killed.

"To go back is to die," said one of the Maya.

United States immigration law defines a refugee as a person who had fled from his country because of political or religious persecution. The Mayan Indians of Guatemala fit that definition to tragic perfection. The U.S. State Department[9], however, has taken the position that the Maya who have come to the United States are not refugees and that it is safe for them to return to Guatemala. . . .

◄ How does U.S. immigration law define a refugee? Did the Maya fit this definition? What position did the U.S. State Department take regarding Guatemalan refugees?

Fortunately for the Mayan Indians, the State Department cannot on its own authority send them back to Guatemala. The decision as to whether they receive refugee status or at least are allowed to stay in the United States until they can safely return to Guatemala is up to the courts. First, there is the immigration court and then, if necessary, the United States Court of Appeals. All of this takes time; and if all else fails, the civil rights lawyers intend to take their case directly to Congress.

A main concern of those helping the Guatemalans is what the effect of being uprooted again might have on the Mayan children. To help answer that question, Peter Upton [an attorney with American Friends Service Committee in Miami] asked Neil Boothby to come to Indiantown and get to know the Mayan children. To prepare his arguments for the courts, Upton needed to know as much as he could about how the Mayan children were still affected by what had happened to them in Guatemala and about how well they were adjusting in Indiantown. Upton needed the insights and judgments of an experienced psychologist.

◄ What was a main concern for those helping refugees from Guatemala? What did Peter Upton do to help address that concern?

That is what Neil Boothby is. Educated at Harvard[10] as a clinical child psychologist,[11] he has worked in both Asia and Africa helping refugee children who are victims of war and political violence. Boothby said yes to Upton and came to Indiantown with his wife and young son. It was not a short visit. They arrived in September, 1984, and stayed until July, 1985.

9. **U.S. State Department.** Agency of the executive branch of the U.S. government responsible for handling relations between the United States and countries around the world

10. **Harvard.** One of the most highly regarded universities in the United States

11. **clinical child psychologist.** One who is trained to assess the mental health and behavior of children by interacting with and observing them

▶ *What kinds of pictures did the children Boothby worked with draw?*

▶ *What did Boothby learn about the children's memories of Guatemala and their feelings about returning to Guatemala?*

Boothby selected a group of Mayan children between the ages of six and eighteen and learned everything he could about them. He talked to each one of them individually a number of times, watched them in the classrooms and on the playgrounds, visited them in their homes and got to know their parents. He talked to their teachers and others in Indiantown who knew them. When he was finished he knew their personal and family histories, and he knew them.

One way of finding out what was in the Mayan children's minds was to ask them to draw pictures about their past life in Guatemala. Some of the pictures they drew were of mountains, birds, flowers, and village life that they remembered fondly from their lives there. But other pictures were very different. They were of planes dropping bombs on villages, helicopters pouring bullets down on people, soldiers attacking a village, guerrillas[12] killing a man. In gently questioning the children, Boothby learned that these were scenes they had witnessed or been a part of, sometimes more than once. Talking about them was hard for some of the Mayan children, and there was no doubt that the memories were indelibly imprinted in their minds.

One of the boys had seen soldiers decapitate[13] a guerrilla. When he told the psychologist about it, he spoke in a whisper and his face was sweaty. "I saw it all," he said, "but they didn't see me."

While the Mayan children had some good memories of Guatemala, Boothby learned that fear and anxiety were the emotions closest to the surface when he asked them if they ever thought about returning to their country. From watching them play at school, Boothby discovered that, when angry at missing a turn on a swing or being left out of a game, the worst threat that one Mayan child could hurl at another was, "The teachers are going to send you back to Guatemala!"

---

12. **guerrillas.** People who engage in warfare against their own government and/or against others of their country
13. **decapitate.** Cut off the head

words for everyday use

in • del • i • bly (in de′ lə blē) *adv.,* that cannot be removed, washed away, or erased; lasting; unforgettable. *The elegance of the wedding invitation indelibly impressed every guest who received one.*

im • print (im print′) *v.,* to mark permanently. *As soon as I saw the sun begin to set over the Grand Canyon, I knew the view would imprint itself forever in my memory.*

Child psychologist Neil Boothby spent nearly a year working with the Mayan children of Indiantown to learn as much as possible about their lives before and after they came to the United States as refugees.

When Boothby asked Mayan children to draw pictures about their past lives, one boy drew a happy memory of his home in Guatemala. The quetzal, a bird with a long, beautiful green tail, is Guatemala's national bird. It symbolizes freedom to the Maya.

Some of the children's other memories were horrific. A Mayan boy drew his village in Guatemala being bombed by army planes.

A young girl drew an army helicopter firing bullets at people praying in front of the church in her village.

Boothby puts it very clearly. "They are children who have been through too much violence, known too much fear. They have seen too much human suffering in Guatemala and Mexico."

His recommendation is equally clear: "If you want to do the best thing for the children, you will let them stay in Indiantown where they have adjusted well and made strong attachments in the school and community. You won't even let it get into their minds that they might be sent back to Guatemala."

◀ *What did Boothby recommend regarding the children from Guatemala?*

To say that the Maya's adjustment to life in Indiantown has been easy would be to deny reality. Moving from one world into another can never be easy. But they have accepted the new life for themselves and their children and have made up their minds that it will be as good a life as possible. Yet they are Mayan Indians and have roots in a culture that is one of the most ancient on earth. Some of the memories, some of the links with the past, will fade, but some will remain.

They brought with them a sense of caring that shows no sign of disappearing in their strange new environment. When they must travel as migrant workers, some leave their children with friends who they know will treat them as their own. Several of the families have with them children left orphaned by the terror in Guatemala. All the Maya want to know what is going on in each other's lives, and they try to help when help is needed.

◀ *What do the Maya do with their children when they must travel as migrant workers?*

They brought with them a gentleness and a contemplative spirit that have not faded. Sister Carol says that in three years she has known of only two fights among the Mayan men, both caused by alcohol. Sister Esperanza describes the way the children love to look for wild flowers and to watch the many birds that inhabit this town on the edge of the Everglades.[14]

Once Sister Esperanza saw three little Mayan girls sitting quietly on a step at school. "What are you doing?" she asked.

14. **Everglades.** Vast swamp region and unique ecosystem of southern Florida

words for everyday use

con • tem • pla • tive (kən tem′ plə tiv) *adj.,* marked by concentration on spiritual things; marked by careful attention and steady regard. *Each summer, I return from my vacation in the woods feeling relaxed and contemplative.*

"Watching the grass grow," one of them answered.

Already the Maya in Indiantown have begun to have a Fiesta of San Miguel in September just as it would be in Guatemala. They eat the special foods, fly kites, sing happy songs and sad songs. They have a mirimba, which is an ancient Mayan musical instrument, and it is made of hormiga wood from the Guatemalan forests, as all true mirimbas must be. The mirimba was brought piece by piece from Guatemala, and it is now kept in the church as a great treasure. At special times it is played all day and all night. Several of the Mayan men know how to play it, both popular songs and the sacred music of the Maya that reaches far back into the past.

© Paul Conklin

A Maya at prayer in Holy Cross Church.

▶ *What does Sunday mass at Holy Cross Church provide for the Maya?*

Holy Cross Church also provides a link with their past village life. Every Sunday a special mass is said in Spanish. The familiar songs are sung, and some words of Kanjobal[15] are always a part of the service. Whole families attend, husbands, wives, children, grandparents. A bus brings those who are living in migrant camps outside of town, and Sunday mass provides an opportunity to find out what is happening in the lives of others and to exchange any news that might have come from Huehuetenango. Such news belongs to every Maya and is important in their lives.

In one corner of the chapel are pictures of priests and nuns who have been killed in the violence in Central America. The pictures of twenty-one martyred[16] priests from Guatemala outnumber all the others combined. The Maya look at the pictures, but they need no reminder of the fury in their country from which they sought and found refuge in this small town in Florida.

15. **Kanjobal.** One of many different languages spoken by different tribes of the Mayan Indians

16. **martyred.** Put to death for adhering to a belief, faith, or profession

Critical Thinking Questions

1. The reading points out that immigration laws were meaningless to the Guatemalan refugees. Why do you think this was?

2. Why did Peter Upton ask Neil Boothby, the psychologist, to come to Indiantown and get to know the Mayan children?

3. Why did Boothby ask them to draw pictures? What did he discover from the pictures they drew?

4. What characteristics did the Maya bring with them to Indiantown?

5. This reading tells the stories of a small group of refugees from one country during the 1980s. It gives you some understanding of the official position that the U.S. government took regarding the refugees from Guatemala. It also shows you how people working together have the power to make a difference. How does this nonfiction excerpt reinforce Esperanza and Estevan's experiences in *The Bean Trees?*

RELATED READING

"Coyotes and the Underground Railway"

ABOUT THE RELATED READING

This article by Richard Kazis from *New Internationalist* magazine was published in 1983, when thousands of refugees were fleeing Central America to escape oppression and death squads. The article summarizes the U.S. response to the influx of illegal refugees, the political reasons underlying the response, and the beginnings of the Sanctuary Movement formed by Americans of strong religious faith to transport and shelter the refugees.

New Internationalist magazine is published by the New Internationalist workers' cooperative based in Oxford, England. According to its mission statement, the magazine "exists to report on issues of world poverty and inequality; to focus attention on the unjust relationship between the powerful and the powerless in both rich and poor nations; to debate and campaign for the radical changes necessary if the basic material and spiritual needs of all are to be met." You can visit the *New Internationalist* website at www.newint.org.

"Coyotes and the Underground Railway"

Refugees from the Fighting

As the fighting intensifies in Central America, so does the human flow of refugees. But despite America's interest in the area few make it legally across the Rio Grande.[1] *Richard Kazis looks at a new, church-sponsored attempt to aid those fleeing their war-ravaged homes.*

▶ *How did most of the refugees from Central America enter the United States?*

Since 1980 at least 250,000 refugees from Central America have entered the U.S. Most have done so illegally, paying 'coyotes'[2] in Mexico to help them slip past the border patrol.[3]

1. **Rio Grande.** River that flows from southwest Colorado to the Gulf of Mexico and forms part of the border between Mexico and the United States
2. **coyotes.** People who, for a fee, act as guides to help people sneak over the border between Mexico and the United States to enter the United States illegally
3. **border patrol.** Mobile, uniformed law enforcement arm of the U.S. government responsible for detecting and apprehending people who have illegally entered the country

words for everyday use

spon • sor (spän' sər) *v.*, to assume responsibility, as a person or an organization, for paying for, planning, and carrying out a project or activity. *The local hardware store will sponsor our softball team and pay for our uniforms.*

The United States government does not regard Central American refugees as political refugees.[4] According to the Reagan administration[5] the majority come to the U.S. as 'economic migrants.'[6] They are quickly deported[7] unless they can prove a 'well-founded fear of persecution.'

◀ How did the Reagan administration regard the majority of refugees who came to the United States?

There are hard reasons why Washington does not want to classify Central American refugees as political. Peasants from El Salvador and Guatemala[8] have the misfortune of fleeing countries which are American allies and staunch enemies of Nicaragua and Cuba.[9]

◀ What misfortune did those fleeing El Salvador and Guatemala share?

The United States provides essential military and economic aid to both Salvador and Guatemala. In effect, by encouraging terror and violence in the region Washington has helped create the refugee problem it now faces. Politically, this is a reality which the Reagan administration cannot afford to acknowledge by giving Central American refugees special status.

◀ What did Washington help create?

To Jim Corbett, a retired Arizona rancher active in helping Central American refugees, 'the violation of refugee rights is an integral part of the U.S. military strategy.' According to Corbett, Vietnam-style pacification programs[10] now being practised in Central America 'require that people *not* leave the area in which they live.'

---

4. **political refugees.** People who flee their country because the actions of their government places them in danger
5. **Reagan administration.** President Reagan and other members of the executive branch of the U.S. government during his term of office; Ronald Reagan was president of the United States from 1981–1989.
6. **economic migrants.** People who move around in search of better jobs; people leaving their own country in search of better economic conditions
7. **deported.** Sent back to the country from which they came
8. **El Salvador and Guatemala.** Central American countries; during the 1980s, both countries were under the control of military dictatorships engaged in civil war against organized groups of citizens of their countries; President Reagan increased military and economic support to the governments of both countries.
9. **Nicaragua and Cuba.** Nicaragua is a Central American country; during the Reagan administration, the U.S. government helped rebel groups overthrow the country's existing communist government; Cuba is a communist country in the Caribbean.
10. **pacification programs.** Strategies used to suppress or eliminate a population considered to be hostile; the pacification programs carried out by the Guatemalan government, such as the "Beans and Guns" program, in which Guatemalan Indians were given food and guns in return for joining the army, were modeled after strategies the U.S. military used during the Vietnam War.

words for everyday use

staunch (stȯnch') *adj.,* faithful; firm; unwavering; dependable. *My mother is a staunch supporter of everything that her children do.*

in • te • gral (in' ti grəl) *adj.,* essential to completeness; necessary; fundamental; indispensable. *Juanita is a fabulous cook and says that great food is an integral part of any social gathering.*

Affectionately known as the 'Quaker[11] coyote', Jim Corbett is a central figure in a new church-based 'sanctuary' movement. More than 60 U.S. churches have actively assisted Salvadoran and Guatemalan refugees to cross safely into the United States. Jim Corbett estimates he has personally helped about 400 people enter the U.S. Many continue along a modern-day 'underground railroad' to temporary sanctuary in churches, where they are helped to find work and housing.

According to sanctuary supporter Rev. John Fife, pastor of the Southside United Presbyterian Church in Tucson, Arizona, 'We came to the conclusion that the problem was U.S. policy. We decided the only thing we could do was show the American people what was wrong with that policy.'

▶ *What did Fife's congregation do on March 24, 1981?*

On March 24, 1981 (the anniversary of the murder of Salvadoran Archbishop Oscar Romero[12]) Fife's congregation declared publicly its commitment to harboring and aiding Central American refugees in defiance of U.S. immigration laws. Since then a nationwide movement has developed. About 60 cities have public sanctuary sites. Groups in 50 other cities and towns are preparing to 'go public'. And over 600 other congregations and religious organizations, Roman Catholic, Jewish and Protestant of various denominations, have given public endorsement and financial support.

▶ *What motivated the sanctuary activists?*

The motivation of sanctuary activists is both political and moral. The political goal is to change American policy in Central America. But the commitment to public sanctuary is seen as a religious as well as political responsibility. In Biblical times, 'cities of refuge' were established as shelters and holy places provided sanctuary 'lest innocent

11. **Quaker.** Member of a religious organization called the Religious Society of Friends; the Quaker movement advocates religious tolerance, equality for all, opposition to war, social reform, volunteerism, a simple lifestyle, and the pursuit of inner spirituality.

12. **murder of Salvadoran Archbishop Oscar Romero.** Catholic archbishop in El Salvador who spoke out for the poor of the country and against the Salvadoran government; in 1980, Romero wrote to President Jimmy Carter to ask him to stop sending U.S. aid to the Salvadoran government, as it was being used to suppress the Salvadoran people; Romero was assassinated on March 24, 1980.

words for everyday use

har • bor (här' bər) *v.,* to give shelter or refuge to. *The stand of pine trees provides safe harbor for numerous birds during the winter.*

blood be shed.' The tradition of church sanctuary has evolved over the centuries. Many congregations have long provided shelter for the homeless. During the Vietnam War some provided sanctuary for draft resisters. Today that tradition is being revived and extended.

According to Kathleen Flaherty, a former Peace Corps[13] volunteer active in the sanctuary movement in Washington DC, 'the sanctuary movement provides a unique opportunity for churches to do a lot of soul-searching. It requires questioning what it means to be a religious person.'

Those who harbour[14] or aid illegal immigrants are subject to five years imprisonment and 52.000[15] in fines. But thousands of Americans are taking that risk. 'It is only eight hours risk for me to drive a family to the next safe-house', says John Fife. 'But the refugees are risking their very lives.'

◀ *What comment did Fife make about the risk he assumed when he aided refugees compared to the risk the refugees assumed?*

The few hundred refugees aided by this network are obviously only a tiny fraction of those needing help. But Kathleen Flaherty believes 'the churches are making a public statement and are publicizing a problem the government would like to keep hidden. The important thing now is to create opportunities for the refugees themselves to speak—to be heard by churches, community groups and elected officials.'

As this happens, the American people will hear a very different story about Central America than they are hearing from State Department[16] officials. 'I didn't want to come here,' said a Guatemalan Indian helped by the sanctuary movement to find a job and a home for his family. 'God willing someday I will return to my home.'

There are legal efforts and a strong public campaign building across the nation to force the US government to grant Extended Voluntary Departure[17] status to Central American refugees.

---

13. **Peace Corps.** Body of trained people sent as volunteers from the United States to assist underdeveloped nations
14. **harbour.** Harbor
15. **52.000.** 52,000 pounds sterling
16. **State Department.** Agency of the executive branch of the U.S. government responsible for handling relations between the United States and countries around the world
17. **Extended Voluntary Departure.** Temporary suspension of deportation granted to aliens from designated countries by the president of the United States

What did sanctuary activists understand?

But sanctuary activists understand that only a reduction of indiscriminate political violence and terror will stem the flow of homeless from El Salvador and Guatemala. And this will require a dramatic turnaround in Reagan administration policies. To people in the sanctuary movement the Central American question is as simple and painful as the banner carried to the White House in a recent protest of U.S. policies: 'More U.S. Intervention[18] More Central American Refugees.'

Richard Kazis is a Boston-based journalist and a frequent contributor to New Internationalist.

Critical Thinking Questions

1. The article identifies two reasons why the Reagan administration would not classify refugees from El Salvador and Guatemala as political refugees. What are these reasons?

2. What did refugees have to be able to prove in order to keep from being deported? This same fact is noted in *The Bean Trees* as well. What was Mattie's opinion of the proof the government required from refugees?

3. What was the Sanctuary Movement and what did it do?

4. Read footnote 13. Why might Fife's congregation have chosen the anniversary of the assassination of Archbishop Oscar Romero to declare publicly their commitment to aiding Central American refugees?

5. How does this article relate to the story of Estevan and Esperanza in *The Bean Trees*?

18. **Intervention.** Interference, usually by force or the threat of force, in another nation's internal affairs, especially to maintain or alter a condition

words for everyday use

in • dis • crim • i • nate (in dis krim′ nət) *adj.*, not marked by careful distinction; haphazard; unrestrained; unselective. *Some students claimed their grades were given in an indiscriminate fashion because they didn't understand why some papers earned an A and others earned Bs.*

"In Case You Ever Want to Go Home Again"

from *High Tide in Tucson: Essays from Now or Never*

by Barbara Kingsolver

ABOUT THE RELATED READING

"In Case You Ever Want to Go Home Again," a personal essay by Barbara Kingsolver, appears in the collection *High Tide in Tucson: Essays from Now or Never.* The author shares her memories of the Kentucky town in which she grew up and what it was like to return after publishing *The Bean Trees.*

In Case You Ever Want to Go Home Again

I have been gone from Kentucky a long time. Twenty years have done to my hill accent what the washing machine does to my jeans: taken out the color and starch, so gradually that I never marked the loss. Something like that has happened to my memories, too, particularly of the places and people I can't go back and visit because they are gone. The ancient brick building that was my grade school, for example, and both my grandfathers. They're snapshots of memory for me now, of equivocal focus, loaded with emotion, undisturbed by anyone else's idea of the truth. The schoolhouse's plaster ceilings are charted with craters like maps of the moon and likely to crash down without warning. The windows are watery, bubbly glass reinforced with chicken wire. The weary wooden staircases, worn shiny smooth in a path up their middles, wind up to an unknown place overhead where the heavy-footed eighth graders changing classes were called "the mules" by my first-grade teacher, and believing her, I pictured their sharp hooves on the linoleum.

◀ *To what does the author compare the brick building where she went to grade school and both of her grandfathers? What are they undisturbed by?*

My Grandfather Henry I remember in his sleeveless undershirt, home after a day's hard work on the farm at Fox Creek. His hide is tough and burnished wherever it has

◀ *How does the author remember her Grandfather Henry? What does he look like in her memory? What is he doing?*

words for everyday use

e • quiv • o • cal (ə kwiv′ ə kəl) *adj.,* subject to two or more interpretations and usually used to mislead or confuse; vague; hazy. *A good lawyer can make even straightforward evidence appear equivocal.*

met the world—hands, face, forearms—but vulnerably white at the shoulders and throat. He is snapping his false teeth in and out of place, to provoke his grandchildren to hysterics.

As far as I know, no such snapshots exist in the authentic world. The citizens of my hometown ripped down the old school and quickly put to rest its picturesque decay. My grandfather always cemented his teeth in his head, and put on good clothes, before submitting himself to photography. Who wouldn't? When a camera takes aim at my daughter, I reach out and scrape the peanut butter off her chin. "I can't help it," I tell her, "it's one of those mother things." It's more than that. It's human, to want the world to see us as we think we ought to be seen.

You can fool history sometimes, but you can't fool the memory of your intimates. And thank heavens, because in the broad valley between real life and propriety whole herds of important truths can steal away into the underbrush. I hold that valley to be my home territory as a writer. Little girls wear food on their chins, school days are lit by ghostlight, and respectable men wear their undershirts at home. Sometimes there are fits of laughter and sometimes there is despair, and neither one looks a thing like its formal portrait.

▶ On April 1, 1987, what two important events happen to the author?

For many, many years I wrote my stories furtively in spiral-bound notebooks, for no greater purpose than my own private salvation. But on April 1, 1987, two earthquakes hit my psyche on the same day. First, I brought home my own newborn baby girl from the hospital. Then, a few hours later, I got a call from New York announcing that a large chunk of my writing—which I'd tentatively pronounced a novel—was going to be published. This was a spectacular April Fool's Day. My life has not, since, returned to normal.

For days I nursed my baby and basked in hormonal euphoria,[1] musing occasionally: all this—and I'm a novelist, too! *That,* though, seemed a slim accomplishment compared with laboring twenty-four hours to render up

1. **hormonal euphoria.** Feelings of elation or joy brought about by hormonal changes that took place after the author had her baby

words for everyday use

pro • pri • e • ty (prə prī′ ə tē) *n.,* the quality or state of being proper; appropriateness; conformity to what is socially acceptable in conduct or speech. *Our English teacher says we can conduct ourselves with propriety and be genuine at the same time.*

psy • che (sī′ kē) *n.,* soul; self; mind. *The poem was short, but it made a huge impression on my psyche.*

the most beautiful new human the earth had yet seen. The book business seemed a terrestrial affair of ink and trees and I didn't give it much thought.

In time my head cleared, and I settled into panic. What had I done? The baby was premeditated, but the book I'd conceived recklessly, in a closet late at night, when the restlessness of my insomniac pregnancy drove me to compulsive verbal intercourse[2] with my own soul. The pages that grew in a stack were somewhat incidental to the process. They contained my highest hopes and keenest pains, and I didn't think anyone but me would ever see them. I'd bundled the thing up and sent it off to New York in a mad fit of housekeeping, to be done with it. Now it was going to be laid smack out for my mother, my postal clerk, my high school English teacher, anybody in the world who was willing to plunk down $16.95 and walk away with it. To find oneself suddenly published is thrilling—that is a given. But how appalling it also felt I find hard to describe. Imagine singing at the top of your lungs in the shower as you always do, then one day turning off the water and throwing back the curtain to see there in your bathroom a crowd of people, rapt, with videotape. I wanted to throw a towel over my head.

There was nothing in the novel to incriminate my mother or the postal clerk. I like my mother, plus her record is perfect. My postal clerk I couldn't vouch for; he has tattoos. But in any event I never put real people into my fiction—I can't see the slightest point of that, when I have the alternative of inventing utterly subservient slave-people, whose every detail of appearance and behavior I can bend to serve my theme and plot.

Even so, I worried that someone I loved would find in what I'd written a reason to despise me. In fact, I was sure of it. My fiction is not in any way about my life, regardless of what others might assume, but certainly it is set in the

◀ *About what does the author worry?*

2. **verbal intercourse.** Exchange of thoughts or feelings through words

words for everyday use

in • som • ni • ac (in säm′ nē ak) *adj.*, experiencing or accompanied by sleeplessness. *Before the big presentation, I had an insomniac night.*

in • crim • i • nate (in kri′ mə nāt) *v.*, charge; accuse; blame; to charge with or show evidence or proof of involvement in a crime. *The chocolate on my little brother's face served to incriminate him for the missing cookies.*

sub • ser • vi • ent (səb sər′ vē ənt) *adj.*, serving to promote some end; servile; obedient; useful. *The head coach is a bit of a tyrant and encourages subservient behavior from the assistants.*

sort of places I know pretty well. The protagonist of my novel, titled *The Bean Trees,* launched her adventures from a place called "Pittman, Kentucky," which does resemble a town in Kentucky where I'm known to have grown up. I had written: "Pittman was twenty years behind the nation in practically every way you can think of except the rate of teenage pregnancies. . . . We were the last place in the country to get the dial system. Up until 1973 you just picked up the receiver and said, Marge, get me my Uncle Roscoe. The telephone office was on the third floor of the Courthouse, and the operator could see everything around Main Street square. She would tell you if his car was there or not."

I don't have an Uncle Roscoe. But if I *did* have one, the phone operator in my hometown, prior to the mid-seventies, could have spotted him from her second-floor office on Main Street square.

▶ *What did growing up in small-town Kentucky teach the author?*

I cherish the oddball charm of that town. Time and again I find myself writing love letters to my rural origins. Growing up in small-town Kentucky taught me respect for the astounding resources people can drum up from their backyards, when they want to, to pull each other through. I tend to be at home with modesty, and suspicious of anything slick or new. But naturally, when I was growing up there, I yearned for the slick and the new. A lot of us did, I think. We craved shopping malls and a swimming pool. We wanted the world to know we had once won the title "All Kentucky City," even though with sixteen-hundred souls we no more constituted a "city" than New Jersey is a Garden State, and we advertised this glorious prevarication for years and years on one of the town's few billboards.

Homely charm is a relative matter. Now that I live in a western city where shopping malls and swimming pools congest the landscape like cedar blight,[3] I think back fondly on my hometown. But the people who live there now might rather smile about the quaintness of a *smaller* town, like nearby Morning Glory or Barefoot. At any rate, they would not want to discover themselves in my novel. I can

3. **cedar blight.** Disease that infects cedar trees, resulting in infected brown leaves conspicuous against healthy green foliage

words for everyday use

pre • var • i • ca • tion (pri var ə kā′ shən) *n.,* lie; white lie; falsehood; untruth. *Occasionally, one might tell a prevarication when the truth would hurt someone's feelings.*

home • ly (hōm′ lē) *adj.,* not attractive or good-looking; lacking elegance or refinement; of a simple or unpretentious nature. *The homely room felt comfortable, warm and welcoming.*

never go home again, as long as I live, I reasoned. Somehow this will be reckoned as betrayal. I've photographed my hometown in its undershirt.

During the year I awaited publication, I decided to calm down. There were other ways to think about this problem.

1. If people really didn't want to see themselves in my book, they wouldn't. They would think to themselves, "She is writing about Morning Glory, and those underdogs are from farther on down Scrubgrass Road."

2. There's no bookstore in my hometown. No one will know.

In November 1988, bookstoreless though it was, my hometown hosted a big event. Paper banners announced it, and stores closed in honor of it. A crowd assembled in the town's largest public space—the railroad depot. The line went out the door and away down the tracks. At the front of the line they were plunking down $16.95 for signed copies of a certain book.

◀ *What big event did Kingsolver's hometown host in 1988? Who was there?*

My family was there. The county's elected officials were there. My first-grade teacher, Miss Louella, was there, exclaiming to one and all: "I taught her to write!"

My old schoolmates were there. The handsome boys who'd spurned me at every homecoming dance were there.

It's relevant and slightly vengeful to confess here that I was not a hit in school, socially speaking. I was a bookworm who never quite fit her clothes. I managed to look fine in my school pictures, but as usual the truth lay elsewhere. In sixth grade I hit my present height of five feet almost nine, struck it like a gong, in fact, leaving behind self-confidence and any genuine need of a training bra. Elderly relatives used the term "fill out" when they spoke of me, as though they held out some hope I might eventually have some market value, like an underfed calf, if the hay crop was good. In my classroom I came to dread a game called Cooties,[4] wherein one boy would brush against my shoulder and then chase the others around, threatening to pass on my apparently communicable lack

4. **Cooties.** Slang term for body lice

words for everyday use

com • mu • ni • ca • ble (kə myü ni' kə bəl) *adj.*, contagious; capable of being communicated; transmittable. *The patient was placed in isolation after being diagnosed with a communicable disease.*

of charisma. The other main victim of this game was a girl named Sandra, whose family subscribed to an unusual religion that mandated a Victorian dress code.[5] In retrospect I can't say exactly what Sandra and I had in common that made us outcasts, except for extreme shyness, flat chests, and families who had their eyes on horizons pretty far beyond the hills of Nicholas County. Mine were not Latter-day Saints,[6] but we read Thoreau[7] and Robert Burns[8] at home, and had lived for a while in Africa. My parents did not flinch from relocating us to a village beyond the reach of electricity, running water, or modern medicine (also, to my delight, conventional schooling) when they had a chance to do useful work there. They thought it was shameful to ignore a fellow human in need, or to waste money on trendy, frivolous things; they did not, on the other hand, think it was shameful to wear perfectly good hand-me-down dresses to school in Nicholas County. Ephemeral idols exalted by my peers, such as Batman,[9] the Beatles,[10] and the Hula Hoop,[11] were not an issue at our house. And even if it took no more than a faint pulse to pass the fifth grade, my parents expected me to set my own academic goals, and then exceed them.

Possibly my parents were trying to make sure I didn't get pregnant in the eighth grade, as some of my classmates would shortly begin to do. If so, their efforts were a whale of a success. In my first three years of high school, the number of times I got asked out on a date was zero. This is not an approximate number. I'd caught up to other girls in social skills by that time, so I knew how to pretend I was dumber than I was, and make my own clothes. But these

5. **Victorian dress code.** Highly formal and stuffy code of dress characterized by the tastes and standards typical during Queen Victoria's reign over Great Britain from 1837 to 1901

6. **Latter-day Saints.** Members of any of several religious bodies who accept the Book of Mormon as divine revelation

7. **Thoreau.** Henry David Thoreau (1817–1862), American author and philosopher known for his advocacy of civil rights and his views on living in harmony with nature

8. **Robert Burns.** Scottish poet (1759–1796)

9. **Batman.** Fictional comic-book superhero

10. **the Beatles.** British musical group of the 1960s and 1970s

11. **Hula Hoop.** Plastic hoop that is twirled around the body

words for everyday use

e • phem • er • al (i fem′ rəl) *adj.*, lasting a very short time; temporary; fleeting. *My mother says beauty is ephemeral, so there'd better be a good and accomplished person beneath the pretty face.*

things helped only marginally. Popularity remained a frustrating mystery to me.

Nowadays, some of my city-bred friends muse about moving to a small town for the sake of their children. What's missing from their romantic picture of Grover's Corners is the frightening impact of insulation upon a child who's not dead center in the mainstream. In a place such as my hometown, you file in and sit down to day one of kindergarten with the exact pool of boys who will be your potential dates for the prom. If you wet your pants a lot, your social life ten years later will be—as they say in government reports—impacted. I was sterling on bladder control, but somehow could never shake my sixth-grade stigma.

◀ *What is the author unable to shake?*

At age seventeen, I was free at last to hightail it for new social pastures, and you'd better believe I did. I attended summer classes at the University of Kentucky and landed a boyfriend before I knew what had hit me, or what on earth one did with the likes of such. When I went on to college in Indiana I was astonished to find a fresh set of peers who found me, by and large, likable and cootie-free.

I've never gotten over high school, to the extent that I'm still a little surprised that my friends want to hang out with me. But it made me what I am, for better and for worse. From living in a town that listened in on party lines, I learned both the price and value of community. And I gained things from my rocky school years: A fierce wish to look inside of people. An aptitude for listening. The habit of my own company. The companionship of keeping a diary, in which I gossiped, fantasized, and invented myself. From the vantage point of invisibility I explored the psychology of the underdog, the one who can't be what others desire but who might still learn to chart her own hopes. Her story was my private treasure; when I wrote *The Bean Trees* I called her Lou Ann. I knew for sure that my classmates, all of them cool as Camaros back then, would not relate to the dreadful insecurities of Lou Ann. But I liked her anyway.

◀ *In what way does the author admit she's never gotten over high school?*

◀ *Which character in* The Bean Trees *grew out of Kingsolver's personal experiences?*

And now, look. The boys who'd once fled howling from her cooties were lined up for my autograph. Football captains, cheerleaders, homecoming queens were all there. The athlete who'd inspired in me a near-fatal crush for three years, during which time he never looked in the vicinity of my person, was there. The great wits who gave me the names Kingfish and Queen Sliver were there.

I took liberties with history. I wrote long, florid inscriptions referring to our great friendship of days gone by. I wrote slowly. I made those guys wait in line *a long time.*

I can recall every sight, sound, minute of that day. Every open, generous face. The way the afternoon light fell through the windows onto the shoes of the people in line. In my inventory of mental snapshots these images hold the place most people reserve for the wedding album. I don't know whether other people get to have Great Life Moments like this, but I was lucky enough to realize I was having mine, right while it happened. My identity was turning backward on its own axis. Never before or since have I felt all at the same time so cherished, so aware of old anguish, and so ready to let go of the past. My past had let go of *me,* so I could be something new: Poet Laureate[12] and Queen for a Day in hometown Kentucky. The people who'd watched me grow up were proud of me, and exuberant over an event that put our little dot on the map, particularly since it wasn't an airline disaster or a child falling down a well. They didn't appear to mind that my novel discussed small-town life frankly, without gloss.

In fact, most people showed unsurpassed creativity in finding themselves, literally, on the printed page. "That's my car isn't it?" they would ask. "My service station!" Nobody presented himself as my Uncle Roscoe, but if he had, I happily would have claimed him.

It's a curious risk, fiction. Some writers choose fantasy as an approach to truth, a way of burrowing under newsprint and formal portraits to find the despair that can stow away in a happy childhood, or the affluent grace of a grandfather in his undershirt. In the final accounting, a hundred different truths are likely to reside at any given address. The part of my soul that is driven to make stories is a fierce thing, like a ferret: long, sleek, incapable of sleep, it digs and bites through all I know of the world. Given that I cannot look away from the painful things, it seems better to invent allegory[13] than to point a straight, bony finger like Scrooge's mute Ghost of Christmas Yet to Come,[14] declaring, "Here you will end, if you don't clean up your act." By inventing character and circumstance, I like to think I can be a kinder sort of ghost, saying, "I don't mean *you,* exactly, but just give it some thought, anyway."

▶ *What can't Kingsolver look away from?*

12. **Poet Laureate.** Poet regarded by a country or region as its most eminent or representative
13. **allegory.** Work in which each element symbolizes, or represents, something else
14. **Scrooge's mute Ghost of Christmas Yet to Come.** Refers to Charles Dickens' story *A Christmas Carol,* in which a visit by the ghost of Christmas Yet to Come scares the ornery and stingy Ebenezer Scrooge into becoming good-spirited and generous

Nice try, but nobody's really fooled. Because fiction works, if it does, only when we the readers believe every word of it. Grover's Corners[15] is Our Town, and so is Cannery Row,[16] and Lilliput,[17] and Gotham City,[18] and Winesburg, Ohio[19], and the dreadful metropolis of *1984.*[20] We have all been as canny as Huck Finn[21], as fractious as Scarlett O'Hara,[22] as fatally flawed as Captain Ahab[23] and Anna Karenina.[24] I, personally, am Jo March[25], and if her author Louisa May Alcott had a whole new life to live for the sole pursuit of talking me out of it, she could not. A pen may or may not be mightier than the sword, but it is brassier than the telephone. When the writer converses privately with her soul in the long dark night, a thousand neighbors are listening in on the party line, taking it personally.

Nevertheless, I came to decide, on my one big afternoon as Homecoming Queen, that I would go on taking the risk

◀ When does Kingsolver say fiction works?

◀ To which character in literature does the author compare herself? What does she say Louisa May Alcott could never do?

15. **Grover's Corners.** Grover's Corners, New Hampshire, the setting of the play *Our Town* by Thornton Wilder; represents "any place" and is peopled with stock characters who represent people everyone knows
16. **Cannery Row.** Run-down waterfront neighborhood of sardine canneries, vacant lots, and brothels in 1940s Monterey, California; setting for John Steinbeck's novel, *Cannery Row,* published in 1945
17. **Lilliput.** One of the fantastical places visited by Gulliver in Jonathan Swift's political satire *Gulliver's Travels,* the city of Lilliput is home to very small, people called Lilliputians who are fickle and narrow-minded.
18. **Gotham City.** Dark and ominous fictional city filled with crime, best known for being the home of Batman
19. **Winesboro, Ohio.** Setting of Sherwood Anderson's fictional work *Winesboro, Ohio,* which depicts the strange lives of the residents of a small isolated town in Ohio
20. **metropolis of *1984.*** Setting of George Orwell's chilling novel *1984,* which shows the reader a society in which personal freedom is taken away
21. **Huck Finn.** Title character of Mark Twain's classic American novel *Adventures of Huckleberry Finn,* in which Huck Finn, a young boy running from an abusive father, and Jim, a runaway slave, travel down the Mississippi River together on a raft
22. **Scarlett O'Hara.** Feisty, self-centered, and headstrong heroine of Margaret Mitchell's novel *Gone with the Wind,* which tells the stories of several southern families just before, during, and after the Civil War
23. **Captain Ahab.** Main character of Herman Melville's novel *Moby Dick,* the story of Captain Ahab's pursuit of a giant white whale
24. **Anna Karenina.** Doomed title character of Russian author Leo Tolstoy's novel *Anna Karenina*
25. **Jo March.** Main character of Louisa May Alcott's novel *Little Women;* Jo is a headstrong tomboy with a passion for writing.

words for everyday use

can • ny (kăn′ ē) *adj.,* careful and shrewd, especially where one's own interests are concerned. *The stockbroker earned a reputation for making canny investments.*

frac • tious (frak′ shəs) *adj.,* quarrelsome; feisty; rebellious; headstrong. *My sister can be fractious if you disagree with her about music.*

of writing books. Miss Louella and all those football players gave me the rash courage to think I might be forgiven again and again the sin of revelation. I love my hometown as I love the elemental stuff of my own teeth and bones, and that seems to have come through to my hometown, even if I didn't write it up in its Sunday best.

I used to ask my grandfather how he could pull fish out of a lake all afternoon, one after another, while my line and bobber lay dazed and inert. This was not my Grandfather Henry, but my other grandfather, whose face I connected in childhood with the one that appears on the flip side of a buffalo nickel.[26] Without cracking that face an iota, he was prone to uttering the funniest things I've about ever heard. In response to my question regarding the fishing, he would answer gravely, "You have to hold your mouth right."

▶ *What does Kingsolver say is the secret of writing?*

I think that is also the secret of writing: attitude. Hope, unyielding faith in the enterprise. If only I hold my mouth right, keep a clear fix on what I believe is true while I make up my stories, surely I will end up saying what I mean. Then, if I offend someone, it won't be an accidental casualty. More likely, it will be because we actually disagree. I can live with that. The memory of my buffalo-nickel grandfather advises me still, in lonely moments: "If you never stepped on anybody's toes, you never been for a *walk*."

▶ *What advice of her buffalo-nickel grandfather does Kingsolver often remember?*

I learned something else, that November day, that shook down all I thought I knew about my personal, insufferable, nobody's-blues-can-touch-mine isolation of high school. Before the book signing was over, more than one of my old schoolmates had sidled up and whispered: "That Lou Ann character, the insecure one? I know you based her on me."

---

26. **the one that appears on the flip side of a buffalo nickel.** Profile of a Native American face appears on one side of a buffalo nickel

Critical Thinking Questions

1. A **personal essay** is a short work of nonfiction prose on a single topic related to the life or interests of the writer. Personal essays are characterized by an intimate and informal style and tone. They are often, but not always, written in the first person, using the pronouns *I* and *me.* Identify several personal details Kingsolver shares with the reader. How do they contribute to creating the informal and intimate tone of the essay?

2. Kingsolver writes, "From the vantage point of invisibility I explored the psychology of the underdog, the one who can't be what others desire but who might still learn to chart her own hopes. Her story was my private treasure; when I wrote *The Bean Trees* I called her Lou Ann." What does Kingsolver mean by "the vantage point of invisibility"? In what ways can't Lou Ann be what other characters in the novel desire her to be? In what ways does she learn to chart her own hopes?

3. Why does Kingsolver contend that fiction only works when readers believe every word of it?

4. Kingsolver says she still lives by Grandfather Henry's advice, "If you never stepped on anybody's toes, you never been for a *walk.*" Why do you think that advice remains meaningful to her as a writer?

5. How does Kingsolver's experience returning to her hometown as a "famous" author echo themes of family and community in *The Bean Trees*?

Creative Writing Activities

Creating Humor through Dialogue

Dialogue is conversation involving two or more characters or people. In Understanding Literature, Chapters 4–7 on page 106, you saw how Kingsolver uses dialogue to create humor during the scene in which Taylor meets Fei, La-Isha, and Timothy. The straightforward Taylor, with her Kentucky dialect, collides with Fei, the human wind chime, and her curd-straining housemates. The reader can't help but laugh at the predictable miscommunication that results.

Follow Kingsolver's lead by having fun with language. Write a short piece that creates humor by using dialogue and dramatic language. For example, you might write about a chance meeting between two people who don't understand what the other is saying—perhaps one character is young and uses lots of current slang and the other character is older; perhaps one character is an adult and the other is a young child (similar to the conversation between Taylor and Turtle in Chapter 17); or perhaps one character is from Earth and the other is from Mars. The possibilities are limited only by your imagination. Have fun!

Writing a Conversation

Imagine that several years have gone by, and Turtle is now ten years old. What might Taylor tell her about how they came to be together? What might Taylor want to tell her about Estevan, Esperanza, and Mattie? Write a conversation in which Taylor tells Turtle about some of these things. Make sure Taylor describes these events and people in a way that a ten-year-old can understand, and in a way that won't scare her or make her feel bad about herself. Have Turtle ask the kinds of questions that you might expect a ten-year-old to ask.

Crafting Images

An **image** is language that creates a concrete representation of an object or an experience. In *The Bean Trees,* Kingsolver offers the reader many strong and beautiful images of the natural world. Look back through the novel, and pick out a few images that are particularly appealing to you. Use them as an inspiration for creating images in your own writing.

Choose something that you love. It might be something in nature or an animal. Or it might be a sport, dance, or music. Craft two or three images related to that subject. Watch your dog carefully as he leaps for the Frisbee. Can you capture that energy and enthusiasm in language? Listen carefully to your favorite guitar part in your favorite song. Can you capture that sound or melody or the feeling that it gives you in language?

Creating a Journal Entry

Choose one chapter from *The Bean Trees,* and review the events of the chapter. Then, create several journal entries that you think Taylor or Lou Ann—depending on which chapter you choose—might have written as the events happened. Try to use language that you think Taylor or Lou Ann would have used.

Writing about Your Rhizobia

In Chapter 17, Taylor reads to Turtle from a horticultural encyclopedia about rhizobia, microorganisms that engage in a symbiotic relationship with bean plants. The roots of bean plants provide home for rhizobia. In turn, rhizobia provide bean plants with a usable form of nitrogen that helps them to thrive, even in poor soil. Taylor likens the role of rhizobia to an "invisible support system" and compares this support system to the relationships between characters in the novel. Which people in your life are your rhizobia, or invisible support system? Write an essay about your personal rhizobia and how they support you—even when your soil is poor.

Critical Writing Activities

The following topics are suitable for short critical essays on *The Bean Trees.* An essay on any one of these topics should begin with an introductory paragraph that introduces the topic and states the thesis, or main idea, of the essay. This introduction should be followed by several paragraphs that support the thesis using examples from the novel. The last paragraph of the essay should be a conclusion that restates the thesis of the essay in different words. The conclusion should also bring a sense of closure to the essay.

Comparing and Contrasting Two Characters

Write a comparison and contrast essay about Taylor and Lou Ann or about Mama and Mattie. Consider what qualities are similar about both characters, and what qualities about them are different.

On your own paper, draw a Venn diagram like the one shown below. In the center of each of the two ovals, write the names of the two characters you are examining. Record similarities between the two characters in the overlapping part of the ovals and differences in the parts of the ovals that do not overlap.

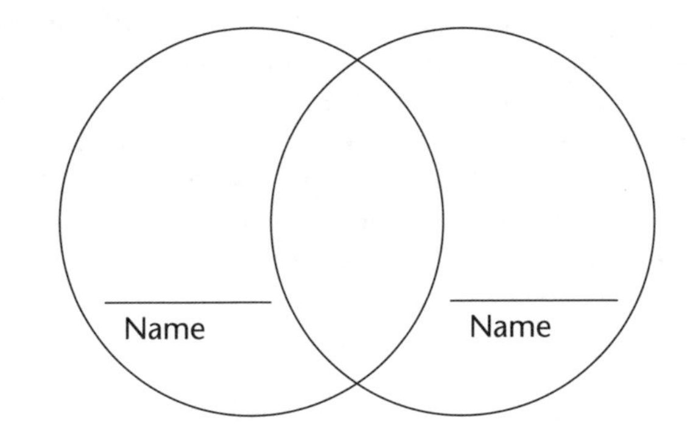

Use the points from your graphic organizer to draft your essay. You will need to decide whether to use point-by-point or block organization. In **point-by-point organization**, you discuss one topic as it applies to the first character, and then discuss the same topic in relation to the second character. Throughout the essay, you move back and forth between the two characters. If you choose this organizational method, be sure to start a new paragraph every time you switch characters. In **block organization**, you discuss all aspects of one character and then discuss all aspects of the other character. Usually, block organization works best if you will focus on one major point of comparison, and point-by-point organization works best if you have several important points of comparison.

As you develop your essay, be sure to include specific examples from the book. Direct quotations from the text, with page references, will also make your essay more persuasive.

In your conclusion, you might suggest how the similarities and differences between the two characters you have chosen relate to the meaning of the novel as a whole.

Character Development

Choose one of the following characters from the novel: Turtle, Taylor, Esperanza, or Lou Ann. Write an essay that describes how the character changes from the beginning to the end of the novel and the causes behind the change.

Your thesis should clearly express the change the character undergoes and the factors that cause the change. Your supporting paragraphs should provide specific examples that express the personality of the character as she is first presented, examples that show how the character changes and the reasons for the change, and examples that reveal the personality of the character at the end of the novel.

To determine the personalities of the characters and the ways in which they change, examine how the character sees herself, how the character sees the world around her, what the character's body language says about her, and how the character relates to others.

Attitudes Toward Policies of the State and Federal Government

The policies of both the state of Arizona and the United States play a role in the stories of Taylor and Turtle and Estevan and Esperanza. The state of Arizona makes the laws that govern adoption and determine whether or not Taylor can legally adopt Turtle. The government of the United States enforces laws on immigration that make it necessary for Estevan and Esperanza to hide so that they will not be forced to return to Guatemala. Throughout the novel, various characters express opinions about both state and federal laws.

Write an essay that addresses the way in which the state of Arizona, the United States, or government, in general, is presented in *The Bean Trees.* Your thesis statement should clearly express the way in which government is depicted. For example, is the government of the United States presented as sympathetic to the Central American refugees? Is the state of Arizona presented as concerned about finding the best home for children who have lost their parents? Is government, in general, shown to be an institution that aids its citizens?

Your supporting paragraphs should provide specific examples of how events in the story are influenced by government policies and how characters in the novel feel about those policies.

The Power of the Individual

Write an essay that examines how *The Bean Trees* communicates the idea that one person has the power to change the lives of others. You may choose to illustrate this by focusing on the difference that one character in the story makes in the life of another character in the story. You may choose to focus on how one character affects the lives of many characters in the story. Or, you may choose to focus on how many characters in the story affect the lives of many other characters in the story. You may choose to address how characters affect each other's lives in a positive way, in a negative way, or both.

Projects

Conducting Research on Making a Difference

The Bean Trees touches on the ugly side of human nature by presenting three characters who have experienced cruelty firsthand. Turtle is a victim of child abuse, and Estevan and Esperanza are victims of the brutal Guatemalan Civil War. But *The Bean Trees* also focuses on the good individuals do for others. Taylor helps Turtle, Estevan, and Esperanza, and Mattie helps everybody.

Form small groups of three or four to research people in your own community who have made a positive difference in the lives of others. You may search on the Internet, locate articles in magazines or newspapers, or contact local community organizations to find individuals who have worked to make the world a better place, either in a big or small way. The group should decide on several individuals to highlight, presenting to the class a summary of the individuals, their contribution, and how it made a difference in someone else's life. After the group presentations, create a list of at least three things that you and your classmates can do to make the world a better place.

Creating a Collage to Represent *The Bean Trees*

With a partner or small group, look back to Chapter 10 of the novel and review the description of the cross that Mattie has hanging over her fireplace. It's actually a collage of images. Share ideas with your group about creating a collage to represent *The Bean Trees*. List the people, events, places, images, and ideas that you think should be included. Then find ways to represent them visually: draw, paint, or cut images out of magazines or newspapers. You also may want to include actual objects, such as beans. Be as creative as you can. Present your finished collage to your classmates, describing the items you chose to include and why you represented them as you did.

Conducting Research on Guatemala Today

Form small groups of three or four, and together research the country of Guatemala today. Address issues such as: the current government, how things have changed for the Mayan Indians, the economy, and the country's relationship with other countries. Write a report based on your research. Each group member should participate both in the research and writing of the report. Once your group report is finished, write your own version of a letter from Estevan and Esperanza, now living back in Guatemala, to Taylor, Turtle, and Mattie. Include your letters with your report, and hand them in to your teacher.

Putting the Landscape to Music

As you have seen, images from the natural world—the landscape, bodies of water, plants, and animals—play important roles in *The Bean Trees*. In fact, nature is portrayed in two distinct environments in the book: One is the wide-open harshness of the Sonoran Desert around Tucson; the other is the enfolding green lushness of Taylor and Lou Ann's native Appalachian Mountains. With a partner, focus on either the desert or the mountain environment. Find five musical selections that evoke the mood of your chosen environment and record a sound track for it. Play the sound track for the rest of the class, and explain why you chose each track and what it suggests about the environment.

Researching Civil Disobedience

The Sanctuary Movement, an initiative undertaken by social and religious activists in the 1980s, provided safe havens for Central Americans fleeing political persecution in their countries. Sanctuary workers like those in the novel—Mattie, Father Williams, Reverend Stone, Mrs. Stone, and, eventually, Taylor—broke the law when they helped refugees cross the border and transported them through the United States. But they did so because they believed it was their moral and religious responsibility. This kind of act is called civil disobedience, which is defined as "refusing to obey government demands or commands," and is usually a collective means of forcing concessions from the government.

In small groups, research other incidents of civil disobedience. Groups might research abolitionists in the 1850s, women's rights supporters in the early twentieth century, labor union organizers in the 1920s, civil rights workers in the 1960s, antiwar protesters in the 1990s, or other examples of civil disobedience that have occurred in American history. Report your findings to the class, describing the people involved, their reasons for breaking the law, and the results of their efforts.

As an additional or alternative activity, discuss causes for which you think civil disobedience is necessary. For what reasons, if any, would you consider engaging in civil disobedience?

Glossary

PRONUNCIATION KEY

VOWEL SOUNDS

a	hat	ō	go	u̇	book, put
ā	play	ȯ	paw, born	ü	blue, stew
ä	fäther	oi	boy	ə	extra
e	then	ou	wow		under
ē	me	u	up		civil
i	sit	ʉ	burn		honor
ī	my				bogus

CONSONANT SOUNDS

b	but	l	lip	t	sit
ch	watch	m	money	th	with
d	do	n	on	v	valley
f	fudge	ŋ	song, sink	w	work
g	go	p	pop	y	yell
h	hot	r	rod	z	pleasure
j	jump	s	see		
k	brick	sh	she		

a • ban • don • ment (ə ban′ dən mənt) *n.,* desertion; the act of leaving without return; the act of leaving a person helpless and without protection.

ab • hor (əb hȯr′) *v.,* loathe; hate.

a • bun • dant (ə bun′ dənt) *adj.,* plentiful, abounding.

am • bas • sa • dor (am bas′ ə dər) *n.,* diplomat; representative, a person chosen to represent one government in its dealings with another.

ap • ti • tude (ap′ tə tüd) *n.,* natural ability; talent.

ar • ter • y (är′ tə rē) *n.,* any of the tubular, branching muscular and elastic-walled vessels that carry blood from the heart through the body; a channel of transportation, such as a river or highway.

as • sent (ə sent′) *v.,* to agree to something after careful consideration; consent.

asth • ma (az′ mə) *n.,* allergic condition marked by difficult breathing, tightening in the chest, and attacks of wheezing, coughing, and gasping.

a • sy • lum (ə sī′ ləm) *n.,* protection from arrest and being sent back to the country from which one flees, given especially to political refugees by a nation, an embassy, or other agency.

be • fud • dle (bi fə′ dəl) *v.,* daze; confuse; fluster.

bel • low (be′ lō) *v.,* make a loud, deep sound.

be • rate (bi rāt′) *v.,* scold; criticize; curse.

be • wil • der (bi wil′ dər) *v.,* to perplex or confuse by a complexity, variety, or multitude of objects or considerations; to cause to lose one's bearings.

bi • ol • o • gy (bī ′ä lə jē) *n.,* branch of science that deals with living organisms.

blanch (blanch′) *v.,* to take the color out of; to boil or steam for a brief period so that the skin can be easily removed.

can • ny (kan′ ē) *adj.,* careful and shrewd, especially where one's own interests are concerned.

can • tan • ker • ous (kan taŋ′ kə rəs) *adj.,* difficult or irritating to deal with; crabby; quarrelsome.

can • teen (kan tēn′) *n.,* portable container for carrying liquid.

ca • reen (ka rēn′) *v.,* lurch; swerve.

chap • er • one (sha′ pə rōn) *n.,* older person who accompanies young people at a social gathering to ensure proper behavior.

civ • i • lized (si′ və lizd) *adj.,* characterized by taste or refinement; domesticated; tamed.

co • ex • is • tence (kō ig zis′ tənts) *n.,* state of living peacefully together.

com • merce (kä′ mərs) *n.,* trade; buying and selling; business.

com • mu • ni • ca • ble (kə myü ni′ kə bəl) *adj.,* contagious; capable of being communicated; transmittable.

com • mu • nist (käm′ yə nist) *n.,* one who adheres to the theory or system of communism, under which private property is eliminated, and all goods are owned in common and available to all as needed.

com • pul • sion (kəm pəl′ shən) *n.,* irresistible impulse to perform an irrational act; urge; drive.

con • done (kən dōn′) *v.,* overlook; excuse; pardon.

con • fis • cate (kän′ fə skāt) *v.,* take possession of.

con • gre • gate (käŋʹ gri gāt) *v.,* gather, assemble, come together in a group.

con • jec • ture (kən jekʹ chər) *v.,* guess; imagine; suspect.

con • tem • pla • tive (kən temʹ plə tiv) *adj.,* marked by concentration on spiritual things; marked by careful attention and steady regard.

con • ven • tion • al (kən venʹ shə nəl) *adj.,* ordinary; customary; normal; lacking originality.

cor • ner • stone (kȯrʹ nər stōn) *n.,* foundation; basic element.

cor • ral (kə ralʹ) *v.,* collect; gather.

croon (krünʹ) *v.,* to sing or speak in a soft, murmuring manner.

cus • to • dy (kəsʹ tə dē) *n.,* immediate charge and control exercised by a person or authority; guardianship; care.

de • bris (də brēʹ) *n.,* remains of something broken down or destroyed; accumulation of fragments of rock; something discarded; trash.

de • cree (di krēʹ) *v.,* command; order judicially.

de • hy • drate (dē hīʹ drāt) *v.,* lose water or body fluids and become dry and thirsty.

dep • ri • va • tion (dep rə vāʹ shən) *n.,* withholding; removal; loss; need.

des • ig • nate (deʹ zig nāt) *v.,* indicate and set apart; point out; make known; specify.

dic • ta • tor (dikʹ tā tər) *n.,* ruler who holds all the power and often oppresses his or her people.

di • lap • i • dat • ed (də laʹ pə dāt ed) *adj.,* decayed; fallen into ruin due to neglect; broken-down.

dis • in • te • grate (di sinʹ tə grāt) *v.,* break down or decompose; fall apart; decay.

dis • si • pate (diʹ sə pāt) *v.,* scatter; disperse; grow thin and gradually vanish.

dor • mant (dȯrʹ mənt) *adj.,* marked by a suspension of growth or external activity.

dus • ky (dəsʹ kē) *adj.,* somewhat dark in color; shadowy.

dy • nam • ic (dī naʹ mik) *adj.,* marked by continuous change.

e • lab • o • rate (i laʹ bə rət) *adj.,* intricate; complete;

detailed.

elab • o • rate (i la′ bə rāt) *v.,* to expand something in detail.

e • phem • er • al (i fem′ rəl) *adj.,* lasting a very short time; temporary; fleeting.

e • quiv • o • cal (ə kwiv′ ə kəl) *adj.,* subject to two or more interpretations and usually used to mislead or confuse; vague; hazy.

em • a • nate (em′ ə nāt) *v.,* flow from; spring; come out from a source.

enig • mat • ic (e nig ma′ tik) *adj.,* mysterious; unexplainable; mystifying.

en • rap • ture (en rap′ chər) *v.,* to fill with joy or delight.

en • ti • tle (en tī′ təl) *v.,* authorize; give a right or claim to.

ex • ile (eg′ zīl) *n.,* the state or period of forced absence from one's country or home.

ex • per • i • men • tal (ik sper ə men′ təl) *adj.,* based on trying new procedures, ideas, or activities.

ex • tract (ik strakt′) *v.,* to pull or take out forcibly.

fa • nat • i • cal (fa na′ ti kəl) *adj.,* marked by excessive enthusiasm and intense, uncritical devotion.

faze (fāz′) *v.,* to disturb the composure of; disconcert, daunt.

flour • ish (flər′ ish) *n.,* wave; dramatic or showy motion.

foist (fȯist′) *v.,* to force another to accept; thrust upon; impose upon.

for • lorn (fər lȯrn′) *adj.,* sad or lonely because of isolation or desertion; pathetic; abandoned.

frac • tious (frak′ shəs) *adj.,* quarrelsome; feisty; rebellious; headstrong.

gar • ble (gär′ bəl) *v.,* distort; jumble; run together; confuse.

gloat (glōt′) *v.,* take great pleasure in; brag; triumph; revel in.

grog • gi • ly (grä′ gə lē) *adv.,* in a sleepy or dazed way.

guard • i • an (gär′ dē ən) *n.,* one responsible for caring for the person or property of another.

har • bor (här′ bər) *v.,* to give shelter or refuge to.

heir • loom (ār′ lüm) *n.,* something of special value passed on from one generation to the next.

hok • ey (hō′ kē) *adj.,* corny; phony.

home • ly (hōm′ lē) *adj.,* not attractive or good-looking; lacking elegance or refinement; of a simple or unpretentious nature.

hyp • no • tize (hip′ nə tīz) *v.,* to cause to go into a state that resembles sleep, but during which, a person becomes readily accepting of suggestions made by the person who induced, or put the person into, the state.

hys • ter • i • cal (his ter′ i kəl) *adj.,* overwhelmed by fear, anger, sorrow, or other emotion; frantic; uncontrollable.

im • pos • tor (im päs′ tər) *n.,* one who assumes a false identity for the purpose of deception.

im • print (im print′) *v.,* to mark permanently.

in • clined (in klīnd′) *adj.,* tending toward; of a mind; likely.

in • crim • i • nate (in kri′ mə nāt) *v.,* charge; accuse; blame; to charge with or show evidence or proof of involvement in a crime.

in • del • i • ble (in de′ lə bəl) *adj.,* lasting; unforgettable; that which cannot be removed, erased, or washed off.

in • del • i • bly (in de′ lə blē) *adv.,* that cannot be removed, washed away, or erased; lasting; unforgettable.

in • sep • a • ra • ble (in se′ pə rə bəl) *adj.,* incapable of being separated; indivisible.

in • som • ni • ac (in säm′ nē ak) *adj.,* experiencing or accompanied by sleeplessness.

in • stal • la • tion (in stə lā′ shən) *n.,* act of setting up for use or service.

in • still (in stil′) *v.,* to impart gradually; initiate; sow the seeds of.

in • te • gral (in′ ti grəl) *adj.,* essential to completeness; necessary; fundamental; indispensable.

in • ten • tion (in ten′ shən) *n.,* purpose; aim; objective.

in • ter • cept (in tər sept′) *v.,* stop, seize, or interrupt in progress or course before arrival.

in • ter • ro • ga • tion (in ter′ ə gā′ shən) *n.,* act of formal and systematic questioning; examination; investigation; inquisition.

in • ter • vene (in tər vēn′) *v.,* to occur between points of time or events.

in • tim • i • date (in tim′ ə dāt) *v.,* to make timid or fearful; to frighten.

jock • ey (jä′ kē) *n.,* person who rides a horse, typically a person whose profession is to ride horses during races.

knack (nak′) *n.,* talent; aptitude; gift; a special talent that is difficult to analyze or teach.

man • gle (maŋ′ gəl) *v.,* crush; cut; tear.

ma • te • ri • al • ize (mə tir′ ē ə līz) *v.,* to cause to appear in bodily form; to come into existence.

me • an • der (mē an′ dər) *v.,* to follow a winding course; to wander aimlessly without destination.

mea • sly (mēz′ lē) *adj.,* of small size or little value; contemptibly small.

mourn • ful • ly (mȯrn′ fəl lē) *adv.,* full of sorrow; sad; gloomy.

non • com • mit • tal (nän kə mi′ təl) *adj.,* giving no clear indication of attitude or feeling.

no • tion (nō′ shən) *n.,* person's impression of something; idea; opinion.

o • men (ō′ mən) *n.,* occurrence believed to foreshadow a future event; sign; premonition.

or • phan (ȯr′ fen) *n.,* child deprived by death of one, or usually both, parents.

pan • de • mo • ni • um (pan də mō′ nē əm) *n.,* wild uproar; chaos; commotion; turmoil.

par • cel (pär′ səl) *v.,* divide into parts and distribute.

pau • ci • ty (pȯ′ sə tē) *n.,* smallness of quantity; scarcity; small amount.

per • turb (pər tərb′) *v.,* disturb; agitate; distract.

poise (pȯiz′) *v.,* balance; to hold suspended without motion in a steady position.

pre • cip • i • ta • tion (pri si pə tā′ shən) *n.,* something that falls, flows, or rushes with steep descent, such as rain, sleet, or snow.

pre • na • tal (prē nā′ təl) *adj.,* occurring, existing, or performed before birth.

pre • var • i • ca • tion (pri var ə kā′ shən) *n.,* lie; white lie; falsehood; untruth.

prim (prim′) *adj.,* stiff; formal; neat.

prod (präd′) *v.,* urge someone on; incite to action.

pro • pri • e • ty (prə prī′ ə tē) *n.,* the quality or state of being proper; appropriateness; conformity to what is socially acceptable in conduct or speech.

pros • pect (prä′ spekt) *n.,* outlook for the future; good chance; well-grounded hope.

pros • the • sis (präs thē′ səs) *n.,* an artificial device to replace a missing part of the body.

pro • trud • ing (prō trüd′ iŋ) *v.,* jutting out; sticking out.

psy • che (sī′ kē) *n.,* soul; self; mind.

pun • gent (pən′ jənt) *adj.,* sharp; strong; harsh; spicy; vinegary.

quo • ta (kwō′ tə) *n.,* share or proportion assigned to each member of a group.

ram • shack • le (ram′ sha kəl) *adj.,* appearing as if ready to collapse.

rec • ol • lect (rek′ ə lekt) *v.,* remember.

re • luc • tant • ly (ri lək′ tənt lē) *adv.,* unwilling; hesitant.

re • sid • u • al (ri zi′ jə wəl) *adj.,* remaining; leftover.

re • sil • ient (ri zil′ yənt) *adj.,* tending to recover from or adjust easily to misfortune or change.

ré • su • mé (re′ zə mā) *n.,* summary of a person's educational and/or employment history.

re • tard • ed (ri tär′ dəd) *adj.,* slow or limited in intellectual or emotional development.

ret • i • cent (re′ tə sənt) *adj.,* reluctant; unresponsive.

rev • er • ence (rev′ rənts) *n.,* honor or respect that is felt or shown; devotion.

rum • mage (rum′ ij) *v.,* to search thoroughly or to search carelessly.

sanc • tu • ary (saŋk′ chə wer′ ē) *n.,* place of refuge and protection; holy place; shrine; haven; shelter.

scrounge (scrounj′) *v.,* steal; swipe; scavenge.

scur • ry (skər′ ē) *v.,* scamper; move around in an agitated or confused way.

shroud (shroud′) *v.,* covered; concealed.

sim • u • late (sim′ yə lāt) *v.,* to copy, represent, feign.

spec • ta • cle (spek′ ti kəl) *n.,* unusual, entertaining, or dramatic public display; an object of curiosity or contempt.

spon • sor (spän′ sər) *v.,* to assume responsibility, as a person or an organization, for paying for, planning, and carrying out a project or activity.

staunch (stȯnch′) *adj.,* faithful; firm; unwavering; dependable.

sub • ser • vi • ent (səb serv′ ē ənt) *adj.,* serving to promote some end; servile; obedient; useful.

thrive (thrīv′) *v.,* grow vigorously; flourish.

tote (tōt′) *v.,* carry by hand.

tox • in (täk′ sən) *n.,* poisonous substance.

tram • ple (tram′ pəl) *v.,* to tread heavily so as to bruise, crush, or injure; trudge; bully.

trance (trants′) *n.,* hypnotic state; state of deep mental absorption or distraction; daze.

tran • si • ent (tran′ zē ənt) *n.,* person traveling about usually in search of work.

trel • lis (tre′ ləs) *n.,* frame or structure of crossed wood or metal strips usually used as a support for climbing plants. *Each summer,*

un • de • serve • d • ly (ən di zər′ vəd lē) *adv.,* not deserved.

vex (veks′) *v.,* distress; agitate; trouble; harass.

whisk (hwisk′) *v.,* to move briskly.

Handbook of Literary Terms

CATHARSIS. The ancient Greek philosopher Aristotle described tragedy as bringing about a **catharsis**, or purging, of the emotions of fear and pity. Some critics take Aristotle's words to mean that viewing a tragedy causes the audience to feel emotions of fear and pity, which are then released at the end of the play, leaving the viewer calmer, wiser, and perhaps more thoughtful. The idea that catharsis calms an audience has been contradicted by recent psychological studies that suggest that people tend to imitate enacted feelings and behaviors that they witness. Much of the current debate over violence on television and in movies centers on this question of whether viewing such violence has a cathartic (calming) or an arousing effect on the viewer.

CHARACTER. A **character** is a person (or sometimes an animal) who figures in the action of a literary work. A *protagonist,* or *main character,* is the central figure in a literary work. An *antagonist* is a character who is pitted against a *protagonist.* Major characters are those who play significant roles in a work. *Minor characters* are those who play lesser roles. A *one-dimensional character, flat character,* or *caricature* is one who exhibits a single dominant quality, or *character trait.* A *three-dimensional, full,* or *rounded character* is one who exhibits the complexity of traits associated with actual human beings. A *static character* is one who does not change during the course of the action. A *dynamic character* is one who does change. A *stock character* is one found again and again in different literary works. An example of a stock character is the mad scientist of nineteenth- and twentieth-century science fiction.

CHARACTERIZATION. **Characterization** is the act of creating or describing a character. Writers use three major techniques to create a character: showing what characters say, do, and think; showing what other characters say and think about them; and showing what physical features, dress, and personality the characters display.

CLIMAX. The **climax** is the point of highest interest and suspense in a literary work.

CONFLICT. A **conflict** is a struggle between two people or things in a literary work. A *plot* is formed around conflict.

A conflict can be internal or external. A struggle that takes place within the mind of a character is called an *internal conflict.* A struggle that takes place between a character and some outside force such as another character, society, or nature is called an *external conflict.*

DIALECT. A **dialect** is a version of language spoken by the people of a particular place, time, or social group.

DIALOGUE. **Dialogue** is conversation involving two or more people or characters.

FIRST-PERSON POINT OF VIEW. See *Point of View.*

FORESHADOWING. **Foreshadowing** is the act of hinting at events that will happen later in a poem, story, or play.

IMAGE. An **image** is language that creates a concrete representation of an object or an experience. An image is also the vivid mental picture created in the reader's mind by that language. The images in a literary work are referred to, when considered altogether, as the work's *imagery.*

MOOD. **Mood,** or **atmosphere,** is the feeling or emotion the writer creates in a literary work. By working carefully with descriptive language, the writer can evoke in the reader an emotional response such as fear, discomfort, longing, or anticipation.

MOTIF. A **motif** is any element that recurs in one or more works of literature or art.

NARRATOR. A **narrator** is a person or character who tells a story. Works of fiction almost always use a narrator. The narrator in a work of fiction may be a major or minor character or simply someone who witnessed or heard about the events being related. Writers achieve a wide variety of ends by varying the characteristics of the narrator chosen for a particular work. Of primary importance is the choice of the narrator's *point of view.* Will the narrator be *omniscient,* knowing all things, including the internal workings of the minds of the characters in the story, or will the narrator be limited in his or her knowledge? Will the narrator participate in the action of the story or stand outside that action and comment on it? Will the narrator be reliable or unreliable? That is, will the reader be able to trust the narrator's statements? These are all questions that a writer must answer when developing a narrator.

Omniscient Point of View. See *Point of View.*

Personal Essay. A **personal essay** is a short work of nonfiction prose on a single topic related to the life or interests of the writer. Personal essays are characterized by an intimate and informal style and tone. They are often, but not always, written in the first person.

Plot. A **plot** is a series of events related to a central conflict, or struggle. A plot usually involves the introduction of a conflict, its development, and its eventual resolution. The following terms are used to describe the parts of a plot:

- The **exposition** is the part of a plot that provides background information about the characters, setting, or conflict.
- The **inciting incident** is the event that introduces the central conflict.
- The **rising action**, or complication, develops the conflict to a high point of intensity.
- The **climax** is the high point of interest or suspense in the story.
- The **falling action** is all the events that follow the climax.
- The **resolution** is the point at which the central conflict is ended, or resolved.
- The **dénouement** is any material that follows the resolution and that ties up loose ends.

Point of View. **Point of view** is the vantage point from which a story is told. Stories are typically written from a *first-person point of view,* in which the narrator takes a part in the action and refers to himself or herself using words such as *I* and *we;* from a *second-person point of view,* in which the narrator uses you; or from a *third-person point of view,* in which the narrator uses words such as *he, she, it,* and *they* to tell the story. In stories told from a third-person point of view, the narrator generally stands outside the action. In some stories, the narrator's point of view is limited. In such stories, the narrator can reveal the private, internal thoughts of himself or herself or of a single character. In other stories, the narrator's point of view is *omniscient.* In such stories, the narrator can reveal the private, internal thoughts of any character.

Stanza. A **stanza** is a group of lines in a poem. The following are some types of stanzas:

two-line stanza	*couplet*
three-line stanza	*triplet* or *tercet*
four-line stanza	*quatrain*
five-line stanza	*quintain*
six-line stanza	*sestet*
seven-line stanza	*heptastich*
eight-line stanza	*octave*

Subplot. A **subplot** is another story told in addition to the major story in a work of fiction.

Symbol. A **symbol** is a thing that stands for or represents both itself and something else.

Theme. A **theme** is a central idea in a literary work.

Third-Person Point of View. See *Point of View.*

Acknowledgments

Brent Ashabranner. From *Children of the Maya: A Guatemalan Indian Odyssey* by Brent Ashabranner. Copyright © 1986 by Brent Ashabranner. Reprinted by permission of the author.

Curbstone Press. From *The Cherokee Lottery: A Sequence of Poems* by William Jay Smith. Curbstone Press, 2002. Distributed by Consortium Book Sales & Distribution. Reprinted by permission of Curbstone Press.

Farrar, Straus and Giroux. "An Overture" from *The Desert Smells Like Rain: A Naturalist in O'odham Country* by Gary Paul Nabhan. Copyright © 1982 by Gary Paul Nabhan. Reprinted by permission of North Point Press, a division of Farrar, Straus and Giroux.

HarperCollins Publishers. "In Case You Ever Want to Go Home Again," pp. 35-45, from *High Tide in Tucson: Essays from Now or Never* by Barbara Kingsolver. Copyright © 1995 by Barbara Kingsolver. Reprinted by permission of HarperCollins Publishers, Inc.

New Internationalist. "Coyotes and the Underground Railway" by Richard Kazis from *New Internationalist,* December 1983. Copyright *New Internationalist.* www.newint.org. Reprinted by permission of the *New Internationalist.*

We have made every effort to trace the ownership of all copyrighted material and to secure permission from copyright holders. In the event of any question arising as to the use of any material, we will be pleased to make the necessary corrections in future printings. We are grateful to the authors, publishers, and agents listed here for permission to use the materials indicated.